Shobhaa Dé

"Shocks India, and much of its literary set like no other writer today."   —*The New York Times*

"The astute descriptions from her deadly pen decide who's in and who's out."   —*Sunday Times of India*

"Her in-your-face wit and immaculately turned-out looks still captivate. . . . Like wine, she's only getting better."   —*Savvy Mumbai*

Praise for
Bollywood Nights

"This steamy saga also includes a bright bindi flash of spirituality that is uniquely Dé."   —*Publishers Weekly*

"A very entertaining, emotional, and moving story that gives a well-rounded picture of the trappings of fame, the fragility of egos, and the effects of a less-than-perfect upbringing."   —*Romantic Times*

ALSO BY SHOBHAA DÉ

Bollywood Nights

Socialite Evenings

Shobhaa Dé

NEW AMERICAN LIBRARY

New American Library
Published by New American Library,
a division of Penguin Group (USA) Inc.,
375 Hudson Street, New York, New York 10014, USA
Penguin Group (Canada), 90 Eglinton Avenue East, Suite 700, Toronto,
Ontario M4P 2Y3, Canada (a division of Pearson Penguin Canada Inc.)
Penguin Books Ltd., 80 Strand, London WC2R 0RL, England
Penguin Ireland, 25 St. Stephen's Green, Dublin 2,
Ireland (a division of Penguin Books Ltd.)
Penguin Group (Australia), 250 Camberwell Road, Camberwell,
Victoria 3124, Australia (a division of Pearson Australia Group Pty. Ltd.)
Penguin Books India Pvt. Ltd., 11 Community Centre,
Panchsheel Park, New Delhi - 110 017, India
Penguin Group (NZ), 67 Apollo Drive, Rosedale, North Shore 0632,
New Zealand (a division of Pearson New Zealand Ltd.)
Penguin Books (South Africa) (Pty.) Ltd., 24 Sturdee Avenue,
Rosebank, Johannesburg 2196, South Africa

Penguin Books Ltd., Registered Offices:
80 Strand, London WC2R 0RL, England

Published by New American Library, a division of Penguin Group (USA) Inc.
Previously published in a Penguin Books India edition.

First New American Library Printing, September 2009
1   3   5   7   9   10   8   6   4   2

Copyright © Shobhaa Dé, 1989
Readers Guide copyright © Penguin Books (USA), Inc., 2009
All rights reserved

 REGISTERED TRADEMARK—MARCA REGISTRADA

Set in Perpetua
Designed by Elke Sigal

Printed in the United States of America

FOR MY FAMILY

Socialite Evenings

CHAPTER 1

I WAS BORN IN A DUSTY CLINIC IN SATARA, A REMOTE VILLAGE IN Maharashtra . . . Even as I type these opening words I find them unexciting. But where else do I start? It is difficult this, trying to tell the story of a life even if it's my own. But do I really want to write about my early childhood, all my memories of which are indistinguishable from the clichéd village and small-town reminiscences one always reads about? No, I don't think I want to do that. Bombay—it is Bombay which has shaped me into what I am now and it's the story of Bombay I want to tell. And when I think about Bombay the person who comes to mind is Anjali and so I shall begin my narrative with her.

My initial memory of Anjali is not unlike those first impressions celebrities are constantly dredging up on request: it is so clear in my head that it unnerves me. I can see the clothes she wore that day, the way she spoke, the way she carried herself—but the thing that transfixed my attention were her nails.

"My precious talons," as she would describe them every now and again. They were truly beautiful. They were, in fact, a little too perfect, or maybe I was just a little bit jealous. I would stare wide eyed at those elegantly shaped and buffed points as she waved her small-wristed arms around to illustrate some point or the other when words failed her. She did this quite often for she wasn't much of a conversationalist. But then, I realize now, she wasn't much of anything. Perhaps that was her problem but it's difficult to be sure.

I

Anjali didn't have to be anything or anyone. She just had to be. Or so I thought then, all my disillusionment coming later. Anyway, the first time I met her she seemed invulnerable. She was still stunning to look at in her midforties. Not classically beautiful, not flashy like a movie star but straight of back and firm of shoulder. Although her nose was too prominent and the eyes far from special she carried herself well and the nails added to the memsaaby image. I should be forgiven for returning to her nails time and again for they were truly spectacular. I never saw them with the polish chipped (until she married her second husband much later and she filed her nails straight across) and I know of at least one of her lovers who was attracted to and could never get over her nails.

She was a prominent socialite and the wife of a wealthy playboy. Like most women in her circle, she had started dabbling in fashion designing and advertising. I had just finished school and started my first term in college. And unlike many of my rich and sophisticated classmates at the time I was terribly self-conscious and awkward and resented with all my being my middle-class origins and the shabbiness of my life as the daughter of a middle-rung government official. No matter that my parents cared for me and my sisters, but subconsciously, and in the previous few years consciously, I yearned to be part of the smart and beautiful set that so many of the girls in school belonged to so effortlessly. Anjali was the portal to that world which is why I remember her so well. I'd been told that she was looking for models for a fashion show, and with what I suppose was an act of tremendous daring for the girl I was then (for though I was a "rebel" I was far from sophisticated), I decided to try out for one of the places. The meeting took place in Anjali's tiny office near Metro cinema.

As she put me through my paces (yes, I did feel like a nervous racehorse trying out for the big race) I remembered that she'd modeled herself—the ads for Tata Textiles and Khatau Voiles rose before my eyes as in a cold voice she asked me to walk. My nervousness threatened to overwhelm me. I even remember what I was wearing that day—awful bell-bottom pants in white, with a funny printed shirt over them. My heels were worn out and scruffy, and my hair teased into a messy bouffant hairdo. She watched me silently as I stumbled about. I was feeling stupider by the minute. This was not at all like the small modeling jobs I'd done earlier for a lark and that Father had got so angry about. She said something to the small intense man beside her in Gujarati and he shook his head. She turned to me and asked, "Are you free to do this show? We start rehearsals next week." Suddenly she didn't appear very fierce. She actually smiled as she gave me her address and telephone number.

It was closing time by the time the interview was over. We left the small office together and walked down the crowded street in search of her chauffeur. "Can I drop you somewhere?" she asked in a preoccupied sort of way. I was dying to say "Yes, back to my college, which is right down the street" but I didn't dare. I just gaped at her satiny nails. Her fragrance washed over me, and it was then that I realized that the rich even smelt different! Her perfume was at once flowery, light and mysterious (L'Air Du Temps I discovered later). I told her I'd wait with her till her car arrived. Then suddenly there it was, an enormous, finned Impala in silver gray. It glided up like a gigantic swan negotiating its way past handcart-pullers, pedestrians, taxis and local busses. It was the perfect vehicle for her. In those days, the only other people in our already flashy city who ran around in these monsters were the movie stars. There was little contradiction in this for, in her own way, Anjali was a star.

I watched her glide into the Impala with the mean-faced man, who I discovered later was her brother Arjun. He worked for her husband in some vague capacity. City gossip had it that this meant he was basically Abe's boozing partner and pimp, the one who drained the Chivas, switched on the stereo and rounded up the pretty Hindu virgins whom Abe was partial to whenever he threw one of his wild parties. Anjali rolled down the window, looked at me and said sweetly, "OK, see you soon." I felt terrific walking to college. Anjali was someone out of all those silly novellas we'd read in school come alive. I wanted to be her. But I was also afraid for she seemed to represent everything I had been brought up to believe was wrong and evil. Perhaps that was what made her so irresistible.

When I got home that evening, I told my two older sisters about Anjali. "I met a real big memsaab today, she's really quite a thing," I said.

I told my sisters everything. Ours was that kind of family. When they asked me to describe Anjali, in my slightly infatuated state I exaggerated everything. "She's very tall and statuesque," I said. (She wasn't.) "She's very sophisticated," I added. (Again, now when I think of it, Anjali could hardly have been described as sophisticated.) "She dresses beautifully," I went on. (She didn't really.) "And she speaks divinely," I gushed. (Well, her voice was sort of throaty and sexy, but she gobbled up all her words, and those that emerged were not exactly dazzling.) Details, details. My sisters had begun to look bored but I prattled on. Anjali had married Abbas "Abe" Tyabjee when she was just nineteen. It had been a little before my time, but I'd heard vaguely about the furor it had caused within her community, the conservative Jains. Anjali and Abe had met on a flight. She'd joined Air India as an air hostess like other attractive girls of her generation. She later explained, "Basically, I wanted to get out of the closed, boring, middle-class environment of my family. I wasn't interested in studies. I wanted to be on my own, independent. To see the world, meet people, buy lovely clothes and perfumes. What else does a pretty girl at that age want anyway?"

Abe had been years older. An experienced rake with a wild reputation. Something about Anjali's almost frigid demeanor had attracted him. Initially, he had imagined she would be just another quick pickup. But, by the time they landed in London, Anjali had managed to hook Abe. Or he her. She told me that part of her life after we became friends many months later.

I remember telling Mother about her one day. We were sitting in the kitchen drinking tea. Mother was preoccupied with what to cook for Father's dinner. It never mattered what the children's preferences were. It was always him. We were left out of their little world. If not left out entirely, then certainly kept carefully on the fringes. Mother gave Father priority, whether it was at mealtimes or anytime else. Whatever little time was left over from looking after his needs was then almost absentmindedly distributed among the three of us. Father rarely spoke directly to us. Anything that he wanted to be said was always routed through Mother except when our transgressions required chastizing. Then punishment was swift and direct. In retrospect, I would say he wasn't an unkind or cruel man. Whatever he did to us was done in the belief that he was bringing us up right. Interestingly, we didn't even resent this. It was just the way things were. And even though the anger and hostility surfaced in time, thinking of it I wonder if I wouldn't have been happier if I had lived the way Mother did. She didn't like it at all when I told her about Anjali. She frowned and said, "Who's this woman? She seems much too old for you." A strange remark that, considering we weren't discussing a future husband. But a revealing one. I've always held that Mother is psychic without realizing it. I tried to describe Anjali to her, carefully avoiding all those areas I knew would alarm her. She wasn't convinced. "Father will be very upset if he hears about this woman. Have you taken his permission before agreeing to model for her? And what is this fashion show business? Girls from decent families do not cheapen themselves by going in for such things. Hasn't your father already got angry with you for those ads you appeared in? I will not take any responsibility for this. You tell him. Don't involve me. Later he will blame me if anything happens."

As it turned out, he did blame her for whatever happened. But that wasn't new. He always blamed her for the children's mistakes.

I began by saying I was born in the country. That I was, but I grew up in a succession of small towns or mofussils as Father called them. This didn't affect me as much as it did my sisters. Perhaps I was too young to notice. To me it didn't matter whether the orderlies (called "oddlies") spoke Telugu or Bhojpuri. Whether there was a chaprassi on a cycle to take us children to school or a tonga. All that mattered was the long, hot afternoons of guileless play with companions of my age—mainly the children of servants. What joy there was in the exploring of the groves outside the compound or clambering up neem trees! Happiness was in finding a bulbul's untidy nest in a low bush and raiding it for speckled eggs. Or playing "soldier soldier" with a young Nepali boy in our unruly garden, or tormenting Billy, the neighbor's pet cat.

The move to the big city came at just the right time—for me but not for the rest of the family. Looking back, I imagine Father was steeped in his midlife crisis, Mother was premenopausal and my older sisters were plain scared. Not surprising really, for we were country bumpkins transplanted for the first time into the impersonalities of big city life. We had never stepped into an elevator before, nor seen a double-decker bus. Bombay was mind-boggling and I loved it. Which seems strange now considering we arrived when the city is supposed to be at its most unattractive: midmonsoon. But the moment we stepped out of the filthy train and on to the slushy platform at Bombay Central, I knew I'd finally found "my" city. Dirty, overcrowded, impersonal and entirely wonderful! Everything fascinated me, including the rowdy railway porters in fire-engine-red uniforms. We got jostled and pushed around as Father went in search of our luggage in the brake van. There was a junior officer waiting to receive us. Mother had on her irritated face (she loathed change—any change, and still does) while my sisters stood around looking terror-stricken, clutching their quaint, rustic frocks to themselves. I couldn't wait to get out of the station and hit town, though I wonder what my expression for my urge would have been then.

We were to stay in a crummy "transit flat" in Ghatkopar while the allotted one was being readied for us. In those days Ghatkopar was a wilderness. Arid hills in the distance, smoky factories belching chemicals, mosquito-ridden swamps and kutcha roads. Not much of anything. But it was Bombay! That was enough for me. Everybody else hated the place. Mother grumbled constantly about everything—no servants, no water, no furniture, electricity cuts, dirty kitchen, unfamiliar language, and worst of all, unfriendly neighbors. Father was too busy trying to organize school admissions for all of us and finding his feet in his new job. My sisters cried a lot and demanded to go back to their old school and friends. I can see why now, though I resented it then, their admission tests to the city's "convent schools" must have been terribly traumatic although they went through them bravely without knowing a word of English. I don't know whether the "government quota" did it but all of us managed to find places in good schools. Within a year, I could eavesdrop on my sisters conversing fluently in a language which had been alien to them not so long ago. My own "progress" from childish rhymes in my mother tongue to "baa baa black sheep" was equally swift. Because I was so young and had been pushed straight into the world of English medium schools, I escaped the "vernac" tag and strange English accent that plagued my sisters forever. My extreme youth also checked my dying over things like shabby clothes and re-heeled shoes.

I took to my new school and thankfully my new school took to me. While my sisters preferred to concentrate on their percentages, I preferred to discover Bombay and Bombayites. While my sisters earned, every now and again, grunts of approval from Father for their high marks, I never did make the grade.

I was the only child with a discipline problem both at home and at school. In the house it manifested itself in small things—not jumping at the sound of Father's voice booming out some command. Not putting my stuff away after school. Leaving a dirty thali on the dining table, whistling in the bathroom, backcombing and teasing my hair, refusing to fetch trays of tea for boring visitors, being cheeky with relatives and, mainly, not cowering in the presence of "elders" as the morose battalion of uncles was called.

At school, defiance took another form. I wanted to be different because I wasn't rich. I didn't like taking the seven-thirty fast train or a double-decker to school while the others rolled up in gleaming Buicks. And so I decided, if the other girls could flash their fancy pencil boxes and smart terrycot uniforms, I would try and attract attention by wearing my sash hipster-style, hitching the hem of my dress higher than was allowed and swaggering around the basketball court like I owned it. Imagine it if you will. A sassy kid, small for her age, oppressed at home and hungering for things she didn't have.

No wonder Anjali seemed heaven-sent: she offered me the opportunity to be everything I ever wanted to be. But at school I had no godmothers. All I did was fret and hunger for things I didn't have: a holiday bungalow in the hills, a personal ayah of my very own who'd call me "Baba" (not "Baby") and carry my imported school bag, a uniformed hamaal to fetch me hot lunch (preferably chicken curry) in the dining hall and lay it all out on an embroidered table mat with knives, forks and dessert spoons, fragrant shampoos to wash my hair with (not cakes of harsh shikakai soap), ham sandwiches and a chilled Coca-Cola waiting for me at home when I returned (not cold chappatis and leftover veggies), brand-new textbooks covered with crackling brown paper (not secondhand, grubbily thumbed copies) . . . My hunger was great and it grew greater by the day for it was never fed. It didn't comfort me much that I was not the only middle-class student in the school. I didn't care that probably half the class consisted of other girls just like me. It was the luckier other half I wanted to belong to.

I guess quite a few of the adages that have survived down the ages have more than a measure of truth in them but whoever said that childhood was a period of innocence didn't know young girls. Young girls are so charmingly vicious that it's a wonder there aren't more bloody deaths and attempted suicides in schools all over the world. How desperately I wanted to be in that charmed circle of rich girls who had everything. And how cleverly, how brutally (even if there was very little physical violence, there was brutality all right) they kept me out. My first reaction was pretending not to care. Then I tried isolating myself. That got me pretty lonely and, finally, almost in a rage, I discovered books. I read whatever I could and I'm glad I found books early considering what was to come later on in my life.

It was when I started reading that Father played a positive role in my life for the first time. And ironically he was all unknowing about it. The one commodity that was never in short supply in our house was reading material. We subscribed to several magazines including the pricey *National Geographic*. Plus, Father had carefully maintained his own highly prized collection of the classics. We sisters had access to Dickens and Jane Austen, Shaw and Shakespeare, Nehru and Radhakrishnan. Also, Father had a remarkable memory for literature—he could quote from Twain, Shakespeare or the Bhagavad Gita. Interestingly, and in this I'm probably unique, though I'm glad to say this lasted only till I grew to adulthood, I'm perhaps the only person who "graduated" from the classics via cult books like *The Fountainhead* (for a long time I was determined to marry a man like Howard Roark and I even had a tremendous crush on an architect in the neighborhood, though it's highly unlikely he even noticed me) to outright trash.

I suppose my lust for pop psychology was of a piece with my immature ideas of rebellion. However, I quickly found a girl at school who agreed with all the ideas of rebellion I held locked within me. Charlie had a college-going brother who seemed to live to masturbate. His collection of "pondies" is what we raided and devoured in the school loo. Naturally, I couldn't bring any of these paperbacks home. But one day I decided to smuggle in a *Playboy* for my innocent older sisters to look at. Which is how I came home with the bulky Xmas issue strapped to my belly under the uniform. All wrapped up in newspaper it still looked exactly what it was—a nudie magazine. We waited till my parents were asleep before flipping open the magazine to the centerspread. Smugly, I watched as my sisters gaped in wonderment at what I was sure were the biggest and the pinkest pair of knockers they had ever seen (my eldest sister claimed, though I didn't believe her of course, that she'd once seen the dhobi's wife bathing in the river and hers were larger). I told them confidently, "In any case all these pictures are retouched. Look at her nipples and you can tell." We stared hard at her gigantic aureoles in absolute awe. "See the edges," I prompted. "That's how you can make out." I think both of them were very impressed by me that night.

Charlie, the college guy's sister, wasn't really a friend-friend. But I hung around with her anyway and often got into trouble. Invariably, we were the "bad girls" who were given blue cards and kicked out of class for misconduct.

Father, expectedly, expressed his disapproval at this but I'm sure he was puzzled by it all. Poor man couldn't figure out how or why the youngest of his three daughters was giving him, and by extension the family, such a tough time. Contrasting me with his other daughters who were passive and obedient, rarely raising their eyes to meet his, made his bewilderment complete. But even I didn't dare rebel openly at home or when he was around. My ploy was simple on such occasions: I'd simply withdraw into myself, especially when he was berating me. "She does this deliberately," he'd tell Mother, who'd scurry off to get extra papads. After a point, I hardly spoke to anyone in the family, not even my sisters. "You wouldn't understand," became the standard line and I'd trot out as I'd lie on my bed for hours together gazing at Rickie Nelson's crew-cut in *Photoplay*.

Because of my intransigence I was lonely. I had always communicated with my sisters and Mother, but in this phase of my life I was almost totally cut off from them. They didn't understand me and I didn't want to understand them. Also none of my classmates came over as I was ashamed to invite them home. And, of course, there was no question of my being allowed to go to their homes considering that even my sisters, who were by now in college, were not allowed any form of social intercourse. "Why do you want to go to the cinema? Why can't you stay at home and improve your mind?" Father would roar, if one of them had the nerve to suggest a weekend matinee. I loathed that phrase "improve the mind." Now that I think of it perhaps that was why I outgrew the classics so quickly. Father hated the sight of comics. I deliberately had piles of them lying around. He hated doodles on the telephone pad. I scribbled all over it. He detested my taking books into the toilet. I always walked in with one. This was all of a piece with Father's ideas of bringing up children. A favorite phrase which I can still remember as though he'd uttered it yesterday was, "A person must have discipline and regular habits." This meant just one thing—regimentation. Lights off at ten p.m. Up at five thirty. No eating between meals. No "idle talk" over the telephone. And no "unnecessary laughter." It was like being in the bloody Army. "How can he decide which laughter is necessary or unnecessary?" I asked my sisters. They didn't answer.

He also knew how each of us would lead our lives when we grew up. "One daughter shall become a lawyer. One daughter shall qualify as a teacher. And one shall be an IAS officer." Unfortunately, not a single daughter obliged him, but that again is in the future. At the time I'm writing of Father's stock phrase to me was, "You'll never amount to anything. With the kind of marks you have it is unlikely that you'll even get into a college." I couldn't tell him that I didn't care whether I did or not. That I found trigonometry disgusting and physics loathsome. That I didn't understand the relevance of chemical formulae in my life. That I secretly longed to become a nightclub crooner and often rehearsed my repertoire in the bathroom, using the plastic mobile shower head as a mike. Get into college I did—but just about. It was really my extracurricular activities that got me in. As I said my chief worry at that point wasn't getting into college—it was what I would wear if I did. School offered protection. Even if my uniforms were made out of rough drill—they still looked like everybody else's. But college! How could I go in my "sensible" pleated skirts and "modest" blouses when all the others would be dressed in clinging sweaters and tight skirts? All the classy girls in school had spent their last term discussing little else. And as the year wound to a close they had begun work on their adult wardrobes in a frenzy and I'd die thinking of my own hand-me-downs. ("They were good enough for your sisters. They'll be good enough for you.") I nearly didn't go to college because of this. I wanted to fail—I prayed that I would. "I'll feel so ridiculous," I confided to my second sister tearfully. She didn't help matters by saying, "Don't worry—nobody will notice you." I glared at her. "But I want to be noticed." "Well, then, you're in trouble. Your sister and I were glad that nobody looked at us. That's why we could concentrate on our studies." "Fuck studies," I said loudly and clearly before stalking out of the room. I think that was the first time my darling sister had ever heard the dreaded "F-word" (as she referred to it ever after). She didn't tell on me, as I thought she would. But from that day onwards I had the feeling that she was distancing herself from me. Or perhaps that's when the madness began to set in. I don't know.

My last years in school and initially in college, until the time I met Anjali, I saw the world mainly through the prism of Charlie. We drifted apart to be sure, she was so much more determined than me to make her life crackle and pop but still I admired her lead and tried to follow her whenever I could.

Charlie was something. She scored so many firsts of the nonacademic kind that she was the envy of every girl in class. She was the first one to start her periods, at age ten no less, and she was, consequently, the first one to sprout breasts. She would proudly pick up her school tunic to show them off to the rest of us during lunch break. How we envied her the pretty pink buds! We consoled ourselves by pointing to the acne on her face. "Pimple Face" some of the girls would jeer when they saw her but she would swagger past unfazed, her little breasts bouncing merrily.

Charlie was the first one to discover boys and soul-kissing. Given the puritanical attitude at school, it was natural that all of us were obsessed with the opposite sex but only she was adventurous enough to do something about it. The "Building Boys," as we'd code-named our gangling schoolboy neighbors (Charlie lived across the street from me), took care of her curiosity and mine. One of them wore surma in his eyes and the other was an Anglo-Indian who played the piano. She was already notorious in the area as a "fast chick," so it didn't surprise any of us when she announced at age twelve that she'd kissed them both—the one with the surma and the piano-player. "Which one was better?" we asked. "Oh, definitely, the Anglo. He was eating a double-bubble gum which he passed on to me with his tongue!" Wow!

But at that stage my interest in boys was only academic, well almost. I don't know what it was that put me off them—perhaps it was their sweaty bodies, perhaps their silly jokes, not to mention my parents, who watched my every move. But I thoroughly enjoyed listening to Charlie's accounts of her forays into the teenage world of "Lipstick on Your Collar" and high-heeled pumps. I shared at one remove all her adventures from experimenting with her father's razor under the arms to stuffing her bra with cotton wool to look "bigger." Charlie, to my adoring eyes, was straight out of Archie and Veronica comics, though not half as innocent. I remember sneaking into a theater with her to see our first adult movie. We were fourteen then. It was *Splendor in the Grass* starring Warren Beatty and Natalie Wood. I'd lied at home that I had to attend netball practice. Instead I sneaked across the street to Charlie's home. We stole her mother's lipstick and money for the tickets and ice cream. (Her mother never found out. She was too busy playing rummy at the club.) I recall we debated whether to take the BB's with us or not but decided against it. "Too dangerous," she said. "Too boring," I said.

On occasion after occasion, Charlie took the lead in pushing us to the limits of our high school respectability. There was the school picnic, for instance, where Charlie decided we were all old enough to smoke. "I've had hundreds of ciggies," she boasted. "My brother pinches dad's fags and we both smoke in the balcony after the lights go off. I know all about it. Come on." None of us dared walk up to a paan-bidi shop and ask for a pack so Charlie volunteered. "First, remove your school badge and sash," Kiran, a tall, awkward girl cautioned, "or someone will report you." She did that and went off. She was back minutes later waving a pack at us. "Cool, my favorites," she laughed. "Look, this is the way to light them—like this. Just like in the movies." We gawked as she expertly struck a match and lit up. "This is a filter-tipped cigarette," she continued. "You put the filter side in your mouth." The smoke coiled up gracefully and all of us sniffed at it with our eyes shut. "Try a puff," she offered. I immediately took one. It was awful and tasted as though I was swallowing dirty steel wool. But I pretended I'd done it before. "I prefer nonfilters," I said airily, trying hard all the while not to cough, and handed the cigarette back.

"Like which brand," asked Kiran, the girl who had cautioned Charlie earlier. I was stumped. "Oh—you know, any of the others—Charminar."

"Go on! Liar! That one is so strong. Only drivers and servants can smoke it. Daddy doesn't allow them to come into the house if he smells them," Manju, another girl, added.

"Well—I like those," I lied glibly as Charlie passed the pack around.

She was also the first girl in school to own a pair of stretch pants. They were the absolute rage at the time, but girls from "decent" families weren't allowed to wear them because they hugged the skin so. Charlie wore her fire-engine-red pair to a school outing once and scandalized everybody. I thought she looked fantastic. She thought so too. And so did the BB's. "I got so many whistles today," she whispered gleefully, as the spinster-principal crooked a finger at her. "You will go home at once," she was ordered. But it didn't matter. She'd wanted to create a sensation and she'd succeeded.

My family detested the sound of her name. "How can a girl be called Charlie?" my sisters would squawk. "She is not a good influence on you," Mother would mutter. "I don't want that girl in my house," Father would rage. And the more they disapproved, the closer we became. The day she got deflowered in the backseat of a borrowed car, she came straight to the house to tell me. She knew she wasn't welcome, so she used the system of signals we'd worked out. I heard the two shrill whistles and ran out onto the balcony. She signaled to me to come down.

"I can't." I gestured. "Father's at home."

"Come to the landing at least—it's important," she urged. I peered cautiously into my parents' bedroom to see what Father was doing. He was on his bed surrounded by a pile of government files marked "Most Immediate." Figuring he was totally engrossed in his work, I was sneaking away when I heard him call out. "Where are you going?" he asked.

"Oh, I've forgotten my science workbook. I have to get some extra notes for the test tomorrow."

"Who was that I heard you talking to just now?"

"A girl from my class."

"Do girls whistle these days?"

"That's her Girl Guide whistle," I improvised.

"Be back in five minutes. I'll be watching the clock."

I ran out of the house. Charlie was looking even more triumphant than usual.

"I did it!" she announced.

"What?"

"Don't be dumb—IT!!"

"You mean—THAT?"

"Yes! What else did you think?"

"How was it?"

"Not all that great."

"Painful?"

"Not really."

"Who?"

"The Anglo."

"Did he know how to do it?"

"Sort of . . . but I showed him."

"How did you know?"

"Come on . . . I've seen books and pictures and things."

"Gosh! Will you get a baby now?"

"Let's see . . . but I don't think so. We didn't do it properly."

"Meaning?"

"You know—it was not exactly like in the books."

"But you did do it?"

"Yes, of course, but I don't think doing it like this can make a baby."

"Are you going to marry the Anglo when you grow up?"

"Don't be mad. Why should I?"

"They always do in movies."

"Yeah—but I'm not in the movies, am I?"

"That's true. OK. I've got to go."

"Swear you won't tell anyone. God's promise."

"Promise."

"You want to do it also? I can ask the Anglo."

"No!"

"Coward!"

"I have to go."

College changed the equation between Charlie and me. We'd conspired to go to the same one and take the same subjects, but somehow it wasn't the same thing anymore. Charlie got more and more involved with boys—real ones (the BB's were promptly abandoned and forgotten) while I didn't know quite what to do with myself. I made a few new friends, but there was no intimacy in these relationships. Charlie and I used to walk to college together and it was only during these morning sessions that we talked. She still attracted a lot of attention on the street and at college mainly because of the flashy way she dressed and comported herself. She was about the only girl in First Year who applied makeup—lots of it. And wore pointy-toed shoes with four-inch heels. I loved the way Charlie put herself together. She no longer needed cotton wool inside her bra cups—her breasts were perky and full. It was no wonder then that she soon attracted the attention of a distant uncle of hers who ran an ad agency. He asked her to model for one of his clients—a synthetic yarn manufacturer. Charlie was thrilled. "Come with me," she urged, "I have to get my photographs taken."

"Have you asked your parents?"

"They won't mind, silly, he is my uncle." I still hadn't learned enough to be wary of all Charlie's uncles and so I tagged along. I wonder sometimes how things would have turned out if I hadn't gone with Charlie that day but I suppose karma is something that cannot be bucked. Charlie had to pose against an enormous plastic shuttle. She was dressed in a clinging sweater and the famous stretch pants. The photographer turned out to be a nervous young fellow from the agency who took hours to set up the lights. It was hot, monotonous and utterly boring. Charlie's uncle looked thoroughly disreputable and his actions and speech did nothing to belie his appearance. The client was around, sweating it out in a three-piece suit. For a novice, Charlie was doing pretty well. Far from being self-conscious, she smiled and pouted with professional ease as the camera clicked away.

"Uncleji" stepped in from time to time to "adjust" her clothes or hair. The client just salivated on the sidelines. As the hours dragged past I began getting jittery. It was time to get home. I couldn't keep pulling off the "extra tutorials" number. Just as I picked up my bags and books to leave the client said, "Just a minute." He and Uncleji spoke for a few moments and then Uncleji said to me with a leer, "Mr. Chopra would like some photographs of you." I looked quickly at Charlie who winked and mouthed, "Say yes!" I was totally confused. I suppose the client thought I would be flattered, but uppermost in my mind was Father's reaction. "I haven't asked my parents' permission." I stuttered. "They'll get angry."

"Don't worry. We will not print these pictures without your permission. These are just trial shots for our files. Your parents will never find out," Uncleji said.

"I don't know . . ." I said weakly.

Charlie came up and hissed, "Don't be stupid. Where's the harm? They won't eat you up—it's nothing. Just photos. Do it, yaar." Which is how I became a model via the perfect con. As it turned out, the client liked my photographs and they got used—without my permission and without any payment. One morning I heard Father calling out to Mother, "Isn't this Karuna?" Mother replied nervously, "Must be some mistake . . . let us ask her." I was summoned. Father flashed the newspaper in front of me. "When did you do this? How dare you? Do you want to disgrace us completely? This is not something girls from respectable families do. How did this photograph get here?" I just stared and stared at the ad. Actually, it looked pretty good, and I looked pretty good too. A smile must have appeared on my face, because suddenly I felt Father's palm hitting me sharply across the face. "Disgraceful! Cheap! Filthy! No Brahmin girl has ever stooped so low. Tell me—how did this photograph get here?" I stood there glumly, too sullen and shocked to say anything. I could feel the sting of his fingers on my cheek.

Mother looking at the photograph said timidly, "She looks quite nice."

Father looked apoplectic. I thought he was going to slap her too. "Nonsense, it is you people who have spoiled this girl. I do not want my daughters to cheapen themselves in this way. I will not tolerate this in my house. You will never do this again—do you understand?"

But the rebelliousness I had cultivated in school now surfaced with a vengeance. The ads kept appearing—again and again and again—but the slaps stopped. I don't know why or how. Perhaps Father didn't know how to handle a situation totally out of his ken. It's strange to think that but perhaps that's what it was.

I suppose it was only the act of rebellion that kept the modeling going for I didn't enjoy it much, not the way Charlie did for sure. But it meant having money of my own and a certain quick thrill of excitement every time someone recognized me as the Terkosa Girl or whatever.

Soon a strange truce existed at home. There was a tacit understanding that I wouldn't do any ads that would truly disgrace the family. I stayed away from all but "safe" and "classy" products. Also, there was an elaborate charade that had evolved—the old staple of "what I don't see I don't know." I never left home with makeup and I always took it off before getting back. The unwritten rules also insisted that I undertook only those assignments which could be fitted into free afternoons and completed before Father got home from the office. This setup worked quite well. Until I widened the rift by acquiring a boyfriend. I still didn't have the interest in boys that Charlie had and I suppose it was really only one more step in my rebellion (added to the fact that I did find him quite nice) that made me begin seeing Bunty. He was from another college and we met in an ad agency where he'd come to audition for a new cigarettes campaign. I thought he was cute. He smoked cheap cigarettes and wore frayed jeans. His language was laced with colorful Hindi epithets and he was what one would now describe as a laid-back person. In other words, a happy-go-lucky bum. We fell into a relationship which was uncomplicated and easy. He hadn't read a book in his life and thought *Anna Karenina* was the name of a new restaurant in town. But we had loads of fun together and even convinced ourselves that we were deeply in love. I think the part we best enjoyed about being an item was people's reactions to us as a pair. "You two look so good together," they'd say and we'd preen some more.

My parents, expectedly, loathed Bunty or even mention of his name. It didn't really matter since I hadn't expected it to be otherwise. By now I was so inured to their disapproval of nearly everything about me that it was really their approval of anything that scared me. But I still played the game by their rules to the extent possible. I never brought Bunty home and I did not even speak to him over the phone when Father was around.

Over a period of time, we just worked out ways that made it possible for us to meet and go out—but we never went out nights. Once exceptionally frustrated or exceptionally daring I asked Mother, "What do you think it is that we will do in the darkness that we can't do during the daytime?" She was too shocked to reply. The matter didn't go further but I think I remember the occasion now because it was so symptomatic of the relationship between Bunty and me. We weren't really doing anything much to Charlie's horror.

"How ridiculous," she scoffed when I explained once. "What's the point in having a steady if you aren't doing anything."

"We'll only do it after we're married," I said goody-goodily and Charlie laughed.

"Weird. Real weird."

We were talking at her place and Simon and Garfunkel sang "Bridge over Troubled Waters" in the background. As Charlie retrieved a carton of tampons from her dresser, I spotted a slim packet of imported condoms—FLs. Charlie saw me staring. "These are for real men and real girls for the real thing. Not for Holy Virgins and Bunty." I was supposed to feel crushed. But I didn't. At the back of my mind lurked the thought—good girls didn't.

CHAPTER 2

As the days passed even the fashion show and Anjali were accepted in that strange shifting compact at home. Father pretended he didn't know I was doing the show. Mother pretended she didn't know where I was going three afternoons a week. And I pretended I didn't notice them pretending not to know.

Today I wonder if I would have gone through all that if Anjali hadn't been all that I aspired to be. Unlikely. But at that stage in my life she was very special to me as a person. Come to think of it, the reason I kept going back to the rehearsals after the first couple of occasions was not so much the chance of being in the show as the chance of being with her. The first time she invited me home I almost cried in gratitude. It was a fancy place in Malabar Hill in one of the early high-rises. It certainly doesn't rate as a hot address today but it was different then. Soon, I was going over constantly, though getting there wasn't easy. It involved a long walk from college to the bus stop, very often skipping lunch to get there on time. It also meant missing afternoon tutorials and additional lectures. The bus stop I had to alight at to get to Anjali's house was at the bottom of a hill and I had to walk up a steep path in the blazing sun to reach her apartment. But, oh, the bliss once I got there: it was cool, carpeted and more luxurious than anything I could have imagined. In retrospect, it was quite a ghastly place with cheap furniture painted over in gilt, ugly chandeliers and shabby Kashmiri wooden screens. As for her bedroom, "my boudoir" as she rather grandly called it, it resembled a bordello from some third-rate Hollywood film. It had a large canopied bed all done up in maroon velvet. One entire wall was covered in mirrors—this was Abe's kinky little secret—the cushions were covered with inflexible shiny brocade, and the dressing table had a synthetic fur covering in plastic pink. But to my untutored eyes this was the height of good living. This was how the rich lived. This was how movie stars lived. It was perfect! It was also the first home with an actual bar that I'd seen. I thought that was terribly stylish—a bar! There was a room reserved for it. Behind the counter were all sorts of naughty stickers—the kind that originate in the touristy kiosks in London or New York. And, of course, this room too was full of mirrors. Mirrors behind the bar, mirrors on the ceiling, mirrors on the bathroom door. It was a cramped little room, really, and on one wall there was a portrait of a waiflike girl, Anjali's only daughter, Mimi (Mumtaz, actually). When I try to recall that picture, its ordinariness points to it being the efforts of one of those slapdash Sunday painters who set up shop in Hyde Park. But maybe I'm being prejudiced for it was quite sweet and it did manage to capture the loneliness in the child's eyes. The bar seemed an inappropriate backdrop for hanging a child's portrait, but even that didn't seem incongruous to me then. But as I later learned a bad portrait in a bar was the least of Mimi's worries. What a life the poor girl led! Sleeping through the frequent fights and showdowns between her parents. And occasionally sharing her small bed with her mother, when she'd take refuge there after a particularly brutal fight with Abe. Or worse, when Anjali would be displaced from her own bedroom while Abe shared the bed with a party guest who'd decided to stay over after all. While incidents like these must have been traumatic for Mimi, they were terribly humiliating for Anjali. But she didn't speak to me about them till nearly ten years after I first met her. "You were far too young then. You wouldn't have understood. Besides I was afraid I would lose you by scaring you off with all these horror stories about my life. I wanted to enjoy your innocence and your admiration for as long as possible."

I suppose I did shock easily in those days for all my forced bravado in school and college. I remember one occasion when Anjali
was too far gone in her misery to camouflage the sordidness of her
life from me. We'd finished rehearsing and she invited me home.
She was uncharacteristically quiet on the drive back and once in the
apartment she took me straight into the bedroom saying seriously, "I
want to show you something." I got my cues all wrong and felt both
thrilled and privileged. Also, very adult. What could she want to
show me? She went to her dressing table, pulled out the top drawer
and extracted a bunch of Polaroids. "Look at these," she said and
handed them to me. They were crude, nude shots of Anjali. I was
too embarrassed to say anything. How was I supposed to react? Was I
meant to admire them? Did she want to shock me? Should I be blasé?
I just didn't know. I met her eyes after several beats of silence and
saw she was crying. She looked very pathetic at that moment with
streaks of mascara smudging the carefully applied blush-on over her
cheeks. Her mouth was twisted up and her nails (those nails!) were
digging into one of the brocade pillows.

"What are these?" I asked in a voice that I somehow managed to
keep controlled.

"Abe took them last night. He'd come back from somewhere
with this new camera. And he insisted he wanted me to pose this
way. 'You have such a beautiful body . . . I want to photograph it,' he
said. I was flattered. We've been going through a bad patch recently. I
just felt so happy he was taking an interest in me again. I didn't really
want to do it—but I agreed. We had fun, and Abe was playful and
loving. After many months, we made love. Not in that old nasty way,
but lovingly, tenderly—like we used to when we got married. It was
so good really. He insisted on opening champagne. We drank it in
bed. He sprayed me all over with perfume. We laughed together. He
kept the phone off the hook. I thought everything was OK. He left a
couple of hours later, saying he had a business appointment. I went
to his cupboard to put back his shirts which had come from the laun-

dry and . . . right there . . . not even hidden or anything . . . were those other Polaroids . . . of that bloody bitch who has been chasing him for a while now. You know—that girl who models—the one who won the Miss India contest two years ago. And that isn't all . . . I also found her panties—awful, dirty ones . . . and a scruffy bra."

I still don't know why she broke down that day and chose to tell me all this. Perhaps she felt I was ready to be her friend and confidante. Perhaps she just needed to tell someone what a bastard Abe really was. Whatever her motives, I didn't feel comfortable in my new role. I would have preferred to remain the wide-eyed fan, and mute admirer. And those Polaroids . . . I wish I hadn't seen them either. They reminded me of dirty pictures, the sort we, as schoolgirls, would stare at and giggle over. And there is something about dirty pictures of familiars that lowers them to the level of wantons and I wanted Anjali to remain her queenly self. Besides, and I hope she won't find this snide, Anjali didn't have the world's best body. In fact, seeing her stripped of all her clothes, I realized just how imperfect it was. The breasts were small ("they fit perfectly into champagne glasses") and freckled. The hips far too wide and dimpled on the fleshly upper thighs. She was pigeon-chested and her ribcage was shaped like a conical jar. But none of this really mattered. Rather it was the battering my image of her received that shocked me. On my way home, sitting on the upper deck of the BEST bus, I also wondered whether she was trying to pass on a message. It seemed a pretty pathetic way of doing it . . . and maybe I'd got it all wrong. I preferred to give her the benefit of the doubt on this one. It wasn't possible, I said to myself. Why would she do that with me? I mean who was I? A nobody! She didn't have to entice me, surely. I hastily brushed away the thought. But even to this day, I often wonder.

It was around this time that I met Si. Anjali constantly brought her up in conversation and I'd formed the idea in my mind of someone even more exalted and high-society than Anjali from the evident admiration in my friend's tone when she talked of her. Besides, Si was quite an item on the gossip hotline: rumor had it that she was a fixture at the "orgies" Abe threw, that she was the first person to wear a mini in India almost simultaneously with its appearance in Europe, the first person to openly declare that she was living with her lover . . .

At our first meeting I was impressed: she sat in one corner of the rehearsal room, smoking incessantly and wearing a Mary Quant wig, false eyelashes two inches long, a mini that revealed her stockinged legs to her upper thigh. It didn't take me long to discover there was something very sly and witchlike about Si. Unlike Anjali, who, as the days went by, often allowed the mask to drop, Si was "on camera" constantly. Not surprising really for she was narcissistic and vain to a neurotic degree. I would watch her gazing at herself in all those conveniently placed mirrors in Anjali's house, studying her image, adjusting her legs, pouting to herself and checking to see if those hideous eyelashes were still around. Aside from the eyelashes which, once the initial awe had disappeared, looked cheap and whorish, the things I detested the most about her were the stockings she always wore. Nylons in Bombay! The mind boggled. Her eyes were always bloodshot; perhaps it was the glue of the false eyelashes that made them so, but it just heightened the generally disreputable air Si managed to project despite all her posturing. She appeared the sort of woman who didn't change her panties for days and left her tampons in long after she was meant to change them.

In sum, she looked a slut and certainly behaved like one. If there was a man in the same room as she was—any man—she would switch on in a flash. The crossing and uncrossing of the legs would then become a little dance and she'd make a production out of lighting her extra-long Kents, pausing long enough to give the man a chance to jump up and do the needful. Once, she offered me a cigarette, saying, "C'mon kid, try it." I hated the condescension in her voice. I refused with as much disdain as I dared to display. In any case, I wanted to laugh. She probably thought I'd never touched a cigarette in my life. But, when one took everything into account, I suppose I did feel gauche and rustic before Si, mainly because she took every opportunity to jerk me around especially when Anjali was present. Perhaps she thought I was competition. Once she asked tauntingly, "Do you have a boyfriend? A pretty girl like you must be having someone around." When I didn't reply she turned to Anjali and said with a laugh, "Hey Anj, why don't we introduce her to Abe—he'd love her. He has this thing about Hindu virgins!"

Anjali looked at her sharply. "Leave her alone, Si. Go play with yourself if you're bored." On other occasions she'd breeze in asking for food saying, "Anj! I'm starving! Screwing is strenuous business." Anjali, to her credit, disliked these mannerisms as much as I did. She'd always try and divert Si's attention by giving her the latest foreign fashion glossy. At the time I thought Si was a bad influence on Anjali but in a while I saw that this wasn't the case. It was all part of the learning process but greenhorn that I was it took me forever to tumble to the realities of Anjali's world, a world where Si and Anjali were only two sides of the same expensive, if badly tarnished, coin.

Finally, it was showtime. The clothes "designed" by Anjali were pretty awful and far from original. Laboriously put together from magazines, they were neither stylish nor attractive. Thankfully, the show wasn't a flop—all her fancy friends showed up—but neither was it a big success. I didn't enjoy it at all, even though she insisted on my wearing her personal jewelry while the other girls used fake stuff. When I now look at those old photographs I feel amused by what was considered fashionable then. Anjali had insisted on my having my hair piled elaborately on top of my head. The hairdo, such as it was, consisted of rolls and ringlets kept firmly in place by a gluey lacquer that made my scalp itch. She also did my makeup herself. It was an era of painted lower lashes, pale lipstick and heavy mascara. I looked perfectly ghastly. She didn't think so. "Just look at yourself," she said. "Just look how gorgeous the effect is." I looked and wasn't convinced. Nobody from my family came for the show, which was just as well. After the show I was more than ever convinced that modeling was not quite my thing. I wasn't an exhibitionist, I wasn't confident, I felt ridiculous on the ramp and I'm sure I looked it as well. But a combination of youthful bravado and subtle manipulation by Anjali (because as I can now see without modeling there would have been no earthly reason for us to meet, something my parents would have used to separate us for good) ensured that I spent a couple of years modeling. I would consult Anjali every time an assignment came up and she would constantly keep tabs on my schedule. Then one of Anjali's sponsors, a successful jeweler, decided the show she had staged in Bombay was good enough to take to Delhi. Naturally, Anjali considered this a major coup. "Delhi—did you hear that?" she told us at a meeting in her flat. "Now all the magazines will be after me. Maganbhai really wants us to do it in style. This time, the accent will be on his jewelry and not on the clothes. In fact, I want you girls to wear simple Grecian-style saris in pastel colors. Something like a jewelry show I saw in Zurich. The accent was all on the fabulous stuff the girls wore around their necks and arms. We'll stick things in your hair—well—you know, like those Ajanta frescoes. This is going to be really big." I listened to her peroration with a growing feeling of frustration. I knew I'd never be allowed to go out of town. Sneaking in a modeling assignment or two in the city itself was tough enough. But this was going to be impossible. Yet, I was dying to go. It was more than just being in another city. This trip, if it happened at all, was the first time I was going to fly and experience the five-star way of living, things I had dreamed about since high school. ("I've told Maganbhai, my girls are used to traveling and living in style. No train business and YWCAs for us," Anjali had crowed at the meeting.)

For two days of pure agony I grappled with how I was going to get my parents' permission. Finally, I decided to tackle Mother when she was alone in the kitchen. "I've got this chance to go to Delhi for two days," I started off.

"It's not possible to go to Delhi for two days. It takes that much time in the train," she said without looking up from the puris she was frying.

"I'll be flying."

"Who is taking you—that woman?"

"Yes. They want us to take the show we did to Delhi."

"Who is they?"

"Some jeweler."

"Father will not hear of it."

"Please Ma, why don't you tell him to let me go. I'm not a kid anymore. All the other girls in my class are allowed to go wherever they want. Why can't both of you trust me?"

"What about your college?"

"I have midterm holidays at that time."

"I will see Father's mood and then decide." I hugged her with joy and went off to the room I shared with my sisters. "I heard you talking to Mother," the older one said.

"So what?"

"So, now you want to go to Delhi and God knows where else with that woman. Do you know what people think of model-girls? They are no better than prostitutes."

"So?"

"Everybody will think you are a prostitute."

"So?"

"Don't you feel ashamed?"

"No."

"You'll ruin your whole life . . . your future. No decent man will marry you."

"I don't want to marry a decent man. He'll probably bore me to death."

"In any case, Baba won't let you go."

"We'll see." Several years later she would display a maturity and grace that I would be grateful for but for now I hated her.

Mother brought up the topic after dinner. Father was listening to a speech on the Five Year Plan on Vividh Bharati.

"Ssh! Don't disturb me. It's an important topic," he said sharply as Mother began. She shut up promptly. An hour later I was called to their room. (We sisters only went there if we were summoned, never on our own.) I stood at the foot of their bed. He said crossly, "What is this I hear about Delhi? Our girls don't go to other cities with strangers. Anything can happen. We don't know these people. Who are they? What if they are racketeers? Do you know their background? Who are the other girls? Are they from good families? Are they Hindus? Brahmins? No—I am sure not. It is not done in our community. This profession is not for us. It is for others—loose-charactered people." I looked down at the floor, sullenly.

"Well, what have you to say? Speak up."

"I'm not doing this as a profession. It is only a hobby."

"What sort of a hobby is this? I've not come across such a hobby before. In our time girls learned how to cook, knit, crochet, embroider, make rangoli. We called such activities hobbies. Yes, a few girls these days collect stamps or learn drawing. But what you are doing is not a hobby."

"I enjoy it and I haven't done anything wrong."

"That is what you think. Once parents allow girls to slip out of their control then everything goes wrong. We don't want that to happen to you."

"I won't do anything to disgrace you," I said meekly though inwardly I raged.

Abruptly he seemed to arrive at a decision. "I will let you know my decision tomorrow, it will be better if you don't go. Your mother and I feel ashamed of all this."

Once again I repeated tonelessly, "I will behave myself. It's only for two days."

I still don't know what made him agree to my going. Perhaps it was just a sense of weary resignation. Mother conveyed his decision to me over breakfast. Before she could finish her sentence, I was on the phone to Anjali. "I can come! Father said yes." She seemed delighted too. "I'll make your reservations," she said and rang off.

All the way to the airport in Anjali's car I mentally scanned the events I hoped would occur in the next few days. Totally preoccupied, even the vast gulf in appearance between Anjali and me didn't depress me. She was dressed in her smart "travel outfit" and even at that early hour everything was perfectly in place—hair, makeup, nails, scarf, sunglasses. There may have been bags under her eyes, but I didn't notice them. The other girls looked like scruffy strays picked up from the street. They were all uniformly dressed in sloppy jeans and T-shirts. Some of them looked like they hadn't brushed their teeth or run a comb through their hair. "All professional models look like this during their off hours," Anjali said when I commented on their appearance. I was wearing my best salwar kameez. I'd barely slept the previous night. Neither had my sisters. We'd set the alarm, booked a wake-up call and told the milkman to deliver our bottles earlier than usual. "Don't leave the house without tea," Mother had warned. I'd packed a brand-new bag that I'd bought for myself from Crawford Market. It was less awful than the ones we had at home, but it was far from good. As it happened, it fell apart on the flight itself, and when we were waiting to collect our luggage at Delhi airport, mine arrived in bits and pieces, with all my stuff hanging out of the broken bag.

That was, surprisingly, the only awful experience that first trip held for me and it did no end of good for my ego. But as with most matters of the psyche it was an illusory high as I discovered when, soon after we had returned to Bombay, Anjali visited my home for the first time. She arrived without warning and I was mortified the moment she walked in. "I wondered if you would be free to go shopping," she announced as she trailed in after my second sister who had let her in, but I just gaped at her in shame and anguish for I knew what she was looking at, things I had lived with and been ashamed of most of my life: the rexine sofas, the distempered walls, the files lying all over the house, the cheap plastic tray and tea cups, the little brass Buddha and the disproportionately large Qutub Minar on the mantelpiece, the embroidered tablecloth and the curtains without pelmets. And that wasn't all: I was, sadly, ashamed of my family and finally ashamed of myself—"caught" in a shabby "house frock" with oil in my hair and chipped polish on my toes. Worse, none of my family wanted to meet her, even my second sister slipping away after announcing her. Anjali sat on one of the rexine sofas, looking slightly uncomfortable but in no hurry to leave. I wanted to push her out, tell her not to humiliate me like this. Instead, I started to mimic Si—not deliberately, but out of nervousness. My voice changed and became high-pitched, and I pretended to be very casual and light. "Have a drink," I rashly offered when I knew perfectly well we didn't keep anything more than Rex orange squash in the house. "What about some fresh lime soda?" I said, again knowing there was no soda around. Fortunately Anjali spared me further embarrassment by saying she'd just had a lassi and wasn't thirsty. Even as she quietly surveyed her surroundings in a curiously masochistic way I hoped she would be disgusted with my middle classness and decide to stop seeing me. It was a ridiculous relationship to begin with. While I had wondered what Si and she had in common, I should have first asked myself what on earth we had in common. At that moment I would have been genuinely relieved if the relationship had ended. Nothing of the kind happened for while I hesitated Anjali took charge of the proceedings. "Why don't you change. We've got to go right now if we are to get to the shop before it shuts."

I ran in to tell Mother I was going out. I saw disapproval written all over her face. "She's not beautiful at all . . . and she's wearing a horrible sari," she hissed. My sisters were standing on the balcony staring at her car. "Is that really hers? You mean she takes you around in that?"

While changing I asked them, "Did you see her? Isn't she lovely? Mother thinks she's awful."

"Mother would," said my second sister, and I loved her for it.

The first time was the worst. Anjali visited intermittently in the years that followed and each subsequent visit dulled the embarrassment I felt. And then I discovered, though this was much later, that Anjali's background wasn't all that different from my own. After that the gulf between us decreased rapidly and I became more equal in the relationship.

Anjali's father was a doctor—a general practitioner. She had grown up modestly in a small apartment located in one of the less posh localities of Bombay—central enough and in the heart of town, but far from plush. Laburnum Road in those days was a tree-lined, quiet avenue full of Gujarati professionals. The houses there had "character" but were certainly not opulent. Anjali had gone to the nearby New Era School, which was not a convent, or even an English medium school. This was why her accent was so strange and this explained also her occasional grammatical lapses when she spoke English. I suppose I would have cottoned on to her background much earlier if only I hadn't been so dazzled by her manner. I must say here I'm not trying to denigrate Anjali; on the contrary I can only give her the most fulsome praise for achieving what ninety percent of India's middle class spend two-thirds of their lives trying to achieve—the step up to the glories of the rich and famous. It is interesting, this business of being part of the Indian middle class and the pulls and strains it inevitably sets up. I doubt I'd have done the things I felt compelled to do if we hadn't been so middle class. Luxury, for instance, was a dirty word in our house, while Education, with a capital E, of course, was one of the great gods. Like in clichéd Hindi films, the world of the rich and privileged was synonymous with the Evil Empire (oh, the hypocrisy of it all). We were trained to regard everything that wasn't "basic" and "essential" as frivolous and wasteful. The key word was austerity. Discipline and denial were the highest prized virtues. Children didn't drink tea, coffee or aerated waters. (Unfortunately, at our place, "children" we remained till the day we married or left home—whichever was sooner. My aversion for milk was understandable—milk was tyranny.)

My parents were not overly religious, but festivals were considered sacred. We couldn't skip any of the rituals—not even in the middle of our exams. Diwali remained the high point of our young lives. But other "minor" religious occasions were important too. How I hated the month of Shravan. It meant bland, "fasting food" on all Mondays, and vegetarian food for the rest of the week. This was torture. Not that we ate meat and fish every day, but Sundays were associated with a spicy mutton curry rich in coconut gravy. To be denied even this pleasure was too much. I cheated. Obliging non-Hindu friends at school cheerfully let me raid their lunch boxes. Only Mother knew but she pretended she didn't.

Our "outings" were strictly en famille. Father decided and we followed. If he was feeling particularly outgoing, we'd make it to the beach, where we children would sit in a huddle, close to our parents, sipping coconut water and staring (slyly) at the boys. Cinemas were out and so was film music. We woke up to the sounds of AIR bhajans. Mother was allowed to tune in to her favorite *Lok Geet* program of songs from popular "dramas," but that was only during the hours Father was away at work. I longed to listen to the Binaca Hit Parade broadcast by Radio Ceylon but I had to satisfy myself by hoping the neighbors would turn their set up or that Father would choose that time to go for his bath. "Love me tender, love me sweet, never let me go," Elvis Presley would croon and I would go weak in the knees and kiss the World War Two radio over the bookcase.

It was quite a while before the family acquired a transistor. The little box with no wires was like a mini-miracle. The servant was sternly told not to touch it. "Don't even dust it," instructed Mother. "I will do it myself." It became Father's exclusive toy with limited access granted to Mother. Her biggest thrill was when she triumphantly took it with her into the bathroom and locked herself in. The transistor lost its glamor when we acquired a record changer. It was installed in one corner of the living room with a laminated box of its very own. The small record collection was handled possessively by Mother who kept the keys to the cabinet with her other "important" bunch. The time for listening to music was also strictly rationed and entirely at our parents' whim. But, for us, the great achievement lay in the fact of the instrument's ownership. It existed. And because of it, in more ways than one, so did we. And of course like the great majority of the middle class in "service" we had "quarters." I forget which class ours were. It was quite complicated to figure that one out each time we moved to bigger premises (with or without servants' quarters) for, to me, all the flats looked depressingly the same. Blue whitewashed walls in the drawing room and bilious green for every other room. The furniture, too, remained virtually identical: numbered government furniture on monthly hire. Our first refrigerator, toaster, geyser, automatic iron, car and television—all these firsts were events that generated tremendous excitement. Especially the car. We spent the first week worshipping it. Literally. Priests were hired, garlands bought, coconuts broken and incense burned, as we propiated the Gods to bless our gray Landmaster. When we finally sat in it, I thought I was Princess Margaret at marriage to Lord Snowdon.

It was this background that made me understand Anjali's basic insecurity and allowed me to put up with her "excesses" once I got to know her better. I remember one of my early trips with her to Bhavnagar to shoot some fashion photographs. We stayed with a friend of Anjali's, a Gujarati heiress who went under the peculiar nickname of Jinx. Bhavnagar was an unlikely setting for Jinx.

She spoke better French than her native Gujarati (having been brought up by a succession of English nannies and then finished in an exclusive Swiss school), was a Cordon Bleu cook (stuck with a shudh vegetarian kitchen), an accomplished horsewoman and frustrated writer. But what she did best was devour men for whom she had an insatiable appetite. Most of the Indian men she went after were terrified of her for she was far too sophisticated and liberated for them to handle. Jinx came on strong and she liked to call the shots. Even sexually, she was the aggressor. Besides, the local men found her ugly (which she wasn't). She had feral looks—catlike, amber eyes, a full mouth and dusky skin. She didn't have a great figure, but she used to giggle so that her "juicy ass" really turned the European guys on. Jinx had one other kink, which I discovered on our first night at the farm. She liked to dress in drag. "Let's all dress up," she announced; "let's make an occasion out of it." I'm not sure for whose benefit she was staging all this. Maybe she had set her cap on the photographer—a scrawny Belgian with bad breath whom Anjali had dug up from somewhere. (What Jinx didn't know was that the Belgie had already been bagged mentally by Anjali.)

Anyhow, when dinner time came around, there was Jinx all rigged out in a dj. She stood dramatically at the door of the vast dining room, holding a fat Havana aloft, and asked how she looked.

"Like someone in drag," said Anjali cattily. Then we noticed Jinx's spats and cane. "Come on, Jinx—what's all this?" Anjali asked.

"It's for you, my darling," said Jinx airily and went off to open the champagne. The Belgie looked bewildered. He'd come to India in search of the exotic. He'd expected veiled women with lotus eyes and small feet. Not spats and cigars. Undeterred by his reaction, both the women put on quite a show for him. It was a terrifically entertaining evening for me as I watched the crosscurrents and stayed out of the firing line. Jinx suggested Dumb Charades— which she was wonderful at. An attempt was made—a miserable one and promptly abandoned after Anjali stumbled over the spelling of Hercules. Dinner turned out to be an elaborate affair. "Traditional Bhavnagari hospitality, darlings," said Jinx as gleaming silver thalis laden with rich food were produced by a small army of servants. Oil diyas lit the room instead of candles and in place of a formal flower arrangement on the table there were fragrant rose petals floating in brass containers. Everybody was high. That is, everybody but me. I was still being the good girl.

After dinner and elaborate goodbyes, Anjali and I returned to the bedroom we were sharing. I went into the old-fashioned bathroom to change. When I came out, Anjali was gone. I thought she might have forgotten something in the living room. I picked up a magazine and waited for her. Two hours went by—no trace of Anjali. I drifted into an uneasy sleep. Sometime at dawn, I thought I heard a shuffling movement in the room but was too groggy to switch on the light and investigate. When I did awake, I found a note propped up on the small bedside table. It looked like a child of five had scribbled it, the handwriting was so unformed and immature. The message had been hastily and crudely written with an eyebrow pencil. "Forgive me, dearest," it said. "Don't hate me for this. I will explane everything." Though I guessed what she was referring to, it was more with curiosity than anger that I looked forward to meeting her.

I saw her at breakfast. She looked sheepish and greeted me awkwardly. "Hi! Angry?" she asked with a weak smile. "Whatever for?" I said cheerfully and saw instant relief on her face. I knew she wanted to confess though this would be the first lime she'd told me anything personal, aside from the matter of Abe and his dirty pictures. As it turned out I was utterly embarrassed by the sordid little confidence and after that for several years there was an unspoken compact between us: I didn't ask or display any curiosity and she didn't tell. I would hear wild stories about her escapades, but whenever the two of us met, she played the vestal virgin—all wronged woman and injured innocence. Sometimes—and this was really much later on when she was getting low on self-esteem—she'd talk about someone she'd met—always someone respectable—like a doctor or a professor and hint about an affair. No, not even an affair—she'd transform it into an antiseptic "relationship" and explain limply, "We have a lot to say to each other. We spend hours and hours just chatting." "I bet," I'd say to myself. But not harshly. It was easy to forgive Anjali. Behind that woman-of-the-world, blasé facade was just an unsure Gujarati girl, trying hard to fit into a world in which she would always be regarded as an alien and an intruder. Which feeling I identified with quite naturally.

What really piqued my curiosity, initially at any rate, was why she stayed with her husband. I could see, anyone could, that she was unhappy in the marriage and chafed at being under his thumb. "Maybe I handled him all wrong," she'd say reflectively. "Maybe I should have asserted myself . . . put my foot down . . . I don't know, done something . . . right at the beginning. Now, it's too late." She never specified "too late" for what. In their circle, nearly everyone was thrice married and divorce was commonplace. In the beginning I was too much in awe of her to ask directly. But every now and then I'd take a swipe at him, like calling him "Ape." At first, she pretended to take offense. Later, we would both laugh over it. But an ape he truly was—brutal and boorish. In some ways, he reminded me of Aristotle Onassis, the same crude arrogance that money breeds. Even the same sort appearance including enormous, tortoiseshell glasses. "Maybe I married him because he treated me like a baby," she once said. "It was a lovely feeling to be indulged. My father never did it. He was too strict and cold. I don't remember him kissing me or any of us. Or even lightly embracing the children. It was not done to express any emotion, other than anger or disapproval." This was something else I understand perfectly. My own father was an autocrat and disciplinarian. He believed it wasn't "manly" to show his feelings. "You are far too soft with the children," he'd admonish Mother. "If you aren't strict with them, they'll take full advantage of you." We never sat in Father's lap. Not did we dare to even tap him to attract his attention. In fact, we rarely addressed him directly—it was always through Mother. Perhaps this was why I also had a thing about older men, particularly those with kind eyes and soft hands. But I would never have married an ape like Abe, for all his money and sweet words. "He wasn't always like this," Anjali would say inef-fectually trying to defend him. "He used to be so generous and con-siderate. He still is. It's just that mussulman part of his nature that ruins everything." I liked the way she'd neatly slotted the most vital area of their differences. The mussulman part. Here was Anjali, a middle-class half-Jain (from her mother's side) half-Hindu girl, who had shunned nonvegetarian food and alcohol till she married a man whose day began with a Scotch gargle and who considered veggie food "fit for milk-producing animals only." His was a large joint fam-ily consisting of other boorish brothers, their wives and countless sisters with their husbands. Presiding over them was the widowed mother, a handsome, strong woman with an imposing personality—the only person in whose presence Abe looked sufficiently cowed. It must have been very hard for Anjali to conform—at least in the first few years. But unlike a movie star friend and rival of hers (another of my schoolgirl role models) who had also married a mussulman, Anjali didn't revel in her Begum status. And in her single major re-volt against her husband she continued to be Hindu outwardly and inwardly: she wore a bindi when she wore saris, she visited the fam-ily temple on festival days and on major occasions, such as Diwali, she celebrated at home. Abe probably put up with it because religion wasn't important to him, but at least Anjali had something.

CHAPTER 3

EVEN THOUGH BY NOW I WAS ALMOST A PERMANENT APPENDAGE to Anjali's sari hem, she still hadn't invited me to a single party she threw (the friend's house in Bhavnagar excepted, but then she was always looser outside Bombay). I suspected this was because she was sure I'd be very critical about her friends, clothes, food and behavior. Maybe she was right. But I always knew when she was having a party because she'd describe everything to me in advance—from the personal idiosyncracies of those on the guest list to her outfits and table decorations. And, of course, we'd have a detailed postmortem the morning after. There was probably one more reason why I was so deliberately excluded. She was afraid Abe would make a pass at me. And succeed. She said once, half jokingly, "I have lost all my girlfriends to Abe. The minute he meets them, he starts his seduction plans. It doesn't take very long. One lunch, two drinks—and boom—they're in bed. I don't want to lose you." I tried to reassure her that I found Abe revolting.

"But do you find him sexually attractive?" she asked anxiously.

"No!" I almost yelled back.

"I know Abe finds you attractive. He has told me so. He even asked me, 'Would you mind very much if I went to bed with her?' I didn't say anything. But he could tell from my expression that I was upset." After this I was even more careful around Abe and tried my best not even to run into him at the house. I succeeded as a rule, but sometimes I'd find him lounging around in a ghastly purple silk dressing gown (purple was his favorite color). At such times I'd be studiedly polite. There were other occasions when he'd hang his bleary-eyed head out of the mirrored bedroom door and demand ice and soda at five in the evening while we were sipping tea in the living room. It was cheap and decadent and offensive. I used to wonder how Anjali could lie next to this beast, how she could bear to make love to him. She shrugged carelessly when I asked her once. "After so many years and so many times—who cares! If he feels like it, he just climbs on. It's easier to just lie there and let him rather than fight him off. Quicker too. I just switch off and think of other things. Sometimes I pick the blackheads on his back or concentrate on my schedule for the next day."

"How awful!" I said.

"That's not all," she said. "Often, my diamond stud hurts as his face presses down hard on my ear, and I can feel the sharp rod of the earring piercing into my neck. I hate it when my hair gets caught in his watchstrap, or when his unshaven chin makes furrows across my face. I hate having to reapply my night cream because it's got rubbed off. And I hate it the most when he drips all over me and there's no Kleenex around to wipe it off. I don't even know what he gets out of it. I've stopped bothering to move under him or even to wrap my legs dutifully around his waist as I once used to. I just lie there, staring at the ceiling, waiting for him to finish off and leave me alone."

"Doesn't he notice your lack of enthusiasm and mind your coldness?" I asked, though heaven knows why I wanted to carry on the conversation.

"Well, if he does, he pretends he hasn't. Sometimes we even joke about it. He says, 'Shall I get you one of those hot films? Maybe you've forgotten what it's all about. You need a refresher course, baby! What about your library of Swedish books? Where are they? Or are you reserving your energy for someone else?' He's quite sweet that way. Once, he got me a funny present from Frankfurt, it was all very fancily gift-wrapped with a huge golden bow. 'What is it?' I asked him. 'Something you'll absolutely love, baby,' he said laughing. 'You won't need me after this.' I tore open the package and what do you think—it was a battery-operated vibrator!"

"Did you need him after that?" I couldn't resist the question.

"No," she replied quickly.

After months of evading him successfully, I finally found myself at the receiving end of Abe's infamous technique. That was the last surprise on a day of surprises (most of which I could have done without) though it did set me on the path to what kitsch writers would call romance. Anjali phoned me on the morning of Holi and asked me to come with them to a beach party they'd been invited to. I was surprised. "Why do you want me to come?" I asked.

"Because there is someone I want you to meet."

I said OK reluctantly. I knew Father would fume and Mother would sulk. I quickly made up some story about running out to collect journals. Neither of them believed me. But by now these daily lies and games had become something of a joke between us. I'd tell myself—"too bad, they don't want to hear the truth." This was so. I was perfectly willing to be frank. But the responsibility of my candor was too much for them. And for my boyfriend. He bought my fibs too. I didn't quite know what Anjali meant by wanting me to meet someone but I hoped she wasn't trying to matchmake. I was perfectly happy with Bunty. But I brushed aside any apprehension I had because deep down I suppose I wanted to see what Anjali's friends were like. Then it struck me that I didn't have anything to wear. I didn't know what people wore at such dos as I hadn't ever been invited to one. It must have struck Anjali too, for she called back ten minutes later and said, "Hey kid—what are you planning to wear? Why don't you borrow one of my thingies? Do you have a swimsuit? Shall I get one for you?" I protested and declined, too embarrassed by the offer. (In our family, we never wore borrowed feathers. It was one of the family rules.) Besides, I didn't know how to swim. I hoped to God I wouldn't need to go into the water. I grew panicky. The simplest thing would have been to wriggle out of the whole thing but then I wasn't thinking rationally. Memories of compulsory swimming classes at the NSCI—during my school days—the water smelling of chlorine and the anonymous urine which stung my eyes, the glare of the sun reflecting from the surface which made me screw up my face, and the subsequent rash on my sensitive skin—floated through my head as Anjali babbled on. Besides my dislike of the water, there was no way Father was going to accept my waltzing around in a swimsuit; he still didn't allow me to wear sleeveless blouses to college or shorts to play basketball. I thanked Anjali for her concern, rang off and began looking through my clothes for something I could wear: all I could find was a maroon handloom shirtlike thing and a pair of pants. Anjali phoned again. "What about jewelry? Do you have any?"

"Jewelry? On the beach?" I asked in amazement.

"Don't be silly, darling, EVERYBODY will be wearing loads of it. It's Holi and our crowd always dresses up . . . even for the beach."

"I'm not coming," I said finally, saying what I should have done all along. "I don't have any clothes and I don't have jewelry." But by then it was too late. "Wear my chains," she instructed and rang off.

We drove to Marve in her red open-top MG. Their "beach car." The Impala was the "office car" and there was a "hill-station car" (a sturdy station-wagon) in addition to the "children's car" which the ayahs used more than Mimi. I was all doubled up at the back. She seemed very tense. Maybe because Abe was driving and he seemed in one of his especially reckless moods. She kept looking back and saying, "Are you all right?" I wasn't. I was still feeling very silly about my clothes, and even sillier with the long strand of pearls she'd flung around my neck. She was wearing a floaty kaftan—very Pucci—with a black swimsuit underneath. And Abe was in shorts, with his hairy, thick calves flexing into knots each time he stepped on the brakes or the accelerator. Revolting like everything else about him.

We arrived around noon. The party was at a sprawling "shack."

We could hear the music and laughter as we looked for a parking spot. I wanted to disappear but Anjali gripped my arm tightly and dragged me through the sand. I recognized a few people. I'd seen them in various magazines—movie stars, businessmen, models, diplomats. The host, in fact, was a German married to an Indian girl—an ex-model. There must have been over a hundred people all over the place. "Have some bhang, baby," said Anjali to me. "Grow up. Enjoy yourself. You're a big girl now." This was a very new Anjali, the Anjali I'd only glimpsed at my first meetings and at Jinx's place. I reverted to my early role of a dependent. "Don't leave me alone," I pleaded. "I don't know a soul. I'm feeling so stupid." But Anjali was off—she'd spotted someone. I spotted him too at exactly the same moment. I knew him. He had used me for an ad film once. I'd liked him, even though he'd made me feel ill at ease and clumsy. He had a reputation around town. People said he was crazy. Rich and crazy. Nobody knew how many marriages he'd run through. But he always managed to get young and flashy wives for himself. Yet he wasn't a flamboyant man at all. Anything but. He was quiet and scholarly. An intense person who made pictures when he wasn't traveling or fooling around with his garage full of racing cars. I don't know how old he was then—perhaps in his forties. But I liked him. I liked the way he spoke. And I liked his arrogance. He was the most temperamental ad man in town. Agencies quaked when he walked in and he terrorized art directors and copy writers into changing all their carefully worked out concepts. But they also respected the high quality of his work. And they respected his moneyed status.

My session with him came back to me. He'd taken one look at me when I walked in for the assignment and said, "Go and wash all that muck off your face. And take down that crappy hairdo." It had taken me two hours and sixty rupees to fix my face and hair. I thought I looked terrific. I was about to say something when the look on his face made me rush out to do his bidding. After that he didn't say a word to me all through the shooting apart from barking a few instructions. But at the end of it all I'd enjoyed myself: enjoyed his professionalism—and loved the results when they came.

And now, there he was, standing motionless under a palm tree, with a soft drink in his hand. I noticed Anjali rushing up to him and talking animatedly. I tried to duck out of sight but he spotted me and waved. Anjali turned around to see who he was waving at and seeing me, her expression relaxed. "Come here. Have you met this divine man?"

We looked at each other. I smiled self-consciously. Then he said, "I'm glad you aren't wearing all that shit on your face. You look so much better minus makeup. And your hair—don't you dare go to the hairdressers. Leave the fucking thing alone." I was stunned. And flattered. Anjali stared and said, "Oh—so you know each other?" I blurted out hastily, "Only professionally."

The man looked amused. He lit a bidi and said, "Would you like to swim?" The question was directed at me.

"I don't swim," I said and reflexively took hold of Anjali's arm.

"That's OK. I don't either," he laughed. "Come on girls, the sea looks irresistible today."

Anjali quickly doffed her kaftan and urged me to come into the water.

"Like this?" I protested.

"Why not—just knock off those silly pants," said the man coolly. What the hell, why ever not, thought the middle-class maiden and took the plunge.

Months after this incident, the man revealed a few interesting details about our morning's adventure. This was after we had become friends—oh hell, why am I being so coy—and the season for true confessions was on. "Your friend Anjali came on very strong that morning," said the man. "She walked up to me and made a crude pass. I was embarrassed and, I confess, a little shocked too. How does one tell a woman to piss off? Besides, I was so taken aback seeing you there, maybe it was at that precise moment that I fell in love.

Later, of course, the sight of your bright red panties suddenly swimming into view, when your shirt floated up to your neck, was what did it. It was quite a sight. I bet you didn't think your shirt would balloon up that way . . . I loved the expression on your face. And I noticed Anjali noticing."

It was quite a disaster, that party. Particularly the point when Abe staggered off with an attractive woman who was equally sloshed. The bhang was working its dangerous magic on everyone. Abe and the woman started to lurch drunkenly across a narrow retaining wall along the edge of the property. He was yelling, "Why don't you remove your top and I take off my bottom and we become one?" She was game. Her husband wasn't. Plus, there was one very jealous young boyfriend in the picture. By this time Anjali had switched off totally and drifted away in a hash haze. She looked old and weary with her mascara smeared untidily under her eyes. The ad filmmaker had climbed into his jeep and driven off quite abruptly after our little swim, leaving me feeling awkward and alone. But I was still enthralled enough by the scene not to want to leave. The two drunken acrobats on the wall were the cynosure of all eyes now. Abe kept threatening to pull down his trunks and the woman was pouring out of her bikini top as it was. To add to the tamasha, a section of the crowd was egging on the husband to slug Abe. Meanwhile, a spoilsport woman rushed into the shack and emerged with a large beach towel. She walked up to the other woman and very dramatically flung the towel over her. There was a loud round of applause at this and the two were persuaded to abandon their caper and cool off with a tumbler full of bhang. The party lost its fizz after that and people started to leave. As we climbed into the car, I noticed the young boyfriend tracing sand patterns on the woman's belly, while her husband puffed moodily at a joint near the retaining wall. The high life, I remember thinking, here I come. But the day wasn't over yet.

Anjali was amazingly cool on the way back and made no reference to the scene. Abe, in any case, had all but passed out. And even though Anjali seemed not to notice, I was worried about getting home in one piece with him at the wheel. How could she be so in control, I kept thinking. How come she didn't jump on him and demand explanations, like other wives did? Or at least wives in movies and books (I couldn't imagine Mother asking Father to explain himself over anything).

The truth about the distance she kept from me on the drive back surfaced a couple of days later. It turned out the reason wasn't Abe at all. "I wasn't shocked by Abe's behavior. I am used to that. I was shocked by yours," she said to me as we sat in her living room.

"MINE? What did I do?"

"I saw the way you laughed in the water when your shirt went up. You weren't in the least bit shy. Maybe you wanted to expose your body to him. Maybe you didn't realize it, but you were trying to seduce him. How could you do that, when you knew how attractive I found him. Besides, you were my guest. I had taken you along. I think you behaved like a bitch. I hadn't expected that from you," she said.

It was my turn to feel outraged. What the hell did she mean? I looked back on the incident and exonerated myself completely. Was I supposed to behave like her sidekick? Handmaiden? Poor cousin? What if I had enjoyed the experience? Besides, she'd never mentioned to me that she found him attractive. Neither had she staked her exclusive claim. And anyway, as it turned out, he hadn't been interested in her at all—so what was she whipping me for?

That was a new side to Anjali. One that I wasn't either familiar or comfortable with. Initially I hadn't realized that she saw me as a threat. But gradually I realized that there was a competitiveness to her that would brook no threat. In our relationship *she* was the star.

On the day of the beach party the first changes in our relationship had begun to make themselves felt and she didn't like it at all. And, before I forget, there was the little matter of Abe on the evening after the party.

After dropping off the smoldering Anjali at their flat Abe offered to take me home. I urged Anjali to accompany us, but she opted out pleading that she was exhausted and needed to catch up on her sleep. Unsuspectingly, I went along with this arrangement. Driving down Marine Drive, Abe turned to me and said, "You know, this is ridiculous. You are the only friend of Anjali's that I haven't screwed. What's the matter with you? Are you frigid or something? Why don't we have lunch together and talk about it?" I can't really say that I was surprised by this, I'd been waiting for it to come too long, but even then I was thrown by the crudity of his approach. Even as I reviewed the various ways in which to put him down, I realized with a shock that however close I had grown to Anjali this was a commonplace occurrence in their marriage: her husband and she quarreling over her friends. I'd been reduced to a precedent. In my anger I chose what was in retrospect the best way to answer Abe: politely, I told him to go look up his own rear end. I told Anjali about this incident when I visited her and I was taken aback by her reply. "But you should have gone to lunch," she said. I had told her about the incident expecting her to acknowledge if not applaud this proof of my loyalty. Her reaction was like a sharp slap in the face. Something snapped within me. Suddenly, I realized the ridiculousness of my position in their lives. I was nothing to either of them. Not even a plaything, any longer. The tension of the hunt was over. They must be looking for a new toy now, I reasoned, and decided to get out. If only it had been that easy!

Soon after this I went abroad—my virgin trip. I'd managed to make enough through modeling to buy myself a cheapie round-trip ticket to New York. And I needed to get Anjali out of my system so I figured now was the time to go. After a couple of weeks in London, I landed in the Big Apple at a school friend's apartment. The setup was pretty weird. Here was this Sindhi girl, involved with a Bulgarian businessman huckster, splitting her apartment with a Swedish spinster, who was a professional masseuse. And in the middle of it all was me—the original yokel, well, perhaps with a superficial polish—in a state of suspended excitement prepared for anything—everything. For the very first time, I felt ready. On my own, free of family influences and pressures, free of Anjali, prepared to discover the world on my own terms. I felt reckless and brave. Adventurous and liberated. It was amazing that Father had agreed to let me go—and without a battle at that. Getting on to that Sabena flight and leaving a world that had begun to bore me behind was, and still remains, the single most exhilarating moment of my life. As it happened this trip became the turning point—and once again without knowing it—Anjali was responsible.

The excitement and jet lag had finally driven me between sheets and I was fast asleep when my Sindhi friend shook me awake. "There's a call for you," she said.

"Me?" For a second I panicked. Maybe it was a long-distance call. And that meant only one thing—someone had died. Who? Nervously I picked up the receiver.

"Hi," said a voice that sounded familiar.

"Who are you?" I asked suspiciously.

"So good to hear your voice and know you are in New York." My God, I thought, thousands of miles from Bombay and it was Him! The ad filmmaker who had driven off so abruptly after being so nice and who had prompted Anjali to sharpen her fangs on me. The ur-bane voice poured smoothly into my ear.

"I ran into Anjali the day I was leaving India—she told me you'd be in New York. I called her up later in the night to ask whether she knew your contact here. And, listen babe, that should be explanation enough. Can I buy you lunch today?" For a moment the almost-awe I'd felt at hearing his voice was displaced by anger. Why the hell had he to complicate my life? I hadn't come all these miles from home to reconnect with the past and with people I'd left behind. This was going to be my Brave New World trip. I was going to find out about myself. America was supposed to be my experiment with adulthood. I wanted to take charge, assume responsibility, find direction. All in a vague sort of way, of course. I mean, these were the "goals" one was expected to arrive at. I had no career to speak of and no real plans for the future. I don't know what it was that I was consciously seeking—but it certainly wasn't an affair. "Say yes," said my Sindhi friend, furiously penciling in her eyebrows. I said yes.

As soon as I put the phone down I began feeling guilty. And the person who dominated my thoughts was someone I'd only thought of infrequently in the last fortnight: my boyfriend Bunty. He was a sweet enough person. Loving, affectionate, accommodating. We were unofficially engaged and it was assumed by the family after all the fights I'd had with them that I'd marry him on my return. He had just landed his first job as a management trainee in a multinational, which meant that he wore Zodiac ties to climb into a bus. But every time I'd thought of him on the trip, I'd seen him in an unflattering light. Our last evening together in his PG digs had really depressed me. Was this where we were going to begin our life together—in someone else's dingy home with smelly dogs and dirty lavatories? I hated the curtains that hung limply on the window over his bed. And the cheap prints of cocker spaniels on the walls. I hated the peeling plaster over the musty cupboard. And the dressing table with the jammed drawers. More than anything else I hated the thought of sneaking into a room that was not our own and feeling like thieves (God, the furtive sex) even while paying nearly half his stipend for the rent each month. Surely life had to be better than that! It was OK to eat frilly cutlets at the neighborhood Irani as students. But it wasn't OK to grab the same in place of a proper dinner, once we'd married and become a couple. Yet, I thought, I loved him in my own way—he was certainly the most considerate man I'd ever met. And now here was this one. "Enjoy," my friend said as she rushed off to work. The masseuse had not come home the previous night so I had the apartment to myself. Tiredly, I sat down on a sofa, tried to put Bunty out of my mind and figure out what I was going to wear to lunch. Perhaps I could cancel. But then I didn't have his phone number. I put my face in my hands and wept: for innocents like me, like Bunty, for the dreams we all weave. After a while the tears stopped and I began lightening up: hey, after all I'm abroad, I thought. Why not enjoy myself? I chose a magenta sari to wear and paired it with an equally bold magenta lipstick and went off to meet my date . . .

He saw me from across the street and waved. Briskly, I started to cross the street without looking at the light and from all sides there rose a clangor of car horns, brakes, curses. My God, I remember thinking, where do you think you are! I finally made it to his side of the street all flustered and jittery. He wrapped his arms tightly around me and planted a great big kiss right on my mouth! I was deeply embarrassed and must have looked it. "Relax! You're in New York, not New Delhi, sweetheart. It's allowed over here. Nobody will arrest you," he said smoothly and did it again!

"That's not the point," I said, struggling to free myself. "I don't even know you!"

"I've been dying to do this for years. Fat chance you had of escaping. God! But you look terrible—what's that purple shit on your lips!" He pulled out his handkerchief and rubbed my mouth vigorously. "OK, I've taken it all off. I bet you're famished and you deserve a great big lunch."

For the four weeks that we spent together, I feel thankful now. For one, he helped me arrive at the decision to break off my ridiculous engagement to Bunty and call off the marriage. "It won't work, baby," he said simply. Of course it won't work, I repeated in my head, as I had a million times before. Only I had to hear it from someone else. Someone older, someone clever and someone who loved me or said he did.

New York lived up to its fantastic reputation. I was introduced to things I'd never heard of before—like quiche lorraines at the Brasserie and Goldberg pizzas. It was the time of salad and singles bars. My girlfriend and I discovered both jointly and lived to tell our experiences. Maxwell's Plum wasn't scary at all. It was plain depressing. We sipped our vodka tonics, smoked pastel-colored cigarettes and tried to look bored with everybody around us. Maybe we resembled Hispanic maids having a little fun during off hours. We were certainly dressed weirdly—I in a handblock-printed maxi (a peculiar version of a ghagra actually) and my friend in a salwar kameez. ("Are you pregnant?" asked a nasty man.) Nothing happened. We grew fat on salads with Thousand Island dressing and frustrated at being a part of the scene and yet out of it. The ad filmmaker was around constantly. The Swedish masseuse didn't approve. Till one day he showed up with a huge bouquet of blood-red carnations the size of cauliflowers. They were intended for me, but the Swede opened the door and barricaded his way. Stumped by the door-filler, he did the next best thing—gave her the bouquet and kissed her hand. Next thing we knew, she was twittering in the kitchen fixing him a cup of coffee.

I wasn't sure what I was doing with him. Learning, I suppose. And, as he never failed to remind me, I had a lot to learn. We talked a lot—mainly about our lives. He described his marriages and I tried to understand the reasons they'd failed. I described my limited experiences with boys (not men) and he tried to connect with them. A lot of the time we talked about Anjali, or at least I did, and he listened. I don't think he was particularly interested in discussing her and often told me so. But I was feeling vaguely uneasy—about her and myself. I didn't know what I was going back to. I didn't know how I was going to handle the breakup with my boyfriend. I didn't know what my parents were going to feel about it (relieved, as it turned out), plus, I didn't know what the hell my next move was going to be or even supposed to be. I didn't have a career—and now, I didn't have a marriage. "Move in with me, love," said the man persuasively. "I'll handle everything—the parents, boyfriend, family—whoever, whatever." It would have been the easiest thing to do—to use him as a stopgap till I found my bearings. But I couldn't get myself to. And I'm not sorry either. The best way out would have been—and I considered it—to just stay on in the US like the thousands of other Indians who melted into the woodwork and stayed put as illegal immigrants till they could legitimize their presence. Once again, I found myself balking at the thought of living like a thief, scrounging around for a job, maybe ending up as a waitress in some seedy downtown "ethnic" restaurant.

Finally after long debates and many arguments I decided that I would be a big brave girl and go home. By then, my worried boyfriend had phoned spending the half of his salary left over from the rent on that call. I was beginning to feel guilty. Carnations and candy were all very well—but I couldn't spend my life swooning over flowers and gorging on chocolates. The man gave me a farewell gift. I had consistently refused to accept any (apart from a fourteen-dollar T-shirt when I ran out of the only T-shirt I'd brought and was told it would cost as much to have it laundered). It was very important for me not to accept presents. As it was, I was beginning to feel like a kept woman.

In fact, for the first few days, I'd almost starved because I'd felt too embarrassed about the man picking up the tab. I'd insist I wasn't hungry and then end up eating an enormous submarine sandwich at some trucker's joint. "You are being loathsome," the man would say. "This isn't pride—this is madness—stop it! Listen, you pricey bitch, I can afford to feed you. I am rich. Do you understand what that means? RICH. Besides, it gives me great pleasure to watch you eat. I have never met a woman who eats as much. Where does it all go? Do you have a wooden leg or something? Come on, let's get you a banana split—I bet you're starving." It was like that. So, we struck a deal—food, OK—presents, not OK.

Anyway the farewell gift was supposed to be a talisman I'd wear on my way home. It was to remind me that no matter what happened, the man was a phone call and a flight away. I was to call (reverse charges, of course) and report my final decision. The man wept. I wept. It was all very Francoise Truffaut.

Until the very end, as I passed into the immigration hall in fact, the man refused to give up. "Live with me—check it out. Don't knock it till you've tried it. What have you to lose . . ." No. No. No. It wasn't for me. It was only a pause. An important one. But a pause—nothing more. The Lanvin watch—far too smart for me—looked awkward on my thin wrist. It was perfect for Anjali, whom I met of all things at Bombay airport as I was waiting to clear customs (she was returning from London).

Unsurprisingly, the watch was the first thing she noticed. "You didn't buy this, did you? Who gave it to you?" she asked, zeroing in perfectly. I didn't want to tell her about the man. I was in no mood for exchanging confidences. Besides at this point Anjali wasn't on my priority list. But she wouldn't let up. "Tell me, idiot. I know you couldn't have bought this. And you couldn't have selected it either. I bet you don't even know how to pronounce the make—go on—pronounce it and show me. Why are you being so bloody secretive? Who was he? Do I know him? Is it serious?" She was being nosey and tiresome and I got rid of her as quickly as possible and headed for home. If my sisters outdid Anjali in anything, it was in their nosiness. They wanted to know everything, particularly the big question—had I done it? Had I finally lost my virginity? I hadn't, but I didn't feel like saying so. They weren't half as bothered about the more important questions—the marriage that wasn't going to be, for instance. They weren't even interested in what I perceived as a major emotional crisis. If I felt my sisters were doing badly, I wasn't doing much better. My short stay in the States had, I felt, elevated me above the rest of the world. I felt assertive and found my sisters provincial and pesky. I resented their superficial questions. I had stumbled on something called "privacy," "space," to give it its Stateside name—a concept that didn't exist in my home. "I need space," I said airily soon after my return.

I tried the line on the boyfriend first. He looked puzzled. "What do you mean—'space'?"

"You know—SPACE—I need my own space. I feel claustropho- bic. I need to find myself."

And then it was his turn to surprise me by saying something that was really sharp and smart. "Yeah?" said he. "Find yourself, huh? What if you don't like what you find. What then? Will you be able to lose yourself again?"

I gave him my best European-heroine smoldering look. "What would you know about such things." Quietly I gave him back the ring he had taken from his mother for me. "I can't go through with it, darling. I'm not ready for it yet."

He had a desperate look in his eyes. "What happened in America? What could have happened in just a few weeks? If you need time— you've got it. OK. Let's not rush into anything. Take your time. Maybe you are upset because you are tired. Maybe the trip was too much for you. Don't see me for a week, if that's what you want."

"I don't want to see you again," I said, in a voice I could hardly recognize as my own. But it had to be done and I didn't know how else to do it.

All in all it was a pretty painful and confusing period for me. Rearing its head above everything else was the guilt of having left a loving companion of four years. One whose only disqualification was his ordinariness. But in those days, the catch phrase of the time was "We've grown in different directions. We don't speak the same language any longer." This was true, of course. Our conversation had been reduced, a long while ago, to absolute basics such as, "What do you want to eat? Where do you want to go? What shall we do on Saturday night?" So long as we were "doing" something, it was all right. But it was impossible to be in a room together with just conversation or rather, the absence of it, between us. He was a genuine person, but as Anjali had so aptly dismissed him after their one solitary meeting, "Sweet and all that . . . but not husband material. You'll tire of him, darling, if you haven't already."

The other man surfaced in Bombay after a month. A month in which I was bombarded with letters, cables and orchids. I remember the first time the orchids arrived—I was mesmerized by their strange, erotic beauty. Two deep purple and white blossoms on one slender, green stem, delicately hanging over the neck of their test tube–like container. They were just so breathtakingly beautiful. "Who sent you these?" Anjali demanded as soon as she spotted them on my shabby table in the bedroom (it was she who visited me now, rather than the other way around). I had got away on the day of my arrival by brushing aside her question about the watch but this time it would be more difficult I knew. I wondered why I didn't tell her outright but even as I dissimulated I knew why I wasn't telling her the truth—it would only lead to a scene involving someone whom Anjali did not own in the first place.

I said I'd bought the orchids myself. "Oh don't be stupid, sweetie. You couldn't afford them. Why are you lying? Go on, tell me, is there someone I don't know about? He's got to be rich if he has sent you these. And he has to have good taste too. Do I know him?" I stuck to my guns and my story. She was smart enough to recognize a rebuff when she saw it. In any case, Anjali was not that interested in me anymore. She only needed someone to talk to for she was in the throes of a crisis. "A MAJOR one, darling," she said. "Not the everyday kind." My first question was, "Have you met someone else?" Anjali didn't reply immediately. She pottered around my bedroom in her impossibly high heels, then said suddenly, "Let's go to the Sea Lounge. I'll tell you all about it." I should have refused to go and then my entire life may have turned out differently. Fate, karma, whatever you choose to call it, is a potent force and I'm living proof that it rules our lives. How else can you explain the fact that as I sat bored in the Sea Lounge, looking out at the sea and half listening to Anjali rabbiting on about what a bastard Abe was, my future husband walked in. Given the two men constantly in my thoughts, you would imagine that a third would be too much but that's the way things work, don't they? One moment you think you cannot take anything more, you are stretched way to the limit and the next you surprise yourself with the things you find yourself capable of. Well, anyway, to get back to the events of that morning, Anjali was playing the injured wife, the pathetic martyr, but I with a combination of my newfangled American ideas and boredom was being militant: "Why don't you fix that bastard—just leave him. You don't need the guy. You're doing OK. You've got a place of your own. Why do you even need another man in your life? Why can't you do this for yourself and on your own?"

"I can't," she whimpered. "I'm not strong enough. I will die if I have to face the world alone without a man by my side."

At this precise moment, my husband-to-be walked into the restaurant. He saw us sitting by the large bay windows and walked up with an easy stride.

"Hi!" he greeted me and held out his hand. I extended my right one automatically.

"No . . . the other one," he said.

"Why?" I asked.

"Just show me."

Half amused, half irritated, I put my left hand into his.

"That's good. I see you aren't married yet. Or engaged. So can we have dinner tomorrow night?" I groaned. "No." If there was one thing I didn't need in my life at that point, it was another man. He wasn't fazed by my reluctance. "Maybe you'll change your mind. I'll call you tomorrow."

Briefly, Anjali forgot about herself, her attention diverted by the new arrival. "Who's he? Quite dishy, actually. Hey—what's with you? Why did you snub him? You know, I think you are crazy! What do you want—to die a virgin spinster?" It didn't take me long to deflect the conversation, distract her with some piece of gossip and switch the topic back to her.

"The new man in my life" called promptly at nine the next morning.

"Listen, I thought I made it clear I wasn't interested," I said testily.

"I heard you. Why don't you tell me all about it over dinner? How about the Rendezvous?"

"Forget it. I do have a boyfriend (two, in fact, I thought to my-self), you know," I continued.

"Yes, I know you had one—that's in the past tense according to market rumors." OK. So, this was one wise guy. Behind my obvious irritation, there was also a grudging sense of approval. I sort of liked his head-on, dead-on approach. There was none of that standard game-playing, the obligatory mating dance. And like he said over a fresh lime soda at the Sea Lounge six days later (when I finally folded): "Look, you have nothing to lose by marrying me. You could do a lot worse. And I need to know now because I've a job offer in Switzerland that I have to reply to. If the answer from you is yes, I'll stay on in India. Otherwise I'm going." I said yes eventually. And all my fancy ideas notwithstanding that's how I got married. Pushed into it by an "acceptable" male who wouldn't take no for an answer.

CHAPTER 4

If I've given the impression that I got married in a mad rush to the first acceptable man, I must be forgiven. For my husband-to-be and I did go way back. Yes, I did have a boyfriend (of sorts) before Bunty and it was he. I met him when I'd just joined college and a few weeks before I met Anjali. He was in his final year. We were introduced by the basketball coach one evening. "He's been wanting to meet you for a long time . . . he likes your game," said the coach, and I blushed.

"Don't worry. It's OK to be complimented," laughed the senior and asked whether I'd like to drink something cold in the college canteen.

"No, thanks. I've got to rush," I said and left to change. When I got out of the ladies' locker room, he was still around, chatting with the coach. He saw me and walked up quickly. "Here, let me take your stuff."

"It's OK. I can manage."

"Reach you home? I've got a car . . ."

"I just have to cut across the maidan. I think I'll walk."

"Mind if I walk with you—I could do with the exercise."

"Why don't you go to a gym instead?"

"Am I bothering you? Do you have a jealous boyfriend or something?"

"No, you aren't bothering me and I don't have a jealous boyfriend."

"Then?"

"Then nothing." I started to walk across the quadrangle briskly and he followed.

"Look, I didn't mean to offend you with that remark about your game. If that's what you are annoyed about, I'm sorry—that Aslam— he should never have told you." I was beginning to feel like Sadhana or Saira Banu rebuffing Dev Anand's or Joy Mukherjee's advances in a silly comedy. I half expected the tall boy behind me to break into a song *Tumse* achcha *kaun hai?* I handed him my books wordlessly and said, "OK, why don't I hitch a ride with you?" I'd seen Suzanne Pleshette doing the same with Troy Donahue in a teen film once.

We dated for a bit . . . not real dates, what we called "group out-ings." Safety in numbers. We'd all pool in and go for a cappuccino to a popular café of the time—Bistro's. Since I wasn't allowed out in the evenings, these dates were generally during college hours or right after, when one could safely lie about tutorials. He was pleas-ant. But bland. He didn't set my heart on fire. We used to go for eleven a.m. jam sessions and dance to "Black Is Black." The Rolling Stones had just arrived on the pop scene and all of us panted to the insistent rhythm of "Satisfaction." And then I met Anjali. She stood my life on its head and one of the first people to get shaken off was my boyfriend. Frankly it meant very little to me that we no longer saw each other quite as often. He graduated soon and faded from my mind entirely. I saw him on one final date before my life went on fast forward.

One afternoon, he was waiting for me outside the college gates. "I came to tell you I'm off."

"Off?"

"Yes—I've got admission. It's not a fantastic university or any-thing, but I'm going to America. Anyway . . . it's something I've al-ways wanted to do."

"What are you going there for?"

"Oh, to study, learn, enjoy myself."

"Scholarship?"

"No, my marks weren't good enough. Dad's paying."

"Where?"

"Texas."

"When?"

"Two weeks from now."

"Good luck."

"Wait a minute . . . I came to ask you whether you'd have dinner with me on Saturday night. Not alone, of course, I've also invited Ranjana and Sumit—by the way, they got engaged last week."

"Good for them."

"Will you come? I mean, this is going to be goodbye—at least for the next three or four years."

"I'll have to ask my parents."

"Shall I call you later tonight? I don't mind coming over and asking their permission, if that'll make things easier."

"No, it's OK. I'll handle it myself."

After he'd left I wondered why I hadn't said no right off. As it was, the cold war with my parents over Anjali was hotting up and I had no desire to exacerbate things. But then I felt sorry for the chap. And I'd probably never see him again. I managed to wangle permission and on the appointed night he collected me at my house (my parents were duly impressed by his quietly rich background) and we went to The Other Room which was considered the choicest restaurant in those days. It was what Father would have described as a "nightclub" (thank heavens he didn't know where we were going), since there was a live band and an antiseptic cabaret. It was certainly the swankiest place I'd ever been to, all red velvet, gilt and mirrors. Just like a whore house in John Wayne westerns. I tasted lobster for the first time in my life and loved it. Also, I had my first sip of a Bloody Mary (didn't love it). It was a fabulous evening—the ultimate I'd experienced in luxury this far. The other three seemed to take it so much in their stride . . . I felt somewhat awkward for a bit then stopped being uptight and we danced to "Blue Moon" and performed an energetic cha-cha-cha to "Yellow Polka Dot Bikini." We walloped down crepe suzettes flambéed at the table and smoked menthol cigarettes. I felt terribly soigneé and sophisticated . . . till the strap of my ugly sandal broke on the dance floor. But even that didn't spoil anything. Though I couldn't have imagined then that I would eventually marry the man who kissed me softly, chastely and said, "I'll write to you from Texas . . . wait for me."

Write he did. One funny letter. I don't remember if I even replied to it. It didn't inspire a response. But I found it amongst my personal possessions years later and we both laughed at the memory. I can't recall how many years it was that he stayed abroad studying law—or was it chartered accountancy? Disgraceful that I didn't feel interested enough to ask such basic questions before I agreed to marry a stranger. A stranger who danced the foxtrot gracefully and enjoyed Dave Brubeck. Maybe at that point those two seemed important enough qualifications. Maybe I didn't really want to know anything further.

I was urged by the ad-film man to find out more about my future husband. There was a feeling of doom about the older man's exhortations (contained only in letters for I refused to see him even though he kept popping in and out of Bombay) during this period. He steadily grew more paranoid and even funded a little investigation into the husband-to-be's affairs. "The man doesn't amount to very much. He's just another rich bum who'll bore you once you're through counting all the diamonds. Get out of it RIGHT NOW, before it's too late." Jealousy, I thought to myself darkly as I read the letter. Nothing but. Foolishly, I even shared these dire warnings with hubby-to-be who dismissed "the old man" and his "warnings" with a careless laugh. Bunty, of course, had obediently stopped calling or trying to see me so he wasn't a problem. When he dies I expect he'll go straight to wimp heaven.

But back to the husband. Sonny boy was expected to take over Daddy-O's hundred-year-old export-import firm—but all the two-hundred-year-olds employed there couldn't quite relate to the younger Sheth's newfangled ideas and methods. To begin with he wore three-piece suits to sit in a stuffy office full of dhotis-topis. He wanted to modernize the musty place, put in air-conditioners, water-coolers, a western-style toilet in place of the squatter's hell. He also wanted to do away with the cabin system and introduce American-style open work stations. He hired the first woman in the firm and never mind that she was only a secretary. He brought in a qualified accountant and sacked the doddering old munimji, who kept the books like his ancestors had done before him, full of strange squiggles and esoteric entries that only he could decipher. Thrown out along with the old earthen matka that held the drinking water supply for the entire office was the bulky filing cabinet. A xerox machine moved into the place vacated by a loyal peon whose only job had been to make sure there was enough masala chai brewing through the day and paans at regular intervals.

The only traditional thing he did in all this time was probably our wedding. We went through the whole ritual but I insisted (and my father backed me up) that there be no Arabian Nights party to follow the wedding. I reckon that was the last battle I won for quite a while in our marriage.

Initially the husband talked to me about his plans for the firm and like a dutiful wife I listened and tried to show some enthusiasm. All this faded to nothing by the end of the first year of our marriage. (It wasn't the only thing that faded.) But even though we no longer talked about the business I could see the firm reflected the husband's attitudes exactly—flashy but lacking in depth. He spent hours and hours at the lush Willingdon Club (golf in the mornings, squash in the evenings and plenty of vodka-tonics in between), presumably courting new clients. His expense account exceeded the firm's billing, and no wonder too. Everything was "charged" including our honeymoon! He ran up fantastic bills all over town and in other cities as well. "I'm leaving on a jet plane . . ." became more than just a funny song in our lives. If my crusty old mother-in-law (very active as a far-from-sleeping partner in the firm) thought anything was amiss, she certainly didn't say so, at least not in my presence. I was studiously excluded from the cozy mother-and-son *après*-dinner business chats. "Why don't you relax in your room? You'll be bored listening to all this . . ." she'd say sweetly but firmly, as she instructed one of the servants to escort me back to our section of the enormous house, with a warm glass of milk to soothe me to sleep.

The one bright thing about the whole business was that my parents finally thought I'd done something right. I could tell from the proud ring to Father's voice when he introduced his only married daughter that he thought I'd done very well for myself indeed. "Good family," he'd say. "Prominent people. Comfortable life. Her husband is a very busy man . . . travels abroad all the time. See that cuckoo clock? He got it from Switzerland. And the pop-up toaster—excellent machine . . . four toasts at one time. Two minutes—and out they come. All automatic. Of course, we never ask for anything, but he's a generous man." I'd squirm through these occasions but also feel happy for them. If my marriage pleased them so much, made them so proud, I reasoned, it must be a pretty terrific marriage. Only . . . it wasn't. We didn't go foxtrotting every night. And after a point, I couldn't bear to listen to Brubeck's *Time Out.* "Brandenberg Gate" gave me a fever. It still does.

CHAPTER 5

ANOTHER CHAPTER, ANOTHER CHRONICLING OF DEFEAT. ANJALI'S DI-
vorce (yes, it finally happened) wasn't easy. While Abe wasn't bothered
one way or the other, Anjali suffered in style: she wept into expensive Swiss hankies or into whisky-sours in various five-star bars. There
were suddenly a whole host of sympathizers—mainly male—willing
to listen to her tales of neglect, abuse and torture. "What a bastard
that man is," would run their refrain, as they counted the minutes to
when their sympathetic shoulder could be switched for an even more
sympathetic bed. The man she had lined up as a prospective mate did
the disappearing act once he discovered she was really serious about
the divorce. "Bastard! Bloody bastard!" she sobbed over the telephone,
slurring those simple words. "Can you imagine—we'd even gone
house-hunting? Now, what will that estate agent think?"

It was a period when I had a whole lot of thinking to do for
myself and I was really tired of her sob stories. Even so, I couldn't
tell her to get lost when she'd show up crying, "Darling one, you are
the only real friend I have. I can't trust any of those other bitches.
They are keeping miles away from me anyway . . . afraid I'm going
to steal their bloody husbands. What shit! Why would I be interested
in those creeps?" I suppose I was "safe." To start with, I wasn't a part
of her charmed circle of so-called friends, so the question of my
passing on her sordid little secrets did not arise. And even though
I had married well in my parents' eyes, well wasn't well enough in
Anjali's eyes.

So, there we were, stuck in our own ways. I was stuck in an increasingly meaningless marriage. And she in a meaningless divorce. Despite my early feelings about what I thought was a horrible marriage, latterly I'd been urging Anjali to be pragmatic. I kept telling her to stick around Abe. "You are used to him. You know what he's all about. How are you sure you'll get a better deal with someone else? And look what the other man did—ran a mile when he realized you meant business." She wasn't convinced. I even urged her to remain single for a while. "I can't, darling. I need a man. How will I go to the club alone? What about parties and plays and things? I hate to walk into a room without a man next to me. And then, no one will invite me without Abe . . . or someone." I didn't see her point. Given my disappointing husband I'd created a liberated woman fantasy persona for myself—passively and secretly of course. I thrilled to the exploits of Gloria Steinem and Germaine Greer, read *Fear of Flying* to bits. Women, it seemed, for the first time, could have control over their lives. The scene was changing, even in Bombay. Women worked, women married, women divorced and women remained single. It wasn't such a big deal. Knowing all this I wonder why I didn't do anything about my own situation and concentrated on trying to get Anjali to stand on her own feet. Perhaps it was because I was a coward or because I didn't want to be known as a failure. Whatever my reasons at the time Anjali seemed a good person to try my liberated-woman ideas on. Life, I would tell her, was about to begin for her especially as Abe was willing to set her up in some style—flat, car, driver, an annuity. But she blew it—as I'd blown it by not walking out on my marriage after that first dreary year.

What was wrong with my marriage? What had gone wrong? Now that there is some distance, I suppose I can hazard a pretty accurate guess. My marriage went sour because I'd married the wrong man for the wrong reasons at the wrong time. My husband was not a villain. He was just an average Indian husband—unexciting, uninspiring, untutored. Why he did marry me, I shall never know. I asked him often enough and he always laughed it off. He wasn't one for introspection or for rocking the boat. Not for him the agony of questioning relationships—any relationship. Unless things went radically wrong he preferred to let things be. He reminded me of a loyal cocker spaniel when we first met, and as we grew older, the canine resemblance became startling. Maybe I accepted him and accepted the marriage, sans passion, sans anything, because it suited me. I didn't have to exert myself. I didn't have to prove anything. He seemed grateful enough for my presence. He wasn't looking for any stimulation, either intellectually or emotionally. And I could have done a lot worse—like Anjali. My friends were stuck with similar husbands. I guess that made us all feel better. We often discussed them and agreed what bores the lot of them were. In a way it was sad that there was no fight in us any longer. We were an exhausted generation of wives with no dreams left. Like our mothers before us, despite the pretensions of our unmarried youth, we concentrated on the lives of our growing children (for the most part, that was one thing I was determined not to do, have children, and thankfully, here the husband concurred). We lived through them, a vicarious, precarious existence. We clung on to the status quo of being "Shrimati so and so," and we refused to take risks. As for the husbands, they came into the picture only in a crisis—a death in the family, a kitchen accident or something that required a man's intervention. Sometimes I felt amused by my marriage and what I had allowed it to become. And as all of us in our little women's club agreed it wasn't the husbands who were the real villains. Poor fools—they were simple and uncomplicated and, therefore, happy creatures. It was us with our denuded anger who were miserable. But how could we communicate anything at all to men who perpetually sat reading the business pages of *The Times of India* while concentratedly picking their noses?

Surprisingly the husband's business, after the initial setbacks it received because of his amateurish enthusiasm, began to revive. His father had died shortly after we were married and all the vodka-tonics he had poured into his contacts seemed to be finally turning to gold. Slowly he rose in the Bombay business community's pecking order until there came a time when he was Abe's equal and more.

And even though Anjali was no longer married to Abe, this elevation in our status really got to her. She couldn't play the grand patroness, which meant that she couldn't play the condescending queen convincingly. I would sincerely have preferred her to go on doing just that. I felt equally uncomfortable in my new-found role in society. I still didn't have satiny nails. Nor did I go to the hairdressers for a weekly oil massage and I still wore local bras and sprayed on English Lavender instead of French perfume. I was in no way close to becoming Anjali, yet I could sense her unease. Sometimes she'd gush over me in an exaggerated manner. "How divine you look, darling. Those must be from Gazdar's," she'd say, fingering my earrings. That would be followed by, "Do get a decent tailor, sweetie, your bra strap is showing." This was to put me in my place and remind me that I may have married money, but I still had to get the details right. Occasionally, she'd show up at home and take an inventory. "Show me everything, darling. What have you bought since I last came here." I would have liked her to go take a powder but a mixture of the old awe and a sense of ennui usually combined to keep me calm. I'd show her my new acquisitions and wait for her verdict. And she would play grande dame to perfection.

We clung on for years and years to this pantomime, much after I had outstripped her in every way and seen through all her acts. There was something fragile and precious about her delusions. I didn't have the heart to hold up a mirror and ask her to study her reflection. She was not aging well. Of course, she was still a striking woman. But now the horsiness had become more pronounced and the lines around her eyes and mouth were harsher, deeper. She'd stare at me critically and say, "Hey! Your hair is all wrong, woman. Why don't you get a proper cut? There's this wonderful Italian guy in town—by appointment only. He's trained at Vidal's and he's a real doll! I could fix him up for you." I didn't have it in me to tell her that my hair had been fixed by the divine Angelo and if it looked a mess to her—she obviously didn't know better!

She couldn't stand my husband and made no bones about it. "Isn't he a little crass, darling? I mean, what do you two do in bed?" That was a good question. I often asked myself the same. Our love-making (if I could call it that) was a listless affair. I would tell my husband, in the days when we still had something going between us, that he generally felt like sex only on the days he skipped his regular workout at the health club. Making love was losing calories to him. I saw it as nothing more than a vague habit. We didn't even bother to remove our clothes. "Most Indians don't, darling," Anjali reminded me, to rub in the view that we were nothing more than the average, native couple. My husband notwithstanding, sex, I'd discovered, rated very low in my life. I could've done without it forever.

We'd lie there in the bedroom with the dull walls reading our respective magazines. He with *The Economist* and I with a film rag. If there was absolutely nothing better to do and we ran out of magazines, he'd turn to me and nudge. "Wife—how about it?" Neither the words nor the tone did anything to allay the disgust I usually felt. But it was simpler to just get on with the damn thing and have it over and done with as fast as possible. I would lie there staring at the ceiling as he pounded away. Or sometimes I'd mentally review the day's accounts. I can never remember my thoughts being anything other than unedifying.

What applied to sex applied to the marriage and I soon realized Mother had been right when, talking to me on the eve of the wedding, she'd said, "Marriage is nothing to get excited or worried about. It's just something to get used to."

Most of the women I knew concurred with this viewpoint. We treated marriage like a skin allergy—an irritant all right, but not something that would totally incapacitate us. We had our own secret lives—and by that I do not mean clandestine affairs. But these were our private worlds, inaccessible to the men we had married. I could spend hours in this world, even when the husband was around talking to me. There was a special thrill in switching off and pretending to be there listening while being lost in a universe created by me, for myself.

Despite this escape hatch, I still dreamed, as I know some of my friends did, of the perfect marriage. The marriage that was as far removed from the uninspiring one I was in as the stars were from us. A marriage full of laughter and conversation. One in which the two of us were perfectly in tune. Speaking the same language, thinking the same thoughts, enjoying the same things. It wasn't that I never tried, but there was no question that my husband and I inhabited different planets.

"So what if he has never heard of Somerset Maugham?" my sisters said once (this was about the time I had begun to make books my refuge). "At least, he's good to you." Good to me? Why should he have been anything else? I wasn't a wicked wife (except in my thoughts). I conformed. I went along with his social cum business entertaining, his house was neat and clean, and he had interesting food on the table. I thought I was doing my bit and paying for my keep. If anyone was shortchanged, I would have thought, it was me.

"Don't be ridiculous, darling," Anjali scolded one day (she was playing her mother patroness role). "Look at it this way—he was quite a catch. You lead a very comfortable life. He doesn't drink and he doesn't beat you. You should consider yourself very lucky. Now, don't go and ruin it all with your funny expectations. If you want to go to Istanbul (this had come up when my husband and I were watching, of all things, a sphagetti western shot in Turkey) or anywhere else—ask him nicely." So even though the time I'd suggested a holiday in Istanbul he'd looked at me as though I was crazy, I decided to try again. And I was extra nice this time. I reeled off a list of names of places that we should go to—Morocco, Tangiers, China, and he came up with one of the few memorable lines of the marriage. "We are not in the movies," he said, "and I'm not Humphrey Bogart. We'll go to London like everyone else." And that was that. There was no meeting ground on the smallest of things. "Why don't we go to the market today, look for some vegetables, I saw some great tomatoes from the car." "What for? We've got servants to do that for us," he'd say and switch on the VCR.

All the husbands of my friends more or less fell into this pattern. They were not evil men, but what they did to our lives went beyond evil. We were reduced to being marginal people. Everything that mattered to us was trivialized. The message was "You don't really count, except in the context of my priorities." It was taken for granted that our needs were secondary to theirs. And that in some way we ought to be grateful for having a roof over our heads and four square meals a day. A friend bitterly recalled how her husband would taunt her during their frequent fights, "What did you marry me for? All you were looking for was a meal ticket." And here was this woman, a qualified surgeon, feeling humiliated and demoralized enough to actually half believe what he was saying. "I can't help it. He brainwashes me constantly. I'm made to feel obliged and in debt. It's awful, but even my insistence on working and contributing to the running expenses of the house has become a battleground. I don't know what to do—either way I'm stuck."

Anjali would sum it up with all the years of experience behind her. "Men just feel terribly threatened by self-sufficient women. They prefer girls like me—dependent dolls. We make them feel like heroes and saviors. You should try it—see how much more you'll be able to get out of him that way." Maybe she was right. But it was not for me. In time, in my own way I worked out a formula that ensured peace if not bliss. I left him alone and I hoped he'd leave me alone. I felt like an indifferent boarder in the house, going through the motions of housekeeping and playing wife but the resentment and rebellion remained just under the surface, ready to break out at the smallest provocation.

It was at one of those utterly boring cocktail parties where one goes to meet the "right people" that a wonderful voice said to me, "You look as if you are about to implode." At that point, I didn't know what the word meant—but it sounded very impressive. I turned around to look into a pair of gentle gray-green eyes behind large spectacle frames. He offered me a drink which I declined. "Offer me even ten minutes of real conversation instead," I wanted to scream. We talked, but I was on my guard. It was such a problem finding a man who I could speak to without having to worry about the message being misread. All I wanted at that point was to meet someone mature, sensitive, intelligent, funny and sympathetic. To my great relief he turned out to be all that. It was a friendship that grew over the months at an unhurried pace. We would speak to each other over the phone and we'd meet from time to time at the idiotic parties that were a staple of Bombay's high life. It remained a formal relationship with well-defined rules. He never asked about my marriage and I never asked about his. I suspected we were in similar situations. His wife was not a vamp—she seemed a studious, sincere, steady sort of woman, who probably regarded marriage as a duty she had to discharge honorably. He was different. And we were similar. But even my overwhelming thankfulness at having met him never influenced my perspectives. As Anjali would've said, "He wasn't husband material." And that made me realize that I wasn't wife material. We were both solitary creatures with solitary dreams who simply weren't cut out for domesticity with all its trappings. That was the truth at one level. At another we were both just chicken. I'm sure about that or we would almost certainly have had an affair.

The gossip circuit spun its own tales ("He likes to screw, sure he does, but only mentally") but I preferred my version. Whatever the truth, in retrospect, I was glad I didn't go all the way (my middle-class background still ruled all my actions at the time and I don't believe I could have coped with the guilt) and that he didn't suggest it.

What we did do was find comfort in each other's loneliness. I would talk to him endlessly about the things my husband found "womanish" and "corny." I would discuss the trips I would never make and the drinks I'd never drink ("Red sails in the sunset?" Why not?). He was also a handy reference library. I respected his scholarship and his literary passions. "Let us go then, you and I, while the evening stretches across the sky," he'd say by way of an invitation he knew I wouldn't take up. (I didn't recognize the poem either!) He would recommend books, stray bits of poetry, an article in the *NewYorker,* a film he'd enjoyed. I discovered Yeats and Kurosawa, Yevteshenko and Maria Callas. Ideas and words swirled around in my head. All sorts of exciting new dimensions opened up mentally and my scattered reading habits began to come together. I couldn't wait to talk to him and share the previous day's discoveries. Apart from all this cerebral stuff, we found comfort in talking about small things. There was just no area of my life that didn't interest him. And the other way around. He had an old, ailing aunt living in his home who he was dearly fond of. Soon after we met, he discovered that she had a gangrenous big toe that needed to be amputated. It pained him deeply to subject the old woman to that operation. And I shared his pain, not because I had any feelings for her—but because it mattered so much to him. There was a certain resonance in our reactions. I could call and crib that the tailor had let me down or that my mother-in-law had behaved like a perfect bitch. I could tell him that I was suffering the premenstrual blues. Or that I was worried about my sister's marriage (my older one, who was a doctor now—her marriage had been arranged to a London-based engineer). When he decided, abruptly and unreasonably it seemed to me, to go away and settle in a distant town, I cried. Would I never really live, I thought, then chided myself and tried to be happy for him.

We went to his farewell party. His wife looked at me as if she knew. Maybe she did. It was a gathering of all the creative, arty brains in the city. The ad people, the documentary guys, the art-film set, painters, journalists, models and others on the fringes of what was a pretty rarefied world. He started to play the piano while his wife surveyed me thoughtfully. My husband may have noticed the crosscurrents, but like everything else in his life, he pretended he hadn't sensed a thing.

I saw my New York flame smoking a bidi in one corner, chatting up the latest "face" in town. And then Si, Anjali's friend, lately back in town, made her entrance, accompanied by a gay arts and crafts guy from Delhi. They certainly were the most striking couple at the gathering. He looked like a Gupta period temple deity, while she wore the ethnic tramp look. By which I mean she had on a bright, mirrored ghagra with an apology of a choli—backless and virtually frontless. A flimsy chiffon scarf served as a dupatta. This she played around with coquettishly, tying herself to her gay friend's wrist with it at one point. I noticed an arty actor from the South, kissing the jeweled toes of a socialite. "Don't worry—we are like brothers," he kept repeating as he begged the woman to take him home. It was that sort of a party. At some point in the festivities an ad man I disliked heartily positioned himself behind the bar and demanded a kiss from every woman before handing her a refill. Most of them obliged will-ingly, and soon his bald head was smeared with lipstick marks. The conversation was of course vintage pseudo-artspeak. "In" references and tart comments. I looked at the phone over which we had spoken so many times and felt sad that soon there would be no one to talk to. No one to "educate" me on *Bonjour Tristesse* and Françhise Sagan. I looked at him with "his crowd," "his guests" and knew whatever we might have shared I could never have been a part of that world. Not really. He moved amongst them with rehearsed ease, a joke here, a quip there, a drink for someone, a hug for another. He was not the same person who discussed Turgenev and Camus, cannelloni and caviar . . . or the color of my eyes. This man was a charming stranger who squeezed his wife's arm each time he passed her and said "naughty girl" to a fierce media controller in granny glasses.

As the evening progressed, I caught myself at one point wondering about who was having it off with whom in that room. It used to be said that a party wasn't successful till at least two marriages broke up during the evening. Which two? It was interesting to intercept sly glances and catch the odd crosscurrent. But all the while that sadness I felt kept its hold on me. My friend began to resemble a beached whale—a huge, clumsy, helpless creature on a filthy beach. Was this the environment I was doomed to spend a lifetime in? Toward the end of the evening my friend went and put on a record of Brazilian tangos. He then walked up to me with a purposeful look in his eyes and, without asking, swept me into his arms and onto the floor.

Soon he discovered a major hitch—I couldn't tango. He turned to me seriously and said, "You, my dear, have to look for just three things in your search for the perfect man. He must tango. He must fence and he must drive a burgundy-colored Lamborghini." And those were his last words to me. He died shortly after resettling in Coonoor. I think he must have died of boredom.

CHAPTER 6

BOREDOM. ONE DAY ANJALI TOLD ME THAT SHE HAD LOST INTEREST in diamonds and I knew she was dead. "Are you ill," I asked her agitatedly. "How can you say no to diamonds?" She answered in a small voice, "What's a solitaire without a man?" I knew this had to be serious. "Let's talk about it," I suggested.

And so we met three days later at the Willingdon Club. The place was like a lush green morgue, and the few old Parsee dowagers collapsed in the cavernous chairs on the balcony looked like corpses with blue-tinted hair. Anjali's divorce would be final in a month or two. Mimi, her daughter, had come to terms with it in her own way. She was sucking her thumb ("but only at night"), apart from that there weren't visible signs of a breakdown. "What are you planning to do with her?" I asked Anjali.

"I'm not sure. Maybe I'll send her to California."

"Why California?"

"Oh, I don't know. She could do some courses or something there. The weather's nice and the boys are well-built. Poor thing, maybe she'll feel funny for a bit—you know, our Mimi doesn't have any boobs. But I can always get her father to fix that. Let him at least pay for a new pair of tits for his darling daughter."

"And what about you?"

"What's wrong with my tits?" she snapped indignantly.

"I wasn't thinking of them at all. I was talking about the rest of your life . . . or isn't it as important?"

She didn't get the sarcasm—or pretended not to. "Oh, my life? It's OK."

"You mean you've found a man?" I said, thinking to myself that this was amazing—in the three days between the time she had talked to me and now she'd found someone! Her voice brought me back to her. "Yes, there is a man. But I don't think he's the right one."

"You mean, he isn't marriage material?" I said.

"Something like that."

"Married?"

"Yes. But that's no big deal."

"Kids?"

"Yes. But that's irrelevant."

"Then what?"

"He's a government biggie."

Heavens! I couldn't imagine Anjali being a government official's wife. "What on earth are you doing with a salaried man, Anjali? You probably spend in one afternoon what the poor man takes three months to earn! You're right—he definitely isn't husband material—not for you."

"But I love him," she sulked.

"So what. You've 'loved' so many before him. What makes this one so special?"

"He makes me feel special. He loves my nails."

God! "So do I, but that doesn't mean I want to marry you. Besides flipping for your nails—do you have anything else going for the two of you?"

"He appreciates my qualities. He values my opinions. He listens when I talk. He doesn't laugh at me."

All that sounded fine. But the picture still remained fuzzy. "Where did you meet this fellow? Have you slept with him?"

"You're awful. You don't have any romance in you. You just want to spoil everything by asking crude questions . . . But to answer your nosiness—yes, I have slept with him. It was wonderful. I felt

the earth move. Just like in those books. For the first time, I felt
something."

"Oh?" I said cattily. "Has the 'Big O' finally happened?"

"You know, you have become quite a bitch. And I don't know why
I'm telling you all this. He's different. He's not like all the others."

"But that's what you say every time. I've heard it on at least
twenty previous occasions. The new twist this time is that bit about
the nails."

"You wouldn't understand something as beautiful and simple as
that. You see, he has never seen polished, manicured, long fingernails
before. I mean—he may have seen them on actresses in movies, but
not on a real woman. He's never touched painted nails before. He is
like a child when he holds my hands. He gets so fascinated by them.
He can't stop touching them."

"How sweet," I commented. "And where do you go for these
fingering sessions?"

She glared at me. "Listen. I don't need any of this. Why are you
being so bloody hostile? Jealous?"

"Of what? Your nails or your government clerk?" I asked archly.

"He is not a clerk. He is a high income tax official. In fact,
that's how we met. Abe had him over to the house to settle some
problems. Nothing happened for months. And then we met again
at Guddi's party. I don't know what it was—maybe the sea air, you
know she has this lovely house on the beach at Juhu. We spent the
evening together . . . just chatting. And then he said, 'Excuse me,
but may I touch your nails? I have never seen such beautiful nails
before.'"

"Where was his wife?" I asked immediately. "Oh—somewhere
fiddling with her sari, I suppose." And then she was off again. "He
has never known someone like me. He thinks I'm so exotic and un-
reachable. He took me to tea once. We went to Malabar Hill—you
know the Naaz Café there? Stop grinning, idiot. I know what you're
thinking—imagine lah-di-dah Anjali eating oily pakoras in that joint.

But that didn't matter. He was so thrilled to be seen with someone like me. He kept saying, 'Everybody is staring at you.'"

I shut off my smile and told Anjali exactly how I felt the whole thing would end.

"Money isn't everything," she said without much conviction in her voice. "It hasn't brought me any happiness."

"But it sure has cushioned your sorrow," I reminded her. I told her to forget the income tax officer and look for someone else.

"But who? There's no one on the scene."

"Someone rich and available."

"You're crazy darling. Do you think I wouldn't have grabbed him if he existed?" She had a point. I promised to keep my eyes peeled for such a person. And if I found him to deliver him to her at once.

"Why would you do that for me, darling? Wouldn't you want to keep him for yourself?" she asked disinterestedly.

"Not really. It's unlikely that I'd find a man who could tango, fence and own a Lamborghini." She looked at me as if I was crazy and turned away.

After the Willingdon Club meeting I didn't see her for a few weeks, though we had a few phone conversations. Truth to tell, her husband-hunting was getting on my nerves. All our talks revolved around her mate stalking. Once on the phone half jokingly I suggested a diversion to her. "Why don't you learn French?" I said. "After all, you do love Paris, you go there often, you've said French is a beautiful language—and the whole thing might be fun." I was amazed when she took this seriously. Next thing I knew she'd enrolled herself at the Alliance Française. She called excitedly, "I've joined the beginner's course. You were right, it's great fun. Of course, all the others are kids, but that hardly matters. At least I know what I'll be doing three times a week." As an afterthought she said dismissively, "It's all over with the income-taxwallah." "Why, what happened?" I said, mentally preparing myself for a half-hour running down of the poor sod. Shows how well I knew her, for that's what happened.

"He was getting too possessive," she began. "Imagine telling me how to dress! I mean it's a bit silly at my age to be told by this man not to wear sexy cholis! I've always worn knotted-up cholis and always worn chiffon saris. In any case, I don't have great big knockers pouring out of them—so what's his problem? He kept saying, 'Men stare at you.' Of course they do. I'd die if they didn't. Initially I found this jealousy business sweet and touching but then it started to crawl up my nerves. Stare at me, indeed! Once he actually instructed me to pull the pallav over my shoulder. What nonsense! I refused to do it and asked him if he nagged his wife in the same way. Immediately he said, 'I don't have to tell her about such things. My wife is a decent woman who dresses decently. She is not one of you society ladies to show her body to the world.' That did it. I told him to go right back to his decent wife and behave like a decent husband himself. And guess what. He promptly went and knocked her up. I hear she's pregnant! Good for them." That closed another little chapter in Anjali's life.

The new one began a month after she had begun taking French lessons. "You've got to meet Pierre—he is *très* terrific." I felt weary just listening. I was positive this new number was one of the teachers at the Alliance—but I had to hear it all from her—the unabridged version. I could almost see her flushing over the phone. Pierre, apparently, was the heartthrob of all the teen elements in the classes. He was young, dashing and debonair. Or so she insisted. She thought he was cute but not her type. Then, one day as she was waiting for her car to drive up after a class, she had found him next to her. "A coffee, madame?" he had asked. She had thought quickly: it was a toss-up between the charming Pierre's invitation and an appointment with her manicurist. This was one round her precious nails lost. On the spur of the moment, she'd agreed. And off they went to the Trattoria, the Italian coffee shop at the President Hotel. As soon as they walked in, the manager had come rushing up to her. "Good afternoon ma'am. Seeing you here after a long time. How have you been? Good to have you back with us." The standard treatment she was so accustomed to. Pierre had looked more amused than impressed.

Barely had they settled down, than he had looked at her, placed his fingers lightly over her hand and said, "I want to make love to you."

Recalling the moment, she said, "I was so taken aback. I thought I hadn't heard right. So, I said, 'I beg your pardon?'"

Slowly and seriously he had repeated it again.

"You must be crazy. I don't even know you," she'd said.

"I know. But I had to tell you. I think it is more honest that way."

A long silence apparently ensued after which she asked him whether he knew she was a married woman, much older and really not one of those sleep-around types.

"Yes, yes, yes. I know everything. But I don't want to go on see-ing you, wanting you, inviting you to coffee and pretending there's nothing more. If you are not interested in making love, then tell me so right now, and we'll never meet again." So she had said she wasn't interested.

"You are saying you don't want to make love to me?" Pierre had asked.

"No. I don't want to," she'd replied. "OK, let's go then. No point sitting here sipping coffee and making small talk." If that was a care-fully thought-out strategy on his part it had worked wonderfully. They had got up in a huff and left the restaurant. "Tell your driver to follow us. I'll reach you to your home," Pierre had insisted. And so they had driven back in his Peugeot in a cold, sullen silence. She had sat clutching her bejeweled hands in her lap and staring at the road through enormous Dior sunglasses while he had concentrated on driving. When they arrived in the driveway of her apartment, he had reached out tenderly and stroked her face with one light touch. "It doesn't matter. I still want to see you." Then he'd taken her clenched hands in his, kissed both of them and said, "Your polish has chipped. You need a manicure!"

Which was how Anjali discovered love—French style. "This is the experience I've been waiting for," she'd trill throatily. "This is what romance is all about. Pierre is the most romantic man I've ever met. I've found a new life, a new world with him. It is so beautiful to be in love, perhaps for the first time." I'd bring her down to earth by asking—"Marriage?" "Oh must you spoil everything with your 'practical' questions. What's marriage? I've discovered something far more important—love," she would say. God! Now where had I heard that one before. For months after she met her Frenchie I had to endure her mooning on about love. One afternoon I reluctantly agreed to have tea with her at the Sea Lounge. Soon after the waiter had taken our orders, she plunged right in. "I've started writing poems," she said.

"In French?" I asked bitchily.

"If you're going to be nasty, I won't tell you anything," she pouted.

"Don't," I hastily told her. "I'm beginning to feel pretty sick." The rest of that evening she criticized me for being judgmental and harsh and not treating her great love with the respect she thought it deserved. Perhaps. Though after I met Pierre, I must say, I changed my attitude. He wasn't the European rake I'd expected him to be. And he seemed sincerely involved with Anjali. In fact, if there was a conversion process going on, it was he who was fast becoming Indianized. Anjali had decided to unveil India for him. And I found this side of her very sweet. She was like a mother hen, a sexy one, and Pierre was firmly under her wing. Apart from the kurta pajamas he began wearing while going out with her to various Indian music concerts and Gujarati (Yes!) plays, he'd adapted on a deeper level. She too had changed, softened, and Pierre suited her. "He makes me feel worthy," she once said. "I don't feel like a fool. He listens to my comments and he truly appreciates me." That was pretty evident and I felt happy for her. She seemed less self-obsessed and more giving. Maybe he had managed to tap something within her that even she had never known existed.

"He touches my soul," she declared dramatically once, after a short, experimental vacation she took with him.

"How did everybody react to you?" I asked her. "Didn't you feel self-conscious traveling with a foreigner?"

"I'm beyond caring, darling. People stared and gawked. They may have thought I'd picked up some gigolo-hippie from the roadside. But it didn't matter. I learned so much from him on the trip. It's one thing meeting in a Bombay flat on the sly and another when you share a room and wake up together."

Perhaps this was for real, but knowing Anjali (as I'm sure she herself did) this was a doomed affair. Pierre was a divorcé so there weren't major complications in his life. But Anjali was not prepared for a long-term commitment to him. And, as always, the decision was based on material considerations. By now, she was too set in her ways. Slumming was fun so long as it was an adventure. And the thing began to fall apart from the time she took a trip with him to Agra. He was unwilling to let her foot the bill at the five-star hotel there. He wanted to do it his way on his money and she went along. It turned out to be a far from exciting experience. They finally ended up in some seedy place without air-conditioning. This in the middle of May! The bathroom was at some distance from their poky little room, and the toilet was an Indian-style *sandaas*. "I took tablets to constipate myself," Anjali recalled. "It was so traumatic seeing that horrible thing. I refused to even pee into it."

"What about Pierre?"

"Oh, my dear, he has become such a dehati, he didn't mind it at all." The food had proved inedible and bat-sized mosquitoes had kept them awake all night. "I'd spray the room with L'Air du Temps five times a day—but still the smell of urine would remain. I felt sick with the heat. Sick with the smell. Sick with the awful food. Imagine asking for tea in the morning and the damn thing arriving on a filthy, battered aluminum tray, with the sugar in a chipped saucer garnished with a dead fly." Poor Anjali. Romance, however feverish, was clearly not compensation enough. "I was so conscious of the noise and dirt that I didn't even feel like sex," she continued. "Even the thought of it was sickening. Where would I wash later? There were no hand towels, no Kleenex tissues, not even toilet paper. The bathroom was one mile off and the bedsheets were full of old semen stains. Ugh! I thought I'd pick up some bug and die there." Immediately, I remembered her finickiness. And recalled the first bidet I'd ever seen in my life, in her bathroom. I'd come out after a wash and asked her, "What's that in the corner? Is it a wash-basin for Mimi?" She'd stared incredulously at me. "You mean you've never seen a bidet before?" After explaining its function to me, she'd giggled coyly, "And I use it after sex . . . you know to wash up and feel clean. I hate that sticky, drippy feeling." And here was this fussy woman in Agra, with nothing more than her Swiss lace hankies to wipe herself with. It was almost funny.

But I was more than glad she'd gone with Pierre on the trip because it had given her a vivid idea of what life with him would be all about if they were to get married. Pierre didn't pretend to be anything other than a lowly teacher. He was not a man with a special mission—he was just plain lazy and unambitious. Money was not important to him. The little he had was spent on books. Kokil's, the rare books place, was where he'd hang around for hours on a free Saturday, looking through musty volumes, digging for a bargain. Books and music were his passions. Besides cooking.

I suppose the high point at this stage in her life was the time she had, as she put it, the first "color-coordinated meal" in her life. She had to tell me about it, "Pierre decided to cook a 'green lunch'— everything was green, starting with the tablecloth and napkins. We had fish with green sauce, followed by green (mint) dessert and crème de menthe on crushed ice later."

"Didn't you puke?"

"No darling. I'd done my green number, too. I'd worn a green sari with my favorite emeralds!"

Before I draw the inevitable veil over this hiccup in Anjali's love-life I must say that the one thing she was uncharacteristically reticent about was her sex life with Pierre. Once I took her up on this—"Is your Frenchie all that the great French lover is cracked up to be? Does he do it differently?"

She started at me glassily and said, "Look, cherie, a fuck is a fuck is a fuck."

"That I know. But is this one done in French?"

"Let me put it this way—Pierre has kissed me in places and ways no other man has before." I nagged her for details but she wouldn't let on. "It's really too beautiful to discuss," she'd say mysteriously. "It's a different sort of trip. Pierre can make love with just his eyes. Sometimes I come when he's only looking at me. Love is music and food and wine and touch. He has black satin sheets. I've never made love on satin sheets. If you ever do, you'll know what I'm talking about. But really darling, I'm finding all this rather tiresome. Why don't I just fix you up with one of the other Alliance bods so you can find out for yourself." I wished my French had not been as nonexistent as it was. I might have had something witty to say to that—in French of course.

CHAPTER 7

WHY DID I KEEP UP MY ANJALI CONNECTION LONG AFTER I HAD NO real reason to be with her? Maybe because I've always needed someone. For what I don't know. To stave off the boredom perhaps. My husband certainly was no help, but with all her faults Anjali kept me occupied. The long and short of it was I was bored, desperately bored with my situation. And as Anjali had gone off to the south of France (the irony) to recover after her affair with the Frenchman, I was left pretty much to my own devices. This simply meant I retreated more and more into my fantasy world. I'd relive my college days—listening to the Beatles, reading Ayn Rand, reliving the superficial intellectualism that was cool.

Those days we thought reading Camus (and not understanding a word) was a vital process in our development, our "organic growth." It all came alive for me once again—heated discussions on Jung and Freud, watching *Ghosts* or *Marat Sade,* discussing *Medusa and the Snail,* crying over a flimsy love story with a haunting background score (*Man and a Woman*).

I don't know what I got out of all this. Maybe I was reminding myself that my life wasn't a total write-off. I suppose the marriage was OK by conventional standards but O God how I hated it. And the social life that went with the marriage was worse. Party time, whether at home or elsewhere, went like this: two or three drinks and the men had reached the backslapping "ha-ha" stage, while the wives spent the evening admiring each other's jewelry and boutique saris.

Sometimes I'd gravitate to the men's section (yes, we were usually as segregated as people under an apartheid regime) after growing terminally bored with fashion talk, until one evening a beautiful Jewish woman, with eyes like opals, said to me, "You know, you give off predatory signals. You are going to be very unpopular with us women if you hang around our husbands." Just like that I asked her if she was the spokesperson of a specially formed committee, and she smiled. "Let's just say I speak for all of us." OK, the message was loud and clear—lay off. Feeling indignant I foolishly went and spoke to the husband about it. "Of course, they're right. Why do you come and join us every time? What do you want to do? Cut us off from the party circuit? Why can't you be like other wives?" That last sentence was most telling. I guess I wasn't like other wives. And didn't wish to be. It was on that night that I decided to stop pretending that everything was fine—to myself at any rate.

The next time we were dressing to go somewhere, I didn't climb into a textured organza from Indian Textiles, and I didn't match it with pearls. I pulled out a ghagra—something I used to wear in my college days.

"Are you *crazy*? You want to go out with me dressed in that? You'll look like a sweeper woman! And don't tell me you're planning to wear that junk?" he yelled, pointing to my precious hoard of old silver jewelry.

Quietly, I said, "I want to wear this for a change. I hate wearing all those saris."

"You mean you hate looking like all the other wives? You want to look 'different' and attract attention. OK, hurry up now—there's no time to argue. But remember, you are upsetting me with your attitude. I don't like defiance." Well, well, he was certainly playing assertive husband to the hilt! I was tempted to ask him about his attitudes. What about all those things he did that upset me? What about his insensitivity and, yes, defiance? What about the nauseating stench of stale cigarettes and the stomach-turning smell of whisky combined with oily tandoori food? What about my revulsion over his horrible safari suits or my anger at the gum he constantly chewed? What about his manners in bed, the loud belches in my face?

"It's only you, wifey. I can relax in my own room," he'd say in self-defense. No, you can't, I'd want to scream. Do I ever bleach my face in your presence? Do you catch me shaving my legs? Do you find used tampons in the bathroom? Or come-stained panties on the floor? If I can be considerate enough to spare you these unsightly "woman" things—why can't you be equally sensitive? "Oh, you're trying to be fancy, are you? Like your friend Anjali," he'd mock if I ever voiced any of this. And I had learned to switch off. Switch off. Switch off. Switch off. Switch off. But I didn't want to any more. I didn't want to deaden myself to life.

It was in such a frame of mind that I went to the party. It was at some finance director's home. As we walked in, I spotted the usual faces, with the usual party expressions.

"You're looking different," one of the usual wives said to me.

"Yes—awful, isn't it, this 'new look' of hers," the husband indelicately added.

"I don't care if I'm looking awful," I said, "at least I'm feeling myself today—whatever and whoever that is."

He squeezed my arm savagely as a sign for me to shut up. "Don't create a scene," he hissed. "There are many important people here tonight."

"Go get yourself a drink and leave me alone," I answered and walked away. As always, I went and sat down on the nearest available sofa. I was hurt and humiliated. Maybe I even looked close to tears. That's when I saw her across the room. She was a new face and a beautiful one. The ugly little episode faded and I began to wonder about her. She was wearing an aquamarine blue chiffon, with a tiny choli. A slim figure, but not curvaceous. Waist-length hennaed hair (a definite minus), and a strange bindi on her forehead. It looked like rangoli. She was smoking but not drinking. I continued to stare, wondering who she was. A little later, she drifted toward me. "I saw you staring," she said with a small laugh and I noticed her eyes. Like shiny blackberries or ripe jamun. There was just a touch of kajal in them. The laugh was open and easy.

"Are you a wife?" I asked, sounding cynical even to myself.

"Of course, I'm a wife. Aren't you?" she countered easily.

"No, I didn't mean it that way, I meant, are you a 'wife-wife'?"

"Oh—like that, huh? . . . No, I suppose I don't come in that category."

"Which one is your husband?" I asked.

"Why don't you try and figure that one out," she challenged. "If you're smart, you'll guess."

I wasn't all that smart, it turned out, since all my three guesses were wrong.

"I can't give you any more guesses. There are only twelve men in the room and one of them must be your husband," she said and wandered away. We spoke a bit during the course of the evening. And though I failed to winkle out the real person from the party personality, I felt the gloom lifting as we drove home for Ritu was the first individual I'd even faintly liked in months. Two days later she called me—"I want to see you in your environment," she said. "What are you doing right now—shall I come over?"

I was delighted to hear her voice. "Do that," I nearly sang and rang off.

She arrived dressed in a canary yellow Lucknowi kurta outfit. "So, this is how you live . . . where you live," she said thoughtfully, as she surveyed the house.

"You approve?" I asked half jokingly.

"No, but I could have guessed this is how it would be."

"Why?"

"Because, you don't really think of this as your home, do you? And that shows."

Good God—how had she figured that out! I asked her.

"Easy. Look at your bedroom. Nobody would guess a woman also lives there. It's a man's room—your husband's room. You merely park yourself in it, because you have no place else to go." This woman was scary.

"OK. Since you are so smart," I suggested, "why don't you also tell me what the problem is and how I should solve it?"

"You're married to the wrong man. I saw it at the party. But I had to come to your house to confirm it. You aren't happy. And you feel trapped."

I hated her and loved her. But more than anything else, I was embarrassed and angry at myself. Had I become so transparent? So obvious? I thought I had my masks so perfectly molded. If she, a stranger, could tell so much, so soon—what about the others?

"Don't worry," she soothed, reading my thoughts. "Your mask is Perfect. It's just that I recognized it instantly since I wear an identical one myself."

She spent the rest of the afternoon with me. As we relaxed in the study she told me about her life—the disastrous first marriage to a sadist. And the second uninspiring one to a chartered accountant. "It's not so bad, really," she said. "It's all a matter of training."

"Who?"

"Oh—husbands, of course." Hers apparently, and I'd noticed it vaguely at the party, was a perfectly trained specimen. He was besotted by her and showed it. She had it over him in every which way and showed it too. "The trick is to make them feel you've done them a favor by marrying them. Once you achieve that, the equation works out.

"The other trick," she confided, "is to make them feel insecure. Let them think you'll walk out on them if they don't toe the line.

That's what keeps them in their place. If you don't believe me, let me give you an example. There's this woman I know, let's call her M., who is married to this very rich guy whose only passion is yoga. He treats it like a religion but what I found interesting about him is that his only other passion is his wife—M. She's not a sex bomb or anything which makes it all the more interesting. So I gradually drew her out on it. What I found was amazing. One day she told me, 'I can get anything out of him.' 'Really! How?' I asked her.

"'Oh, by using sex.'

"I sort of guessed what she was getting at, but wanted her to tell me. I prodded her to explain, pretending I didn't know what she was talking about.

"'You know, you're a pretty funny person,' she snapped irritatedly.

"'You mean, funny—ha-ha? You like my sense of humor?'

"'No. That's not what I meant. You think you are smart. You believe in all this independence-shindipendence stuff. But what do you get out of it? This way, you won't get anything out of your husband.'

"For the sake of argument, I baited her. 'Maybe I don't want anything out of him. Maybe I'm too proud to use my body for gain.'

"'Then you're a fool. Every wife who likes good things knows how to get them. I don't have to beg my husband for anything—he gets it for me even without asking. Do you know why—I let him think he is superior.'

"'But isn't that a horrible game to play? Don't you feel manipulative?'

"'It may seem horrible to you. But I don't think I'm doing anything dishonest. I'm not cheating him in any way. I look after his mother, his home, his needs. Why shouldn't I expect something in return. If I didn't fulfill him in bed—he'd look elsewhere. Maybe go to a prostitute.'

"'Where does love, affection, that sort of thing come in?'

"'Love-shove is OK yaar. Of course, I love him in my own way.

I'm not looking at other men. And what is love? I do what he wants. Do you think I enjoy sex when I've got my come? Ugh! I hate it. It's so messy with blood stains all over and gooey stuff on my thighs. But I do it knowing that he knows I dislike it. This makes him feel grateful and guilty. After that—anything I want is mine. Arre, we are different creatures. You've been to college, you have certain ambitions. So it's OK. I would feel miserable in your place. What do you do all day—just sit in this room and think and think and think? Where does it get you? Be like me—*pretend*. Call your husband "darling," at least in front of his friends. Pamper him in public. Press his feet sometimes. All this works like jaadu. But you're useless, yaar. You think too much. A woman who thinks is not good for a man. Look at me. I hardly ever think—and there's nothing wrong with my life. I'm happy, yaar, and you're not.'

"Listening to her," Ritu said, "I realized here was a woman who had beaten the system. She got everything she wanted by making her husband grateful. And if she made the slightest signs of leaving he'd give her anything and everything she wanted. You've got to play him, Karuna, that's what you've got to do, play him subtly."

"I wish I'd met you years ago," I said and thought, my God, this friendship is too easy, much too easy, let it not fade. Years later I would still remember what she'd told me: that men, like dogs, could be conditioned through reward and punishment. It was a lesson I'd never forget.

It was about the time I met Ritu that my marriage took a turn for the worse. I'd be sitting pensively in a chair when my husband would say, "Oh no! You aren't thinking again." It was worse when I tried to share any of my thoughts with him. "Not now, I'm reading," or "Not now, I'm watching TV," or "Not now, I've got important business problems." "Then when?" I'd seethe. Soon it became never. I just stopped wanting to share anything with him. Initially, I felt stifled by

this lack of communication. I used to experience a sensation not unlike physical suffocation. I'd start to choke and turn pale. Yet Ritu's
advice notwithstanding, I found it quite impossible to even consider
pandering to him the way she'd suggested. So I opted for my own
way out and the husband went along. Simply put, we kept out of each
other's way. We became quite clever at anticipating an emotional
outburst and avoiding it swiftly. I taught myself to suppress my rage
and switch on a button in my head that would instantly transport me
to safer, more manageable terrain. When things became too tense,
we switched to exaggerated politeness with plenty of "pleases" and
"no, thank yous" sprinkling our nonconversations. He may not have
been a monster like Abe, but he still horrified me. In fact things had
got to the point when I'd get irritated by his smallest action. The
sight of his underpants would bug me. I used to wonder why he
couldn't wear sexy undies. The sort I saw in foreign magazines like
GQ. Why didn't he throw away those hideous Victor Y-front briefs?
Even the gargling sounds he made over a basin after a meal would fill
me with revulsion.

I recall an incident once, when he had invited a minor actress
and her brand-new husband to dinner at the Taj. The husband was
all out to impress both of them—and I couldn't stand his obvious
awe and adulation. After all, as Anjali had told me, this actress was
nothing more than a hard-up extra who had made her way up the
film industry ladder by the most trusted method in filmdom—the
casting couch. Why would anybody waste time trying to impress
her? Anyway, the husband ordered champagne and tried to show his
familiarity with the stony-faced maître d'.

"Oh, Gomes." He clicked his fingers to summon him.

"The name's D'Souza . . . sir," the man corrected and I almost
died. The actress wasn't at all interested in either of us. She merely
wanted to show off her nonfilm "friends" to her dull bridegroom,
a semi-literate moneybags from Delhi. The meal was ordered with
much throwing around of fancy names and French dishes . . . till

husband asked for some "jerkins." I'm certain D'Souza understood perfectly what he meant, but stood there with a blank face and said, "Jerkins, sir?" I was furious and deeply embarrassed. "Perhaps, you're looking for gherkins?" "Of course, ha-ha. How could I have mixed it up," laughed my oafy husband. I saw the actress's eyes glazing over. She was, in any case, busy surveying the room and admiring all the new rings on her fingers. With a stupid flourish the husband got up and stood with his hands on her chair. "Shall we dance?" he asked. His expression was that of a hungry puppy. I wanted to kill him. If she accepted, it would have meant my dancing with her paunchy husband. I'd already noticed the dandruff flakes on his jacket. The thought of those fat fingers being placed on the bare portion of my exposed waist (I was in a sari) gave me the creeps. "Later, perhaps," said the actress with a practiced smile and the matter ended there: I'll never forget the expression on the husband's face. But, from my point of view, he deserved much more than a snub from a faded actress.

Now that the soul baring is on, I might as well say it all. I couldn't stand his bada saab act, for instance. And, even if I'm repeating myself, I was sick to death of his compulsive socializing. He wanted to be out every evening and it didn't matter with whom or where. "Why don't you call up someone?" he'd say almost as soon as he'd stepped into the house and flung his briefcase down. "Anyone in particular?" I'd ask, knowing full well he wouldn't come up with the names. His mother would come by at seven thirty to ask "Dinner?" also aware of the fact that her darling son probably had other plans. This had become an oppressive exercise for me. Phone. Fix up. Dress up. Buzz off. Get bored. Come back. Sleep. When I expressed my resentment he'd ask, "Do you have better alternatives, wifey?" Frankly, I didn't. But I had my books and my fantasies. I was happy enough with those. I also had the phone and my few girlfriends. "Don't you get bored sitting in the house all day?" he'd ask with fake concern. "I plan our evenings just for you. You need an outing." No, I don't. Not these kind of idiotic outings anyway, I'd want to yell. But even yelling required an effort. It was easier to dutifully climb into a mother-in-law-approved sari (with matching jewelry, of course) and go along. How I detested those empty evenings. The men would talk "bijness" over their Black Dogs and the women would stare at their diamond-studded Piaget watches and wait to go home. Did he embarrass me or I him? Thinking about it now I'm not sure. If I found him gauche and pretentious, he probably found me the same. If I got impatient with his tactless attitude, he probably got pissed off by my passivity. There was just nothing for me to do all day and there was nothing I wished to do at night. "Let's both learn bridge," he suggested brightly one day. "Or golf."

"Why?" I asked without a trace of enthusiasm.

"Oh, all our friends play and that way we could spend more time at the club—make new friends, maybe."

"But I'm not interested in bridge or golf," I protested.

"Then what are you interested in?" he asked with irritation. Good question. One that I hadn't dared ask myself. I didn't have an answer, really.

"Why don't you join Bonsai or Ikebana classes, like Varuna?" he suggested.

"Why?" I asked.

"So that you find something to do with yourself. It's not enough just being a wife."

While the husband's little lecture should have amused or irritated me (it was he, after all, who had reduced me to this zombielike state) it had the disastrous effect of making me feel guilty. I suppose I had become resigned to the prospect of being a nondescript wife but now I began to feel guilty each time my husband walked in and caught me reading. I had to do something with myself, I'd think. But what? One of the symptoms of this guilt complex was that I began trying to get my precious books out of my sight—and out of his. I needn't have bothered. The lecture had been a sort of irritated eruption on his part and our lives soon settled into their normal pattern. My books even began, as before, to play a major part in our sex life. We'd both be in bed reading, after watching the news on television. He'd be flipping through London financial papers or a folder, and I'd be hooked on the current book. For many months it was *The World According to Garp*. The book drove me out of my mind. It was so brilliant, I didn't want to finish it. I would be stingy and read five pages a day (my self-imposed quota). Then I'd reread them, till they were practically memorized. Each new day would mean just one thing—five fresh pages. The husband was intrigued. I'd watch his eyes half closing over his papers. He'd turn to look at me. "Sleepy?" I'd shake my head and go back to the book. With one hand on his table lamp switch, he'd ask, "Want to read . . . Or . . . ?" "Read," I'd reply hastily. A look of relief would come over his face. "Good night, then, sleep well." He'd pull the quilt over his shoulder, turn his back to me . . . and leave me to my *Garp*. I felt something very close to love at those moments. I'd watch his sleeping form for a minute or two, and feel grateful. Truly grateful. I'd been spared one more passionless, mechanical encounter. Our "frequency" had been reduced to maybe once every three months. And even during those sessions, I'd be lying there thinking of the book of the moment and wondering what was going to happen next. The minute he was through, I'd rush to the bathroom to wash myself off, come back to my side of the bed, switch on the light and dive into my book. The other man in my life was a hardcover.

One day, like an idiot, I revived the topic of my doing something. "I feel like going back to college," I said.

"College? What on earth for? You weren't such a brilliant student or anything. You've got your second-class BA degree. What will you go to college and study?"

"Anthropology," I replied without thinking.

He snorted in disbelief. "Now I've heard everything. Do you even know what it means? What it's all about?"

"Of course, I do. It was part of my sociology course. I did one paper in it."

"That's not enough. I bet you just scraped through. When did you have the time to study during college? You were so busy running around with your boyfriend—what happened to that creep? You were quite a girl then. I heard all about it when I came back. So what's wrong now? Why this sudden college trip?"

"It was just a thought. Forget it. But I did enjoy those years tremendously. And it might surprise you to know that even though I was not a first-class student I liked studying. I found it stimulating to discover how other societies lived."

"Let me tell you, wifey, you aren't Margaret Mead material. This college business sounds like another one of your crazy ideas."

"OK. OK. Let's just drop the topic."

"Have you fixed up anything for tonight?"

"I'll do it right away."

I took to crosswords like a maniac. And newspaper chess. I'd forget to have a bath sometimes. My mother-in-law would arrive for her midmorning rounds and discover me with uncombed hair, still in my night clothes. "Didn't find the time for a shower?" she'd ask sweetly, and I'd look up guiltily from the crossword. Even the servants were beginning to regard me as cuckoo. I'd overhear them sometimes. "*Hamara memsaab pura din akhbar mein ABCD likhta hai.*" The driver would knock discreetly on the door. "Any duty, memsaab?" And I'd realize it was five p.m. I'd forget small things around the place and neglect to check whether there was enough soda in the bar. Often the ice in the ice trays would run out or we'd be stranded without tonic water. The husband wasn't amused. "What on earth do you do all day that you can't remember things? What are you so busy with? Look at my mother. If you spent more time with her, you'd learn how to run an efficient home. She is so organized—and she also goes to work, mind you. Yet, her house is tip-top. Everything in place. And she herself—always tip-top. Have you ever seen her in a crumpled sari? Doesn't she always carry matching handbags?" My only defense was silence.

Initially, his mother had tried to train me but I hadn't been a very good apprentice. The only time we actually went to the market together was never repeated after she saw that I'd never make a good, tough, penny-pinching daughter-in-law. "It's no good buying fruits and vegetables from the neighborhood vendors," she said as we set out. "Not only do they cheat you, but their stuff is substandard. You save a lot by going to Byculla or Crawford Market." I tried to reason that the petrol spent on these excursions probably added up to much more than the few rupees saved. But she worked by her own logic. "In the mango season, we issue a contract to one wholesaler. I will introduce you to him. He gives us ten dozen raw mangoes which we bury in rice. They ripen gradually and one servant is kept in charge of sorting them out daily. We save more than five hundred rupees this way." I nodded my head and tried to look interested. (After this little pep talk had finally wound to a close, and I had some time to myself, I wept at the irony. Once I'd tried to inveigle my husband into accompanying me to the vegetable market to inject some color into our lives, and now I was resisting my mother-in-law's attempts to get me to the market!)

The lectures rolled endlessly on, mostly in the morning when the husband was away at work. "Oranges and juice mosambis are always bought in Byculla. We do not buy them by the dozen. As for detergents—never buy the known brands. We make our own for the entire year." That went for the grains and the masalas that were laboriously pounded in giant pestles positioned in the garage.

Women from Andhra Pradesh with glittering nose-rings in both nostrils would arrive with naked babies at ten a.m. I'd hear their lilting melodies as they pounded sacks of red chilies rhythmically while the babies bawled in unison, their eyes stung by the chili powder that filled the air. My mother-in-law would watch from the balcony with immense satisfaction and pay them five rupees or some such pittance for their labor. Once I made the mistake of sending down some lunch for them. She came up to my room, her eyes blazing. "What have you done?"

"Nothing—why?"

"Did you send food down to the laborers?"

"Yes—why?"

"It is not a part of our arrangement. Now they'll expect it every day, every year. Food costs money. I'm already paying them such a lot."

"But I only sent them some leftovers."

"Leftovers aren't free. You must be more careful with money. This way the monthly budget will go out of control. We give them one cup of tea twice a day, that's all. Please remember that. These people get spoiled very easily. Tomorrow they'll come and sit on my head and demand a full thali."

"I'm terribly sorry—I didn't know."

She'd hassle the raddiwalla too. I'd hear her haggling over twenty-five paise and accusing the man of cheating. "I know your weights are wrong. I don't trust your scale. I saw you putting your finger in between. You are trying to take advantage of my goodness. But I don't get cheated so easily. I have purchased my own scales. You will use them henceforth. I don't want this nonsense, you've been robbing me for years, you scoundrel."

Once during the monsoon I noticed that the poor man's torn shirt was sopping wet and sent him one of the husband's discarded shirts. My mother-in-law nearly burst a blood vessel. "What are you trying to do? That's a shirt baba bought when he was in England—

Turnbull and Asser. You are giving this rascal an expensive, imported shirt!"

"Yes, but it is over ten years old, and it doesn't fit baba anymore."

"That's not the point. You feel sorry for all these people. But let me tell you they are crooks. Absolute crooks—thieves, all of them. Next, you'll give him an old suit because it doesn't fit baba. Whatever doesn't fit can always be sold at a good price. You leave it to me. I know a lady who buys used clothes, especially imported ones. I'll contact her tomorrow."

I would wonder at the husband's unquestioning acceptance of his mother's view of things. Mama's boy was too pat a solution, for surely there were some things that their views could differ on! After all they belonged to different generations and he and I belonged to the same generation. We'd been to the same college. We had friends in common. Then why were we constantly at loggerheads? Why did I hate to supervise the detergent-making operation when various chemicals ate right through the rubber gloves given to the servants to "protect" their hands? Why did I prefer crosswords to conversation? And Scrabble to cocktail parties? And most of all I wondered why I didn't get the hell out of the marriage. If I'd had the gumption to show my displeasure, as I had at the time of the party when I had met Ritu, why couldn't I go the whole way and walk out? I don't know, perhaps it was because, for all my little rebellions, I was a well-trained Indian wife!

CHAPTER 8

THE MORE MY MARRIAGE DEADENED, THE HARDER I TRIED TO CON-
vince myself that I was happy enough as I was. I began to see myself
as a drifter, letting life happen to me. If the husband was unhappy
I'd try not to argue, only do things the way he wanted. It was easier
that way. I felt passive and powerless and tried not to think about my
problems. For if I thought about them I'd have to make some decisions, the last thing I wanted to do.

Then, Anjali phoned. She had returned from her vacation in
France a fortnight or so ago and apologized for not calling earlier. I
welcomed her phone call with a gratitude I'd not felt for her presence in a long time. We arranged to meet and I unfolded my unhappiness over a long lunch at the Apollo bar at the Taj. Her comebacks
were vintage Anjali.

"You are bored with your husband. You need an affair," she said.

"Like I need a hole in the head," I said wryly.

"No. You need an affair," she repeated firmly.

"Affairs are not the ultimate solution Anjali," I argued.

"No? You'd be surprised, darling."

"I sure as hell would. Frankly, Anjali I'd rather scratch my head
for a four-letter word beginning with an 'f' which means to adore,
rather than the other one. Get what I mean?"

"You're nuts."

Anjali's attentiveness to my problems lasted only about half an hour. For, surprise, surprise, she was in love again, but this time she managed to stun me.

"My new guy," she said, "isn't a man . . . He's a boy." One thing I had to hand it to her, she certainly wasn't predictable in her choice of specimen.

"Now, where did you meet your latest find—this 'boy'—how old is he by the way?"

"I'll only tell you if you promise not to be cynical."

"I solemnly promise not to be cynical."

"All right. I met him at the health club. The one right here in this hotel."

"Oh, I get it. He's one of those pumping iron studs is he? The hunks who rub you down after a sauna, while you rub them up?"

"Another Bloody Mary, please," she shouted, without bothering to answer. After a long pause and three drags of her Kent lite, she continued. "I used to see him working out every day. Later, we'd meet in the yoga class and smile."

"Really, how sweet!"

"Go on, bitch away, you frigid bitch. I don't care. Yes, that's how it started. We used to smile at each other, and I would feel self-conscious, because I'd catch him staring at my hips. Now, you know how I feel about my hips. I hate them! I want to slice them off. Remember, I have those little things jutting out—what are they called—saddle bags or something?"

"Forget your hips and get on with the story. OK, so he stared rudely at your saddle bags and you felt self-conscious. Next?"

"One day he didn't turn up for the class."

"How sad, *ma cherie*," I said deliberately, just to remind her of her Frenchie.

"Yes—it was very sad. He didn't turn up for three more classes—that's when I panicked. I thought he'd given up. Or that he was sick or something. Then I realized I didn't even know his name. I was literally moping, like a lovesick schoolgirl. Finally, he showed up a week later. 'Hey, where were you all these days?' I asked.

"'Why? Did you miss me?' he asked boldly and winked. I must have blushed or something, because he added, 'You know what? I missed you too, kid!'—KID!! Can you beat it. How cheeky!"

So, they'd got off to this great start, and it was presumably all going wonderfully.

"I wish it was. But I haven't told you the most embarrassing part as yet—his mother turned out to be one of the women in my Bonsai class!" she said.

"Oh no!"

"Not just that. I quite like her."

"Does she know you are having it off with her son?"

"You know, sometimes I wonder why I bother to be civil to you. I hate your sarcastic tone. What do you mean 'having it off'? This is the most beautiful thing to have happened to me. You know how bruised I was after the last episode. What Karan and I share is a very tender and beautiful relationship."

"You mean—no sex?"

"Sex. Sex. Sex. What's wrong with you, woman? Obviously you don't get enough of it. You seem to have sex on your mind all the time."

"That doesn't answer me—just say a simple yes or no."

"OK, I'll give it to you straight—we've been to bed just once. Rather, I forced him into it. Poor darling was so overcome, he is still in a state of shock."

"You mean you raped a minor?"

"He's not a minor and I didn't rape him, well, not exactly. But it was a major mistake. He refuses to touch me now."

"That translated means that you want it and he doesn't—am I right?"

"It's not so simple. He is a very sensitive and artistic boy," she said in a voice filled with rapture.

"You mean, he's a bum."

"No, I mean he's an Aquarian. You know how Aquarian men vibe with my sign?"

"No, I don't and I'm not interested either. But do go on."

"He was sloshed at the time but I knew he wanted it desperately. He was just scared."

"How old is the guy, Anjali? Twelve?? What do you mean 'scared'?"

"He comes from a very conservative Punjabi family. He has had girlfriends in the past—but those relationships didn't go beyond petting and necking. He is still very young, you know."

"How young? Come on, out with it. How young is very young?"

"Twenty-four."

I exploded when she confessed. "Anjali, you are disgraceful. He's the same age as Mimi. What's wrong with you? Why don't you find someone more of your age? What's your new number now? Are you doing a Mrs. Robinson on him?"

"It sounds terrible. But it isn't. I realize I shouldn't have forced him. He wasn't ready for it. I should have waited a little."

"Hell—poor fellow must've thought he was screwing his mother. This is getting very Freudian and complex."

"But he loves me—he told me so."

"Yes, but like a mother, honey, like a mother."

"No, no, no. He wants to spend the rest of his life with me. I've tried to break up many times, but he begs me to see him again and not leave him. He's told me all about his life. I know about his girl-friends. But he has never met someone like me. Someone mature and sensitive."

Oh Jesus! Anjali and mature? Sensitive—maybe. "But listen, you dope. This isn't going to take you anywhere. There is no future with the stud. What's in it for you? It's not even as if you're having a great time in bed."

"You wouldn't understand. We spend hours just talking. I'm

planning to take him to Delhi with me. Maybe in a new environment he'll feel differently. Maybe he'll be more relaxed."

"Does his mommy know?"

"Yes, I told her I want to take him in hand and groom him. I've offered him a job."

"What? As what?? A live-in gigolo??? What is his designation—chief nonscrewer?"

"Why am I paying for your drinks and lunch? You know, I don't need this crap, I really don't. I could be with Karan right now. He's waiting in the bookshop downstairs."

"Go ahead," I said, getting mad. "I'm beginning to feel pukey. I don't know what you expected from me. Did you think I would jump with joy and pat you on the back for this? I think you're disgusting and this is disgraceful. Why don't you leave the kid alone. What about Mimi? Does she know? Or are you both fighting over his crotch?" Anjali was fuming.

"By the way," I said, "I hate to remind you, but this lunch was supposed to be for me. I wanted to talk about what's happening to my life. I wanted to unwind. But I guess I should have known better. It's always you, you, you, you and your men. You and your tits. I'm pretty sick of the whole thing. But let me tell you, if I'd suspected that I'd be sharing canapés with a cradle-snatcher, I wouldn't have come."

I thought that was quite a speech. But Anjali just looked moonily at me. I might as well have spared the effort. "Do you want to meet him? Let's call him up. I'll go bring him—or wait. I'll call downstairs for him. I'm too drunk to walk."

And that's how young Karan and I met. I hated him on sight. Callow youth, I thought, as he walked up with a cocky John Travolta swing. He looked like one of those typical Punjabi teddy boys from Delhi's Karol Bagh. The kind who whirl round and round in the skating rink at Simla during the summer, hoping to pick up a girl. His second disqualification was the scruffy beard and sleeveless T-shirt with masses of underarm hair hanging from the armpit. He was wearing an expensive watch and gold chain. I wondered whether Anjali or some other Anjali had given him that out of eternal gratitude. She intercepted my thoughts. "Isn't Karan's watch and chain gorgeous? His mummy gave them to him on his twenty-first birthday. Oh Karan, remember I told you about my old friend? Well, this is her." Then turning to me, "And this is Karan, my young friend." OK. She'd made sure we got that right. It was a pretty awkward afternoon once Karan joined us. I noticed she couldn't keep her hands off him and he seemed visibly embarrassed by her attention. He had a good voice, but his speech was all wrong. Obviously, he hadn't been to the right school. And I doubted whether he'd been to college. His body? It was a good enough body but not a great one. But then, I was never much of a body person, so I wasn't surprised that left me cold. He seemed polite enough—he rushed to light her cigarettes and stood up to hold her chair when she lurched off to the loo, but I got the impression he was playing some game—acting dumber than he really was.

My hunch proved right. Three months later Anjali came over unannounced. The first thing I noticed was that she hadn't done her nails. Not only were they yellowish and discolored, they looked like she'd been chewing them! She had a desperate air about her—but worse than that, she had a great big black eye.

"What happened?" I asked alarmed.

"Nothing. I walked into a doorknob!"

"Listen, don't be stupid. Tell me. Did Karan do that?"

"I told you the doorknob did it."

God! It was going to be one of those sessions. I wasn't feeling patient enough. "OK. Have it your way. Now don't tell me you were attempting to screw the doorknob and it jumped up and slugged you?" I shouldn't have said that for Anjali collapsed. She just folded into a heap and lay sobbing on the bed. I felt awful. I tried to comfort her but she pushed me away. "Leave me alone. Just leave me alone." I asked the servant to get her some strong coffee in the hope that this would calm her down. Frankly, in addition to concern for her I was worried the husband would walk in and discover this strange scene. Maybe I was being selfish but I was in no mood to explain anything to him.

Fortunately, the coffee did it. She recovered sufficiently to tell me what had happened. The Delhi trip had been a disaster. She'd taken him around and introduced him to all her contacts as a senior sales executive ("I'd even bought him an expensive suit for his sales calls"). They'd discreetly booked two adjoining single rooms at the Taj Man Singh, but she'd hoped that he'd walk in through the connecting door at night. When that didn't happen, she'd decided to walk into his room, except she found the door locked. She'd called the room and there was no reply. She'd decided to wait up for him. Around three a.m. she'd heard the sound of the toilet flushing and had immediately called the room. When he answered, she'd demanded angrily, "Where the hell have you been?"

"Just cool it, lady," he'd replied calmly. "You don't own me, remember. I went down to the coffee shop because I couldn't sleep. I ran into some Bombay friends and we decided to go to the disco. OK. And will you please lay off now. I need to catch up on my sleep before all those appointments tomorrow!"

"You're fired! Do you hear me? Fired. You bastard. How could you do this to me? You are here at my expense. You'd better do what I tell you to."

"Good night," he'd said and put the phone down.

The next morning she'd woken up seething. He'd come to her room with a cheery "Good morning! Wakey, wakey!" but she wasn't about to be mollified that easily.

"I told you, you are fired. Get out!" she'd screamed.

"Hey, easy does it. That was last night. This is today—a new day.

We've got work to do. Come on. Get your ass off the bed—let's go."

As she said it, she couldn't believe his gall. "There he was, so cool and controlled, while I was ready to die. I don't know what got into me, I hurled an ashtray at him. He ducked and it missed him. Then he came at me like an animal and gave me a left hook that sent me flying across the room. And that's the last I saw of him. I should have seen it coming."

I wish that's the last I'd seen of Karan. But that was not to be. He popped up again with the last person I'd have expected, but by then I was beginning to be less and less shocked by life's twists.

Anjali took the breakup very badly. Suddenly she was forced to confront an ugly truth—she was getting old. This was particularly evident in the way she looked at men now. I had noticed this at our long lunch when her eyes kept darting all over the Apollo bar. But even as I sympathized with her I was angry in a strange sort of way. Why, I would ask myself, did I allow Anjali to upstage me even in our low moments? But I could never sustain my indignation for long and would invariably forgive her. The husband commented on this once during one of his rare perceptive moments. "Why are you so generous and loving with that friend of yours? I don't see this side of you with any of my friends. With them you are harsh and judgmental. But Anjali—oh, she's treated like a visiting maharani. Let me tell you something. You may think she's fantastic, but her reputation is awful. You should hear what the guys at the bar say about her." I cut him short, "Listen, I haven't as yet descended to the level of listening to cheap bar gossip. I happen to like Anjali—that's all." He beat a hasty retreat, as he usually did on the infrequent occasions when I stood my ground, and switched on Handel. I always knew when he was crushed. Phut! went the stereo switch and on came Handel full blast. What he'd said was perfectly true of course. Anjali was teetering dangerously on the brink and her actions had begun to match her emotions. She'd lost her father recently, and from what she said, she hadn't been very welcome at the funeral and other associated functions. Her mother had made it very clear that the presence of a divorced, and therefore debauched, daughter was nothing but an embarrassment to her. Almost viciously, she had instructed her to stay away from the besana—the wake two days after the funeral when the women of the family received mourners. "We have suffered enough because of you," she was told. "First you marry a mussulman. That was when dadaji got his initial attack. Then you go and divorce him. That is what killed your father. It is our misfortune to have such a daughter. But that is fate. Now, do us one last favor—stay away. We don't want relatives and members of our community to ask us awkward questions at a time like this."

That just about put the seal on Anjali's misfortune. Hounded out of her own home, she had nowhere to go, no one, with the possible exception of me, to turn to. Even her tenuous links with her ex-husband were almost sundered since Abe had taken on a full-time mistress: an anglo-Indian woman who must have been attractive at some point, but now looked blowsy with bags under her eyes and enormous boobs that nearly reached her toes. "The Udder Woman" Anjali would joke when in a savage mood. Abe had sold off his interests in the family business and was perfectly content to spend his days gambling or in bed. His woman Gigi slopped around the place stoned witless, her dressing gown forever open with those unbelievable breasts swaying in and out.

With her world arrayed against her, Anjali plumbed the lowest depths she would ever reach. For a start she began running with a cheapie film crowd. I did what I could but a nympho starlet was Anjali's main woman now and she'd shrug me off. Once I made an uncharacteristically long speech on the phone. "These people aren't your type." I ended, "Why are you wasting time with them. And that new fancy piece of yours—Nisha—come on, what's going on? She's a foul-mouthed slut."

Anjali didn't seem to want to discuss her new "friends." "You're being a snob. They're people too. I enjoy them. They are uncomplicated and fun. Why don't you stick to playing Ms. High-and-Mighty and leave me alone. Anyway—Nisha is great company. I get all the gossip firsthand and I find her most relaxing."

"If you don't watch it, you might end up getting more than just gossip from her. Heard of herpes? VD?"

"You're so full of shit, you know. I can't bear your prejudices. Besides, you haven't even met her. Why do you believe what the film magazines say?"

"OK. So, introduce us."

"Why? Just to give you the pleasure of tearing her to pieces?"

"No. Maybe I'm feeling protective about you. I don't want you to die a painful death. I want to save you from AIDS."

"I hate you," Anjali spat and slammed down the phone.

I did meet Nisha eventually. This was months later.

Anjali called one afternoon, all breathless and excited. "Listen— is that bore at home?" referring to the husband.

"No, sweetheart. He isn't Abe, you know. He works for a living."

Ignoring that, she continued, "Guess what? Nisha is with me right now and she wants to show you her body."

"WHAT?" I nearly screamed. "What makes you think I'm interested in seeing that whore's diseased body. Please—stop—I'll bring up my lunch."

"Don't be such a stick-in-the-mud. I tell you, this woman has the most fantastic figure—it's perfect. She just wants to show it to you—that's all. You don't have to sleep with it or anything."

"It!" Imagine that. Grudgingly I had to admit I was curious. I had heard and read so much about this body. Of course, I'd also seen most of it in all the cheesecake shots Nisha so obligingly posed for. But that wasn't the same as seeing the Indian Marilyn Monroe in flesh and blood—and what's more, in my own bedroom. I tried to keep the excitement out of my voice. I pretended I was doing them both a big favor. "OK," I said. "But come quickly, I want you out of the house before he gets home."

Twenty minutes later, they were there. Nisha looked very demure in a white sari, with an enormous red bindi on her forehead. I asked Anjali about this. "Oh, she's just been to bed with DK," she said in a low voice. "You know—that old sod? He has the hots for her and hires a suite at the Sea Rock for their fortnightly fucks. And, you know about his white sari hang-up. He tells her, 'I like to see you in white and with a big tikka on your forehead. Then I imagine I'm screwing a devi and not the "pros" you are.'"

"And she doesn't mind being talked to like that?"

"Well, five thousand bucks is five thousand bucks. Plus, he recommends her to his producer buddies and she gets the odd role."

"Oh, great! She sounds real classy," I said with calculated irony. It went completely over Anjali's head.

"Yes, yes, yes. She isn't like the other film girls. She's studied in a Bandra convent. She speaks English with a good accent. She has even heard of Barbara Streisand. You must ask her to sing 'Woman in Love' for you."

"While she's stripping—or later?" I asked.

Again, Anjali gushed, "Oh, anytime. She does a beautiful slow strip to it. We have it on video—she did it at the Khan party recently. Everybody just loved it."

"I'm sure they did. All right, then—let's get on with it."

All this while, Nisha had been walking around the place taking an inventory. I could almost hear her counting. I half expected her to pull out a tiny calculator and tot it all up. She'd kept her distance with me, but had obviously sized me up with a glance and had concluded "harmless." I could almost hear her telling Anjali on their way home, "Your friend is harmless, yaar. Very sweet and all that. But what do you do with her? Discuss how to make papads and achaar?"

The show began after Nisha and Anjali had both fortified themselves with a stiff shot of vodka from the husband's bar. As Nisha swigged her drink, I took Anjali into the bedroom and asked her, "Why does she want me to see her body? Or is that a stupid question?"

"Oh—I don't know—let's ask her," she said and we went back to the bar. "Hey Nisha, babykins, why do you want her to see your body?"

"Because it's perfect," said Nisha and took a large sip of her drink. She seemed to remember something suddenly. "Girls. Is it OK if I keep my panties on?"

Anjali groaned and then yelled, "No! How can she see that lovely mole on your bum then?"

"I should have told you this earlier—but I'm having my period. And I don't wear tampons."

"Listen," I whispered fiercely to Anjali. "Why don't we keep this for another day? Really, let's forget the whole thing."

"No way. She's here, you're here, and the show must go on." She turned to Nisha and instructed her firmly, "Why don't you be a good girl and just take yourself off to the loo. Do whatever it is that needs to be done and come back."

"Look, Anjali," I intervened still whispering, though it appeared that Nisha wouldn't have minded if I'd been shouting, "my loo happens to be across the corridor. I don't want this crazy nympho running around naked for all the servants to see."

"Give her one of your kimonos, darling. Don't be difficult." Like an obedient fool, off I went to fish out a kimono. I was racked with visions of contracting some unmentionable disease and had already decided to throw it away when she was through.

Nisha emerged from the bathroom with what she thought was a sexy pout. I thought, "How utterly vulgar this woman looks even fully clothed! And that mouth—it's vile and obscene. An overused fellatio mouth." She swayed into the bedroom and struck a pose against the door frame. Anjali whistled.

"Ready?" asked Nisha.

"You're ON!!" shouted Anjali.

"I am a woman in love and I'll do anything . . . to get you into my world . . . and hold you within . . ." She dropped one shoulder and stuck out a leg. "Note, girls, I'm keeping my heels on. They give a better shape to the legs." Then with one great swirl, the kimono was at her feet. "Voila!" she exclaimed with her arms raised, her hands in her hair. I didn't know where to look. While I certainly was pretty curious, I felt embarrassed to stare.

"Go ahead! Have a good look," urged Anjali. "Look at that mole—isn't it too much . . . Nisha, turn around so that she can see how narrow your waist looks at that angle."

Nisha was moving in slow motion, softly humming under her breath. "You seem eternally mine . . . in love there is no measure of time."

Anjali nudged me. "Look, look she bleaches and shapes down there. Doesn't it look cute?"

"Doesn't it burn?" I asked despite myself.

"Of course not. You've got to know how to do it. Nisha was saying it drives DK wild."

At this point Nisha interrupted. "I give my men the works, girls. The absolute works!" There was one question I'd always been dying to ask experienced women. This seemed an appropriate enough time. "What do you mean by 'the works'? I often read about woman being 'good in bed.' What exactly do they do to qualify?"

"Well, darling. Are you asking me to reveal all my trade secrets?" Nisha asked archly.

"No—just asking you to educate an illiterate woman."

"I can only tell you about myself. And I'm the best. But I don't think you're old enough to hear it—ha! ha!"

Anjali whispered, "Nisha does stuff with crushed ice, oil, spirits you know, that sort of thing." I was still clueless but thought I'd be wasting my time trying to push it. Oh, yes, and Nisha's "perfect" body—I must admit it looked pretty grotesque to me, with bulbous breasts and a small ass. If there was one feature that was indeed Perfect—it was her navel. But, as she sardonically pointed out to me, "It is cute, yaar. But what use is it to me?" She had a point.

CHAPTER 9

AT THIS TIME MY ELDEST SISTER, THE ONE WHO'D MARRIED THE EN-
gineer and moved to London, dropped a bombshell. She was divorc-
ing her husband, she wrote, but would be staying on in England.
Mother told me all this in a tired voice over the phone and almost
before she had stopped speaking I had the driver take me to the house
in the suburbs they'd retired to. I'd seen my family but infrequently
after I'd married, primarily because Father as usual had laid down the
law. "Parents do not go and sit around in their daughters' homes," he'd
said. So their visits were reserved for ceremonial occasions—like
Diwali. And these were very formal affairs. Everybody was stiff and it
was a relief when they left. The husband wasn't one of those men who
marry the whole family along with the daughter. Being reserved (and
boring) he didn't have much to say to anyone, and even less to my parents. But he maintained what he called "cordial relations." Anyway, as
I sat talking to Mother I realized the conversation was veering around
to children. "It's a good thing she didn't have children," I said. "The
children always come off the worst in a divorce."

She raised her head. "Well I hope you'll have one soon."

"Mother," I said, "we've been over this before. I don't want children and neither does my husband."

"Why don't you have a proper checkup?" Mother asked, obviously not listening to me. "Do you get your periods regularly?"

"Yes, Mother, I do. I'll show you proof if you're that interested.
But I don't want children. I don't like children."

She stared at me thoughtfully. "You'll get a beard by the time you reach forty. And then you will regret your decision."

"I'll risk sprouting whiskers. Mother," I told her, "electrolysis is cheaper than children."

I felt bad immediately, being facetious at a time when she was obviously upset, but Mother seemed not to mind. Or perhaps she was past caring. I thought about her who, to my eyes, had served out a life sentence as a domesticated wife, still able to be concerned about my sisters and me and I felt small and unheroic. But later, as I was driven home, I envied my sister. At least she'd had the guts to break free from an unhappy situation (her husband had taken an English mistress) while here I was still playing out a witless little charade. As usual I thought to myself that I should get out, that I should break free, but some spark had been extinguished in me.

My sole comfort was Ritu. She had been away for six months in Switzerland with a married sister and I was delighted she was back. At least she was someone to talk to and be with. With Anjali lost to the filmi set (though she'd never been any great help in pointing me in any direction given that I did most of the nannying in the relationship) Ritu began dominating my life and not because of our talks alone. I was fascinated by her way with men. Whatever it was she had, she attracted all sorts, from little servant boys she mothered to silver-haired industrialists, who drooled at her feet and begged for a smile. "All the men I've ever known have always fallen in love with me," she'd say without a trace of boastfulness. At one of our early outings together, I found her in the hostess' bedroom, sitting on the bed, with a slobbering man at her feet. He was weeping while she was murmuring soothing words.

He repeatedly clutched her feet and slobbered all over them. "Trample me, walk all over me—but let's spend one night together. Just one. Is that too much to ask?" She signaled me to sit next to her.

"Have you met my friend?" she asked her tearful admirer.

"Look, I don't care a turd about your friend or anyone else. I want you. Just you." And he burst into a fresh round of tears.

She looked at me and winked. "He wants to drink champagne out of my slippers. He wants to lick wine off my toes. Isn't he sweet?"

"Come home with me, Ritu. We'll never get a chance like this. My wife's in Vienna, your husband's in Hyderabad. This is too good an opportunity to blow." He turned to me desperately. "Friend . . . tell her."

I looked at her and said, "Maybe you should go with him."

Her eyes widened with alarm and she shook her head violently. Very gently, she removed her foot from his clutches and retrieved her sandals. "Shall we leave? Your husband must be waiting," she said, and got up.

The poor man collapsed in a heap on the floor and started to flail his limbs about like a child throwing a tantrum. "You are a cruel woman," he moaned.

Just then, our hostess walked in. "Well, well, well—what do we have here? Ritu, what have you done to this poor man? He looks destroyed!"

I thought it was pretty perceptive of her to address that remark to Ritu and not to me, though, on reflection, I guess I didn't look the sort men would grovel on the floor for.

"He's OK," Ritu said. "It's the wine, smoke and air-conditioning that's got to him. I think he needs a doctor." I was amazed by her cool handling of the situation.

"Why did you go into the bedroom with him in the first place?" I demanded as we rejoined the party.

"I didn't. I'd gone to the loo and he followed me in.

"You were encouraging him. You led him on. Why did you flirt if you weren't interested in him?"

"Don't be silly. You call that flirting? Then you haven't seen me in action."

Ritu, I realized soon enough, had managed to cope extremely well with the circumstances that straitjacketed wives like me. Her only grouse against her husband was his lack of drive and general un-adventurousness. And so she maintained the other satellites in her orbit for temporary amusement. She sent out messages, maybe without even meaning to do so. But I'd watched her at parties, a few at my own home and I concluded that she was what the glossies always described as a "natural flirt." She couldn't help herself. "It's all terribly harmless," she'd insist. "Plus, I think you are far too uptight and old-fashioned." Her husband, well-trained by her, to make the right responses, reveled in her glamour and sex appeal. I'd seen him sidle up to her at parties and whisper, "Did you see the way that guy has been staring at you all evening?" It was innocent enough on her part. The men always made fools of themselves. At one party in their home, a prominent businessman said to her, loudly, "I'm going to Singapore next week. What shall I bring back for my lovely one?"

She looked embarrassed for a minute but recovered fast enough to say, "I'd love a Big Mac—Can you manage that?"

"Why not? Your wish is my command, lady."

Ritu was holidaying with the family in Mahabaleshwar the following weekend, when a chauffeur-driven Mercedes drove up. The driver leaped out and gave her a large package. "With compliments from Mr. Gupta." Gift-wrapped elaborately and presented on a silver salver was the Big Mac she'd asked for. Soggy and stale—but there it was. Her husband was even more tickled than she was.

I suppose the reason I really hit it off with Ritu was because she was everything I wasn't. She was spontaneous, I was inflexible. She was shallow, vibrant, buoyant and fun. I was anxiety-ridden and tense when I was not anxiety-ridden and bored. And the best part about Ritu was that while she enjoyed every nugget of the attention she got, she didn't use the power she had over men the way some women did. For her it was all just fun.

"Isn't it wonderful to be pampered?" she'd ask with a twinkle.

"I wouldn't know, never having experienced it," I'd say flatly.

"That's because you're too tense. You scare men."

"Maybe they scare me," I'd say defensively. Invariably, when she'd be spending an afternoon at my home, the phone would ring. "It's for you," I'd say. "Now, who's the new one on the scene?"

She could seduce someone over the phone, she was that good at it. But like she always maintained, "I don't really do anything. I don't sleep with these men. They don't threaten my marriage."

"Then why?" I'd ask.

"It's nice to have them around. It's flattering. It keeps me going. There's an incentive to dress up." Oh boy! She could say that again. If there was one woman I knew who spent a major portion of her time planning her wardrobe and jewelry, it was Ritu. She loved dolling up. She loved to watch herself dressing. She would lavish at least an hour and a half before a party going through the whole routine—a leisurely perfumed bath, maybe a shampoo, a face scrub with some imported grains, feet and hands scrub with a pumice stone, a good rub with a fluffy towel ("Don't you love the texture of a Turkish towel against freshly bathed skin?"), deodorant, perfume (always the latest one), and then the short but effective makeup routine. Her dressing room resembled the makeup rooms of Hollywood stars. Professional lights all around the long mirror, lights inside the wardrobe, a basketful of brushes and accessories hanging in a corner, the closet neatly divided up into sections and rows upon rows of sandals. Ritu had a shoe fetish. She had more than two hundred pairs of shoes, and was truly surprised when the world made a fuss over Imelda Marcos' collection. "I thought all women bought sandals," she commented. "Yes, of course, they do," I told her, "but it's not a disease with them." "Really? How strange," she said, looking genuinely puzzled. The same afternoon she added five more pairs to her collection. And then Ritu, the only woman I'd known who'd taken up the destructive challenge of high society living and turned it right around to her own advantage, lost her touch—if briefly. And the one who put her life on the skids was, of all things, Karan. Yes, Anjali's ex-huckster-gigolo and the last person I'd have expected to bewitch the enchantress herself. They met on the tennis court. She was wearing a sexy T-shirt with a sequined melon on it. He was sitting on the sidelines watching her powerful game. She saw him staring and, as was instinctive to her, pulled in her breath and pushed out her breasts. At the end of a set he came over and said, "Your melon looks tantalizing. I feel like biting into it." Corny, but it worked. She giggled and asked him whether he was a player or just an ogler. "I'm equally good at both—playing and ogling," said Karan in true gigolo-fashion and swept Ritu off into an affair she'd have preferred to forget.

Naturally, when I heard about Karan's entry into her life I was aghast. "Don't be ridiculous. I know how that man operates. You don't need a toyboy at this stage. Just drop him." "I can't. I've never felt like this before." This was lunatic. First Anjali and now her. "Why don't you tell him that you know all about his past. Tell him you're a friend of mine and that I'm a friend of Anjali's. See his reaction." Ritu promptly went and repeated what I'd asked her to. "Oh, you mean that old hag and her chamchi? Forget it, sexy, let's not waste our time over those two." Ritu preferred his version to mine and that was that.

After this I decided to keep well out of her personal life. If she wanted to get taken, it was not my concern. But I'd underestimated Ritu. Where Anjali would have twisted herself into knots every which way to keep her man hooked, Ritu, for all her claim that Karan was an event in her life, still kept her cool and her distance. She'd come over to see me and Karan would never be mentioned. Not out of any desire to spare me embarrassment but simply because he didn't rule her iife. Gradually I began to look upon her as a sister, the sort of sister my sisters had never been. This showed in all sorts of ways. For instance, on one occasion Ritu was around when I was cleaning out a cupboard. She joined in spontaneously and started to sort out my clothes and then exclaimed, "God! You live like a refugee. What are all these tied-up bundles?" Suddenly, I noticed, for the first time, that my cupboard really was a hopeless mess with several little heaps all tied up in old saris, a hangover I realized from the time I had to share an ugly Godrej cupboard with my sisters. The only way of separating our belongings then was to tie them up in individual lots. It hadn't occurred to me that now that I had these wonderful rosewood cupboards from Chor Bazaar all to myself there was really no need to squeeze my clothes into ugly heaps. Then she looked at my jewelry. "Good heavens! Look at the way you've kept your jewelry! You'll spoil it like this. You've just thrown stuff together—the pearl strings will break and the stones will get damaged." A couple of days later, she arrived with a determined gleam in her eyes. "Look, why don't you empty out the drawer and let me line it for you. I've brought the felt, fevicol, scissors—everything." For over two hours I watched her bending over the drawer and painstakingly pasting the felt pieces into place. It was a treat looking at her hands moving so efficiently, her entire self concentrating on doing a neat job. An elder sister, I thought, or perhaps an adoring younger sister. For a flash I liked myself as an object of adoration and then the self-deprecation set in and I began anxiously and ineffectually to help her until she shooed me away.

As the months passed it became obvious her Karan affair wasn't really going anywhere. She'd mention it casually every now and again and usually, to my amazement, it would be with an amused air. God, I'd think to myself, the woman has a soul of ice.

Then Karan started becoming jealous and possessive. If she did her usual forty laps at the pool after a game he'd snap, "You are showing off." If she stopped to chat with someone else, he'd ask, "Who was that guy you were making eyes at?" Ritu lapped it up in the beginning and said it was like being back in school. The puppy love syndrome. Then Karan began to get on her nerves with his suspicions. "The bloody fellow is not even a real boyfriend," she commented exasperatedly one day. "Why do I need this? Even my husband doesn't ask so many questions." Karan's demands on her time started to increase. Apparently, he didn't want to remain a "swimming-pool friend." He'd said, "I want to date you. I want to take you out to dinner. Go dancing."

"That's impossible, idiot," she'd told him. "What do I tell my husband? 'Look, sweetheart, I hope it's OK with you, but I'm hitting the nightspots with this stud friend of mine?' You're crazy, Karan. It's not possible." And then for the only time in those early years of our friendship she asked me what to do. "Drop him," I said. "I've told you what a jerk he is." "I am scared to. What if he slugs me like he did Anjali?" she asked half seriously. "He won't dare," I assured her. "You aren't Anjali."

The matter ended there but a fortnight later, as I was rushing through the shopping arcade at the Oberoi hotel, I ran into both of them. I would have thought Karan would feel embarrassed at the sight of me.

No way. He greeted me coolly and had the nerve to ask jauntily, "Oh, by the way, how's that friend of yours, Anjali's the name, isn't it?"

Something snapped inside me right then. "Listen, asshole," I heard myself saying, "don't give me your fancy lines. You're nothing but a cheap male whore. Why don't you leave Ritu alone?"

I was stunned by my own venom, but the sight of him standing there in his Calvin Kleins, fingering the gold chain around his hairy chest and playing with his Carrera sunglasses was too much.

And then Ritu redeemed herself completely in my eyes. "Bravo!" she said. "You stole the words right out of my mouth. Why hadn't I thought of saying them earlier?" With that, she linked her arm affectionately through mine. "Let's go!" she said and threw a few shopping bags full of shoes at Karan. "I'm booting you out, baby. In style."

When we reached the escalator I couldn't resist looking back. Karan was on all fours on the floor, gathering up the scattered shoes. He saw me looking—and then he shrugged, grinned broadly and blew me a kiss!

CHAPTER 10

Just as we were getting into the car, we spotted Anjali. She was obviously coming out from the beauty salon as she had her nail varnishes and hair-conditioners in her hand. She saw us and waved urgently. "This is straight out of a C-grade film," I said to Ritu, as we walked over. "Imagine running into her of all people."

Before I could tell her about the Karan scene, she announced in a thin, high-pitched, semi-hysterical voice, "Guess what, girls? I'm getting married!" Her nails gleamed in the afternoon sun. Frosted peach with eye shadow to match.

"Great!" I said unenthusiastically. "Let's celebrate!"

"My treat!" Anjali squealed. "Let's celebrate!"

"I have to call my husband first," I said.

"Oh! Don't be such a bore. Honestly, you and your 'duties.'"

"It's not that. He might wait lunch for me," I said defensively.

"Call from the bar," Anjali commanded and herded us into her car.

"Listen, let's skip the bar bit," I suggested. "I'm hungry. So is Ritu. Why don't we just get ourselves a quick lunch?"

"You girls are such drips. It's such an occasion for me, and you don't want to be a part of it," Anjali pouted.

Ritu piped up, "Of course we do. But we have to be getting back—at least I do."

Anjali didn't say anything. She pulled out her Charles Jourdan sunglasses and stared at her nails.

"Lovely glasses," Ritu said.

"Wait a minute," I interrupted. "Look at that ring! Anjali—no—you mean, this time it's for real?"

"What did you think, you horror? Of course, it's for real—and it's pretty soon. No point in waiting. The wedding is a few months from now. Now, stop gaping at the ring and have the decency to ask me the name of the man I'm marrying."

Ritu giggled, "What does it matter? Any man who can give you a rock that size must be fine. Even if he's the hunchback of Notre Dame, to hell with it!"

We decided to "grab a crab," as Anjali put it, at Nanking.

"It's crawling all over with cockroaches," I protested.

"So what, darling? You don't have to eat them!" Anjali insisted.

"I'm not so sure—but what the hell, now that we're here." I first made my "duty call." The husband didn't sound pleased. "So you just ran into those two women—did you? Anyway, have fun, what else can I say. And, by the way, there were no hand towels in our bathroom this morning. And don't forget to pick up my shaving cream on the way home." Those remarks were meant to kill me. I'd taught myself to shrug them off. I rejoined my friends at the table. "There's fresh broccoli today," Ritu announced. We ordered the broccoli and crab to follow. The crab arrived. It wasn't stuffed with cockroaches. I checked.

"So, let's hear it," I urged Anjali. "Who's the guy? What does he do? Where did you meet him?"

"Let me get myself a drink first," Anjali said.

"Tough luck, honey. All you'll get here is ginger ale. And cockroaches. But carry on . . ."

"Oh, his name is Kumar, Kumar Bhandari."

"Punjabi??" Ritu and I chorused.

"Well—half and half. His mother's from Coorg."

"That's OK. He's all right then. Next."

"He's a businessman—some sort of an engineering company.

Now, don't ask me what and where. He has a factory outside Bombay and they export machine tools or something like that. And I met him at a party—where else? You know—the party at the Mehras I'd told you guys about?"

"No—I don't know anything about this party," I said, "but it doesn't matter. What happened there? What were you wearing? Tell us everything—and make it fast. I have to buy shaving cream."

"Is that fucking shaving cream more important to you than my future?" Anjali asked.

I spoke soothingly and she seemed mollified enough. Besides, it was obvious, she was dying to tell the story. She'd gone to the party reluctantly, since she had a migraine. But the Mehra wife phoned and insisted. Anjali wore her sequined black chiffon ("The one Abe used to adore me in"), slapped on lots of glitter dust ("even between the titties"), wore her favorite diamonds ("my first Cartier set—remember it?"), and went migraine and all. She'd expected it to be a smallish affair, but as it turned out, there were over a hundred people. As she had been chatting with some impoverished princeling, a man nearby who had obviously been overhearing their conversation ("Such silly stuff, you know, who's sleeping with whom, and all that") said, "A refill?" Without looking up, she had held out her glass and said, "Yes please, but forget about the olive."

"Any other instructions?" the voice had asked politely.

"Yes—no ice either."

"You've got it," the voice had replied and moved off. It was only when she saw him walking back toward her with the drink that she had really noticed him. ("Nothing special. Average height. Slightly paunchy. Nice hands. Firm mouth—you know what an average Punjabi businessman looks like.")

"My name's Bhandari. Kumar Bhandari. I already know yours. Pleased to meet you, Anjali. I've wanted to for a long time."

Anjali had felt slightly confused. "Do I know you? Have we met. No, of course not, you just said so."

"May I?" he had asked, before sitting down beside her. The princeling taking the hint had picked up his wine and walked away.

"Lovely sari," he'd said.

"Nice cuff-links," she'd answered.

"Are we going to spend the rest of the evening complimenting each other like school children? Come on, why don't we go get ourselves a decent drink somewhere."

"What shall I do with my car?"

"Sell it. I have a feeling we aren't going to need it in future."

"Is that a proposal?"

"Thought you'd never guess. Yes—it is. Do you accept?"

"You must be insane. But I accept your offer to go and get ourselves a drink."

They had landed up at the Café Royale. Kumar had said, "I love fondue. Do you?"

"Cheese, yes. Meat, no," Anjali had replied.

"Then cheese it shall be. With a crisp wine." It had extended into a long evening. He'd told her about himself. He'd been married twice. The first wife with their two daughters lived in Madras. The second one with their son lived with him at Juhu. "So, you aren't divorced. Do you go proposing to every single woman you run into?"

"No, not every single—just the odd one now and again."

"What if I'd taken you up on it and said yes instantly?"

"I'd have been delighted and worked toward a quick divorce."

"Are you rich?"

"Sufficiently."

"What do you mean by that? Can you afford me? I have very expensive tastes."

"Yes, I noticed. And I think I can."

"Your Mercedes isn't the latest model. It's at least five years old."

"This one is for slumming. The other two are reserved for driving the likes of you around."

"What about your wife—the current one?"

"What about her? She's a sweet person, but I'm bored. I can't see myself spending the rest of my life with her." And so it had gone with Anjali questioning him closely. ("The only thing I didn't ask him was the number of his Swiss bank account. And that too, only because I forgot.") He had remained candid and amused throughout. "I'd love to see you again," he had told her. "And the next time I'll bring the 280 S."

"Make it a Bentley—and you're on," she'd said—or claimed to. Anyway, they had embarked on a dizzy courtship, which included a quick trip to Mauritius. He was generous and attentive, plus "honorable" in his intentions—he had stuck steadfastly to his marriage proposal, even though Anjali had been quite prepared to settle for an affair.

"What kind of a woman are you?" he had asked her, when on their first evening out, after the fondue dinner and two bottles of St. Emilion 1978, she had saucily asked him—"Your place or mine?"

Indignantly she'd replied, "Just an honest one. Why? What's your problem?"

And then Kumar had sprung his first big surprise at her. "I don't want to go to bed with you. No, please listen. This isn't a rebuff. It's just that I value you too much. I'd rather wait till we're married. Now, be a good girl, wipe that fondue off your face and I'll take you for a great big orange juice at the 1900s . . . come on."

Both Ritu and I snorted when she told us this. Then I asked her, "Are you still pure and untouched? Has he broken his vow of chastity or not?"

"If you're asking whether we've been to bed yet, the answer is, we haven't."

"Don't be ridiculous. You've been out with the guy night after night. You've been on a vacation with him—and you haven't screwed?? This is too much! It sounds fishy. Are you sure he's OK? I mean—can he get it up?"

"How crass you've become. Of course he's OK. He's just sentimental and old-fashioned."

"What do you do then—hold hands—or isn't that allowed?"

"Yes—we hold hands and kiss—soul kiss—and all that . . . but nothing more."

"This is the silliest story I've heard in years. At your age and his. It's almost obscene. And unnatural."

"Look who's talking. My! My! What has happened to Little Red Riding Hood suddenly? Seeing too many wolves lately? Besides he isn't ninety-five or something. He's fiftyish."

"Dentures? Or haven't you found even that out?"

"You disgust me." Anjali stuck to this version, while Ritu and I listened in disbelief. Kumar had taken her to the 1900s where he did order this great big Orange Julienne with lots of crushed ice. He had asked her to dance, held her close and whispered, "I like your body. We fit well into each other, I knew we would."

Great, we told her. Just terrific. But what about the wife? Mimi? Abe? Anjali's parents?

"My parents . . . you mean, ba? She's happy enough. Her first reaction was, 'Thank God, he's not another mussulman.' That's all she was interested in. Mimi was more practical. When I told her the whole story, she said, 'Look, Mama, it is your life. I can't tell you what to do with it. But if he could dump two wives just like that—he could as well dump you in the future. But if this decision makes you happy, it's fine by me.' Abe—oh, I don't know about him. I went over to break the news. He was pretty plastered. That cow was around. He looked blearily at me and said, 'God bless you! Inshallah, everything will turn out OK.' Then, out of habit, he asked, 'Do you need any money?'"

"When did he give you the ring?" Ritu asked her. Anjali caressed it lovingly and said, "Oh, that was really romantic. One day, he arrived early to collect me. I forget where we were going. In my rush, I'd forgotten to wear my own ring. He looked at my hands in the car and said, 'What's this? Naked fingers? Let's go get you something glittering.'"

I was instantly suspicious. "Anjali, confess. Are you sure you didn't plan this?"

"I swear I didn't. Don't believe me? I swear on Mimi—I'm not so calculating."

Well, for a "spontaneous" buy, it was quite a whopper. A three-carat, flawless marquise. Even after listening to the whole story, I remained skeptical.

"This not-going-to-bed business—I don't know. It doesn't make any sense. Why don't you tell him it will lead to hormonal imbalance or something?"

"Do you think I don't want to? I'm dying to make love. But he is determined to do it his way."

"Next you'll tell us he has planned a special deflowering ceremony on the wedding night, complete with a flower-decorated bed and shehnais. What happened in Mauritius? Did you have separate rooms and were you wearing a chastity belt?"

"It was understood that we'd abstain, so I didn't have to do anything."

"You mean you slept on this springy king-size bed in a seductive negligee after dousing yourself with Passion and nothing happened? This is getting filthy. Are you sure the guy isn't a eunuch?"

"Don't be idiotic. Why would I want to marry a eunuch?"

"Well, a eunuch with three Mercedeses and a bungalow in Juhu, is better than a down-and-out stud, wouldn't you say?"

"That's a cheap comment, but I'll ignore it. OK. Listen to this—I know he's not a eunuch because I have felt him."

"Oh sweet lover of God! You've FELT him? What's going on? Are you guys playing 'back-to-school' or what? Where did you feel him, for Christ's sake? Don't tell me you go parking à la Sandra Dee?"

"I don't have to do that—I can feel him against me when he holds me in his arms. Or when we're in bed together. I'm telling you—it's OK. He's all right, the only thing that worried me was when he once let slip, 'In five years time I'm going to need a snake-charmer to get it up.'"

Ritu interjected, "I'd make very sure, if I were you. How do you know that what you are feeling is really him? I mean, he could have stuck a rubber hose into his briefs like Mick Jagger does."

"You know what I think?" Anjali finally exploded. "I think you women are sick. Sick. Sick. Sick. And I'm sick of this conversation. Let's get out of here. Rubber hose! Honestly! How disgusting can you get! Anyway, remember you said all this about my future husband."

"But do you love him?" I asked as a parting shot. Anjali was honest for once. "I haven't really thought about it."

She got married six months or so later. I hardly saw her during this period. She was in such a flurry, getting her trousseau together. She preferred to take Nisha with her on these shopping expeditions. Or even Mimi, who was looking even more emaciated and anorexic than ever.

We received the card inviting us to the wedding and a champagne reception at Kumar's Juhu residence. I was pretty excited, but my husband wasn't.

"Do you really want to go?" he asked grumpily.

"What do you mean? Of course, I want to go! Anjali is a good friend of mine."

"Friend?" he snorted derisively. "Friend? That's a laugh. Anyway, if you want to go that desperately, I suppose we'll go, but don't expect me to hang around for hours and hours."

I rang up Anjali to ask her about details—what she was going to wear and so on. She sounded very happy and surprisingly relaxed.

"My first Hindu marriage," she said, "at last I'll feel really, really married. You know how weird the whole thing was with Abe. I was too young, my family wasn't with me, and I felt so out of it—you know, the nikaah and all that. Plus, I was dying of guilt marrying a Muslim. It didn't really feel like a wedding at all. This time, I'm going to have the works, including a Vedic ceremony, our traditional Gujarati sari, mehendi, haldi, everything."

I felt very glad for her and touched by her enthusiasm. I still hadn't met her Kumar. Perhaps after the disastrous Nanking lunch, she'd decided to keep him away and maybe she was right. I still felt prejudiced, but there was no hostility. I was genuinely glad for Anjali and wished her well. She told me about his divorce. "It was easy. His wife was told—cooperate and you'll be well looked after. Act tough, and you'll be on the streets." Sounded ominous and awful, but I didn't say a thing. I quizzed her about the rest of his family. "The old girl is quite something. Do you know she guessed everything much before he told her? She saw me at a party in their home soon after I met him at the Mehras and apparently told her son, 'That woman in white—you're in love with her aren't you? I knew it the moment I saw her walk into the room. Your face changed immediately.'"

"Does that mean she approves?"

"Oh yes—she's quite sweet, actually. I don't think she was crazy about my predecessors. She loves the children, though, and will miss little Bobby—but *c'est la vie.*" Anjali's little "frenchisms" were still there. I liked that.

Anjali's wedding made it to the pages of a city glossy as the "Event of the Fortnight." It was quite spectacular. Mr. Mercedes-Benz had obviously gone to town on the production. The entire street leading up to his palatial marble palace on the beach was strung with tiny lights. The marble chips in the driveway had been shampooed for the occasion and were gleaming white. There were "instant palm trees"

in the garden—hauled in a couple of days earlier by his company's heavy-duty cranes and a special police bandobast had been organized with extra traffic police on duty for almost a mile down the road. The enormous swimming-pool had been emptied out and resembled a brightly lit womb. This was supposed to be the discotheque for the night. All in all, pretty weird. While Cyndi Lauper wailed in the blue-tiled pool disco, live shehnai players greeted guests at the entrance with wails of a different sort. Traditional marigold garlands were strung up over all the doors, while enormous western-style flower arrangements wilted in strategic places under strong spotlights. Anjolie Ela Menon hung cheek-by-jowl with vague European painters on the wall, and an obscene-sized Husain dominated the living room where a huge bar had been rigged up. A Vithal bull stood in a neglected corner of the garden.

I watched women on tall, thin heels wobbling their way through the marble chips. Each time they took a step, they sank four inches into the ground. Champagne and feni. Dahiwadas and caviar. Like I said—weird.

I went in search of Anjali and found her in one of the rooms on the second level. She was looking dazzling.

"Wow!" I said, giving her a hug. "The radiant bride herself! So what's this big bridal routine at your age!"

"Sweetheart, I'm not eighty yet you know." She gave me a beseeching look. "Spare me your sarcasms, at least on this day. You can go back to bitching tomorrow."

Even then, I couldn't resist asking, "Did you do it last night? Or have you reserved it for tonight?"

"Ssh—everyone can hear you," she hissed.

"Quick—tell me."

"I'll call you in the morning."

"Which means you haven't. Are you sure he's up to it?"

"Go away!"

"But I've just arrived." Just then someone came up to hug her.

I stood at a distance to take in the details. Anjali—I had to hand it to her—had chutzpah. There she was decked out in an elaborate Rajasthani ghagra in gold tissue. It was intricately embroidered all over and must have weighed a ton. She had the odhni demurely over her head, and her face was made up like a Bengali bride's. I felt yucky looking at her. And I felt even yuckier when I saw Mimi standing miserably in the shadows with a pinched smile on her face. I went and put my arms around her.

"Isn't Mom looking fabulous?" she asked me.

"Sure she is. So are you Mimi," I said to her.

"You don't have to be kind," she said quickly. "I know I'm looking awful. My mascara's smudged and the lip gloss is all over my teeth."

"No, it isn't," I said. "Here, take my hankie. Or let me fix it for you."

She was in what was the hot outfit that season—a bhopali. It didn't suit her at all. For one, she had bleached and permed her hair on her last visit to LA. She looked like a Mexican waitress at a Tex Mex drive-in. Poor Mimi. At that moment, I felt intensely protective. She held my hand and said, "Did she ask you before she agreed to marry Kumar uncle?"

"Well, she told me, Mimi. But she didn't *ask* me. Why should she? I'm not her mother or someone."

"No, I just wondered whether she'd asked. I'd told her to."

"Really. Why?"

"You're the only sensible friend she has. And I was sure you'd tell her not to go ahead with it."

"No, Mimi. I didn't tell her anything of the kind. In any case, she'd already made up her mind when I found out."

"Do you think she'll be happy?"

"Let's hope so, Mimi. For her sake."

I left Mimi standing near a French window, clutching the drapes and still gazing at her mother.

Even as the pool filled with gyrating bodies, people kept arriving in mobs. Michael Jackson screamed "Beat It," in his inimitable falsetto. That's what I felt like doing. I went looking for the husband . . . and caught sight of the bridegroom instead. He was wearing a well-cut sherwani with wonderful minakari buttons. I suppose this was in keeping with her Rajasthani gear, for he sported a leheriya saafa on his head. I must say I was quite surprised to see that he was almost presentable. Tallish, not as paunchy as Anjali had made him out to be, and altogether dishy. He was wearing far too much jewelry even for a bridegroom, but I pardoned the excess, thinking the poor man must've got carried away and if not on his wedding day, then when? He was standing amidst a cluster of men knocking back their drinks with exaggerated gusto. Punjabi high spirits, I figured. Out of this bunch, my attention was drawn to a dark-complexioned young man standing beside Kumar with a scowl on his face. What seemed odd was the manner in which he hung on to Kumar's right hand, refusing to release it even when the other wanted to light a cigarette. Perhaps he's a young brother or nephew, I thought.

I strolled into the dining room where a stupendous spread awaited the guests. The sight of all that food made me ill. Kumar had gone overboard with the ordering—mixed cuisine in great big heaps sat all over the long tables. Chinese, Mughal, Gujarati, Polynesian, Continental. Everything seemed far too opulent, almost vulgar. I recognized several faces—movie stars, the Juhu Pack, businessmen, socialites, the usual bunch that drifts from one party to the next, often climbing into Airbusses to make it to Delhi and back, if the host was important enough. In fact, there were quite a lot of out-of-towners present that evening, including a clutch of Pakistani cricketers. Someone was talking about a laser show Kumar had organized the previous night. I overheard snatches of conversation referring to the stag party the week before.

"Poor Murty—he looked heartbroken."

"But Kumar's been so generous with the boy. I hear he's sending him for a long holiday. Disneyworld, I think."

"Yes, but what happens later?"

"Well, that depends on the wife—what's her name—Anjali—doesn't it?"

Suddenly, there was a minor commotion. I looked in the direction of the noise. A few people had started running. A man rushed past me. "Call an ambulance. I think Feroz has killed Zafar." "What do you mean—is Zafar dead?" a woman shrieked. "Maybe," panted the man while trying to locate a phone. I walked past the pool where "Join the Party" was blaring. That stopped and Gloria Gaynor started to belt out "I Will Survive." How ironic. And perfectly appropriate. Almost as if the party coordinater had ordered it.

Zafar, the Paki vice-captain, lay bleeding on the floor. Feroz, Bombay filmland's machoest star, was sitting near him with his own nose bleeding profusely. A few of the traffic cops who had filtered in stood around indifferently. I heard my husband saying urgently, "Let's get out of this madhouse before the police arrive. I don't want to be hauled in as a witness."

It made the front pages the next morning. Anjali had achieved the fame she always longed for at last, even if it was in such a bizarre fashion. The two men had fought over a trampy starlet and the local hero had pulled a gun. Fortunately for everybody Zafar didn't die that night, but recovered fast enough to marry the starlet and take her across her border. It was all very exciting, and my husband couldn't get enough of "I was there" mileage out of it. He drank out on the story for weeks.

Anjali finally phoned nearly a month after her wedding.

"Hi!" she said, but there was no cheer in her voice.

"Have you been deflowered yet?"

"Sort of . . ."

"What do you mean 'sort of'?"

"What are you doing?"

"Nothing special."

"Feel like some mushrooms?"

"Have I ever said no to mushrooms?"

"I'll collect you in half an hour. Be downstairs."

"Which Mercedes has been allotted to you? Have you made the 280 SE grade yet?"

"Shut up and come down."

She drove up in an electric green Porsche. Before I could say anything she said, "Wedding present."

"Not bad," I said. "Not bad at all."

"Everything costs," she answered.

"That a loaded remark or what?"

"What do you think?"

"I don't know . . ."

"Now what?"

"I guess I'm stuck again."

I slid into the seat next to her and put my hand over hers. The three-carat monster had acquired a companion. An equal-sized emerald ('because green suits you so well'). Anjali was wearing a beautiful mangalsutra. I knew how much that meant to her. She hadn't been able to wear it in her previous marriage. She also had sindoor in her hair and a prominent red bindi. "You look beautiful," I said sincerely. And then I noticed she'd changed the shape of her nails—they weren't perfect ovals any longer. She'd filed them straight across the fingertips into blunt squares. "What's this?" "Oh, Kumar didn't like my nails. He said they reminded him of knives." The car attracted a lot of attention all along the road, particularly at traffic lights. She pulled out a pair of Balenciaga glasses ("got these in Madrid") and stuck them on top of her head. Red glints bounced off her shiny hair ("too much henna, this time"). We pulled into the Taj portico and the hefty sardars came salaaming up. "*Sat Sri Akaal, memsaab,*"they saluted smartly. She handed them the keys and we walked in. On the way to the rooftop, she fidgeted nervously with her brand-new Gucci bag.

Her slim arms were weighed down with bracelets ("Milan"). A curious German riding up with us couldn't take his eyes off her. She still had that effect on people.

She didn't ask for a Bloody Mary in the restaurant. In fact, she turned it down when the waiter came up familiarly and said, "Bloody Mary, ma'am?"

"Get me a Spritzer . . . and don't forget the twist of lime." She turned to me. "Why don't you have the same? Go on—it isn't evil. It's only mildly alcoholic. You'll think you were drinking a Limca with a slight kick."

"No, thanks. I'll stick to an orange juice." There was a long silence as we both gazed at the harbor. The light was beautiful outside. Maybe we were thinking the same thing—our last meeting there and the Karan episode.

She broke into my reverie. "You knew it wouldn't work, why didn't you tell me?"

I was taken aback. "To start with, Anjali, you hadn't asked me. I was not on your advisory panel at the time."

"Yes but when you knew, you could have told me then."

"It was too late," I said without the faintest idea of what she was talking about.

"What rubbish! You're supposed to be my friend. Even Mimi has faith in you. I should have listened to her."

"Why don't you start where you're supposed to, what's wrong?"

"Just about everything. Kumar's gay, you know, he's a homo."

"Then why did he marry you and those two other women?"

"Because he needed a front—he couldn't possibly marry Murty or any of the other boys."

"How come you were dense enough not to sense it?"

"How could I? I thought he was being very romantic when he insisted on that no-going-to-bed-before-the-wedding clause. I was so touched. This was the first time a man was treating me like a decent woman. I thought it was his way of showing respect."

"What a fool, Anjali. Remember our teasing you about it? But surely you must've noticed Murty lurking around the place—what did you think he was doing there?"

"I believed Kumar when he told me that Murty was an orphan he had picked up somewhere. He said he'd felt sorry for the boy and decided to 'adopt' him—not legally. But he paid for his education, gave him a roof over his head, employed him in his company—and generally looked after him—that's all."

"Then, when did you discover that Murty was his bedmate?"

"Kumar broke down on our wedding night. Maybe he was drunk or maybe Murty had created a scene. He told me I would have to accept him in our life—like his previous wives had."

"What's the deal then?"

"Isn't it obvious? The Porsche, emeralds, holidays in Biarritz, shopping along the Champs-Elysées, a villa in Ooty, parties every night, unlimited champagne—and the choice to pick my own bedmate but discreetly."

"Sounds perfect. What are you cribbing about?"

"I suppose I'll get used to it—eventually."

"It's better than being stuck in some poky little place with an accountant or someone. If you have to suffer at least do it draped in French chiffon."

"I guess you're right, but I don't know. I was really looking forward to a proper married life with a proper husband and a proper home. Maybe it's not in my horoscope."

"Maybe he'll be proper every which way but bed. And, like you said, he hasn't closed your options. I'm sure you'll be able to work something out."

"Yeah, like what? Suicide?"

"Don't be silly, you've been reading those cheap paperbacks again. Why don't you relax and make a buddy out of Kumar. Gays do make excellent friends. Go on, try and do that. Imagine, you could have so much fun together. Maybe you could swap lipsticks and eyeshadows."

"I knew you wouldn't be sympathetic. You have to be vicious and rub it in. Kumar isn't into drag. He doesn't wear lacy panties or stick-on falsies. He's just a straight guy who prefers boys—that's all."

"That's all?! Then why all this tragic stuff? Maybe it's just as well—he'll leave you alone to work your sexual trip out with whoever, and you leave him to cuddle Murty. The trade-off seems simple enough. He keeps you knee-deep in diamonds, you keep up his image. I think it's very fair. Besides gays have a great sense of humor and terrific taste. You'll pick up lots of jokes and a fantastic wardrobe. Look at it that way."

"He can keep his jokes. Give me sex any day."

CHAPTER 11

My husband and I had just had one of our long and meaning-less fights and it made me very despondent. I knew Ritu had just got back from one of her periodic holidays so I called her. She sounded chirpy as always. And game for anything. Atta girl.

"You're like instant coffee," I told her, "an immediate pick-me-up."

"Is that a compliment?"

"No, you dummy, I'm insulting you. I'm marginalizing you. I'm reducing you to a beverage. Satisfied?"

"Having a fight with the husband are you?"

"No, listening to Joan Baez."

"Same thing."

"You're horrible."

"And in the same boat."

"You mean you are fighting with your husband?"

"We never fight. We just cancel each other out. I can go for days pretending he doesn't exist."

"But I thought you couldn't get any sleep without cuddling him in the night."

"You don't have to talk to cuddle."

"But how can you bear to touch someone you aren't speaking to?"

"It's easy—try it."

"Doesn't he throw your arm away? Push you off?"

"No. He can't sleep without cuddling either."

"What happens when he goes out of town?"

"I pop pills."

"And he?"

"Never asked. Maybe gets bombed. Or finds someone else to cuddle."

"Go on—you don't believe that? Has he ever cheated on you?"

"He tried—just once. But I threatened to castrate him. And he knew I meant business."

"When was that?"

"Oh, a couple of years ago."

"Who was she?"

"Some little tart—a secretary somewhere."

"How did you find out?"

"Someone told me."

"You mean a friend phoned and said, 'Guess what Ritu, your husband is having it off with this tart.'"

"Yes—just like that."

"Then what did you do?"

"Waited for him to get home."

"Did he confess?"

"No way. He looked terribly shitty and said things like, 'You have a nasty mind. Don't jump to conclusions. She was helping me out with some confidential filing.'"

"And you believed him, of course."

"No, I didn't. I just pointed my knitting needles at him and said, 'Whatever it is that she's helping you out with—just forget it. Unless you want these stuck in your eyes.'"

"Did he listen?"

"No. It went on for a while. I knew it was on since we'd receive all these blank calls with someone breathing heavily at the other end. Often, he'd be late coming from work and give me some bullshit excuse. Then they were spotted in Bangalore together. That's when I decided to do something about it."

"Yeah—like what? Replace the knitting needles in the eyes with a dagger in the gut?"

"No. I just went across to her office and told her to leave my husband alone—or else."

"And what did the tartlet say or do?"

"She was very cool. She had the nerve to tell me, 'Why don't you ask him to leave me alone? I'm not the one chasing him. In fact, it's very embarrassing for me when he calls or sends flowers.' I was stumped for a bit, but then I remembered to act tough. 'Don't give me all that shit, you whore. Just lay off—is that clear? Or your husband is going to hear about it!'"

"Did that matter?"

"Not at all. She said in a bored voice, 'If I were you, really, I wouldn't bother. My husband already knows. Besides, you're a fine one to be lecturing me. From what your husband says, you're a hot number yourself.'"

"Sounds sleazy. Did your husband find out about this encounter?"

"You bet he did. The minute he walked in, I pounced on him. 'So what are these flowers you're sending these days? They sure as hell aren't coming for me.' He looked thrown for a minute and recovered fast enough to say, 'You mean those? I'd sent them for Gloria and Peter's wedding anniversary. I'd also put your name on the card.' I couldn't believe it. I saw red and went mad. The next thing I knew I'd grabbed this huge vase and flung it at him."

"Did you aim for his crotch or his head?"

"I would have missed either—but what happened later was awful. He came at me like a maniac. First he pulled out his leather belt from the trouser and then he stood over me with his eyes blazing. Phatak!—I felt the leather on my arm, and I was so stunned I couldn't even scream. Before I could open my mouth, it landed on my arm again. I lost my balance—I was sitting on the edge of the carpet. He was still standing at the same spot with his arm raised. Suddenly I felt a sharp kick in my side. And another one. Then I heard him say, 'Shit! There goes my Bally shoe.' Can you believe it! Then he threw his belt away and started to slap me around. One hard hit cracked against my nose. Before I knew it, my favorite Anokhi dupatta was drenched in blood—my nose was like a geyser with blood gushing from it. Maybe it was the sight of all that blood that made him panic. He stopped and yanked my face up by the hair. 'Shit! I'd better get a doctor. Is there any ice in the fridge?' I was still on the floor with the dupatta stuck to my nose. Some of the blood fell on the carpet—the stains are still there. I walked to the kitchen slowly to get some ice. It was so unreal, the whole thing. When I went to the bathroom to wash my face, I was shocked out of my wits. The whole thing was swollen—twice its size. My eyes were beginning to puff, and one side of the face was turning purple where it had got badly bruised. There were thick welts across my arms. But do you know something—I quite enjoyed the whole thing. You must think I'm crazy. But really, it was thrilling in its own way. Not the pain—but the experience. He didn't look like a pipsqueak anymore. I thought of Marlon Brando in *A Streetcar Named Desire,* have you seen the film? You must."

"Was that the only time it happened or are you both now heavily into the S & M scene?" I asked incredulously.

"It's not as sick as it sounds. In fact, I think I deserve a beating now and then, especially since I boss him around so much. I feel so much better after it. Now, we've worked out the rules—he doesn't touch my face."

"Isn't that darling of him?"

"Don't be so shocked. In a way, I think the beatings have brought us closer. I respect him more. He looks so macho in those moments."

"Do you know that you have joined the ranks of battered wives? It's horribly humiliating, Ritu—this is awful. It's demeaning. Don't you have any dignity? Self-respect?"

"Come on, you've got to be joking. He'd do the smallest thing

I asked him to. And how can it be humiliating when it's me who's doing the asking? And between you and me these slug-outs lead to terrific sex. It's the only time I feel I'm not in bed with his mother."

"Seems one hell of a price to pay for a lousy orgasm," I said. "I can think of other less destructive ways."

"Since when have you, iceberg, become the expert?" she teased.

"I may not be a Hamburg hooker; but I read books. I know all about these things."

"But that's paper knowledge, academic knowledge, whatever you call it. I can't imagine you letting yourself go ever. In fact, I'm sure you have such an antiseptic sex life, you probably keep rubber gloves and a bottle of Dettol by your bedside."

"How did you guess?"

The phone rang again, almost as soon as Ritu had rung off. It was Anjali. Apparently Si (who was Si? it took a moment and then I remembered, ah yes, Anjali's trampy friend from long ago) was back in town having tired of a long holistic experience with a Swedish hippie in Kodai, and wouldn't I come over. The idea was that the three of us would spend the day together. I said I'd have to check with the husband. Anjali sneered, "Surely your husband can manage on his own for a few hours. Or does he need you to brush his teeth?" "I'll have to check with him," I insisted. "I don't know if the car is free."

"You mean after so many years of slavery you haven't earned a car as yet? Not even a teensie-weensie Maruti of your very own? That's bad. You'd better renegotiate your marriage contract."

"Ha! Ha! You are so-o-o funny, Anjali, I'm dying to laugh. I guess you wouldn't know the difference between a moll and a wife now, would you."

"Female dog—how I detest you. Sometimes I wonder why I put up with your two-bit remarks. So, can you come or not?"

"Have you invited any hangers-on? That is, besides Si? Or do you have a live-in harem these days."

"I'm offering you a gourmet meal—as good as if not better than the last La Tour D'Argent one. Take it or fuck it."

I took it. I collected Si from her seedy digs. She was even more tramped up for the occasion. Her hair looked unwashed and she smelled so high it was difficult to have her beside me in the car. All along the way I kept thinking, "I mustn't use the same toilet seat . . . I'll probably pick up a bug and die." She was wearing Elton-John-style sunglasses with golden spangles all over them. Her legs had a three-day stubble and she hadn't done her underarms. Ignoring my coldness, she kept up a steady chatter. "I was with Abe last evening," she giggled. "It was just like the good old days, except that Abe has started serving Indian whisky—ugh! Gigi was around in a red dressing gown and rollers in her hair—imagine! I think she was drinking bewda. Poor Abe. That woman is going to see him to his grave. He really misses Anj—he told me so."

"You must have made him feel vastly better, I'm sure."

"Well, I sure as hell tried. I even gave his toesies a nice massage."

"That was too sweet."

"You think so? Do you think I should tell Anj about Abe or will it kill her?"

"I think she'll be able to survive it."

"What fun! I can't wait to see my old friend. I wanted to get her something but I was broke. Everything's so expensive these days."

Anjali was waiting for us. She all but ran toward the car as it pulled in, muddying her marble chips. She gave Si a big hug and I winced. We were never on hugging terms, so she just patted me awkwardly on the shoulder and said, "Nice sari." After a long time I had taken the trouble to dress up, so I was happy that she'd noticed. Anjali was overpainted. Great big gashes of color over her cheekbones, a very shiny mouth, too much green over the eyes and a fancy bindi to boot. The sindoor had disappeared. "Seems a bit much, doesn't it?

And it's awfully difficult to wash out. After a shampoo, the tub looks like somebody was murdered in it. Doesn't it?"

"But why have you slapped on so much gook?"

"This is how wives of prosperous Punjabi men are supposed to dress at all times. Kumar has told me never to emerge from my bedroom in a dressing gown. I have to be 'properly' clad in a sari, makeup, jewelry, the works."

"Your bedroom? You mean . . . ?"

"Don't be silly—of course we have separate bedrooms. You know that. Thank God. I've always thought it more civilized. We women have our own little secrets, best left behind in the boudoir, don't you agree? And I'm sure most men like to do their thing on their own as well."

"Lucky you," I said, and meant it. "I would have preferred to have a room of my own, but the husband wouldn't hear of it. 'What will Mother think? As it is, we don't have children.'"

Anjali fluttered all over the place, while Si, as was her disgusting habit, went around inspecting everything in the house, opening cupboards, examining bathrooms. I wouldn't have been at all surprised if I'd seen her pocketing a Lalique anemone or a silver supari box. Anjali insisted on taking us on a grand guided tour. She showed us her bedroom proudly, threw open the padded (yes, padded) door with a grand sweep and announced "Sleeping Beauty's boudoir." It would have given Barbara Cartland nightmares with its pinkness. Everything in sight was pink, not baby pink, but shocking pink. There were satin bows and lace insets, frills and canopies—and heaven help us—wallpaper with rose-buds all over it. "So girls—what do you think? I designed it myself! Kumar told me, 'You have such wonderful taste. Why do we need an interior designer? Have fun—do it all yourself and don't worry about the budget.' Of course, I had to wait for a long time for some of the imported things—you know, like the gold taps in the bathroom and other fittings, but the rest of it took just eight months. Even the contractors were surprised. They said to me, 'Madam, we have worked with so many professionals, but nobody has such good ideas.' Come and see my Japanese rock garden. I've created it just outside my bathroom, to give me the feeling of showering outdoors—super idea, no? I saw it in *House and Garden*—some countess had one in her villa. I thought it was so cute. Kumar is very generous that way—he doesn't mind my spending on such things. And did you see the shower curtains with the tulips? Harrods. I'd seen them on my trip two years ago and loved them. The taps aren't really made of gold—it's plated. But it looks classy. And the canopy over my bed—divine! I love it. It's like sleeping inside a cozy tent. Remember, Liz Taylor posed in a similar bed? Don't remember? Anyway, I do, and I sketched it for my contractors. They were so impressed. 'Madam, you have a lot of talent,' they said. See those porcelain figures? And that vase—Baccarat. Costs a fortune. I'm not very happy with the chandelier. I wanted a pink one—you know—from that famous place in Italy—what is it? Morana, Moreno—something like that? But the dealer here said, it's better to wait and buy it from some maharaja—you know, when they sell off their stuff? I said OK, but in the meanwhile you don't expect me to live in the dark. Give me something as a stopgap—and that fool produced this. It's not too bad—but it isn't pink."

I asked her whether we were going to be fed a pink meal to match the bedroom decor. Even as I said this my mind flashed back to her green luncheon with the Frenchie. Anjali caught on. "Naughty girl," she said, "you're taunting me about Pierre, aren't you? I can give you a pink falooda if you want. Or strawberry ice-cream. But the Western cook has really taken trouble over our meal today."

"Western cook? You mean you have an Eastern one, and a Southern one and a Northern one?"

"No, silly. This guy used to work for some British family. He prefers to work for foreigners since they appreciate his food."

"But Brits eat the most awful food in the world. Don't tell me you've lined up mulligatawny soup for us? If you have—I'm leaving. I'd rather eat at an Udipi."

Si came over sniffing. "I went to the kitchen while you girls were yacking. Something was smelling very yummy. In any case—I haven't had a decent meal in years. All those bean-sprouts and raw vegetables. Ugh. Anj—since you are in a pink mood, how about a pink gin?"

"Let's go to the upstairs bar," she added. "We have another one in the basement—but that's for the boys. They play darts and things there. It's a bit too macho for me."

"Is the upstairs one pink like your bedroom?" I inquired.

"Are you being bitchy as always? The answer is no. But in case you're interested, it has also been designed by me and everybody just loves it. Most of Kumar's friends actually prefer it to the other one, but they dare not say so. The basement bar has been done up by Kumar himself and he's very proud of it."

We trooped upstairs behind Anjali. Once again she flung open the door. I must admit, this was an improvement on the boudoir. It was color-coordinated, but in pleasing tones. There was lots of cane and plenty of green all over ("plastic ferns, from Hong Kong"). The Shyam Ahuja dhurries were not on the parquet floor ("Everybody throws them there, darlings. But I prefer them on the walls—like works of art") but stared at us from just about everywhere else including the ceiling. The inevitable mirrors were fixed behind the bar and reflected the soft hues of the room. Anjali told us proudly, "It looks even better at night, because the lighting is so clever. I spend a lot of time here—not drinking, mind you, but just lounging. When the bearer sees me here, he knows what to tell people over the phone. I have trained him to say 'Memsaab is lounging and cannot be disturbed.' Sounds good, huh? That's one thing about Kumar—he knows how to train servants. I don't have to supervise anything in this house. He has all his old fellows who know exactly what's what. I only have to ring this bell." With that she picked up a silver bell on the bar and went ting-a-ling-a-ling. "You know electric call bells, are so inelegant, darlings, so I've scattered a whole bunch of silver bells all over the house. And, you know, the servants are so alert, that in two seconds after I ring someone knocks." Someone didn't. She scowled impatiently and went ting-a-ling again. I burst out laughing. "You look so comic ringing that silly bell," I couldn't resist saying. She pulled herself up, gave me a drop-dead look and reached for a button under the bar. There was a call bell, after all. And it worked. A slave materialized in no time.

The lounging got boring after a while and as I wasn't drinking I said, "Show us Kumar's room."

"I don't know if that's a good idea—he doesn't like intruders."

"Intruders? What do you mean intruders? We are not intruders, we are his wife's friends."

"Still, he gets jumpy about things like that."

"Oh come on, what's he hiding in there—whips and chains? Little boys? Skeletons rattling in the cupboard? Cross our hearts and may we die, but we won't tell."

Si piped up, "Maybe wifey has not been given the key to the kingdom. What say, wifey, are you allowed to enter or do you come under the intruder category too?"

"You women are so shameless, I don't believe it. All right, I suppose it's OK. But don't go and drop your hankies in there."

"What about the slaves floating around the place. I'm sure Kumarikins has a spy to keep tabs on you. Won't they squeal?" Si asked. She was already sloshed, after two quick pink gins and a swig from Anjali's Spritzer.

"I'll take you when the servants retire to their rooms to watch video after lunch."

"Wait a minute—what was that? The servants have a video in their rooms?" I said.

"Yes. In fact, I suggested it to Kumar. It was one way of keeping them out of my hair."

"That's smart thinking woman. What other tricks have you come up with?"

"Take it easy, or I won't feed you any lunch. What tricks? I'm being good these days."

"And chaste too?"

"Let me convince you girls—look at my eyes, skin and hair? Do I look like I've been screwing around? Everything is dull—eyes, skin and hair. That happens when a woman stays off sex. I used to glow in the old days, darlings—glow!"

"I'm sure. So what's it now—'just me and my friendly vibrator.'"

"I don't have to dignify that question with a reply. Let's have lunch."

"Listen, you fancy broad, you've promised us a Tour D'Argent lunch—it had better be good."

Si chimed in, "You mean that swanky joint in Paris? The one that's better than Maxim's? I nearly went there one night—but my date stood me up."

"I'm not surprised," I said under my breath, but Si flared up.

"What did you say—I heard you, you bitch. I never did like you. I always used to tell Anjali that. So holier-than-thou and all that shit. What makes you so virtuous, huh?"

Anjali put a restraining arm around her and hissed, "Si, Si. Down girl. Now behave yourself. She didn't mean it."

Then turning to me, "Tell her you didn't mean it even if you did. You both are ruining my lunch."

We went into the dining room, Anjali still playing tour guide. "Oh, this was practically the way you see it now. I haven't really done anything much to it. Just fooled around with the curtains and bought that painting for the wall. Like it? It's by a Delhi painter—Krishen Khanna. Very classy, don't you think? Just what this room needed. And I picked up that fruit bowl somewhere—where was it—in New York, I think. Stuff like that—nothing major."

She reached for one of her silver bells and rang it with a delicate twist of her wrist. "Don't you love the tinkling sound it makes?" she asked. Again no bearer appeared but a sleek cat did. "Oh, come here, my darling Cleo. Look girls—isn't she just too gorgeous? Kumar gave her to me on some occasion—I forget which—saying, 'The only pussy I can bear to touch.' Cute I thought."

"What? The remark or the pussy?"

"Oh both. He's quite funny really. When we first met—you remember he was still pretending he was straight in those days?—he put his hands inside my choli and commented, 'Hmm—quite a handful.' I was quite surprised when he said that, I mean, you girls know the size of my tits. And then he added, 'Aren't you lucky I have such small hands?'"

"I would've killed him," Si said. "How awful. Maybe he was trying to give you a complex. You should have reached for his crotch and said something nasty like—I don't know—'Is dicky-boy away on vacation?' or something like that—but anyway, that's typical gay humor. I should know. I'm a gay groupie myself. I was heavily into the gay scene sometime back. That's how I knew about Kumar even before you told me. I must say that husband of yours has managed to keep his little secret very secret—over the years. Three wives, not bad."

Actually that was something I'd been dying to ask Anjali. How did Kumar manage to seduce beautiful women and talk them into marriage, quite apart from the money angle that is. "He is utterly charming," Anjali said as if in reply to the unspoken question. "He is very attentive, generous and attractive in his own way. I have seen him at parties. Women fling themselves at him—and he flirts away. He isn't one of the 'obvious' gays—I mean, he isn't limp wristed and he doesn't mince when he walks."

"He wears far too much jewelry for a straight guy," I said. "But so do all the movie stars. And living in Juhu, that's the crowd we hang out with, so nobody really notices his chains and rings."

Finally, lunch was served with a great deal of ceremony. The bearers were indeed perfectly trained. They brought in warm Royal Doulton plates ("this is our informal luncheon set"), and removed them after each course. The food was superlative, with mellow wine to wash it down. The cheese platter had an impressive assortment of the best, and we were even offered Havanas and cognac later. "Let's cut out the crap and invade Kumar's room," I suggested. Hesitantly, Anjali led us to another section of the house and put a key into an intricately carved wooden door. ("Chettinad. Must introduce you to this guy—he has the most phenomenal old furniture")

We walked into total darkness. "Kumar likes the dark," she explained.

"It figures," I said.

She reached for the lights. "Concealed." So they were. But at least we could see the room now. It was enormous, with the largest bed I've ever seen.

"Large enough to have an orgy in," Si giggled.

"That's the general idea, I suppose," I added.

"You're both wrong. This room is sacred. No fooling around here. He just likes a large bed, that's all."

"Did you do this one up too?"

"No—this is Kumar's domain. He has picked everything down to the potty." There was a mahogany table along a wall with an exquisite Japanese vase. The wood paneling had a rich grain, and the colors were very discreet—beige, walnut and salmon. Si landed on the bed without warning and started bouncing around.

"Stop it," Anjali warned. "Don't do that. He'll be able to smell you."

"Is he a bloodhound or what?"

"Just get off that bed."

"OK. OK. Take it easy. I'm not going to pee on it or anything. Don't get hysterical." While this was going on I was surveying the row of bottles on his dressing table. Anjali saw me looking. "He has a weakness for aftershaves and lotions. The minute a new one appears in the market—it's on his table. He loves women's fragrances too."

"Of course, he would," I hitched.

"It's not just gays who like perfume. Abe used to constantly finish all my favorites. And you know how un-gay he was."

"Don't I just," Si giggled. I pretended I hadn't heard.

"Let's see the loo," I suggested. Anjali opened the door and we stepped into miles of marble and granite. Everything was gleaming and perfect. A sunken bath tub, Jacuzzi, a stuffed chair in one corner and a fair-sized library.

"What does this man do? Spend half his life in the bathroom? It's so well-equipped."

Anjali missed the irony. "Yes—it even has a mini-fridge and a bar. Anjali showed us where these were cleverly hidden within easy reach of the tub.

"Hey that's pretty neat," Si said. "I once spent the night with one of these Sheikh types in Dubai—he had a similar one in his bathroom. It was such fun—we spent all our time in the tub, filled it with bubbles and drank lots of champagne. I even shampooed my hair with what was left over in the third bottle. It was the swankiest shampoo I've ever had—Dom Perignon."

"Kumar keeps a small hoard of Godiva chocolates hidden somewhere—but Si don't you dare touch them. He counts. He'll know if even one is missing."

"Tell him you fed them to your pussy—and don't specify which one," Si laughed.

"You are so low class and cheap. I don't know why I tolerate you. You pollute the atmosphere. And, please, the next time you come here—if I invite you again, that is—kindly shave your underarms and put on a bra. My bearers were staring at lunch."

"Fuck your bearers," Si said.

"You do it. You'll probably enjoy it more. But I'm not sure they'll oblige. They have high standards."

"Touché, Anjali," I said and clapped.

"OK—now lead us to his gizmos. Where does he keep his naughty things? Where does he, well, bugger his boyfriends?" Si said, unfazed.

"I am too disgusted for words. And really horrified," Anjali said. "You girls go too far sometimes. You're talking about my husband, you know. This is his house. You've just had a meal at his expense. Drunk wine from his cellar. Really!"

"Now that you've said your loyal-and-outraged wife piece—let's go. Lead us to kinky-land."

But Anjali surprised us both by saying, "Let me show you my puja room, instead."

"Your what? Puja room? What a minute. When did you get on to that trip? What's with this puja angle? I didn't know you prayed," I said.

"You don't know many things, Ms. Know-it-all—I can still surprise you."

When we got to the puja room Anjali instructed us solemnly: "Please remove your shoes before you go in."

Si asked saucily, "What else? No bath?"

"Well you could certainly do with one," Anjali countered. I kept my silence as she unlocked a door and ushered us into a smallish room. She'd covered her own head demurely with her sari pallav. Once we were in, Anjali went down on her knees and touched her forehead to the floor. She remained in this position for about a minute, while Si and I shifted uncomfortably with Si's eyebrows dancing up and down, silently demanding, "What's going on?" I didn't think Anjali was acting for our benefit. As soon as she'd entered the puja room, she seemed lost in a trance. When she finally raised her head, she had a beatific expression on her face. "I have found him," she sighed. "I am at peace at last." Seeing our expressions she blushed and pointed to an exquisite deity of Krishna which she had installed in an ornate shrine.

"Anjali—have you been reading Mirabai?" I asked her.

"I knew you'd say that. You've become so predictable. You girls haven't lived my life. You won't be able to understand what spiritual bliss is all about."

"Next you'll tell us you've joined the Hare Krishna guys. They operate from Juhu, don't they?" Si laughed, "I can just imagine you jumping around with them on the beach every evening like a hijra."

"Nothing either of you says will affect me now. I have Krishnaji with me constantly." Then she reached inside her low-cut blouse and pulled out a locket. It was a beautiful image of Shrinathji painted on ivory and framed in gold. "This gives me a lot of strength, nothing can get me down now. But enough of all that—it's a very personal thing, and I don't want to talk about Him like we gossip about other people. Why don't you look at my mandir? When I asked Kumar if I could have one, he was so delighted. 'It's yours!' he said. 'You don't even have to ask me. Go ahead, spend as much as you like. I think religion is wonderful.' Wasn't that too sweet of him? He even helped me to choose the marble. I wanted the best Italian, but I couldn't get this pure white shade so I got the Makrana one instead. It has a lovely milky tone which I thought was appropriate for Krishna—the naughty makhan-chor."

"All this is marvelous, my dear," I said, "but does it also include a vow of celibacy?"

"What is sex compared to religion? Nothing! The ecstacy I experience when I'm praying or listening to my bhajans is far better than an orgasm. I'm into this totally, and sex has become irrelevant. In fact, I hate to use the sort of language we used to—you know—fuck-shuck and all that. I feel impure. I go and gargle immediately if these words come out by mistake. If I'm not near my own bathroom and it happens in someone else's house, I quickly take out my mint breath-freshener pump and do a fast whoosh whoosh."

Si looked at me and said, "I think the woman has flipped. Come on, let's get out of here before she tries to convert us. I don't believe it—bhajans, malas, prayers. Anjali, dear heart, why don't you see a shrink and get this whole nonsense out of your system? It's sick. You're sick. You need treatment, not a temple. Doesn't that bloody bugger realize this? I may be a screwed-up bitch, but I ain't cuckoo."

Anjali continued to look at us calmly while fingering her locket. "I have not joined an ashram or given up on life. As you girls can see, I still love my luxuries—nice saris, jewelry and all that. I'm just in a heightened state now, and I can feel my kundalini rising and lifting me out of the mess I was in. What's wrong with that? What's wrong with peace and love?"

"That kind of crap went out in the sixties for Christ's sake. It's so unfashionable to be a peacenik these days. Anjali, if for nothing else, give all this up at least to remain 'in' with the trends. Everybody will laugh if you come out with your peace and love rubbish," Si advised seriously.

I felt obliged to put in my two bits' worth. "I don't agree with you, Si. Hindu revivalism is going to be the big trend of the 80s—Anjali is, in fact, ahead of her times. Have you joined the RSS yet? I think it's very chic to rediscover your roots and proclaim it to the world."

"This is getting spooky. I don't think I want to know either of you. I prefer sin anyday to this holy shit," Si remarked and reached for a ciggie.

"Not here," Anjali stopped her sharply. "Oh, forgive me, Mirabai," She bowed with folded hands.

We left the house and strolled out toward the pool. Si wandered off by herself. Anjali put her arms on my shoulders and stared intently into my eyes. "You believe in what's happening to me, don't you? You believe I'm on the right track?"

"Yes, Anjali. If it means so much to you—it really is entirely your business. And you don't owe anybody any explanations, least of all someone like Si. Just forget about her cheap remarks.

"I forgive her, I really do—I forgive everybody. My heart is filled with love."

"That's great. But don't overdo this trip. You know how disappointed you feel when things don't work out the way you've planned them? But your temple is very beautiful. It smells lovely—better than your Nina Ricci and I'm glad you've got this room to escape to when things get rough. We haven't really talked today. How are things between you and Kumar?"

"There's a lot to tell you—but I made a mistake. I shouldn't have asked Si to come here. I can feel her bad vibrations everywhere. She spreads *paap* wherever she goes. She is so morally corrupt."

"Let her be—she's not really evil—just mixed up. Maybe she'll find her Krishna also—till then she won't be able to understand what you're going through."

"Thanks for being gentle. And for sticking up for me. It's important you know. I feel so friendless and alone. As it is, living at Juhu I'm cut off from my world in South Bombay. At one time these filmi types seemed OK. But now. Oh God, they drive me up the wall. And then—Kumar—I call him K now—entertains compulsively every night. I have to organize a banquet for twenty or more people at least thrice a week. It is a bore—but I've got used to it. Plus, we do have excellent servants."

"What about the rest, Anjali. You haven't said anything about Murty or your life with Kumar—surely, it doesn't begin and end with parties and pujas?"

"Murty, look, I don't want to discuss that little jerk. I detest him and he detests me."

"Does he live with you guys?"

"Off and on—K has given him some sort of a job. So, he hangs out at various branch offices doing God knows what. When he's in town, he shacks up here. But not in K's bedroom—servants talk, and it's just not done."

"Do you and Kumar discuss this relationship?"

"Not really. I'm supposed to go along with the pretense that Murty is like an adopted son of the family. At least, for public consumption. I've told K to make sure he stays out of my way. We rarely run into each other—if he's around at a party, he stays behind the bar, fetches and carries for K and makes himself useful."

"But what does Kumar see in him?"

"Hard to say. Murty is cute in his own way, like Sabu the Elephant Boy—remember that movie? And he's great for Kumar's ego. He absolutely adores K, worships him."

"That's the least he can do, considering the style he's kept in. Is he given pocket money?"

"K controls that very strictly. As I told you, he's on a salary, and K gives him presents from time to time—watches, shirts, shoes, plus an extra allowance on his birthdays. By the way, his birthdays are big numbers. We have a huge party—not a gay party—just about the entire city—and the birthday boy cuts a cake, is given birthday bumps—and the whole thing is recorded for posterity on video. Then, till his next birthday comes around, we have to watch the previous year's film at least once a fortnight. Oh, and K gives him jewelry on the occasion—a thick chain, cuff-links, ring. Plus, Murty insists on National Savings Certificates for his future and his security."

"Sounds like a neat arrangement. What have you worked out for yourself?"

"We have a joint account which I operate. I draw from it whenever I require cash. He gives me the housekeeping money at the beginning of each month. If I run out, I show him the accounts and he supplements it. I'm supposed to buy my own stuff out of this—the smaller things like saris, bags, shoes. But if there is a major piece of jewelry to be bought he clears it."

"No pension plan? No contract in case the marriage collapses? No nest egg of your own?"

As usual, she missed the sarcasm. "The Lonavala property has been transferred to my name. And I already have the apartment Abe gave me. So that's OK. I have given that to Mimi—poor child, she needs a place of her own. He gave me substantial shares in his company when we got married. Plus the jewelry. I think I'm pretty well provided for. Oh yes, there's the insurance policy and some other blue-chip shares. I'm being careful with my money these days."

"Good girl. Just don't blow it this time."

"I'm becoming very professional, my dear. I have hired Abe's old tax consultants to help me sort out all the money angles. Abe had given me enough after the talaq—that's been invested too."

"That makes you quite an heiress. And what does Mimi do?"

"Shuttles between homes. She prefers living abroad, and has decided to go back to school and take courses. Abe has money there, so that's no problem. She is keen to earn her own—though she doesn't need to. But I encourage her. A woman has to be self-sufficient these days."

"She's not a kid anymore. Let's see—how old is she? Late twenties?"

"Yes. She's nearly thirty, you know. Mimi has always been very hyper—you remember her as a kid? Far too sensitive. Sometimes I think she can't handle this whole situation."

"What about K? How's he with her? And what about his two exwives? Where are they?"

"The first one keeps out of his way. She sends the older kid during the vacations. A sweet, sad child. The other one is not as easy. In fact, she's left a lot of her stuff behind."

"Don't you mind that?"

"Well, I did, in the beginning. But K said, 'Look, Anjali, she did share my home for a few years and she does have some rights. So what if she leaves a few things behind? She'll remove them once she settles down. You don't have to feel threatened.' But you know something—I resent her shadow in our home. Not that she's done anything to me or said anything. But I still don't like reminders of her all over the place.

Albums full of photographs, books with her name in them, records which she has dated and signed. Two enormous wardrobes full of her clothes, cosmetics and shoes. Why would a woman want to leave her bras and panties in an ex-husband's house?"

"Maybe she really loved the guy, maybe she thinks she'll be coming back one day."

"But isn't that evil? She still phones the servants and asks after their health. As if she cares! It's all a strategy to keep tabs on me and find out what's going on in the house. I think it's cheapo. I don't keep calling Abe. She also tries to act very palsy-walsy with Murty. Once or twice I heard them on the extension—but I think they knew I was listening."

"Why don't you be firm with Kumar about this and tell him it bothers you."

"I've tried—but he laughs it off. 'You are my Kohinoor,' he says. 'Nobody else matters.'"

"Then, I guess it's best you leave it at that. Now, if you don't mind, I must leave. Shall I abandon Si? I can't bear the thought of driving back all the way with that stinky creature."

"Where is she?"

We went to look for her and found her in the pool, stark naked, swimming up and down like a tadpole.

"What the hell are you doing there?" Anjali screamed. "Get out this minute. Are you mad? I'll have to empty out the pool and disinfect it—you little tramp—get out immediately."

Si took her time to emerge, then she walked slowly up to Anjali and said with great deliberation, "Darling, I should be the one screaming about infection, with all these faggots floating around. Your fucking pool stinks—and I don't think it's just urine. If I pick up some unmentionable disease, you, my dearest Anj, can bet your sweet ass, I'll be the one doing all the suing." Then turning to me she spat out, "As for you with an Arctic Zone between your legs, I don't need your frigging lift into town. I'd rather hitch."

The last the two of us saw of Si was her small figure in ugly mules going clomp, clomp, clomp through the marble chips.

It was obvious Anjali didn't want me to go. When she asked me to stay on longer, her eyes pleaded as well. I knew I'd be inviting the husband's wrath, but I decided to stay.

"Tea?" she asked brightly once she knew I wasn't leaving.

"Why not? I could do with a cuppa."

"We have our own blend which one of K's planter friends sends us every three months by the case. But if you want something else—we have quite a variety. K's an absolute tea freak. Murty, being a southie, sticks to coffee. I must say I hate the smell of idli sambhar on Sunday mornings—so does K—but he spoils that boy—silly. Anyway . . . what's it going to be—Darjeeling? Orange Pekoe? Jasmine?"

"Let's not get posh, Anjali. Red Label is what I usually drink at home, which I don't suppose your servants would deign to have. But what I'd really love is some real Gujju masala tea, well-brewed and strong."

"That's a good idea. Why didn't I think of it? Silly me!" There'd been something strange about Anjali (apart from her conversion of course) that I couldn't place but now I discovered what it was. She hadn't touched a cigarette in all the time I'd been there. I asked whether she'd quit. She nodded and explained: "K's second wife used to chain-smoke. He hated it. The whole house used to smell of cigarettes—the drapes, carpets, everything. When he asked me to marry him, my quitting ciggies was part of the deal."

"What else did you agree to give up?"

"Come on, it wasn't so difficult. In any case, I'm glad I did— give it up, I mean. I would have, in any case, after I met Krishna." For a minute I started to wonder who this new guy was, when I remembered.

"You must attend one of the bhajans at our place. K is very enthusiastic about them. He says they purify the atmosphere. We call mainly ladies, but a few husbands also show up. Why don't you come with yours on Janmashtami day—that's twenty days from now—let me look at the calendar. Yes—that's it. Come then, that's when we have one of our really big functions. We put up a shamiana in the garden and serve free prasad to everyone. At night, all the poor zhopadpattiwallas come for a free meal. Mind you, we don't cut corners. They're served on banana leaves, and what they get is a full vegetarian meal with puris and everything. There's practically a stampede that night and we have asked for extra police. It's quite a tamasha. The previous time we did it, the young girls from the locality organized a raas, and they came dressed up in ghagras and things. We got a lot of filmi people too. But that's really a nuisance, because all these crowds hang around outside the gates to gape at them."

She gushed on. "My Krishna is brought out at midnight in a silver palanquin. One section is kept for reenacting his birth. We have a cradle decorated with flowers. It's really, really pretty. I make a new outfit for him and change all the silk cushion covers and coverlets on his little bed. We generally have everything in one color, with one theme. Like, we use only dry fruits or only fruits or only vegetables. Or only flowers—like lotuses last year. It's very creative. I start planning months in advance. Don't ask me what the theme is this year. I want it to be a surprise. You'll come, won't you? And stay to dinner. I fast on that day—but you don't have to."

"I'd love to, Anjali, but don't expect me to become a born-again believer, an instant convert. You know how I feel about religion. I only celebrate some of the festivals because the old girl will squawk otherwise. As it is I'm not hitting the high spots on her popularity poll."

"That's all right. I'd just like you to be there. This means a lot to me."

We sipped our masala tea in silence. I thought I saw her lips moving.

"What are you mumbling?"

"Nothing. I'm repeating my Krishna mantra. It calms me down."

"I didn't know you were agitated."

"Not agitated. Just a little tense. I always get like that before K comes home."

"I know that feeling all right. I feel the same way every evening. Which reminds me, I should be off. It will take me at least an hour to get back, that is, if the traffic isn't too heavy."

Just before I got into the car, I saw a quick flash of the old Anjali. She picked up a stray strand of my hair. "Split," she said tch tching. "Do you know your hair is splitting? You must take care of your appearance. I saw your feet also. You haven't been going for pedicures obviously. And am I imagining it or have you gained around the waist? This is the time a woman has to watch it—you let yourself go—and you're finished. I have this wonderful bai who comes and gives me a daily massage. Warm almond oil—divine, divine, divine. I could send her to you once a week. You might have to pay her something extra for coming that distance. But she's worth it. What about workouts? Are you working out regularly? That waist, darling, I don't like what I see there. Middle-age spread. Most Indian women have a cow mentality. Get married and get fat. Disgusting. Anyway, you're lucky to have a good skin. Have you started weekly facials? In case you're looking for someone—this woman who comes home—remember that Parsee female, Panda?—she is now into natural stuff. Apricots, seaweed, cactus—takes care of the lines. Want her?" I smiled and said nothing at all. I didn't feel like defending myself. Maybe she was right about the lethargy. Maybe I had turned into a complacent cow. But there was no incentive. My husband barely noticed me. Whether or not my waist had expanded a couple of inches was of little interest to him. He'd put on quite a bit of weight himself. And it didn't matter to me either.

The car was nearly out of the gate when I saw the durwan running toward us. "Memsaab is calling you back." There she was waving frantically. I asked the driver to reverse and we backed to where she was standing with a small container wrapped carefully in foil. "I forget to give you this—it's the house pâté. Francis does a marvelous one—smooth and silky. You'll love it. I would've given you a full-bodied burgundy to drink with it—but the cellar's locked. And here—a small box of homemade pedas—pure ghee and malai. We make them fresh daily." "Thanks," I said and left.

Pâté and pedas—how perfectly contradictory, yet appropriate. They summed up Anjali's present life. I popped one of the pedas into my mouth—it melted. It was very good. And very rich. I pinched my waist to see if it had gone straight there. I could have sworn I felt a small lump.

A couple of days later, I got an early morning call from Anjali. I was a little surprised, knowing that, for her, anything before eleven a.m. was "the crack of dawn." But that was the old Anjali. The pre-Krishna one. Now, she told me she was up at the real crack of dawn to wash her mandir herself and start her morning prayers. "It's so invigorating. Everything is quiet in the house. The servants aren't up, except for K's valet. K is an early riser, he goes for a jog on the beach before leaving for the golf course. He doesn't expect me to hang around fortunately. I switch on Lata Mangeshkar's bhajans and light agarbattis. I've instructed the mali to make sure I have fresh flowers on a special silver thali that I've given him—he won't steal it because it's Krishna's—then I string my own garlands. Sometimes it's hibiscus, sometimes it's champak. Then for one hour I pray. Bliss, my dear. But that's not what I called about. I wanted you to be the first to know—I'm in business."

"Business? What kind of business?"

"Interiors, darling, interiors. I'm just too excited. Have you heard of Mrs. Kripalani—'Kuku'? Remember, she was once a movie star—never really made it. Then she married that hairy producer and produced half a dozen kids? Attractive, in a brassy kind of way. Anyway, she and I are in this together. She has all the contacts—film stars, hotel people, richie rich Sindhis—and I, my dear, have the talent."

"Good for you, Anjali. How does Kumar feel about all this?"

"Oh—he's delighted. He'll be able to boast to his buddies that his wife does something besides sing bhajans. And if this thing takes off and makes money—then he will back it all the way. There's one small catch—he wants Murty to be involved before he gives me the initial capital."

"What does he want Murty to do?"

"Handle the finances, I suppose. Make sure his own interests are looked after. But he's not saying that. He told me, 'The boy is talented. He is artistic. I want him to have this break—why can't you let him handle details—run around getting fabric samples and that sort of thing?' What could I say? It was clear—no Murty, no money. Simple."

"I still don't see why Murty should get a piece of the action. Besides, why do you need Kumar's money? You have enough of your own. Why don't you invest the lolly Abe gave you?"

"I can't. It's all locked up in a trust. It's too complicated to explain—just believe me when I say I'm a rich woman on paper, but I don't have any cash liquidity."

"The idea sounds fine—but partnerships can be extremely tricky. I don't know anything about business—but I do overhear phone conversations—a partnership—that too with a Sindhi—forget it. She'll take you to the cleaners."

"Don't forget I have some Kutchi blood in me from my grandmother's side. Kutchis can eat even Sindhis when it comes to money matters. I'll chew her like a rotla and spit out the leftovers. Besides, we are hiring the best solicitors to draw up the agreements."

"What are you going to call this firm?"

"Something very French or at least foreign-sounding. You know what a hang-up we have about anything that has a foreign tag on it. I was thinking of Chez Nous or La Maison—except that nobody will be able to pronounce either. It will end up being 'Chaze Noose' or 'La Mason'—horrible. But Kuku has come up with a few suggestions. I'm sure they aren't original, but she gets all these fancy magazines from abroad—*Architectural Digest* and all that."

"When do you start?"

"I thought I'd combine it with my Janmashtami celebrations. It will be a good mahurat to launch a new venture. And I couldn't think of a better day than on my Krishna's birthday. Since I'm superstitious I won't have a booze party—that we'll do later, in style. Maybe have a press conference. I can call up all my old contacts. We'll organize publicity in the women's magazines—what do you think?"

"Sounds terrific. Have you got any jobs on hand at all?"

"Yes, we've got one bungalow of a producer-friend of Kuku's husband. And through him, we've landed that female, you know Bina?—the heroine who posed in a wet sari with her nipples showing?—Well, she's only given us her bedroom to start with, and if that comes out right we'll get the rest of the house. Then we are trying hard for that booze baron's beach house. He has just got married to some starlet and he wants to splurge. That project involves big money, but he hasn't been convinced so far. We are working on him. He wants to get some Spanish designer whose work he'd seen in Dubai. We told him, we'd do the same job for half the price. The man's an ass. Have you met him? You must have—he's unbelievably dumb. I remember Abe making a killing out of him years ago. It was so easy. Not that we want to take him for a ride. In fact K has warned me. They play golf together, and he doesn't want to be embarrassed. I say, in case you are going partying over the next couple of weeks—just spread the word around. But do it discreetly. Don't make it too obvious that you are pushing me."

"No fears, Anjali, people might get the wrong idea."

"Like what?"

"Like you're giving me a commission or something."

"Don't be ridiculous. Anyway, you must see my new visiting cards. They are so stylish. Embossed and all that—with a little touch of gold, very classy. I copied them from a New York woman's. She was also in a similar business. The letterheads will be ready next week."

"Where are you going to operate from?"

"Initially from home. But K has promised us premises if we behave ourselves and make money like good girls."

"Right. I guess I'll see you at the birthday bash."

"Remember to have your hair fixed. Oh yes—there's a sale at the Taj—you know the shoe shop—Joy—remember I used to take you there? I've placed an order for six chappalls—be a darling and pick them up for me. Will you? Otherwise I'll have to send the car all the way just for that."

"Why don't you send Murty? Might as well start the training program—and what better way than to collect the memsaab's chappalls?"

"You're horrid! But useful. Bye for now." She'd had the last word as usual.

The husband was less than enthusiastic about the Janmashtami party. "The last time we went there someone was nearly murdered. What's it going to be this time—gang rape?"

"How can you say that? It's not one of their rowdy evenings. This will be sedate and religious."

"Sounds awfully boring. Why don't you go and make some excuse for me. Say I'm out of town or something."

"She'll misunderstand. Besides, I accompany you to a lot of dreary evenings. And I don't complain. How can this be more boring than one of those business parties?" That did it. We raged at each other for more than an hour and he finally refused to come. As I changed I saw he had the Sherlock Holmes tape on the VCR. I'd seen it a million times. I used to wonder what fascination the film had for the husband for he never tired of it. His eyes would light up and his lips would mouth the dialogue silently. On one occasion I'd suggested a change. "Let's see my favorite film," I'd said, and produced *Gone With the Wind*. He hadn't read the book; naturally, I hadn't expected him to. The film had bored him, which didn't surprise me. What did was the anger it produced. "How can you like such trash? I suppose you admire what that woman did. What was her name—Scarlet, Magenta or some such thing. I know she's supposed to be a great actress, this Viviene Leigh (which he mispronounced as 'Lee')—but what is so fantastic about her performance? I didn't like that woman's role at all. She was a real bitch. Unfaithful, selfish, treacherous. Like all women." I tried to tell him to relax. It was only a film. But he was really worked up. I'd rarely seen him so mad. I could guess why the film disturbed him—but he didn't want to discuss it rationally. He had turned on me instead. "All you women—you're just the same. You have no gratitude, no loyalty, nothing. Think of yourselves all the time, that's all."

"Are you accusing me of something?" I had asked finally.

"No. Why are you taking this so personally? Guilty conscience or something?"

"Then why are you being so aggressive? I don't compare you to Charles Bronson and start a fight over it. What's the matter? Is something upsetting you? Stop playing the silent, suffering spouse and tell me. I don't understand what's wrong these days. You seem so switched off. Is it something at work? Your mother? Money problems? You're drinking too much. And smoking too much. You've put on a lot of weight—what's wrong?"

"What weight? I'm OK. Maybe a couple of kilos here and there. You expect all men to be Clark Gable. That's your problem. You live in some fantasy. Life is not a movie. Or a book. You don't like reality. I have seen how you react when there is some real situation. When Mother comes here. Or even when your own parents visit.

You prefer your dreams. I think you are too pampered. Maybe you are bored. How many times have I told you to join some classes and learn something? All day long you are on the phone talking to all those worthless friends of yours. Other women work, get into a business. Or at least they have children to look after. Look at you. Whenever I come home you are reading a book. With all the servants and everything, you don't have to bother about running the house. Mother is not like other mothers-in-law. She leaves us alone, she doesn't interfere, but even she was saying the other day, 'Your wife should do something.'" I heard him out without reacting for it was obvious that there would be no way he could bring himself to see things from my point of view. And why should he be interested in my life? Then a small anger rose in me as I remembered the besotted man in New York, who was interested in everything about me—even the small mole on my upper arm that only I knew existed. My mind flicked over my time with him and his mad jokes. His insistence on buying me a hideous green plastic Empire State Building souvenir ("You can't be different from other tourists"), and how we laughed over kiddish things—the expression on my face at the sight of a large pizza (it was two feet in diameter).

Through mutual acquaintances I knew my New York flame remarried one of his wives. I forget which one. That had ended in a divorce soon after. He'd all but given up his first love, films, and switched to photography. He was immensely successful here too, and had quite a collection of awards. I'd read about him in various magazines. Everybody felt obliged to ask him his opinion on women, beauty, sex appeal, marriage. He'd dish out quotes that made great copy. None of those articles had evoked a reaction but today I remembered him fondly. There rose in my mind's eye the image of us walking down Fifth Avenue, hand in hand, humming "Touch Me in the Morning . . ." The husband didn't notice the expression I wore. He was staring goggle-eyed at a frog-faced Dr. Watson on the screen. The resemblance was remarkable.

CHAPTER 12

I'D ARRANGED FOR RITU TO PICK ME UP FOR THE JANMASHTAMI party. When she drove up with her husband I felt slightly ashamed of my pink crêpe de Chine sari for she was looking gorgeous. She had her hair in a careless bun and wore a colorful ghagra choli with a bandhani dupatta, and loads of rustic silver jewelry.

"You aren't playing Radha, are you?"

"No. But I felt like looking the part. Just for fun."

By the time we reached Anjali's, the celebrations were well under way. "Come on in, girls. Welcome to Vrindavan," she said by way of greeting. She looked slightly comical in a heavily embroidered lehenga. Ritu took one look at her, turned to me and said, "Bet her husband designed it—it's not her at all." Kumar came up clad in an unusual Bengali dhoti with a starched kurta. "Welcome, welcome." We were escorted to where a group of women were singing lilting songs about Bal Gopal. Right next to the temple in the garden (this was the latest addition—a marble shrine next to the pool) I noticed an extraordinarily good-looking man, clad in a sadhu's saffron robes. He must have been in his late forties or early fifties. His eyes were piercing and he used them well. His posture was ramrod straight, and his body gleamed in the sun. I stared at his bare torso, with just a zari-bordered *angavastram* thrown over it. Ritu saw me staring. "Dishy, huh? One of those sexy sanyasis. Wonder who he belongs to—Kumar or Anjali? Let's find out." The man saw us looking at him. He was obviously vain. Immediately he straightened his already straight back and adjusted his dhoti. He looked arrogantly at one of the devotees and snapped his fingers. Someone rushed up to him with a thali full of fruit and a tall glass of pomegranate juice. He waved it away and asked for Anjali. She all but ran when summoned, not forgetting to cover her head with the dupatta. When she reached him she fell at his feet, eyes closed, head bent. He patted her head and whispered something to her. The sunlight caught the stones on his fingers and showered fire. As he leaned forward, four or five long gold chains left his torso and dangled over Anjali's hair. It was quite a sight. As soon as he sat back again, instructions issued, Murty came up from behind and began to massage his neck and back. Ritu promptly concluded, "He's Kumar's." Anjali went off to do his bidding and we saw her talking to her husband, who went inside their home and emerged with a manila envelope which he handed to Anjali.

We moved off to look at the birthday boy. Little Krishna looked very cute indeed. He had on emerald green garments with jewelry to match. Anjali joined us and gazed at him adoringly.

"Doesn't he look sensational?"

"Him or the bare-bodied hunk out there?" I asked.

She turned to me feigning deep shock. "You aren't referring to our Babaji by any chance, are you? Please be respectful. He is our spiritual guide."

"Oh, I would've imagined he'd be on a more down-to-earth level looking at him."

"He is divine."

"He sure is—whose is he, by the way. Ritu and I are dying to know. Or are you both sharing him—Kumar and you?"

"I don't know what to say—you are perverts, the two of you. You have no higher feelings. I didn't really expect you to have any—but this is the limit. You are insulting His Highness—he is an enlightened being. A Sufi saint. The reincarnation of Gautama Buddha and the final avatar of Krishna."

"Wow! But you haven't answered us—where did you find him?"

"We didn't find him—he found us. Just ten days ago."

"Pray how? Did a star rise over your home and guide him here?"

"Stop being horrible—it wasn't anything like that. Mataji brought him to us when she felt the right vibrations."

"Now who is this Mataji?"

"You mean I haven't told you about her? She is the Godly Mother, who leads all our bhajan evenings. She makes our kundalini rise and tells us about our past lives and past sins."

"Sounds boring. I'd rather know about future sins—at least it's something to look forward to," Ritu said.

"Don't make fun of subjects you know nothing about. These are all highly evolved people. After knowing them, our lives have changed. K is a different man now."

"You mean he prefers girls these days?" I said.

"Shut up, will you? But if you must know, he has taken a vow of total celibacy for a year."

"Poor Murty. How does he get his kicks?" Ritu said.

"Oh, Babaji is working on him too."

"Oh wow! I love this—you mean he has stolen Murty from K and convinced both of you it's for your good? This guy has to be smart. I'd love to talk to him. Is that allowed?"

"I'll first have to seek his permission. And I'll have to route it through Mataji. If you give her the right vibrations and she feels a cool breeze against her palms in your presence, then she'll take you to Babaji. He doesn't meet just anybody. By the way—it's considered a big honor that he is with us today. Half the people here are his followers. He has brought them for the prasad and puja."

"I get it—him and his wild bunch. We call people like them freeloaders."

"They are not freeloaders—have you seen how they've been sitting next to my Krishna and looking after him?"

"Yes—I also noticed the thali they've placed in front of the deity.

At the end of the day, they'll clear at least five thousand bucks. Not bad. And a free meal too."

"You won't understand what all this means. We are into bhakti and charity is a part of it."

"Then why don't you feed a few of the urchins and beggars at your gate? Or adopt a few kids from one of the orphanages?" Ritu said.

"All that is so obvious. To each his own charity, is what I say." We left it at that.

I strolled across to where Babaji was seated, Ritu by my side. One of his disciples was busy applying sandalwood paste on his feet which he had stretched out before him. "He was getting hot vibrations from someone in the crowd. This makes his feet sweat. It means there is an evil presence amidst us. When Babaji feels very sorry—his feet start to weep. We are trying to cool them down," one of the crowd surrounding him volunteered, unasked.

"Sweat." I whispered, "Nothing more than sweaty feet."

Ritu was staring at him with her eyes twinkling. "No, Ritu. Don't you dare," I said, knowing what she was thinking.

"I've never made it with a sadhu before. And it would be so easy too—off goes the lungi."

Babaji had noticed her as well. I saw him giving her his hypnotic special. "Let's go and chat him up," Ritu suggested. I demurred but she went ahead anyway and kneeled in front of him and asked for his blessings. He said to her, "*Beti, tum bahut dookhi ho.*" She nodded her head vigorously. They started a conversation, with him telling her how he had immediately recognized her disturbed state of mind. She got to the point pretty quickly and told him that she also knew the minute she saw him that he alone could help her.

"I am in your hands, Babaji," she said, and gave him one of her soulful looks. I noticed him peering at her cleavage from his vantage point. He placed both his hands on her head and let them linger there. Then he drew them down her nape and onto her shoulders.

"Come and see me tomorrow at noon. You will find me in the Taj Mahal hotel. I forget the suite number."

Ritu folded her hands, bowed and walked back to me. "I did it," she crowed.

"What will you tell your husband?"

"I don't have to tell him a thing. I'm so excited, I can't wait."

"You're behaving like a raging nympho. Control yourself, woman."

"It's not the seduction part that's turning me on—it's the novelty of the experience. I wonder how he'll handle it."

"Expensively," I told her.

"What do you mean? You think I'll have to pay for it? You must be joking."

"I kid you not. If I know how this game works—you'll pay." As we were conversing Mataji waddled up. She was a huge, ugly woman with stringy hair and mean eyes. Her teeth were heavily paan stained, and she wore two big rudraksha malas around her neck. Like Babaji she had rings on practically every finger. She smiled a phony smile and touched Ritu—"Give me your hand, beti. Open it and give it to me." She extended her right hand, palm up. Mataji shut her eyes and held it between both hers. I looked at her thick, stubby fingers and thought, "I'm sure she can't count notes fast enough." After a bit, she started to breathe heavily and say between short gasps, "Yes, yes, yes—I can feel it. The breeze—yes I can feel it blowing. Cool breeze, cool, cool breeze. Beti—your kundalini *is* rising, I can feel it." Ritu was ready to giggle but I stopped her with a frown. This was getting interesting. Mataji nearly swooned over Ritu's hand and finally opened her eyes. "Kneel down, little one. I want to touch your head. I want to feel your spine." As soon as Ritu knelt, Mataji was all over her. It made me ill watching those sausage-like fingers pummeling Ritu's back. "Your chakras . . . something is wrong . . . here, right here. Your kundalini gets stuck at this point. We must ask Babaji to do something. He will help you, beti. I saw him talking to you, you will be all right now." After that initial fit of suppressed giggles, Ritu played along marvelously I thought. She bowed low with gratitude and asked softly, "Tomorrow? At the Taj? What shall I bring with me?" "Beti, you are a blessed woman, you are fortunate, you are wealthy. Do not ask what offering to bring before God. Your inner voice will guide you. Babaji has already entered your body now."

Once Mataji had lumbered away, I said to Ritu, "Let's get the hell out of here. This is getting a bit much—are you really serious about going tomorrow?"

"Of course I am."

"Listen Ritu, I don't want to play Agony Aunt, but you should be careful. This isn't one of your games. These guys can be dangerous. Maybe he's a hypnotist. Or a blackmailer. Or worse—maybe he's one of those tantriks. He could cast a spell on you. Black magic and crap like that. I wouldn't fool around this time. You can live without a holy you-know-what for heaven's sake."

But Ritu was already halfway there. I could tell from the moony expression on her face. This was one conquest she wasn't about to pass up.

"What if Anjali finds out?" I asked her, hoping to shame her into changing her mind.

"So what if she does? Babaji isn't her property."

"No, but Kumar could turn nasty. Maybe he'd set Murty on you."

"Calm down—nothing has happened. Maybe nothing will. It may turn out to be just an ordinary darshan—that's all."

"You're sounding disappointed already. There are other, less tricky ways to get your kicks. This is heavy stuff. Maybe you won't be able to handle it on your own."

"Are you hinting? Do you want to come? Well—why don't you just come right out with it and say so? I'm not dying to go alone. The more the merrier. Maybe we could set up a mini-orgy and throw in Murty."

"Ugh! and ugh again. No, my dear. I'm not interested—well, let me be truthful. I don't want to participate. But I don't mind being a fly on the wall. I'm at a loose end tomorrow anyway. The husband will be in Delhi, and I don't feel like lunching with the mother-in-law. If it doesn't cramp your style too much, I think I will come along. Maybe Babaji will bar my way when he sees me."

"Let's play it by ear—we'll both present ourselves on his doorstep and take it from there."

"Fine. But one thing—let's leave all our jewelry at home and carry twenty bucks between us—that way, even if we are robbed, we'll be all right."

"Yes," giggled Ritu. "Let him steal our chastity, but not our purses." "Precisely."

The encounter which we were both so keyed up about turned out to be disappointingly tepid. When we presented ourselves at Babaji's suite, he was being given an almond oil massage, and we were asked to wait. We were amused to hear romantic ghazals being played on the music system instead of bhajans. Mataji came bustling out and her piggy eyes narrowed further at the sight of us. "Nice. Very nice. Good. Good. Good," she said. "Babaji will be happy. Very happy. You wait. If you want, we can meditate."

We declined her offer. She sat in front of us staring unabashedly. "What your husband is doing? Business? Or naukri?" she asked Ritu.

"Naukri," she said.

I thought Mataji looked disappointed. "Nice. Very nice. And your husband? He is also having job?" That was for me.

"Having job," I lied.

"Good, good, good. Officer—no?"

"Yes—both officers," we chorused.

"Government? Police? Or private office?" We pretended we hadn't heard and started talking animatedly to each other. But Mataji wasn't the sort to be put off so easily. She butted in. "Babaji is a very holy man. Very holy. Faith—so much faith people are having in him. Simply they worship him. See that rose there—one disciple gave him two years ago. Fresh—it is still fresh. It has smell like best Paris perfume. Ask me why? Because Babaji blessed it. It is always here now. He travels, he takes rose. Never it is fading. Always smelling. Touch it—see, good smell. Soft. That is called faith."

"How long does Babaji's massage take?"

"Depends. Sometimes the chakras are all right. So it is shorter. Babaji takes the world's troubles on his own head. If there is riot, war, floods, anything bad, his chakras take time to calm down. Then the massage is longer."

We heard a new ghazal tape being switched on. I was getting quite bored. Mataji left us to attend to the phone which had begun ringing almost nonstop. Other devotees began drifting in. Babaji, it seemed, had quite a following and it appeared an exclusively female one. Ritu and I exchanged glances as a beautiful woman, fortyish, came in with two teenage daughters. What seemed strange was the way the girls were dressed. Both of them were in long, lacy gowns—the sort English flower girls wear at weddings. And to top it all, they were wearing tiaras—that's right—tiaras. Their mother was dressed like an aristocratic Gujarati woman in a standard white organdy sari with tiny daisies embroidered on it. Whopping big diamonds glittered on her shapely fingers, and she was wearing a pretty mangalsutra. She had a pinched, thin face with high cheekbones and very sad, sunken eyes. She would have been stunning had she looked happier. The three of them sat stiffly while Mataji chatted to them (another minion was answering the phone now). They were obviously known to her. One of the girls was holding on to a gift-wrapped package and kept fiddling with the satin bows. Soon the masseur appeared. He resembled Hercules unchained. He must've been a wrestler in his youth. Now, he was overweight—gross, in fact—and bald. Mataji rushed past him, signaling to us to wait. She was back in a minute.

"He is being bathed," she announced.

"Note," I said sotto voce to Ritu. "Being bathed—did you hear that?"

Sure enough, five minutes later, a young woman appeared, wet towel in hand. "Mataji, there is no shampoo in the bathroom. What is this? Please call room service at once."

After a terse call, a basketful of shampoo sachets were delivered. We waited and watched.

By now it was well past lunchtime. Mataji was busy arranging sliced fruit on an enormous silver thali.

"Babaji eats only fruit at this time. And goat's milk. Arre baba, it's so difficult to get goat's milk in your city. Behenji here is very kind—she bought a bakri for Babaji, and her driver brings fresh milk in the morning. Thank God! What would Babaji have drunk otherwise?" she said to the room in general.

"Coffee?" I said deliberately.

She slapped her hand to her forehead. "Chee! Never. That upsets the chakras."

Ritu decided she'd had enough. "Mataji, we can't wait anymore. Please tell Babaji we'll come again some other time after checking in the newspapers about war, riots, accidents, floods."

"As you wish, beti. But Babaji will be disappointed."

"Tough," I muttered.

On the way home, I said to Ritu, "What a waste of time. Don't tell me you want to go again?"

"No. I'm not sure I'd like to. I got bad vibes today." Which was just as well. Subsequently, we heard all sorts of vile stories about the guy—but never from Anjali. She continued to be faithful and protective. There was one particularly delicious scandal Ritu heard about, but Anjali hotly denied it when we asked her. It involved one of the young Gujarati flower-girls we'd seen in Babaji's suite that afternoon. Apparently, the doting devotee, the pinched-faced mother, had "offered" her daughter to Babaji on the very day we'd seen the trio—which was the child's sixteenth birthday (that explained the gift-wrapped parcel on her lap—a cake??). Babaji had blessed her with his ministrations and decided to adopt the other sister as well. Now, he had himself a threesome including the mother—the recent widow of a wealthy businessman. The woman had stripped her home of all the priceless antiques her late husband had collected over the years to buy a bungalow in the hills for Babaji. She had installed him there, along with a menagerie and her daughters, who had, by then, dropped out of school. One day another devotee driving up to the air-conditioned ashram in the hills had been surprised to see Babaji's car parked at a lonely, wooded spot, a little distance from the road. He also recognized the driver who had been standing at a distance, smoking indifferently. The disciple had rushed up to inquire whether anything was the matter—maybe a flat tire? Engine trouble? "Babaji is blessing a disciple." The driver had smirked. The older disciple had gone up to the car for a closer look and had found Babaji in the back seat with the flower-girl going hell for leather at it.

The story did the rounds and died a quiet death. Anjali refused to discuss it insisting Babaji's enemies were spreading ugly stories to malign him.

"Jealousy. Nothing but jealousy," she assured me on the phone.

"Just make sure you keep Mimi away from him—just in case," I cautioned.

"Nonsense. Mimi loves him—like a father. Of course, Abe doesn't believe in such stuff and discourages her from accompanying me. But I know that Babaji's heart is pure."

"His heart may be pure as driven snow. But what about lower down? Are all the other parts of his anatomy equally pure? And that ugly cow—Mataji? Don't tell me her heart is pure too."

"She represents the Earth Mother. She is shakti. They need each other."

"Indeed they do—one has to hustle and the other to con. They make a super team. Who manages the lolly? And how much of it have you parted with?"

"Don't talk like that, please. It really hurts my feelings, we give what we can. K is a total believer you know. He is into yoga these days. He is feeling fit and cleansed."

"Other people use an enema for the same purpose."

"I meant he is spiritually cleansed—free of sin."

"You mean he's going straight and that you are sharing a bed?"

"Rubbish. We both value our privacy. I only mean that he is leading a constructive life, thanks to Babaji. We are thinking of setting up a foundation—of course, both of us will be the managing trustees—or whatever the term is."

"You mean, you'll control the funds."

"That's important, isn't it? It is our money."

"True."

"So we'll probably organize that in a year's time and then all the activities will be monitored by us."

"You will be in charge of marketing Babaji—is that it?"

"Somehow you have the knack of making everything sound ridiculous and petty."

"Not at all. I think you are on to an excellent thing. If you handle it carefully and professionally you will clean up."

"We are not looking at it as a business venture. This will be for mankind. We want the world to discover Babaji. We want people to find love, peace, joy, happiness."

"You can find that in a hash joint."

"Stop talking nonsense—you know what I mean. This is a very important thing for humanity. Babaji has the answers for nuclear war. He has a message for the universe. In fact, K has sponsored a few ads bearing Babaji's message. They will appear on his birthday. You will see the response for yourself. Then maybe you'll feel convinced also."

"Are you going through an ad agency and getting artworks designed? Or are you doing a straight paste-up job?"

"I don't understand all these terms. But watch out for these ads. K has really worked hard on them. He got one of his film contacts to put us on to the best photographer in town—remember the chap who photographs Sri and all the others? He's fantastic. Costs the earth. But worth it. He did a session with Babaji last week. Black and white, color, video, everything. And guess what. I designed his outfits!"

"Outfits? What do you mean 'outfits'? I thought the guy only wears loincloths."

"No, for these pictures, we wanted to show him as a modern-day saint. He had to look contemporary. So I had these fabulous robes stitched at that men's boutique at Juhu—you know—Maharajah? We had to get the bead work and sequined stuff done by someone else. The clothes turned out really lovely. In fact, I felt like wearing them myself."

"I can't wait to see these ads. Maybe Babaji will get a few film roles. Or at least modeling offers."

Anjali giggled despite herself. "Actually, all the Juhu crowd, especially the actresses, just die to be photographed with him. They keep calling to ask when he's coming to our home. He has so many women drooling all over him. Especially these hard-up heroines. Babaji isn't at all interested and he discourages them all the time. But what can he do if they throw themselves at him and send all these gifts?"

"Poor chap. Must be really hard."

"It is! I see him telling Mataji to send all those crazy women away—but no—they refuse to go."

"By the way, I notice your godman is very nattily rigged out. Nothing but the best for him, huh? Silk lungi kurtas, diamonds and sapphires, gold and silver."

"Naturally, silly. He's a rajyogi—a prince on earth. How can he wear ordinary clothes or behave like an ordinary man? Besides, he doesn't buy anything for himself. Ask him and he says he doesn't own anything. He isn't attached to anything. He wears whatever his devotees give him—that too, only to make them happy. He doesn't want to hurt their feelings. I have never seen such an unselfish man. I wish you wouldn't misunderstand him."

"I don't. Believe me, I don't. On the contrary, I think I understand him only too well."

For the next few months Anjali was virtually incommunicado. I assumed this was because she was busy with her Babaji. Every now and again I'd hear stories about their latest joint activity. Maybe an ambulance donated to the local hospital, or a scholarship set up for needy students. I knew the number of Babaji's devotees was growing, because he began to appear in the press frequently. His pronouncements sounded almost comical, but they were carried without comment. He took to holding press conferences at various five-star venues and declaring his views on everything from virginity to sati. Sometimes, I'd spot Anjali and Kumar on the dais. Mataji was fairly active on her own as well. Maybe she was tired of being Babaji's sidekick. She'd started to hold discourses in school and college gyms. She'd come up with strange theories about the nails telling the whole story. She'd read finger and toe nails for a fat fee, and depending on their pinkness or the absence of it she would make her predictions. But all this was very much a part of the background noise of my life for I had finally plunged into an activity that wasn't merely going to parties with friends or the husband or reading books. My initiative was entirely due to the husband—but I don't mean this in any complimentary sense. We'd had one of our usual fights and sometime during the course of it he had yelled angrily at me—criticizing me again for a no-hoper and saying that I would never amount to anything. Why, he asked (for the millionth time), didn't I involve myself in some activity instead of making his life miserable. Once again, as had happened earlier, I felt guilty: maybe he was right, I told myself, perhaps I was as frustrated as I was because there was nothing I was doing.

Which is how I became involved with theater and with Krish. Well, more Krish than theater; but that will explain itself. Krish was a friend of my husband, but he was the first of them I found fascinating—a hot-blooded Bengali rebel from the late '60s, he had flirted with all the right things—poetry, theater and politics. After a particularly tumultuous decade, during which he staked his claim to fame as a fiery college union leader and activist, he disappeared. Just like that. Everybody assumed he had gone underground, though nobody could figure out why. He may have been sympathetic to the Naxalites, but it was well-known that he wasn't one of them. Neither was he a card-holding commie. In fact, he came from an affluent background with a noted barrister for a father and a school principal for a mother. They lived in one of the larger badis in Calcutta and he was amongst the chosen few in college who actually drove up in a car each morning. But, as it was fashionable at the time, he rejected his bourgeois roots (but only in theory) and decided to work for the toiling masses. This went on till his father decided enough was enough and packed off sonny boy to law school in America. Krish was too ashamed to let this dark secret get round, so he fled without telling anybody—and that's how my husband and he met.

When Krish returned to Calcutta, he refused to join his father's firm! He turned his back on law altogether and took up a job in an ad agency. He was perfectly cut out for that world—glib, good-looking, convincing. The kind of guy who could sell crocodiles to a fish farmer. He still wore the khaddar kurta pajama uniform of his revolutionary days, but now it looked more of a fashionable pose than a symbol of anti-establishmentarianism. Like a lot of his peers, theater had become his main love. Poetry was now relegated to the odd session in someone's garage, where scruffy versewallahs gathered to compare each other's doggerel.

It was on one of his visits to Bombay (he'd brought some obscure play here, I forget which) that we met. Someone had sent us free tickets. I think a cigarette company was sponsoring the scheduled four performances. We went because we had nothing better to do—and I'd run out of books. A few minutes after the play started, the husband suddenly perked up.

"I know that guy."

"Which one—the pansy or the hunk?"

"The one with the beard."

"And the eyes?"

"I don't know about his eyes—but that's him—that's old Krish. I'm sure—why don't you check the program? I haven't brought my glasses—go on—just check the names."

"All right. Don't get so excited. The way you're going on, one would think it was Robert Redford himself."

"It's not that. I used to know the guy. We were at college together. He was quite a fellow in those days—one of those anarchists or something."

"What fun. Maybe he's a terrorist in disguise. Maybe he'll blow up this theater at the end of the performance. OK—I've got it—is his name Krish Mukherjee?"

"Yes, that's good old Krish. We must meet him backstage. I wonder if he'll remember me."

"Why shouldn't he—you remember him—don't you?"

"That's different. I told you he was a revolutionary or something."

"Anarchist. You said anarchist."

"Same thing."

"Not quite." Somebody in the row ahead of us ssh-ed angrily and that ended our conversation.

But we did go backstage. I remember it vividly. Krish was standing in front of the dressing table with a towel around his neck. He would have looked like a Davis Cup player, only he was removing his makeup. He looked so absurd, this bearded brute carefully removing the rouge from what little one could see of his cheeks!

"Krish?" my husband said with some hesitation.

"Yes?" He turned to look at us.

"Hey, fatso—it's you! What a surprise. So, how's the business? Minting money?" he shouted, throwing an affectionate arm around the husband. For the next couple of minutes, there was much horseplay with Krish punching his old friend in the belly—"soft underside"—and generally indulging in the sort of juvenile play men invariably fall into when they're meeting up after a long gap. Suddenly, the husband noticed me standing awkwardly with a forced smile on my face. The sort of smile wives have to put on with a matching "men will be men" expression.

"Meet the old girl, Krish," said the husband without mentioning my name. Krish grabbed my hand roughly and bent low over it with an exaggerated bow.

"Charmed," he said and straightened up.

"Hey Krish—what are you doing tonight? Come on home with us. Potluck—don't know what the old girl has rustled up—but it will be edible. And of course, there's plenty of daaru shaaru. You still drink like a fish, don't you?"

Krish handled this exchange with suave tolerance. "Well, let me see—I do have a cast party to attend—you know, it's the done thing—postmortem and all that. But maybe I can run away early and catch up with both of you. How about that? Don't wait dinner—but save the booze. I'll bring my own straw."

A hastily scribbled address was pressed on him and off we went to check on what the "old girl" had "rustled up."

I deeply resented the husband's patronizing tone. I hated being referred to as "the old girl," it made me feel like a bag of bones. I didn't like the put-downs about potluck and the expression on my husband's face when he introduced me. Had I imagined it, or did he look slightly ashamed? I'd begun to wonder about that lately. Maybe I was being oversensitive, but I thought he was invariably apologetic about me in the presence of his friends. As if I was not good enough. I'd even asked him once. He'd dismissed it irritatedly. "What's the matter with you? Chip on the shoulder or what? Why should I feel ashamed of you? Have you done something shameful?" Oh hell—it wasn't any use at all. But that feeling stayed and that evening it was more pronounced than ever. My husband was lost in a reverie on the way home. I wondered what it was that these two unlikely persons had shared? Women? Books? Music?

"What do you have in common with that man?" I asked.

"Which man? You mean Krish? I don't know. I just liked the guy. He was different, full of mad ideas. He tried to organize a protest march, then he got arrested for doing something stupid. I forget what—maybe breaking tables in the cafeteria. He was always up to something. He tried to stage Shakespeare in Bengali. Then he knocked up some Swedish girl. He used to write poetry—I didn't understand it, but the college magazine published a few of his poems. He dropped out for a while to write subversive articles for some underground paper. Mad fellow. But a great guy."

"You still haven't answered my question—what did you have in common with him?"

"Oh—I don't know. Wait a minute—I know—food. We both used to die for Indian food. When we got desperate we'd attempt to cook together. He'd fry the fish and I'd make the dal chawal. And we both liked music. He'd play Nikhil Banerjee while cooking and I'd switch on Aida while eating. Food and booze. We had some good times drinking—going to all the bars, or just getting some bourbon and staying home watching television. I used to listen to him talking—without paying much attention. That man doesn't stop talking once he starts. You'll find out when he comes home tonight."

CHAPTER 13

WHAT I FOUND OUT WAS SOMETHING FAR DIFFERENT. INSTEAD OF THE fiery revolutionary who went wenching in the West, waving his libido like a lal nishan flag, I found a shy, sensitive, mixed-up man who I instantly fell in love with. He arrived pretty late, clutching a paper bag with a bottle of rum in it. In the other hand, he awkwardly held a chameli gajra, which he thrust at me saying, "This is for you—someone was selling it at the traffic lights."

The husband repeated the back slapping routine with plenty of '60s American slang thrown in. "So, what's cookin'?" he asked and Krish looked embarrassed.

"Oh, nothing much—the usual, work, theater, that sort of thing."

"Family?"

"No—I mean, yes. Actually nobody would have me, but I am married."

"Great—finally joined the club, have you? Let's have a drink to that. With or without ice?"

"What?"

"Scotch, of course."

"No, no, don't waste that stuff on me. I don't touch it. If you don't mind, I'll stick to rum—actually, I've brought some along."

"Forget it, yaar. What is this rum-shum? Since when? This is a celebration—Black Label—that's it." So Black Label it was, with a sweet-lime juice for me. I could see Krish recoiling each time the husband hollered for a servant or yelled at the ayah for not replenishing the ice. I sat silently as I generally did when his friends were around. At one point, I picked up a book and started to read.

"Are we boring you that much?" Krish asked and I put away my book guiltily.

"My wife is different, yaar," the husband explained with what I thought was a sneer. "She reads books and sleeps—those are her two main hobbies."

"What are you reading?" Krish asked gently.

"Something stupid—one of these cheapie bestsellers. Ludlum."

"That's a fun read."

"Fun?" scoffed the husband. "Waste of time, if you ask me." And he excused himself to go to the loo.

Krish waited for him to leave the room, leaned forward and touched my hand. "I thought the chamelis would cheer you up."

I quickly withdrew my hand and looked at the door.

"It's OK—he's still in the loo."

"It's not that."

"Then?"

"I don't know."

"I think you do."

"What are you talking about?"

"You'll find out—if you're interested. By the way, I like your feet. They have a lot of character."

Bloody flirt, I thought angrily—my feet—I hated my feet! They were truly awful, with a big toe like a fat, overboiled potato. Character! Maybe he was being bitchy. I was relieved when the husband walked in and asked in his irritating ha-ha way, "So have you two become friends or is the vow of silence still unbroken?" I excused myself saying I had my sleep to catch up on. Krish caught the irony of the remark, but not thick husband, who waved me off gladly and even planted a kiss on my cheek to impress Krish.

❖

He called at noon the next day. "We are planning a little workshop at around four today. I think you'll enjoy it. Why don't you come? You can bring your book with you, but please don't fall asleep while I'm talking—that will hurt my ego and damage my reputation." I nearly chickened out but then my husband's taunt about my being feckless suddenly surged through my mind and I thought why the hell not, theater is as good an activity as any to be involved in. Besides, though I didn't want to admit to it, I wanted to see Krish again. Once again, I had nothing to wear. I didn't want to look "dressed up" but I didn't have anything attractively casual either. Khadi would have been an affectation, jeans—well, I was never the jeans sort. I picked a sari at random, thinking—what the hell, why am I acting like a schoolgirl, I bet he'll be too busy to notice. I reached late and the workshop was well under way. Quickly, I surveyed the room—there were more women than men, and all of them were frighteningly attractive. There was one chain-smoking woman in particular, who gave me an instant complex. She looked so self-assured, so studiedly elegant. I detested her. But more than that, it was the way she was look-ing at Krish—hungrily. He too was obviously aware of her pres-ence, directing most of his remarks straight at her. I wanted to leave. Suddenly, he stopped midsentence to greet me. "Lovely to see you, glad you could come. The chamelis are waiting for you." Everybody turned around to stare. It was one hell of a way to make a pass and start an affair.

I won't trot out the standard line—I didn't know what I was doing. I bloody well did. The affair seemed inevitable, and was the best thing that could have happened to me. I didn't feel mortified then, as I don't now, when I think of it. Neither do I regret it coming to naught. As Anjali would've promptly reminded me, had she met Krish, he was not husband material. But he couldn't have been a better lover. For three years we plunged into what the tabloids call a "torrid affair," the better part of it conducted through letters. There were days when we scribbled over twenty sheets each, in three batches, and sent them off QMS. It came to a stage when the postman was the most important individual in my life. I would wait like a lunatic for the fat envelopes to slip into my hands as I waited this side of the door. I would pounce on Krish's words and gobble them all up, savoring each one, hungry for more.

The affair was cockeyed from the very beginning. The logistics of it even crazier. He would engineer a trip to Bombay every couple of months. The question of my going to Calcutta did not arise. Though once, when I was feeling really desperate (no letters for a week), I told my husband I felt like going to Calcutta. He was surprised but not suspicious. "Why Calcutta? You don't know anybody there. Of course, Krish can take care of you. Maybe you could stay with them—I hear his wife is a sweet girl—but how come you want to go to Calcutta?" I just burst into tears and sobbed like a fool. This puzzled him further. "Are you all right? Is there something wrong? Do you need a holiday? Why don't you visit your family? Maybe you need a checkup. Shall I fix up an appointment with Dr. Kapadia?" I just continued to cry which was pretty uncharacteristic of me. For one mad moment I actually considered "confessing" but something stopped me. What was I going to tell him—I'm having it off with your pal from America? How do you like that? Fortunately, I shut myself up . . . and allowed him to dismiss me as yet another hysterical woman.

In my more rational moments I found the whole thing awfully depressing—the subterfuge and tricks we had to resort to. I don't suppose Krish had the resources to make long-distance calls. So I was the one calling. Then there were all the rules that adultery immediately imposes: no calls on Sundays, no calls at home, letters to be destroyed immediately after reading (I didn't follow this rule faithfully and it got me into a lot of trouble later on—but I'm getting ahead of myself), no presents. There were times I would die to hear Krish's voice, and quite often this coincided with a Sunday.

I remember one occasion distinctly. Krish was leaving for London. He was going to be away for a fortnight. I wasn't sure he'd find the time to write or call, and I had to speak to him before he left for the airport. I decided to break the rules for once and rang him. It was a reckless decision and one that I regretted later. After much difficulty, I got through. It must have been around seven in the evening. The servant answered. "*Saab, memsaab bahar gaye hai,*" he said in heavily accented Hindi. I couldn't resist asking where they'd gone. Innocently the servant replied that his saab had taken the memsaab for an ice-cream. I gagged hearing those words. I honestly thought I'd throw up all over the phone. I couldn't believe it. It seemed like such a betrayal. How could he do it—ice-cream! The effect of that word ice-cream lingered for a long time. I couldn't get myself to eat it for over a year. I never asked Krish about this episode. In fact, it proved to be the turning point in our relationship. When he returned from London, I felt tense and hostile. All of me was knotted up. Maybe I was heading for a breakdown. Even books didn't help.

My husband knew nothing. Sensed nothing. He seemed terribly preoccupied and I assumed it was a complicated business deal. For the first time in my life, I felt like dying. I felt sick of myself and full of self-pity. I hadn't told anybody about Krish and me. It was a secret I felt extremely possessive about.

But Ritu managed to pry it out of me one evening. I was at my lowest. Out of some sort of crazy defiance, I'd enrolled myself in a suburban theater group. It was to prove something to Krish, something nebulous—what even I didn't know. His letters were less frequent now, though I continued to write mine (at the office address, of course) as feverishly as before. I would drive myself into a state if three days went by with no contact. I'd imagine he'd found someone else or that he had rediscovered his wife. And for all this I'd detest myself. It was a demeaning experience and I felt I was wasting away, draining myself physically and emotionally. It was beginning to show. I looked wan and wild-eyed. My day began and ended with the letter or the absence of it. Everything hinged on it—even my meals. I'd make insane promises to myself. "If the letter comes, I'll eat my lunch—if not, I'll starve." I began to imagine that fasting or punishing myself in some way would make the letter arrive. In saner moments I'd tell myself this was crazy—the letter had assumed a life of its own. It was as if it had become independent of the sender. I'd feel angry or happy at the letter, not at Krish. I'd blame the postman, the weather, Indian Railways—everybody and everything else. My own letters must have sounded manic, but I didn't know it. Obsessed with the thought of love, I was behaving like Adele H, chasing an illusion like a woman possessed.

Intuitive and shrewd, Ritu zeroed in immediately. "It's some man isn't it?" I suppose I was bursting to tell someone. And Ritu had the knack of being sympathetic, particularly in matters such as these. "Don't forget I have a doctorate in the subject," she laughed and urged me to tell all. It was such a wonderful feeling to be able to talk about Krish. It all came gushing forth in schoolgirlish garb. Ritu said later that my entire appearance underwent a dramatic transformation as I spoke. She said I had looked twelve years old, and even my voice and accent had changed as I broke my silence on Krish. She may well have been right for once I had begun talking Ritu became unimportant, irrelevant, it was just the sound of my own voice talking about Krish that was thrilling me.

I heard her ask, "What is it that you like about him?"

And I said, "His teeth. I've never seen such sexy teeth. Strong, white, large."

"What about the rest of him?"

"He has knobby knees and they hurt."

"And the rest, you know, the rest??"

"He's not exactly *Playgirl* pinup material—but I love him. I absolutely love him. I want him. I can't bear the thought of not having him as my own."

"You mean, you want to marry him?"

"Yes."

"Does he want to marry you?"

"I don't know. I don't care. I want him. I'll go crazy."

"Wouldn't it be simpler to get all this straightened out—why don't you ask him whether he has marriage in mind? From what you tell me, and to quote our friend Anjali, this man doesn't sound like husband material. It's best you have him as a lover—even a long-distance one—till one of you decides to move on—let's hope it is you. I know your marriage isn't fantastic, but it isn't a total write-off either. If you can have both—a boring husband in the home and an exciting lover on the sidelines—perfect."

"You are making it all sound so sordid and cynical. For the first time in my adult life, I'm feeling ready to give of myself, to risk love, and you are saying it's not worth the effort. Just imagine if I let it go now, it will never happen to me again. I don't mind the hurt, but I want to give it all I have, or I'll regret it always."

"Then, why don't you, for starters, come clean with your own husband? Why don't you make a couple of hard decisions? Why don't you get to the bottom of this with Krish? Ask him if he's told his wife. I am certain he hasn't. Men like him don't. And why should he? It would only complicate his comfortable existence and cause trouble."

"But look at it this way, Ritu. We are both free in a way—freer than most other couples. There are no children in both the marriages, and the respective spouses aren't the sort to create hurdles. The whole thing could be handled in a civilized way without creating too many ripples. Divorce isn't such a dirty word anymore. I'm sure my mother-in-law would feel pretty relieved, maybe the husband too. I've always felt like such an imposter in this house."

"You are speaking about yourself and your setup. You don't know anything about his. You haven't seen him in his environment. You only have what he tells you to go on. How do you know he's ready to leave his wife for you? Has he ever told you that? Or even hinted?

If I were you, I'd make a trip to Calcutta to find out a few things for myself. But before doing that, I'd first check with the man himself. You wouldn't want to go there and stumble on a few unpleasant truths, would you? The next time you speak to him, just say casually that you want to come there. See his reaction—that will tell you plenty."

I swore Ritu to secrecy. Told her I'd kill myself if I ever found out she'd spoken about this to anyone. And then I called Krish. He was busy with someone. His secretary with whom I'd palled up (and worked so hard to cultivate) told me she'd pass on my message, but she'd been instructed not to interrupt the presentation—the agency was angling for a new client—a big fish. I chatted her up as I usually did. I don't know why I felt the need to ingratiate myself. Maybe I imagined that her approval of this faceless voice from Bombay would somehow make a difference to Krish. That she'd be able to influence his attitudes toward me. I'd even thought of sending her perfume for Christmas. That's how desperate I was.

The flip side of my raging passion for Krish and all its attendant anxieties, was the guilt I felt that rose up every now and again—often with frightening intensity. More than any other regret, I felt awful that now I too had joined the ranks of all those women I'd so easily condemned in the past. I had become an "adulteress." What an ugly, judgmental, biblical-sounding word that is! And so old fashioned. Yet, we haven't coined a better one to replace it so far. I would wonder how the parents, particularly Father, would react to the discovery. Would they damn me? Ask me never to set foot in their home? Insist on my telling all to husband and family? Expect me to die of some awful disease? Pay for my sins? Or would they blame themselves instead—don a hair shirt and wonder, "Where did we go wrong?"

I wrote to Krish about this and he scribbled back some blank verse which didn't make any sense at all. This was another habit of his that maddened me. I'd ask him a specific question and get back an unrelated poem instead. Typed at that. Sometimes I'd wonder darkly if he kept a drawer full of typed poems which he instructed his secretary to mail out periodically. I even asked him that—I only got back another poem!

All through the affair the thing that bothered me the most were our assignations. I found them very depressing and sad. The furtive phone calls to announce his arrival in town and give me the room number. Then the little details—between meetings and after meals etc. So horribly mechanical and unromantic. Yet, I would wait with my teeth on edge, canceling everything for those frenetic couplings in impersonal hotel rooms. How I'd hate walking through the lobby to the elevators. I'd imagine everyone staring at me—knowing where I was going, sneering at the thought. I'd feel like a harlot self-consciously sneaking up to solicit customers. Once inside the room, I'd get preoccupied with small things. Overripe bananas in the fruit basket would bother me, wet towels on the bed drive me nuts, clothes discarded sloppily all over the carpet and trays with stale leftovers make me sick. I'd look for things to take my unhappiness out on—wilted rosebuds in the flower vases, underclothes and socks on the armchair, files and papers scattered on the sofa, stubbed-out cigarettes in a saucer, shoes under the table, toiletries on the writing desk—anything.

The first time I set about tidying the place Krish said impatiently, "Your secret desire must be to make it as a room service girl—the perfect chamber maid. I can put in a word for you with the head of housekeeping."

"Very funny. But how can you live in this pigsty?"

"It's not a pig's abode. Or maybe it is—a male chauvinistic pig's."

The light banter would continue, as phone call after phone call interrupted us. This then was the pattern. There was never time for a real conversation. Or maybe we maneuverd it that way. Krish was a clown. And it was impossible to stay angry with him. Besides, what could I be angry about? His lack of commitment, his insensitivity, his selfishness, the way he had absolute control over my emotional life, his power over me. Yes, I hated him for all this. I could imagine myself advising another woman, "Don't waste your time on that bum—he has nothing to lose. He is exploiting you, using you. At the end of this you'll be dumped—join the heap of his other discarded women. Where's your self-respect? Get him out of your system. He's no good for you. Never get involved with a married man." And so on, and so on, ad nauseam. But all it needed was a letter or a call from him—and I'd go running, telling myself, "There should be no ego, no pride between lovers." I'd plan gifts—plan them for months making them as unique, as original, as possible. I'd try and impress him in other ways. Drop names of Russian poets and Czech playwrights. Talk about the progress I was making in my little theater group, discuss future plays I knew I'd never act in. It mattered so much what he thought of me, my worth, my standing.

All of this, he took for granted. All my offerings were accepted as of right. It astonishes me, in retrospect, how grateful I'd feel for his gracious acceptance of me and my presents. I remember getting him a beautifully enameled, old silver pocket watch. It was something I'd seen with a dealer and lusted after. It was meant for Krish—just perfect. It suited his personality and I wanted it for him. I had it engraved, placed in cotton wool, put into a velvet box, gift-wrapped and hand-delivered, with a bunch of wild roses that I knew he loved. When I spoke to him an hour later, he even forgot to thank me for it! I had to ask him, as casually as I could—"What's the time by your watch—the pocket one?"

It was only then that he remembered. "Oh shit! How could I forget? Thanks—that was real pretty."

I didn't want to say another word, but didn't want to sound petulant either. With as much control as I could muster I asked him, "Liked it? Did you read the inscription?"

"What inscription? Hold the line, let me find it—oh hell, where did I put the damn thing? Look, I'll locate it later and call you back. OK? Got to run. You're coming later this afternoon, aren't you? In case you can't make it, leave a message at the counter so I'll reorganize my appointments accordingly. Bye now."

That was one of the more egregious putdowns but whatever he did, detesting myself all the while for doing so, I'd go along with his plans—taking hours over my appearance, changing in and out of a dozen saris, checking my legs and underarms for fuzz, wearing Dior panties, my best lacy bra and far too much perfume.

And then he was scheduled to go to London again. On an impulse I decided to go too. I told the husband about it, and absently, as it were, he agreed.

"Yes. I think it's a good idea. You can stay with your sister."

"That's the main reason," I lied. "I haven't seen her for ages. I think she's having a rough time. I should be with her."

"Speak to my secretary—she'll arrange all the details with the travel agent. Do you want to go somewhere else as well?"

"No. Just London."

"How long for?"

"Maybe ten days."

"Just ten days? Don't be silly—stay longer. I'll be OK. My mother will organize the food and everything. You take your time, enjoy yourself. Don't worry about foreign exchange and things like that. I've kept some money there with friends—you can have it. See some good plays, shows, get yourself a new watch—I hate the one you've been using. Get an elegant one this time—Longines or Cartiers."

While he was innocently instructing me, I was already planning where, when and how I'd meet Krish. At the airport? Hotel? What we'd do together—how liberated and free we'd feel without any pressures on us. I didn't feel I was taking advantage of the husband, deceiving him—nothing.

Krish sounded almost pleased when I told him.

"Excellent planning, dear girl," he said. "Why don't we go on a little side trip somewhere—where would you like to go? I've never been to Venice—have you? Let's spend four days there before heading back—what say you?"

I jumped at it. I hadn't been to Venice either, but had always longed to, particularly after seeing *A Death in Venice*. And I was sure Venice would be the turning point in our relationship—and a turning point for the better in that ethereal city of my fantasies. We'd discover how perfectly in tune we really were and how it would be madness not to be together forever. It wasn't the touristy Venice I was chasing. I didn't see Krish and me floating around in gondolas being serenaded by gondoliers. My Venice was going to be a golden dream where Krish and I would luxuriate in each other, sip capuccinos in small cafés, hold hands in the piazza and kiss on the Bridge of Sighs. There was nothing I wanted more in the world—just nothing. The thought of the trip transformed me. Soon I was tripping around like a teenager, making plans, just stopping short of a song on my lips and a spring in my step. Everybody noticed the difference, particularly Ritu. But this was one secret I wasn't going to tell anybody. I didn't want to risk it. I didn't want to blow it. My plan was foolproof. I wouldn't even involve my sister. I schemed day and night and bombarded Krish with letters. He seemed excited as well, and sent back quite a few missives. These were loving notes, full of warmth and affection. I thought it was all going the way it should. Krish was finally coming around to looking at things my way. Venice became the ultimate test and I wasn't going to flunk it.

I mentioned Venice in passing to the husband. He seemed amused. "But you don't know anyone there. Besides, have you checked your ticket? Is Venice on it? Rome maybe. And your Italian visa? Have you arranged for that? Where will you stay? What about hotel bookings? I think you're crazy to want to go alone. You are not used to traveling that way. Why don't you wait till we can do this together—maybe next year? I promise I'll take you, leave it till then. Go somewhere else if you want to. Why not a weekend trip to Paris or Amsterdam—I know people there. Or, ask your sister to come with you. I'm sure she could take two days off—ask her right now." But I refused to discuss it further or go into details. I had already spoken to the travel agent and fixed up the dates. Krish had left all that to me saying it would be easier to do from Bombay. He'd organize his own ticket from Calcutta. I still didn't know where he'd be staying in London but these were minor things. I planned my wardrobe with care, selecting the sort of saris I knew Krish liked—saris closer to his home—Dhakais, Tangails, Jamdhanis. I wanted to look like a wife—his wife.

When the husband saw me off at the airport, I didn't feel even a tinge of guilt, remorse or shame. I waved to him cheerfully, even gave him a warm goodbye kiss at home with a long embrace. He was being very sweet—red and yellow roses, a new handbag and a small note saying, "I'll miss you, wifey. Our home won't be the same without you." Even so, I felt dead and cold. It wasn't cruelty, it was indifference. At that moment the one thing that mattered was being with Krish—everything else was irrelevant, secondary, practically nonexistent.

I couldn't eat or sleep on the flight. I asked for stationery and wrote a long epistle to Krish—I planned to hand it over to him in person. My hands shook as my fingers raced across the pages.

Swati, my sister, was at the airport. I was too self-absorbed to even notice how old and ill she suddenly looked. My first question to her was, "Are there any messages for me? I was expecting a call or a letter."

"Aren't you going to ask me how I am?"

"I'm so sorry—of course, I want to know how you are. How are you?"

"Tired. Bone tired."

"Health?"

"I don't know. I just feel exhausted all the time. Come on, let's go. We have enough time to talk about all that—I'm just so happy to see you, it's been such a long time. I haven't met the family for nearly three years. You're looking well—in fact, better than when I saw you last. Is everything OK? Husband? Mother-in-law? And you?"

I felt so protected in her presence. Even though we weren't very close, we had an understanding of our own that was a very undemanding one. She was the gentle sister, the giving one and I was truly sorry that her marriage hadn't worked out. I wished I could've found some way to offer her my support but I hadn't anything to give. Everything was reserved for Krish. I suppose I should have talked to her about Krish for she was the sensible one in the family—the person all of us turned to in a crisis. But I didn't.

Unfortunately, on the very next day, my wonderful secret was out. And it was the husband who spilled the beans. Before my sister and I were fully awake, the phone rang. It was him. "We need to talk," he said quietly. "I'm arriving tomorrow night."

I knew from the tone of his voice that he knew. And my sister knew that something had happened—something major. I didn't really have much of a choice, so I told her the whole sordid, messy story, as calmly as I could. I was relieved by her reactions. Like my parents, she too was a stoic—strong and silent and deep as the Ganga. She just looked at me for a long time and said, "You were always the strange one, right from childhood. I couldn't ever figure you out. I used to think you were slow or vain or both. But there was always something secretive going on inside your mind that none of us knew about. You weren't like the others. After you grew up and got married, I stopped trying to figure you out. Even your marriage was funny—the husband you finally chose."

"Why do you say that?"

"I don't know, really. In all departments he was all right, I suppose. In fact, better than most. Yet, I always felt he was the wrong man for you—maybe because I never saw you talking to him. Not idle chatter—you know—but the sort of conversation husbands and wives have. Then I thought it was because you didn't have children. But it wasn't that. Your worlds were different and you didn't want to belong to his.

"Mother used to say, 'It's all right if a woman marries above her, but a man never should.' Though your husband was a rich man, with you he didn't feel confident. Your coldness kept him away. In his own way, I thought he loved you sincerely. But you didn't—love him, I mean. And he had to live with that and pretend he didn't know."

I was all tensed up and in no mood to listen to her analysis. "What shall we do tomorrow? How shall we handle him? Do you think he'll create a terrible scene? What am I going to tell Krish?"

Suddenly, it had become "our" problem. "Let him first get here and then we shall see. For all you know, he may have a surprise for you. What makes you think he's coming here to accuse you? Maybe he has a mistress tucked away somewhere and your absence has helped him to reach a decision. You must not initiate the conversation. Remember not to incriminate yourself by volunteering any information. Let him do all the talking. You merely say yes or no. Silence is your best defense."

I was quite taken aback by her attitude. Maybe I had underestimated her over the years. The truth is I hadn't really thought about her too much one way or the other. She didn't make me curious. I'd dismissed her as a dull, mousy, studious creature whose interests began and ended with microbiology or anatomy or some such subject. Though I was fond of her in a vague sort of way, there was never any great communication between us.

Perhaps this was because I felt she disapproved of me on some level. Or regarded me as an outsider. And, I suppose, it was the inevitable comparisons that arise in families that drove us further apart. I could still see the day, when there had been some disagreement at home, I forget what, and Father saying of her with pride, "she has moral fiber." And here she was now, providing me with the sort of sisterly support that I needed. I couldn't even show her how much it meant to me, since we were never great ones for displaying our emotions. I wanted to hug her or place my head in her lap. Instead, I held out my hand awkwardly to shake hers. "Thanks a lot," I said while pumping her dry, bony fingers up and down in a ridiculous handshake.

She decided to accompany me to the airport. "I'll drive you," she said. "Why waste money on a cab?"

On the way, we were both silent. Her only comment was, "It's a pity your holiday is spoiled. I was looking forward to taking mine along with yours. We could've gone to Brittany together. Or the Lake District. I rarely get a chance to relax—and this would've been fun."

As we waited by the gates for the husband she remarked, "Look. He's carrying just a tiny case—hand luggage. Maybe he isn't planning to stay. Maybe you were imagining things. Perhaps he's on his way somewhere—could be an urgent business trip. Remember, mum's the word."

The husband was remarkably restrained. We drove back making desultory conversation about the weather in London and the weather in Bombay. Back at the apartment, Swati left us alone, discreetly saying that she had some papers to attend to for a long day tomorrow. (Swati was now on the seminar circuit in a big way.)

The husband busied himself unpacking his small bag, carefully taking out his shaving things, toothbrush and toothpaste. His voice was controlled as he chatted about the talk show that was on the tube. Once he'd changed into his pajama kurta, I could see he felt himself and in control.

"Right," he announced, like he was the convener of a Rotary Club meeting. (I half expected him to add—"the first point on the agenda today," but he disappointed me.) He pulled out a couple of familiar-looking envelopes from a folder and handed them to me. "Do you want to tell me about these?"

"Where did you find them?"

"That's hardly important."

"It is—to me, it is. You've been going through my things—my cupboard. The key's with me—did you break it open? I hate people prying—what a sneaky thing to do."

"Wait a minute, I asked you a question. I think that is far more important than how I got these letters. Besides, I didn't break open your cupboard—my mother had the spare key."

"What the hell was she doing with a spare key to my cupboard? I always knew she was a sneak."

"Listen, you'd better watch your words. My mother was given the spare keys to all the cupboards in our house as a precaution—just in case we misplaced them. And the only reason she opened your cupboard was to clean it out in your absence and air the warm clothes."

"Oh, I bet! Like I'm incapable of cleaning out my own cupboard. Tell me another. She was just snooping. She's always snooping. I've heard her pick up the extension in the living room often enough when I'm talking to someone from the bedroom."

"Thank God she did do that or else we'd never have found these. Don't bother to explain anything—yes, she has heard you talking to your lover on the phone. But she didn't tell me earlier hoping you'd be sensible enough to end it on your own. Now the whole thing has gone too far, even for her. She felt she just couldn't keep it from me any longer."

"Well, since you already know so much and have obviously read the letters, what's the purpose of this trip? Have you come all the way just to confront me with the 'evidence'? It could've waited till I got back—would've been cheaper too."

"Don't worry about the expense. I'm attending to some business here—the fare is taken care of by one of the clients. But that's really no concern of yours. Let me hear the whole story. Don't you have anything to say? Is this nonsense going to carry on? I'd like to hear your decision before I leave. And yes—in case you have any plans of staying on, forget them—you're coming back with me. I've told Mother I'm bringing you home."

"What for? To face a joint inquisition? Does she want to grill me separately? Haul me over the coals? Or am I expected to fall at her feet and beg for mercy?"

"We'll come to all that later—I'd like to know who this K is. I think I know—though I'd like to hear it from you. But first, I need a drink. Where's the liquor cabinet, or doesn't your sister keep any booze in the house?"

"It's in the drawing room, near the lamp—and while you're at it, get me one too, I could do with a drink today."

"Is that also a new development—something K has taught you? So what is it that you drink, rum?"

"You obviously know everything—why do you want me to go into details?"

"I always knew Krish was a lowdown bastard. I'm not surprised at all that he is doing this—but you? And with Krish? Have you lost your mind? That man is not your type. He is a pseudo through and through. He is weak—and he is broke—by your high standards, that is. What do you see in that creep? What about his poor wife? Didn't you think of her at all? When did all this start—don't tell me it was that night when he came to our house and drank up all my scotch."

(I felt like putting the record straight on that one but refrained.) "Bastard! Drinks my booze and steals my wife. Lowdown bastard. I'm going to expose him. I'll fix him. I'll see to it that he loses his job and is out on the street. I know his MD very well—we are on several club committees together. All it needs is one phone call from me—that's all. And then we shall see where this Mr. Intellectual goes. He'll be begging on the streets of Calcutta. I'll see him in the gutter. He will pay for this. But before that I have to deal with you."

"Deal with me, indeed."

"I admire your nerve. The way you are playing the high and mighty role, one would imagine the whole thing was my fault. Just get off your high horse and face life—you aren't in one of your books now, and I'm not the understanding husband they show in films. I have come here to thrash things out—and I mean business. I'll get myself a drink. If you want one, you can bloody well fix it yourself. I'm not your goddamned bartender."

He came back with a tumbler full of whisky. He held a can of Coke in the other hand. "Here. I think you should stick to this. Next you'll tell me you've taken to smoking his brand of stinking cigarettes. God! I just can't believe how you could have got involved with a man like Krish. He's scum. Maybe you like scum."

"I thought you said he was a great guy and that you liked him. If you hadn't forced him on me this would never have happened."

"So now you are trying to turn the whole thing around and blame me! I like your cheek. So I am responsible for your affair!!"

"I wouldn't have met Krish otherwise. You really sold him to me, made me curious. I'd never heard of this man before."

"All right, now that you have more than heard of him—what do you intend doing?"

"Go to Venice—with him."

"You must be mad. You think I'm going to sit by and allow you to go to Venice with your boyfriend?"

"Let's make a deal."

"A deal? What are you talking about? I haven't come here to make any bloody deal with you. Get it straight right now—you see him one more time and you're out of my house—out! I've thought over the whole thing carefully. I would've thrown you out right now—but I'm prepared to give you one more chance. I'm not a mean man. You've been a good wife. I don't really have any major complaints against you. I'm prepared to cancel this one black mark on your performance record and start with a clean slate. But you have to swear you'll never see or keep in touch with that man again. I think I'm being more than fair. No other husband would've reacted like this—but I said to myself, you are human, you have sinned, but I must be generous and forgive you."

It was incredible the turn the conversation was taking. And the slight display of anger the husband had shown earlier had disappeared completely. He continued talking. "What do you say—we forget about the whole thing—and go on as before? Tell you what—I'll take you to Venice. I know you've always wanted to go there." Saying which he lapsed into silence and waited, rolling the cubes of ice in his glass.

"You make me sick," I said, and I thought he'd topple over with astonishment. "You really make me sick. I think our marriage was over the day our awful honeymoon started. We've got nothing going. I don't love you—never have. As for you—I really don't know to this day why you chose to marry me. I don't think you even know who you married. You don't have a clue what sort of a woman I am. I'm tired of your smugness, your irritating mannerisms, the way you take me for granted and expect me to fall into your overall scheme of things. I really don't care one way or the other if I ever see you again. So just get off my back. You've found out about Krish and me—so fine. Don't expect me to give you the gory details. And thanks a lot for the Venice offer—but if you don't mind—I think I'll pass."

"What does that mean?"

"It means, I don't wish to discuss my relationship with Krish.

And it means that I'm going to Venice on my own. And you can take a jump if it doesn't suit you."

"Suit me, huh? A lot of things about you don't exactly 'suit me.' I think I've been far too much of a gentleman and kept quiet for too long. My mother used to warn me. She sensed what was going on long ago—ever since you started all your theater rubbish. She noticed all the changes. She'd phone the house in the afternoon to check with the servants and they'd tell her you were out. She asked me a few times if I knew where you were going and like a fool I told her that you had enrolled yourself in theater classes because you wanted to do something new. She showed me the telephone bills. I don't know how I didn't suspect even after that. She asked me whether I was making all those STD calls. But I trusted you so much, it never occurred to me that you were a woman of such low morals. I think it was all your friends, those cheap women, who influenced you. I told my mother when she came to the airport to see me off—it was those women. All of them cheating on their husbands, telling lies, screwing around. And that was the sort of company you kept—you chose to keep. How could you have been any different? I'm cursing myself for being such a fool—but, like I told my mother, these women changed you. You were not like them when we got married, otherwise I would never have married you."

"What did you know about me then? As much as you know now—nothing. Just nothing. I was another one of your well-calculated deals—though I really never could figure out what there was in it for you in this case. You could easily have grabbed any of the other, far more desirable girls from your own community. Your mother never tires of telling me how many proposals you turned down and how wealthy those other girls were. Maybe you wanted to feel superior. You wouldn't have felt half as complacent with one of these richie rich girls. You know what your problem is? You never cared to understand me as a woman."

"If it was as bad as you now make it out to be—why did you

get into it. What was in it for you? Security? Luxury? Prestige? Why don't you be honest and give me an answer to those questions? By having this affair what were you trying to do—I'm sure you weren't going to leave all this and marry that bloke? He doesn't have the resources to keep you in the style you're accustomed to. Be truthful—would you have shacked up with him in some poky little flat filled with cockroaches where you'd have had to get up at six o'clock to fill water? No way. You are a spoiled woman—like your other friends. You women want it both ways—your kicks and your comforts. Well sorry lady, but you married the wrong man in that case."

Suddenly, he looked vulnerable. I felt sorry for him and surprised at my own aggressiveness. "Let's not fight," I urged. "Why don't we talk about this thing calmly and figure out a sensible solution?"

"What solution are you talking about? I haven't come here to work out solutions with you. Let me make it very clear—you want out, you've got it."

"I'm not sure I want out—I'm kind of used to you."

"Ha, if you think I'm going to wait around till you make up your mind—forget it, just forget it. You don't deserve me and my family. My mother had told me at the very beginning—'Find out more about this girl and her family. Are they like us? Will they fit in? Will she?' and I'd given her a guarantee that you would be OK. How wrong I was and how right she'd been!"

"There's no point in postmortems, I don't believe in them. Let's get on with the story. I love this friend of yours, and I want to be with him—in Venice. There is a good chance that I will feel thoroughly disillusioned after that. Maybe he will have some truly foul personal habits that will disenchant me. In which case it will really be *A Death in Venice*. You know by now that I'm not the flighty sort. I don't flirt at random like my other friends. I'm steady and grounded. It's the Taurean in me that's surfacing these days. Treat this as a short-term mania that will wear itself out—and then we can go back to business as usual."

"You do overestimate yourself, don't you? After all this do you imagine you can just stroll back into the house as if nothing's happened and expect my mother to swallow it."

"I am not concerned about your mother—she's not the person I married—though I'm beginning to wonder. I'm talking about us—you and me. I think we are OK. We leave each other alone. You try not to get into my hair and I try not to get into yours. That's the best possible combination."

"Since when have you reached this conclusion? I thought you are looking for romance *à la* films. A white knight on a charger, soppy songs—not that I can picture that selfish bastard doing any of this. If at all, he must be sitting back, expecting you to provide the frills. Which reminds me—how much of my money have you spent on him? That two-bit gigolo—all his life he has lived off women. That's why he married this girl—not out of love or anything. Has he ever told you that? I'm sure not. Well, I found out a few things before getting here. She's the only child of a wealthy zamindar. Your Krish lives off her—the car, driver, the holiday home in Kalimpong—do you think he's paying for all that? Do you even know what kind of a job he's in? It's a joke—he's treated as a joke. What does he do when he gets to the office? Drinks fifty cups of coffee, smokes two hundred cigarettes, makes thirty phone calls, flirts with the secretaries, bullshits around and heads for the club. He gets away with it because he is in a phony business where the likes of him rise to the top on all the hot air they produce. It's all big talk, nothing else—and like a fool—you fell for it too!"

"Anyway, what's the point in dissecting him? I don't think he's Jean-Paul Sartre. I know he's a phony—but what to do? I like him. I love him."

"He's never going to leave his wife for you. After he chucks you where will you be? You don't have a job. You can't support yourself. I'm not going to give you a dime and I don't think your parents are going to welcome you with open arms. By the way, I went and met them before coming here. I must say their reactions were strange. They didn't seem to care at all. Any other parents would have been shocked or at least pretend to be. They went on watching television as if I wasn't there."

"You shouldn't have gone to them. They are old people, and you can't hold them responsible for my life."

"Well, you should have thought of that before jumping into bed with that bastard." Abruptly he said, "I'm hungry. Is there anything in the house or am I expected to eat out."

"I'll fix you some eggs." More and more this was beginning to feel like something out of the theater of the absurd. He followed me into the kitchen swirling his ice cubes around and looking at me with his cognac-colored eyes. Incredibly, I wanted to play mother and put my arms around him, saying, "There, there, it's OK. Mummy will take care of everything." We sat down at the kitchen table and I invited my sister to join us. She looked at my face anxiously and asked, "Everything OK?"

"I don't know," I replied.

After dinner, I asked him, "Do you want me to sleep on the couch or is it OK if we share the bedroom? I won't bite." Suddenly I felt very self-conscious changing in front of him or doing any of the things I used to do only a week earlier without even noticing. I felt silly having him watch as I brushed my hair and applied a nourishing night cream on my face. I didn't like him staring at my silhouette through the flimsy nightie. He had become a stranger overnight—and he sensed it.

"Why are you behaving in such a funny way? As if I've never seen you before."

I didn't answer but got into bed, taking care to remain on "my side," and hastily switched off the light.

"Don't want to read? What's wrong? Ill or something?"

"Save the sarcasm. You must be tired—why don't you get some sleep?" And then with a sense of horror I realized the husband was feeling amorous. Perhaps the fact that his wife had taken a lover excited him. It seemed immoral that we should make love under the circumstances, but there was no point in resisting—it would have only consumed more time. And I needed time—to think. How was I going to phone Krish and tell him about the husband's arrival? That was the only thought spinning in my mind as the husband went through the motions, grunting whisky fumes into my face and hurting my knees. Before he rolled off and fell asleep, he added, "Your great intellectual can't even spell. His letters are illiterate. You should present him with a dictionary on his birthday."

Krish phoned the next morning when the husband was in the bath. I promptly interpreted it as a good omen. I spoke to him on the kitchen phone and turned the TV up to muffle my voice.

"Guess who's here," I croaked.

"Who?"

"Your friend."

"Which one?"

"Black Label." (We had nicknamed him that in memory of the first night.)

"You're kidding! What's he doing there?"

"He has found out about us."

"Oh hell! What a bore. So what does he want to do? Kill me?"

"No—he wants to take me to Venice."

"That's jolly sweet of him! So what do you want to do? Or have you booked your gondola already?"

"Stop being a bitch. I've told him I have to see you in Venice."

"And has he meekly agreed or is he going to join us for a Venetian ménage á trois?"

"I don't know as yet—he's in the bath. Give me a number where I can reach you. As of now our Venice plan stands. Don't you dare chicken out. I've got to run now."

I saw Black Label by the door. He was looking very rested and rather natty in his Benetton T-shirt and faded Kleins.

"Were you talking to the jerk?"

"Yes."

"Did you tell him I was here?"

"Yes."

"And?"

"And nothing."

"OK. I've thought about it. I've got a proposal for you. Why don't you and I go to Venice two days before you are scheduled to be there? Then I leave, you stay on—see that creep, and come back to Bombay on your own. But there's one condition—this has to be a farewell. You will never see him again after this. That's the deal—and I think it's a fair one. You get that rat out of your system once and for all—and we will close the chapter."

"But what will you tell your mother?"

"That's my problem. Think about it. I'm looking forward to Venice and I'd like to see it with you. Another thing—separate hotels. You stay on in the one I book for us. And that shit can stay wherever he likes. I don't want you to move in with him or he with you."

"Let me sleep over it."

"There's no time for that—I have to speak to the travel agent immediately and book our flight." On an impulse, I agreed. I'm glad I did.

Venice with Black Label turned out to be quite an experience. Strange as it may seem I actually found myself enjoying his company. And in the strange warp I was in I found myself even laughing at his jokes about Krish. "When that bum gets here, you'll end up starving—I'd better leave enough money with you." We did the whole tourist bit, the museums and the boat rides to the islands.

"What is left for you and that swine to discover now?" the husband taunted. "In any case, he'll only be interested in checking out the bars. Make sure he doesn't get arrested, or fall into a canal—or wait a minute, that might be the best way to get rid of him. Just give the guy a small shove after a night on the town—call it an accident. No one will ever know." This was when I actually found myself laughing—laughing at Krish!

We were booked into a magnificent old palace hotel with a sprawling suite at our disposal. We drank champagne in the sunken green marble bath and lunched alfresco. We had great weather and great fun. In fact, I was sorry to see the husband go. We had steered clear of the subject of Krish, except for the occasional little asides from the husband, but the weird calm that had hallmarked the confrontation kept things easy.

CHAPTER 14

WHEN KRISH ARRIVED, HE BROUGHT THE RAINS WITH HIM. The canals looked forbidding and dark. The squares were completely deserted, and the only people on the Bridge of Sighs were a group of Japanese tourists who enlisted our services to snap their pictures. All this did not deter Krish in the least bit. He was his usual breezy self, ever ready with the throwaway line. He'd picked a seedy hotel to live in, and I was both guilty and glad I didn't have to spend the nights on those beds with the springs gone. He went along with Black Label's plans happily enough, which rather surprised me. I'd been expecting him to explode, to be outraged, to throw at least a token tantrum. Nothing. He cheerfully agreed to the deal and slapped me playfully on the bottom saying, "*Theek hai, yaar*. Poor guy has a point."

"You mean you aren't going to challenge him to a duel? There's going to be no bloodshed? No suicides? What's the matter with you? Or is it me? How absurd this is. I'll kiss you goodbye in Rome and fly off to rejoin Black Label. You will get on to the next flight and go home to strawberry ice cream. This is worse than an anticlimax. If I'd known the grand passion was going to end so stupidly I'd never have accepted your chamelis."

"Don't do so much dramabaazi. Life isn't a Chekhov play. For that matter it isn't even a Badal Sircar one. You aren't Anna Karenina. And I'm not Valentine. We are all adults. Don't behave like a kid. Now, eat your pizza and shut up. If you're a good girl, I might even break a rule or two and hop over to your hotel for a long soak in your sunken tub."

"Do that, and I'll make you pay for the room."

"Forget it—I'm a maamuli ad guy—not a Black Label. By the way, has he left you enough money for us to buy ourselves a goodbye gift? I saw something wonderful in a boutique this morning." That's when, as the cliché goes, the scales fell from my eyes and I saw him for what he really was—a shallow, exploitative, utterly ordinary, no he was even less than that, human being.

"You are so shameless, it's unbelievable."

"That's what you saw in me, jaaneman, and that's why you are here."

I bought him the Armani jacket and, just to rub it in, I bought another for Black Label. "Coordinated jackets—isn't that cute? His and his. I'll think of you every time he wears it. And he'll think of you too."

"You are so charming—I'm overwhelmed. But thanks for the jacket. It's got Venice written all over it."

"Don't thank me, thank your friend. It's his money, not mine."

It still amazes me to think that that's how it went and that's how it ended with Krish waving and blowing kisses at the airport, looking smart and trendy in his new jacket. I didn't feel a thing. Not even that I'd been had. I'd enjoyed Krish, no regrets there. But I knew too from this experience that I wasn't up to adultery for adultery's sake and the grand romance I was looking for just seemed not to exist. Books were safer. And less time-consuming. I dived into the one I'd just bought at the airport, and forgot all about Krish.

The homecoming was as I'd expected it to be. The husband was at the airport and looked genuinely pleased to see me. He looked very sweet standing outside the customs enclosure awkwardly clutching a bunch of roses. The hug and kiss were almost formal. It felt good to sit beside him in the car and I felt glad he hadn't brought the driver with him. He started the music—and it was Ravel's "Bolero" which I absolutely adored. "I couldn't find the tape this morning—then I looked on your side and there it was."

He didn't ask me a thing—not a thing about Krish. He just picked up my wrist and smiled. "You didn't get yourself the watch. I knew you wouldn't. Never mind—I've got it for you. Someone was coming from Dubai." There was an instant flashback in my mind to the time he had picked up my hand at the Sea Lounge and said, "No ring?" We didn't speak very much all the way home. I was dying to ask about his mother but shut up. "I've asked the cook to make puranpolis for you."

"Thanks. That's awfully thoughtful of you."

"There's some wine in the fridge, but it won't go with the food tonight."

Then, a little later, "Did you at least get your bras and panties? What about perfume? I saw a new range in the flight magazine, but Alitalia didn't have it. They had the usual stuff—Dior and all that. I got you Caleche anyway, because I know you like it. And Je Reviens—you like that too, don't you? And something else—what's that—Blue Gras—I'd seen it on your dressing table once."

Back at home, there were flowers everywhere, in each room and the servants had lined up at the entrance to greet me. I should have felt guilty or remorseful. But I didn't. Only happy to be back. Happy and safe. Krish was forgotten for the time being and I gave up chamelis for ever.

CHAPTER 15

THE ONLY PEOPLE I WANTED TO TALK TO ABOUT THE WHOLE EPISODE
were Father and Mother but even that was not to be for they were in
the middle of a far greater crisis than a daughter's unsuccessful affair.
The emergency had to do with my second sister Alak. She had always
been a reserved, moody girl but now there seemed to be something horribly wrong. No wonder my parents had paid little heed
when the husband had complained about me. Alak seemed to have
lost her equilibrium—with all that this entailed: frequent memory
lapses and the occasional dysfunctioning of her motor coordination.
Mother told me in whispers that a few times she'd wet her bed and
soiled her clothes. I was alarmed at hearing this. She'd quit her job.
And she lapsed into frequent depressions. I was summoned home
by Mother. "You had a friend in college—he was a mental doctor, I
forget his name. Why don't you take your sister to see him? I think
something has happened to her. Your father and I are afraid she's
going mad." I wasn't really surprised to hear this. In a way I'd seen
it coming years ago. She'd never been completely there, often going
into her black spells without any warning. She was like the proverbial girl from the nursery rhyme who, when she was good, was very,
very good and when she was bad, was horrid. I'd been unable to
keep up with her swings in mood and had learned to leave her alone.
She used to puzzle me by her obsessive secretiveness. It was impossible to figure out what it was that she wanted to hide so desperately.
I'd hear Mother teasing her, but never Father. With him she shared a .

strangely intense relationship, though they hardly spoke to one another. I would notice their silent exchanges at the table, or see her gazing at him intently while he worked on his files. She was always there to fetch him tea or press his feet. He was gruff with her as he was with all of us, but there was tenderness in his manner when he put an extra helping of fish into her thali. And the only time one saw her animated was when she went to Father with something she had created, even a crochet doily. She would wait for his reaction, her eyes lighting up with each compliment.

As I tried to reach my psychotherapist friend I tried to figure out where we'd all gone wrong. If we'd only tried to help her when we'd first seen she was not normal. I remembered asking Mother once why there were no plans for Alak's marriage (this was after both Swati and I had married). Mother had replied uneasily, "Your father thinks it's better she stays with us. She is a difficult person as you know. Very moody and emotional. She does not wish to marry—she has told us both the same thing many times over."

"But why? How long will you be able to take care of her? Can she live alone later? Why would any woman want to remain a spinster? There's nothing really wrong with her. She is attractive enough. She speaks well, has a good job, dresses well—then why?"

Mother had looked over her shoulder to see nobody was near before replying hesitantly, "I think—and your father also thinks—that she is afraid of men—you know—of marriage, because it involves having a relationship with a man."

"Don't be ridiculous," I had answered. "Why should she feel afraid? Has anything happened to scare her? Did she have some bad experience when she was a child? Has she ever told you her reasons for being afraid."

"No—how can I ask her such a thing. I feel ashamed. But I remember when she was about eight years old. We had all gone to visit my sister in Nagpur—her husband was posted there. It was a large house—do you remember it—an old mofussil bungalow. One afternoon we couldn't find your sister. Everybody got very worried. We searched the whole house. Finally she was located in the coal shed, sitting in a corner, looking very scared. Her mouth was full of coal—she'd been eating it. She had done that before in our own house and the doctor had told us to give her extra vitamins or calcium, I don't remember. So we all thought she was hiding there because she was afraid she'd get a scolding for eating coal. But maybe something else had happened—who knows? She never told us. But after that day she definitely changed. Your father noticed it too. When we came back to Bombay, she didn't feel like going to school. And she stopped changing her clothes if any of you were in the room. She became very shy of even me. She started to lock herself in the bathroom and stay inside for hours. When she got her period three years later she became hysterical. She came running to me screaming, "I am dying." I tried to calm her down, but she kept asking for Father. I told her that these were female problems and it wasn't done to bring a man into it, but she wouldn't listen. She continued to scream till I phoned your father and asked him to come home. He was actually very annoyed with me. He said I hadn't prepared the girls for these changes and that it was a mother's duty to handle a daughter at a time like this. It was no use telling him that I had told all of you and that this girl was acting strange. She became uncontrollable—wouldn't allow me to help her to clean her up. She just sat there screaming, 'Help me! Help me! I'm dying.' We had to call the family doctor, who gave her a tranquilizer. It was only after that that she calmed down."

Why hadn't any of us done something then? I wondered. Or later? Events from the past came to me: Swati and I ganging up against her and making fun of her kinks; Alak glaring at us and then even attacking us sometimes, flinging whatever was handy—saucers, scissors, cushions.

As I sat there, telephone in hand, trying to work all this out in my head, the only reason I could think of for our disregarding of the first signs of Alak's madness was that she was so quiet and orderly after she landed her first job that we all forgot about her as we got on with our own lives. And all the while she had been going quietly and desperately nuts. Occasionally Swati and I would wonder why she never dated or received any calls. Surely, there must have been some eligible men at her office? I had concluded one night, "She must be lesbian." Swati had gleefully agreed. But she didn't receive calls from women either. Each morning, she'd dress carefully, put a few drops of Tata's eau-de-cologne into an ironed handkerchief, check her bag for pens, money and other essentials and leave. She'd return on the dot of five forty-five p.m., go to the room, lock herself in for half an hour and emerge in a full-length housecoat. Mother would then serve her tea, which she always had with two Marie biscuits. If Mother ever ran out of Marie biscuits, she'd push the tea cup away and leave the table in a huff. The remainder of the evening would be spent crocheting or watching television. She never went to the movies and had no curiosity about any sort of entertainment. She'd wait for Father to return and then there'd be some spark of life in her dull eyes. She'd rush to the kitchen to make his tea and sit with him at the table while he drank it. Mother would sometimes show her resentment by snapping at her but that was all. Alak's days continued as always, unchanging and dull.

A year or so later I got married and then, Swati. We'd get the occasional report that Alak wasn't well, but we lost all sight of her illness so well did my parents hide it from the two of us. It was only now that I was finally told everything by Mother. Apparently the first sign of Alak's worsening condition was her rapid losing of weight. And then she had started talking to herself. At first this was restricted to low, unintelligible mumbling. Soon it had become excited, extended conversations. Then her speech had come out slow and slurred. Her movements had become catatonic. Old aunts had insisted it had all to do with her "unnatural state." "Marriage," they had said. "Marriage cures everything. But who'll marry her now—it's too late." Mother had despaired, as Alak sat on the family rocking chair and rocked away, smiling sadly to herself. An uncle had suggested calling in a vaid—a bearded, bare-chested man from Andhra Pradesh. After picking on an auspicious time, this man had arrived and put Alak into some sort of a trance. Amidst a great deal of chanting and shouting, he had performed a peculiar puja, which he had "taught" my mother. "The girl must fast for thirty-six Tuesdays. She will observe a strict vegetarian diet and wear plain cotton clothes. No tea. No coffee and no bed. She will sleep on a mat on the floor. Every morning you will say this mantra over her head and give her this packet dissolved in milk. At the end of thirty-six weeks, you will report to me." He had been the first of several tantriks and quacks who had been brought along to solve Alak's malady. But all it had resulted in was Alak being hastened along the path to a quiet madness.

My psychotherapist friend was sympathetic but discouraging. "I don't deal with cases like this," Praful insisted, "but because she's your sister, I'll take a look at her." I took him to my parents' home one evening after his regular clinic. Alak was in one of her off moods, totally isolated and withdrawn. He didn't talk to her directly, but all of us sat around and chatted, trying to involve her in our conversation. She seemed not to hear. Praful addressed a couple of casual questions to her, but she ignored him. She looked like a skeleton, wrapped in a housecoat several sizes too large for her. We talked some more. She continued to rock. Her rocking was beginning to drive me crazy. Rock. Rock. Rock. After a while, Praful got up and gestured to me to come down with him. "I think she requires immediate hospitalization. Your sister is gravely ill. I'm not competent enough to say what exactly is wrong with her, but she needs expert medical attention. Speak to your parents and let me know. I'll try and arrange it. By the way, what was her relationship with your father in the past? Was she very scared of him? Did he ever beat her? And your mother—were they ever close? I wish you hadn't waited this long to see someone. I'm afraid it might be too late."

He was right. It was too late by the time we removed her to a psychiatric ward. About a month after her admission, she suffered a stroke that left her paralyzed waist down. With intensive therapy, both psychological and physical, she improved a little—but only marginally. She was restricted to a wheelchair and required a day and night nurse. We never really knew whether she was aware of our visits or even if they mattered. Her condition continued to be a cause for grave concern and it destroyed my parents. They withdrew into a self-created whirlpool of guilt and spent most of their time blaming themselves for Alak's fate. It was that and television. Numb and afraid to face anyone, they remained closeted at home, listening to taped discourses and praying between serials.

I withdrew as well (thankfully Swati was far away—but who knew what she went through) from the people I knew. The husband was very understanding and I think I liked him better than I'd ever done before for his grace. It was Anjali, surprisingly enough, who finally pulled me out of myself. Her two businesses (Babaji and interior decoration) were both flourishing and she sounded exuberant when she invited me to come over and see her in her new office. I knew I had to get away from myself, so I went. When I arrived at the place I was amazed at the change in her. Gone were the chiffons and pastel silks. Anjali, the most wanted "interiors" woman in the business, had switched to something like business suits though not exactly Brooks Brothers stuff. The day I met her she had on a strange creation all her own—a pin-striped, shirty, padded-shouldered version of the traditional salwar kameez. Her nails matched the new look. "These are my executive nails," she explained showing me the blunt-filed versions, buffed and varnished with a transparent polish. No lipstick either—just a little lip gloss. The cheekbones continued to be colored with slashes of blush-on, but otherwise this was Anjali's idea of looking serious and professional. "It's a nuisance, dealing with lechy businessmen. Saris look far too sexy and, in any case, they aren't practical in the workshop. I tore up too many French chiffons. I had to stop leaving my hair free because each time a lock fell across my face, I could see the lech wetting his pants." She now wore it neatly coiffed at the nape of her neck. I liked this new woman, she was so brisk and together. I suppose I needed someone like this to get me out of my own depression. "I heard you dumped that no-hoper ad man." God, I thought, there wasn't anything private in this society!

Paying no heed to my silence, Anjali went on. "Good, it's a good thing you did. It would have come to nothing." I didn't want this to continue. Hoping to distract her I got up and walked around her office. "So how are both your careers doing?"

"What do you mean both careers? I have only one. And you know that perfectly well."

"OK. I take that back. What about that little punk—Murty—is he still hanging around?"

"You bet. I have got used to him actually. Don't mind him all that much. He has his uses."

"Such as?"

"He's the person I send off with my partner to the Gulf to get more business there. The Arabs just adore him. He adores their generosity. Each time he comes back with a gold Rolex or a CD. That, plus a new contract for us. The Sheikhs are willing to trade a couple of their prize white camels for him, but K isn't biting!"

"Are they still in love?"

"Murty is more relaxed now. He knows K doesn't sleep with me. K does go off sometimes for a sneaky quickie—generally foreign pursers he picks up at the Holiday Inn pool, but even those one-afternoon stands are getting rarer. Age—he's getting on. He still has a glad eye for the boys, but he doesn't come on strong. Besides, Babaji has a very strong influence on him."

"What do you mean? Are they a number?"

"Rubbish! Don't even talk like that. Babaji has shown him an alternative lifestyle—a purer one. K now keeps animals."

"Really! Now I've heard everything! Kumar isn't into bestiality is he? Anjali, this is too, but too shocking!"

"Your mind is worse than a garbage can. Can't you think of anything besides sex? Woman—you are hard up. Really hard up. Finished." Suddenly Alak's poor sorry face came into my mind and it occurred to me how flip I was being. I excused myself hastily and left.

All the rest of that week Anjali phoned but I refused to see her and kept our conversation short. I'd call Mother and cry into the phone until one day that patient, long-suffering woman said firmly to me: "Look, we all should have done something for Alak but we didn't and now it's over and done with. She's happy as she ever can be, she doesn't feel or know a thing and there's no use your crying and wishing you had done more. You've got to lead your own life, so do it." That was the toughest speech she'd given in her life and it succeeded. Gradually I began climbing out of my depression. And after refusing Anjali's invitations a couple of times (it had become a habit) I agreed to have lunch with her at one of our favorite old haunts: the Apollo bar at the Taj.

She was her old self. After making a couple of throwaway remarks about my reclusiveness and after cursory inquiries about my well-being she was off again on the topic of her beloved Babaji. The focus was still his love for animals.

"It's amazing how cats, dogs, deer, monkeys, even tigers behave when he goes near them."

I held my peace.

"And birds, he has an extremely valuable collection of birds—he's given me a Brazilian parrot—he is so attractive that I'm thinking of using him as a prop in one of the restaurants I'm designing. So what are you planning on doing?"

"I don't know just yet. I'm very keen on theater, but I'm not too fond of acting so I'm thinking of taking a course in directing at Bharat Bhavan. Or maybe I'll go to Pune to do a course in film direction. I'd like to try my hand at documentaries."

"Goody! Do that. Then we can hire you to do one on Babaji. We have all his foreign disciples here at the moment. There's also a TV crew from Germany. Babaji is deeply into environment these days. He quotes from scriptures and everything. We are planning to launch an international movement to adopt a tree or an animal. I'll let you know."

"Sounds fascinating. A little old hat—but the more the merrier."

"I've got an ad agency to design the campaign with the Peepul tree as our symbol. Babaji is very pleased with that—Peepul—People—you know—the connection? I'm very excited. All my new designs have something to do with trees. It's my motif for the year. I've done a whole new line using the Tree of Life as the theme. The Arabs just love it. An American buyer also flipped for it."

"Whatever has happened to Mataji and her pink nails?"

"She's around, but she's concentrating on doing her own thing."

"You mean she isn't a part of your zoo—she doesn't vibe with the animals and the birdies?"

"In case you are really keen to know, the animals can't stand her. Bad karma or something. They start baring their teeth and growling."

"I must've been an animal in my last life—or maybe I'm one in this life too without knowing it, because that was my precise re-action on meeting Mataji. I would've bitten her had she come any closer."

"You are a vicious female canine—I've always known that. It's surprising more people don't think the same. You have a pretty good market image—very goody-goody in fact."

"Isn't that a wonder considering all the pains you've taken over the years to ruin it? Must be my good karma. What news of Ritu? Why is she lying low?"

"Oh, she's jouncing around in Hong Kong with her husband. Expected back Tuesday."

"God, what a lot of holidays that woman takes. I miss her," I said. "Say what—why don't you throw one of your obscene parties. Throw a theme party—'Come as your favorite animal.' Most of your friends won't even have to spend on costumes. They can come as themselves."

"Talking about theme parties," Anjali said, "we went to one two weeks ago. It was hilarious. Guess what the theme was—'Whores and Pimps,' and you are absolutely dead-on—most people came as themselves and looked the part."

"Whose place?"

"That crazy couple. Remember them from Abe's days? They used to be neighbors. The woman is half-Swiss and half-Sardar and the guy is Assamese. You must remember that apartment—it was the talk of the town in those days because they were the first to have a glass disco floor with lights underneath. And a huge bathroom with one glass wall that overlooked Bombay—a bird's-eye view of the city from the potty."

"I remember them vaguely. Particularly the woman. Each time she came back from Goa she'd show off her all-over tan to anyone who cared to see it—same one?"

"Yes—not that she had anything to show—tan or no tan. But she'd display the two little pimples on her chest like she was Brigitte Bardot."

"So how was the party otherwise?"

"Fun. You remember that other woman—also a neighbor, the one who Abe had a brief thing with?"

"How can I recall her with that description? Abe had a thing with every single neighbor and her maid."

"Come off it—he wasn't that bad. But this woman was the buxom Marwari who had a yen for Rajasthani cooks—the Maharajs. You must remember her, she was rather attractive in her own way."

"Well, what about her?"

"She was there. Met her after years. Obviously she's heavily on the booze—and maybe other stuff. At one point she disappeared into the bedroom and stripped down to her blouse and petticoat."

"Why on earth did she do that?"

"She said it was terribly hot outside—and she was cooling off on the bed. Soon that slobbering egghead—you know him too—the computer guy—decided to join her on the bed and cool off as well."

"What fun," I said sarcastically. Anjali missed it as usual.

"No, it wasn't very funny—at least her husband didn't think so. He charged into the bedroom and ordered her to wear her sari. She refused and he started to get aggressive. The baldie just sat around with that silly smile on his face repeating, 'Let's all have a drink and talk about it.' Her husband bellowed, 'There's nothing to talk about—get dressed, you bitch.' Soon the entire party shifted to the bedroom and it became a sort of makeshift theater with an impromptu performance."

"How did it end? Did everybody strip and join the party on the bed?"

"No. But the woman removed her blouse as well and pulled her petticoat up over her huge breasts. It refused to stay there and kept slipping off. The hostess very sweetly offered her a kimono from the bathroom. She put that on and removed her petticoat, leaving just her bikini panties on. The kimono kept opening, so there was this terrific scene, especially when the husband tried to rough her up. She ran straight out of the flat and toward the elevator—and who do you think came out of it? A khadi-clad minister—the hostess' great friend. He had his security guys with him, plus the usual hangers-on. This woman knew the minister slightly from one of the earlier parties at the couple's place, so she flung her arms around him and cried, 'Save me! Save me! I'm being raped!' There were also a couple of journalists around—not the scruffy ones—these chaps were

Oxford-Cambridge types. The minister recognized one of them and nearly collapsed at the thought of the headlines this incident could make."

"Sounds like a super party—the sort Abe and you used to have in the good old days. What's with him? Is he still alive?"

"He's alive. Still drinking. The cow is still around, also drinking. And that's all I know."

"Are you coming to the Patel party next weekend?"

"Well, we're invited but we have one of these Arab types in town that day. I'll check with them if I can bring him along. He's coming with another builder—Gul—you must've heard of him? He has bought up half of Bombay?"

"Vaguely. That shady NRI fellow—is that the one? He's supposed to be the front man for that local slimo—isn't he? How's your Krishna? You haven't mentioned him in a while."

"I went to Dwarka in between, and to Mathura too. This year we'll spend Holi at Vrindavan. I've changed the temple a bit. I thought Krishna needed a little more color around him."

"Don't tell me you've given him a disco of his very own to dance the garba raas with his gopis. How hep!"

"Choke up. I've merely changed the marble and added one more air-conditioner. It used to get very hot in their during aarti time."

After I came home I felt better. Anjali's inanities were the sort of thing I could cope with, I decided, not my sister's madness. A day later Ritu called. She sounded despondent. Her first sentence to me was: "Where are all the men?"

"Oh—oh, that sounds ominous. I thought you were having a great time in Hong Kong."

"Well, Hong Kong's Hong Kong. Big deal. You know I'm beginning to ask myself basic questions."

"Don't. That's dangerous."

"Can't help it. They pop up even when I don't want to think about them."

"What kind of questions? Men-related?"

"Naturally. But not the silly kind. I'm sick of my life. It's so empty. What do I do all day—smoke and embroider."

"Doesn't sound so bad. You could be a junkie. Or one of those kitty-party wives."

"I'm feeling worthless. I want to do something useful."

"Why don't you get on the hotline to the Sisters of Charity. Or organize an anti-sati cell in your locality. It's very 'in' to involve yourself in women's issues these days."

"It's not all that simple. I'm looking for an alternative life."

"You mean another husband—why don't you just say that? Thought of putting in an ad? Let's work out something naughty for the Classifieds—just for the heck of it . . . Are you coming to the Patels?"

"Yes. Maybe I'll feel more cheerful by then."

"Maybe you'll find a husband there."

The Patels, who'd made their money in cement, were the hottest party-givers of the season. And the husband was determined we should go. For once I agreed for I was trying my best to distract myself. The Patels turned out to be quite an event all right for that's where I saw Ritu, perhaps my closest and calmest friend, go totally down the tubes. It had to do with a man of course—Gul, the crooked builder Anjali had brought along. I was with Ritu when she saw him for the first time and I instantly recognized the mutual attraction. And their being introduced was a mere formality for the die had already been cast.

Thinking back on it everything seemed to happen freeze-frame. First Ritu said to me: "Omar Sharif. He reminds me of Omar. Isn't he too much? Look, I'm trembling." Kumar brought him over to meet the husband and I saw Gul leaning over his shoulder and whispering something into his ear. The husband laughed, looked up and pointed at me. Gul looked relieved and Ritu piped up, shouting over to him: "Share the joke with us—we're feeling left out."

The husband told her, "Oh, he just wanted to know which one of you two was my woman. I was tempted to say 'both,' but I thought your husband would slug me."

Ritu laughed uproariously and dropped her pallav. I saw her husband shrink further into his chair.

She turned to Gul and said, "I haven't seen you here before but you look very familiar. I never forget a face."

He smiled but said nothing.

Her husband excused himself and headed for the bar.

I whispered, "Behave yourself. You're making it far too obvious."

She ignored me and carried on. "I know where I've seen you. It was at a fashion show in Delhi ten years ago. You were standing at the entrance by yourself. I remember you distinctly—but you wore your hair in a different way then—with a parting."

Gul's hand flew to his hair and he laughed. "You have an excellent memory. Yes, I remember the show—but it's my misfortune that I didn't see you there, or I wouldn't have forgotten your beautiful face either."

She beamed and turned to me. "See, I told you I never forget faces."

I whispered, "Bet you made it all up and he's a sharp one, the way he caught on and played along."

"Nonsense, I swear I remember the guy." She pulled out her Charles Jourdan cigarette case and, in a flash, his gold Dunhill was on the ready.

"Baby, won't you light my fire . . ." she said huskily. My husband glared at her and went to join hers at the bar. I felt awkward hanging around and told her I had to go to the loo. And that was it.

A week later, Ritu moved in with Gul even before the gossip rags got wind of the whole affair. She phoned me from her new penthouse sounding ecstatic. "This is it," she said triumphantly.

"What am I supposed to call you now—Begum something? What have you done, Ritu? Rather, what has that scoundrel done? Are you wife number thirty-four?"

"Gul is the best thing that could've happened to me. It was fated this way. We knew it that night itself. He said to me, 'I've waited all my life for you—you are my new moon.'"

"Don't tell me more. I'll probably puke. You must be out of your head. That man's a don—a smuggler. He might bump you off once he's through with you. How could you, Ritu? Why didn't you treat him like all your other men—why couldn't he also just hang around like them?"

"Because it had to be all or nothing. If I hadn't moved out immediately, I would've lost my nerve and then everything would've gone back to square one like before. You know how often this has happened in the past. It would have been one more affair. Another ten years of nothingness. I feel I have taken my first major step—whatever the consequences. Maybe Gul will get rid of me when he finds someone else, someone younger; but right now, I'm confident and I'm happy."

"Why were you in such a hurry? And Gul? How did it all happen?"

"That night he told me he found me terribly attractive. I replied that he was the most devastating man I'd met. Then, just to tease him, I asked, 'You look so dangerous, do you carry a gun?' and he thought I was being cheeky. He got his own back by saying, 'I like what I see of you. But it isn't enough. I'm a leg man basically. Why don't we go to the garden? You pick up your sari and let me see your legs. If I like what I see, I'll take you to bed.'"

"How crass. Did you do it—behave like a hijra and hitch up your sari way up above the knees?"

"Yes. I was beyond caring. I wanted to show him that his challenge was nothing—that I dared!"

"Obviously, your shanks impressed him, though, if you ask me, they aren't your best assets."

"Now, let's forget all that and tell me, when can you come over?"

"You must be kidding. I won't be caught dead in your smuggler's den. If you want to be the kept woman of a criminal, that's your business. But count me out of that scene. The husband will be horrified. I'll just have to disown you till you work this one out. Call me after he ditches you or you ditch him, whichever is sooner. What about your divorce—or is that irrelevant?"

"I want to see how this arrangement works first. I'm not such a fool."

"Is this a trial marriage then?"

"I haven't thought the whole thing out as yet. I'm having a wonderful time—and that's what matters. Gul is unbelievable."

"Spare me the details. Good luck, girl. I can see you are going to need it. Dollops of it. Don't forget to call if you need something—like a gun, a butcher's knife or a rope."

Anjali phoned three months later and filled me in on more details about the Gul-Ritu business in the midst of telling me about a "tragedy" that had taken place in her own life: Kumar had been raided by the income-tax authorities. But to take things in order. Apparently Ritu, in the short time she had been with Gul, had changed out of all recognition. As her lover (and by extension she) belonged to what was called the Duplex Sindhi set—vulgar, nouveau riche builders with nefarious reputations—she was now regarded as something akin to the chief gangster's moll and looked the part. Anjali had seen her at a party. Her hair was hennaed to an alarming shade of red with blond highlights scattered through it. The bright-eyed girl who shunned makeup in the past, now wore loads of the stuff particularly around the eyes. Her taste in jewelry (never discreet) now ran the gamut of glitz. Indeed, according to Anjali, she'd looked as though she'd raided a gold souk in Dubai and worn all the loot in one go. If she wore saris at all, they were at crotch level with bralike cholis in lamé.

Anjali told me to speak to her—"As a friend you should tell her not to look so whorish. And did I tell you, she now smokes through a foot-long holder? People in their group were saying that Gul and she are also fooling around with drugs—sniffing coke. You should stop her."

"I'm not her keeper. She might tell me to take a jump."

"Try talking to her anyway."

"Why don't you—I wasn't the one who introduced her to Gul."

"Don't blame me for that—Gul is, or rather was, just a client. We get all types."

"Why did you say 'was'? You mean you've fallen out so soon?"

"We've actually been doing work for him for some time. But finally we sacked him—he didn't pay our bills. It was all terribly messy. I asked Murty to go to his office and sit there till he paid up. Poor Murty, he went there and Gul's goons roughed him up. Murty told us one of them pulled a gun. It was awful. K told me to just forget the whole thing—write it off."

"And yet, you continue to socialize?"

"That's different. We don't invite him to our home, but if he happens to be at the same party—what do you expect us to do—run? But, my dear, that's not why I called you. K's in trouble."

"What?"

"We were raided a couple of days ago. I can't tell you how traumatic the whole thing was. About a dozen ugly men just walked into the house with warrants and all but stripped the place down—including my Krishna's mandir. I kept screaming, 'Look everywhere. Do what you want in the other rooms. But leave my Krishna alone.'

One of them laughed and said, 'All businessmen tell us that—and do you know how many times we've found key evidence and incriminating documents in the puja room? We've even confiscated murtis made of solid gold.'"

"Did they find anything? Is the whole affair closed?"

"They didn't find very much. K is very careful about money matters. But they found gold coins and jewelry in Babaji's room. Unfortunately Babaji had forgotten to tell us that he'd kept some things in the cupboard, so we were very surprised when they opened it and found all that. Apart from the gold in his room there was one other thing that made me die of shame. You know K and Murty often watched blue films. It was innocent fun. Whenever they felt bored they'd switch on one of these. K used to pick them up at Frankfurt. And he'd bring back a few other sexy things—again just for fun. We used to laugh at the latest 'inventions' and compare them to last year's. Nobody actually used them or anything. In fact, at one party we'd strung up all these fish-tailed condoms and other thingies all over the bar as a joke! But they were all lying there in Murty's room. Along with some foreign exchange—a ridiculous amount—just small change, really—maybe thirty or forty dollars. That was careless of Murty—but it was too late. Those fellows pounced on these things. Then they started gossiping among themselves, cracking vulgar jokes. It was very humiliating. And can you imagine their cheek? They were there for over fourteen hours, so they used all our loos and kept asking for tea and coffee. K told me, 'Be nice to them even if it kills you. Give them plenty to eat and drink. Don't antagonize them.' I told the cooks to feed them constantly. They made such a mess of our beautiful home. Tore up the garden, wrecked the marble in the patio. I nearly had a nervous breakdown."

"What happens now? Has Kumar fixed things?"

"Well, he has been going up and down to Delhi to talk to his contacts. They all tell him, it's difficult to hush up things after the raid has taken place and incriminating documents found. Let's see how it goes. But the friends I've told about it laugh. 'Join the club,' they say. It's quite a status symbol these days, I suppose. But I can tell you it isn't worth the agony."

"But what about Kumar's business—has that been affected?"

"It's too soon to say."

"I suppose Babaji is blissfully out of the whole thing. Why wasn't he arrested?"

"He was out of the country at the time. His disciples in California had organized a major celebration. Babaji couldn't refuse—besides he likes the weather there and his allergies behave themselves abroad."

"That's all very well—but in the meantime you got screwed thanks to him. When does he get back?"

"We don't know. We've called several times. His disciples here are getting restless and his animals are missing him. I try my best to cheer them up. Babaji had given me some holy water for them. A couple of birds died after drinking it—I don't know why."

"Maybe it was poisoned."

"Nonsense. Now, my supply is nearly over. But some of his devotees say that all I have to do is take ordinary water in a silver vessel and pray over it repeating Babaji's name. Then I have to place the vessel near his chappalls and seek his blessings. Automatically, the vibrations charge the water and it becomes holy."

"I think you have gone completely mad. How can you believe in such shit?"

"This is all a matter of faith, my dear. Had it not been for Babaji's presence in our house the day those fellows raided us, we would have been in even bigger trouble. K and I both know it was Babaji who saved us. Now my worry is about K's health. He tries not to show it but the raid has affected him. We went for a thorough investigation and he has been recommended an open heart job—two of his arteries are blocked. These days that's not considered serious at all—but we have to go to the States for it—the problem is our passports have been impounded."

"Oh dear! All this is *très compliqué*. Where does it leave Murty?"

"That's another problem. He has nowhere to go as you know. Legally, he isn't our responsibility. K might even agree to get rid of him—right now he is far more worried about his own health. But Murty isn't willing to let go of his golden goose."

"What do you mean—'not willing'? Just kick the runt out."

"It's not all that easy. Haven't you heard of a word called blackmail? He has told K very plainly not to try any funny stuff with him—or else."

"Maybe he's only negotiating for a bigger slice of the cake. Why can't Kumar pay him off? Can't they arrive at a sensible settlement?"

"Difficult. Murty is a greedy little bugger. He wants to milk K dry—pardon the pun."

"How about trading him for some camels—didn't you tell me a Sheikh wanted him for his harem?"

"Murty is far too smart for that. He will not let go till he finds another K. Also, K is still attached to him in his own way. He may say anything, but I don't think he'll let go all that easily himself."

"I have a brilliant suggestion—why don't you find a bride for Murty? Sounds like a cruel joke—but you have to safeguard your own interests first. Talk to K—let him convince Murty. I'm sure you'll be able to find a rich enough girl to palm off on him. He's reasonably good-looking, and smart where business is concerned. He'll be able to manage her money and you'll get him off your hands."

Anjali thought for a moment, then said, "It's an idea worth pursuing. Let me talk to K."

The whole of the following week I felt uneasy. I thought it was my period coming on and tried to carry on as normally as possible. It was during this time that I read about Babaji's arrest in the papers. He'd been caught trying to bring in a suitcase full of gold at the airport.

When I phoned Anjali, she was very agitated. "He's being framed. I tell you—the whole thing is a frame-up. He is a saint. A God. And they are treating him like a common criminal. I haven't stopped crying. Handcuffs—can you imagine him in handcuffs? Never mind, these people will have to pay for their sins. Even Jesus Christ was persecuted. This is a great test. Babaji is totally innocent and he'll prove it. I know who's behind this—all those enemies jealous of his success. But Babaji is pure. He didn't resist when those animals pounced on him. He just laughed. He kept on laughing—mocking them. But do you know what they said, 'He is high on drugs. That is why he is laughing.' Imagine! High on drugs! That man is high on life—he doesn't need drugs. But how can these sinners see that? They even charged him of smuggling drugs into the country. And you know what they suspected of being a drug—the holy powder he distributes to his disciples. Prasad, nothing more than prasad—a little sugar with something else that only he knows. Perfectly harmless stuff—and they're calling it drugs. K and I have been so upset by all this. K's contacts don't want to get involved in this case. They say it's too dangerous and feel they might get implicated. We've been told that it's a conspiracy, but nobody is saying who's responsible. The one person who can help is Gul. Everybody has told us to approach him. He has all the underworld fellows in his pocket. But K doesn't want to be obligated to him. I also feel funny about contacting Ritu. I don't even know whether they're still together. How can I ring her up out of the blue and ask for a favor?"

"There is something like 'for old times' sake.' Give her a ring and see what she has to say. What's the worst you'll hear—'Sorry, but it's not possible.' So what? Take the chance and call her. If you want to set up a meeting, I don't mind coming along. Let me know."

CHAPTER 16

SOON AFTER THE WHOLE BUSINESS OF BABAJI'S ARREST I MISSED MY period for the first time in my life. At first, I thought, "Oh well, every woman faces some irregularities sometimes—this is one of those freak things." But when I was three weeks overdue and feeling sick and had vomited off and on for a couple of days I decided something was wrong. But I really didn't know what to do or who to call—certainly not Mother; she had enough problems as it is. And I couldn't bear to go and see our family doctor either—a filthy old man with overactive salivary glands and a deformed forefinger. After much deliberation, I decided to phone Swati in London—surely she would know and suggest what to do next.

There was of course no question of discussing it with the husband—we never talked about such things. In fact, the first time I got my period after marriage, there was so much awkwardness that I began to wonder whether I'd be asked to shift into the adjoining room till I was declared "clean" once more. No, talking to the husband was out. The first question my sister asked me when I phoned and told her the problem was: "Have you had your urine examined?"

"Of course not—should I? What for?"

"Well, you could be pregnant."

"Are you crazy! That's impossible!"

"Why, have you taken a vow of celibacy or something?"

"No. Not that. But how could I be pregnant?"

"Like everyone else—you know—the birds and the bees?"

"I don't think that's likely—but since you've suggested it—I might as well check it out."

"Could it be Krish?"

"KRISH? Don't tell me! Oh my God! Now that would be the bloody limit. Heavens! How sickening—imagine producing a little Krishlet!"

"Don't wait. Do it tomorrow and let me know."

The result turned out to be positive—and I practically died. How was I going to break it to the husband. If my sister could've come up with Krish—wouldn't the husband? I phoned her again in a panic. "What am I supposed to do now? I don't want the bloody baby. I've never wanted one—Krish's or anyone else's. I don't even know what women are supposed to do when they find themselves knocked up. Should I get myself into a clinic? Which doctor? How do I explain it to the husband? And the mother-in-law—she'll guess like a shot. She's a hawk, always watching me."

"You'd better tell your husband. For all you know, it might even be his—unless you haven't been sleeping together for years."

"No, I don't think it could be his. You know, we only do it rarely, and we're very, very careful. And what if the kid speaks Bengali from the womb and looks like Krish? But maybe I should tell him. After all, as you say, it could be his. I guess I'll just have to tell him and get rid of it. But tell me, just in case I'm in big trouble and the husband refuses to help, are there any of your medical friends here who can help me out?"

She gave me a number and I wrote it down. For two days I didn't call the number. Then finally, when I was almost at breaking point, I dialed. And was given an appointment for the following week. During the week I found an amazing shift taking place in my attitude to things. To begin with I found myself noticing children, something I'd never ever done. First it was an idle, cursory kind of curiosity ("so this is what they're all about"), and then I actually felt some strange, new emotion—what was it—tenderness? Our Gurkha had produced three children in the past whose presence I had barely noticed: they could have been kittens or puppies—wiggly little things that wailed all day and peed all over. Then, on Thursday, the Gurkha announced that his wife had delivered another baby. On an impulse I told him I wanted to meet the mother and the child. He looked very surprised but also pleased.

We went to his tiny, ill-lit room and found the mother lying on a heap of rags. The family's latest addition was sleeping close to her, on a smaller heap of rags. She made an attempt to get up when she saw me but I waved her down. That done, I didn't know what I was supposed to do next. Coo to the baby? Pat the mother? Offer money? Congratulate the father? I stood around awkwardly asking meaningless questions about the mother's health. Just then the baby woke up and the mother turned to pick her up. She offered the thing to me to hold and I almost jumped. At the same time I was ashamed of my reaction. It must have seemed awfully graceless. So I gingerly extended my arms and waited. Once the baby was placed in them it felt easy—there was absolutely nothing to it. The creature fitted perfectly into the crook of my arm and it stopped yelping. It was a pleasant feeling and I found myself rocking back and forth making peculiar noises in my throat.

When I came back to my room, I started to feel a little annoyed with myself. Was I weakening in my resolve to get rid of the kid? Did I really enjoy the experience? Had I changed? I must've imagined this, but even my body felt different. The breasts were tender and sensitive, and felt heavier, fuller. I quickly looked at myself in the mirror—my face seemed wider. I tried to picture how I'd look pregnant. I would not be a pretty sight—I saw myself with a bloated belly and pendulous breasts, my thighs dimpled with fat, blue veins crisscrossing my torso, the navel flattened out and funny. Why couldn't baby-making be easier or at least more aesthetic? How could any woman come to terms with a gross, disfigured body? And the birth itself—the pain, blood and slime. Who needed that? I recalled meeting a svelte actress at a party who had confessed that she was all for babies—if she could get them through a vending machine. I'd identified with her totally. What a distasteful process it was—and with a lifelong responsibility attached to it. Despite all this there was certainly some sort of "stirring" within me. Could've been just a guilty conscience. Or the novelty of the experience. But I was far enough gone to allow myself the luxury of dreaming about a baby I didn't really want. And then the other problem cropped up. Was it fair, I asked myself, to go ahead unilaterally on something that after all did involve two people? On the one hand, it was my body, but someone else (which of the two?) had also played a part in this mess. Again, I felt it would be injudicious to go ahead and drop the baby without informing the husband. What if he found out on his own and jumped to the wrong conclusion (there was an equal chance that it was his)? Was it worth the secrecy and stealth? Besides, things had been pretty good between us since my return. I felt close enough to confide in him. It turned out to be a bad decision.

The husband was incredulous to start with. "How did it happen? When? Where?" He behaved like I'd been bitten by a poisonous snake rather than impregnated.

"It can't be mine, anyway!" he said, after blustering a bit.

"What do you mean by that? It could well be ours—we haven't exactly abstained I might remind you."

"You don't have to remind me about anything. I'm sure it isn't mine. Now you'd better ask yourself whose child you're carrying. Poor Krish—I suppose you'll palm it off as his. But I have my doubts even about that."

"That's a filthy, cheap remark! 'Poor Krish'—I really love that! What makes you feel so sympathetic toward him all of a sudden? Or is it some brotherhood that I don't know anything about? Who the hell else's baby can it be?"

"How would I know? These days you are up to all sorts of tricks. You might call your activities 'theater-related' but I don't trust you. If you could screw around with my friend Krish, right under my nose, you could be screwing the whole town. Adultery is an addiction—it's only the first time that's difficult. After that, it's only a matter of one fuck here or there—isn't that right?"

"You are being detestable. What's got into you? I thought we'd ironed out our differences, I really believed we were finally on to a good thing. I must be crazy but I thought you'd be happy with the news. That your mother would be happy too."

"My mother—and happy about your producing someone else's child? You must be out of your mind! Do you think she's such a gullible fool? She has lived life."

"If that's how you feel—fine. I had planned to terminate the mess anyway—so why don't we change the subject? It will all be over this time next week."

"Fine, fine, fine. But my fine lady it's not all that easy. You may walk into some clinic and get your dirty little secret removed. But how do you think I'm going to live with this? I'm not prepared to forget about the whole thing and pretend nothing's happened. Why should I? I don't trust you any longer."

"What are you trying to tell me?"

"I think you are clever enough to know. I don't think there's any point in continuing this farce. I've been thinking about it. We'd better call it off."

"Call what off?"

"Our marriage."

"Are you serious?"

"Of course, I'm serious. I've discussed it with my mother."

"Before even talking to me?"

"Why should I consult you, my dear? Did you expect me to seek your permission? You didn't 'consult' me when you jumped into bed with Krish. Fair and square."

"But this involves our lives, our future—where does your mother come into it? How could you talk about this with her before telling me?"

"I don't owe you any explanations. I mean, look, did you really believe you could have your little tryst in Venice and come back like nothing had happened? Do you know what I did the moment I reached Bombay? I saw a lawyer. I wanted to check on the legal position. Let me tell you a few things—you don't stand a chance in hell. I'd suggest you go along with my plan. Let's file for divorce by mutual consent. That way we'll save a lot of time, money and headaches. My lawyer has briefed me on this. I'm not interested in prolonging the proceedings and going through a bitter court battle. In any case, there's nothing to contest."

I stared dully at him. All this was happening with frightening speed and I didn't know what to do, think, say next.

I knew the finality of what he was saying—that had registered all right. I also knew he didn't generally say things for effect. This was something he had worked out systematically and in consultation with his mother.

Slowly my mind got into gear. I began worrying about the implications—where I'd live, and how I'd break the news to my parents. I didn't want to live with them. And I didn't want to move in with anyone else like Anjali. Would the husband grant me enough time to find alternative accommodation? And did I want to hang around his house till I found it? How badly timed the whole thing was! That's what I couldn't get over. Why had I been so dense as to not have seen the signs earlier? Had I really been so sure of myself that I'd thought I could pull it off? I think not. I'd been full of a fool's optimism and played ostrich. I'd indulged in some wild, wishful thinking in hoping that finally we'd arrived at a workable equation.

The husband had stopped talking. He paced around for a while and left abruptly. I thought the appropriate thing to do was to pack a few belongings and move out. That's what women in my position did in the movies. But I was not in the movies, and my concerns were more mundane—I didn't have any money. I couldn't possibly ask him to bail me out. Nor could I seek a loan—not from him. I hated the thought of touching my parents for money. They had more than their share of problems, including an invalid child to care for. I really didn't have much of a choice. Reluctantly I picked up the phone and called Anjali.

Her car came for me an hour later. I was feeling dead. Mechanically I dumped a few essentials into a small suitcase—my first Samsonite. I thought it would be too movielike to leave some silly goodbye note. I didn't want to face the servants either. What was I going to say to them anyway—"Guess what, folks. I've been thrown out of the house—so goodbye guys. It was great knowing you." It was hard to decide what to take with me. I wasn't going on a weekend trip to the beach. What did one take on these occasions? What constituted "essentials"? Toothbrushes and dressing gowns? Face cleansers and lipsticks? Bras? Panties? Sanitary towels? Oh God—I was so confused. What did Ritu take with her when she left the house? If I knew her, it must have been all her jewelry. I didn't want to touch any of mine ("Foolish," Anjali scolded later. "Now you'll never get it back!") Shoes? Chappalls? Watches? Or was one supposed to leave all the things the husband had paid for behind? In which case I'd have had to walk out stark naked. When Anjali saw my small bag her first reaction was, "Is that all—where's the rest of your stuff?" I sheepishly told her that I'd left it all behind and that I preferred it that way. "This is not the time for false dignity and pride, woman," she advised. "Don't be a fool. You are entitled to your things."

"I feel like a thief. I don't want to sneak out of the house with things. I don't want to be accused by anyone. Tomorrow his mother might turn around and say that I ransacked the place."

"She's going to say it anyway."

"What did you expect me to do?" I said flaring up. "Get in car-penters to strip the place clean? Unhook the chandeliers? Unscrew other fittings? Take down the paintings? Roll up the carpets? Pack up family heirlooms? Pack up all the crystal and silver? I couldn't do that. I don't care how stupid that makes me. That's just not my style. I'd hate myself."

"Screw all that darling. You need money. I wasn't suggesting you rob the guy. But you are entitled to compensation. You have invested all these many years in this marriage—don't you think it's your right to claim something? If I know that family, they'll cut you off with-out a dime. That's not fair either. I call that exploitation. And don't you dare go on a guilt trip. I don't want to know what you've been up to. But whatever it is—just shut up about it. You'll weaken your position by opening your mouth. I'll talk to K's lawyers, they'll be able to advise us. Don't take any calls and for heaven's sake don't in-criminate yourself with any stupid 'confessions.' Do you understand? Now just relax. I'll talk to my gynae and let's see what can be done about the other problem. Get some sleep. You have to look your best tonight—we're having a big party—it's our anniversary today."

I nearly groaned when I heard that. A party! That's all I needed right now. But Anjali was being sweet and well-meaning. I know she was trying to distract me and really help. But I wasn't in the mood to meet anyone—not even her. She gave me a pill to pop and told me to sleep it off. I was thankful for the privacy. She'd put my things in one of her fancy guest rooms, away from the main house. It was a tranquil room done up in quiet colors. I switched on the a/c and fell instantly asleep.

I didn't hear the loud and steady knocking on the door. Anjali told me later that they were thinking of breaking open the door as she was nervous I'd done something drastic like slash my wrists. "No such luck," I laughed weakly, as she sat by my side on the bed, running her fingers through my hair. She was dressed in some floaty white thing—and looked like an angel or a nurse. Was I tripping? Was it really her? She'd go in and out of focus, and I thought I saw a halo around her head. Was I going mad? I tried to raise myself up—I couldn't. Maybe I was dead, I thought with relief.

The party was just an hour away but I didn't have the energy to do anything. There were no tears, they seemed to have been absorbed into my body making it seem bloated. Or maybe it was just my imagination. I did what I had been putting off: I called my parents. My misfortune hadn't stopped—Father picked up the phone. I asked for Mother but was told she was having a bath. I should have put the phone down then, but I wasn't thinking, I just told him the whole story—expecting what—sympathy, I guess. All he said was: "What you've done is unacceptable, totally unacceptable. Nobody in our family has done it before, nobody will do it in the future. You've made the mistake, now you pay the price. We're old people and we cannot help you. You were the one who wanted to marry your husband, it was your decision. Now we don't want to get involved. We have only a few years left to us, let us live them as peacefully as we can." Having said this, he put the phone down. If I'd been alone I'm sure this would have prompted me to do something pretty drastic. But with Anjali around this was not to be. Thinking about it now, I suppose I owe Anjali a lot more than she will ever know. Anyway she bustled around and fussed over me, and eventually I found myself in the middle of the party. It was the usual circus with plenty of high jinks but I went through it in a daze, moving from room to room, place to place every time someone tried to include me in the festivities. I do not remember a single conversation or incident that took place that night except my meeting with Ritu. And it tells you something about the change in her, that it even penetrated my own misery. When she walked in with Gul and a few of his lackeys, it took me a moment to recognize her. In less than six months, she had bloated to an unbelievable size. She looked puffy and unwell. I watched her waddle across the pebbles. Even her walk was unsteady—but I thought she'd probably had one too many. She was dressed in a garish, sequined chiffon—the sort Dubai or Abu Dhabi Sheikhs present to their harems for Id. Her beautiful hair was permed and cut in an unflattering, shaggy style. Yes, she was loaded with jewelry, but it was hideous. Overrouged, overweight and over-dressed, she looked pathetic. She saw me and attempted to sneak away but I stopped her. Gul looked on indifferently, his eyes were already scanning the room and had found their prey—a starlet in a bubble dress. As he walked away Ritu hugged and kissed me warmly and I thought I saw tears in her eyes. "I am so-o-o-o tired," she said, "let's sit down somewhere and talk."

"What's wrong?" I asked her.

"What isn't?" she said.

"You're still with the guy, aren't you?"

"There is nowhere else to go."

"What do you do with yourself these days?"

"Procure."

"What!?"

"That's right. Organize virgins for him and his friends. It's a full-time occupation."

"Why don't you opt out?"

"And do what?"

"Surely you can do something—come on—how can you allow yourself to become like this? Just look at you—you've put on tons of weight. Are you ill?"

"Not exactly ill. Sick in the head, definitely. But not ill. I just drink too much. And pop too many pills. Without that—I'd be dead."

"Have you seen a doctor?"

"What's he going to tell me that I don't already know—don't drink, don't smoke, don't do drugs? It's too late already. I'm about finished, I can't go on much longer."

I knew I couldn't go on much longer myself, so excusing myself,

I hunted out Anjali and told her I was going back to the room. She nodded and said, "Go and lie down for a bit—I'll see you later." It was much, much later when she finally came. It must have been early morning since I'd been fast asleep for a few hours. She looked very distraught.

"Wasn't it a successful party?" I asked her sleepily.

"Oh sure, it was. But something awful happened after you left. Gul got into a fight with Ritu and struck her straight on the face. He also called her some filthy names—in Hindi. And do you know something? Nobody dared interfere. She just lay there on the ground while he kicked her, yanked her hair, spat on her and tore her blouse."

"Why? What happened? What did she do?"

"She attacked that creature—Sonia—remember the starlet in that funny little dress? Well, Ritu thought she was playing up to Gul, so when he went to the loo she walked up to her and threw cold water on her dress—her crotch, actually, saying, 'That should cool you down even if you are in heat.' Sonia started screaming—she became hysterical. Gul came out of the loo and saw this. He went straight for Ritu. His first swing itself sent her reeling. It was so terrible. The Princess tried to intervene, but Gul chucked her into the pool. By the time K was alerted, the whole thing was over."

We heard about Ritu's halfhearted suicide attempt the next afternoon. It didn't surprise either of us. After that scene, she'd been hauled home by one of Gul's henchmen and dumped in her bedroom. (Gul no longer spent his nights with her unless she'd organized a party for his friends with her "girls." Otherwise she slept alone, after taking a couple of tranquilizers in a warm glass of milk.) That night, instead of milk, she opted for whisky and a handful of pills. By the time her servants found her and phoned Gul she'd been unconscious for a few hours. They pumped out her stomach and she pulled through—but neither Anjali nor I were sure whether it was a good idea.

Anjali's gynaec was a kindly old lady who reminded me of a distant aunt and so I decided to go with her instead of the doctor my sister had recommended. She didn't ask too many questions and went about efficiently fixing an anaesthetist and operation theater. The same day that I was making these preparations the husband phoned for the first time since I'd left his house. "I knew I'd find you here," he said, his voice as friendly and casual as in the past. I didn't feel anything at all—no anger, no hostility. Just the standard indifference that had defined our marriage. I found myself making the sort of small talk I used to in the past, when he made his duty calls from Madras, Delhi, Calcutta, wherever. I even asked about his mother. That surprised him. After ten minutes of this, he came to the point. "Look—let's be civil about this. I've thought over it, and there is no reason to sulk or accuse. My lawyers will be in touch with you next week. We've worked out a package. You can have your jewelry and all other personal belongings. In fact, come and pick them up anytime you want to. We'll figure out where you can live. I've identified a flat in Juhu—nothing grand. But you'll like it—it has a small garden, plus, you'll be close to your beloved Anjali. My tax consultant is looking into a monthly maintenance scheme. You have your insurance policy, of course, and the income from shares and the other investments we made jointly. I'll have your portfolio reorganized and give you the details in a month. The only hitch is the car—I'm afraid you'll have to do without one for some time. Maybe, we'll be able to lay our hands on a second-hand Maruti. I know it's small. The driver will be tricky, because I won't be able to keep him on the company rolls—you understand. But maybe you could take driving lessons, so that you don't need a driver. It's better to be independent. How does all this sound?"

"Sounds sweet," I answered unenthusiastically.

"Hell! What do you mean 'sweet,' I thought you'd be jumping with joy. Not too many husbands, rather to-be ex-husbands, are this generous, let me tell you. And what about the problem—what have you decided to do about it?"

"Which problem?"

"You know—the . . . whatchyoumaycallit—pregnancy?"

"I'm attending to it—the appointment is for next week."

"Oh—do you need any money? How are you for cash? Is your check book with you? I'll send some money across tomorrow. In any case, you can't go on living in Anjali's house. My mother wanted me to tell you that if you need anything, you can phone her. She's not at all angry. You left in too much of a hurry—she would have helped you pack. Anyway no point in talking about all that now. The papers have been prepared. I think we should use the same lawyers. It will make things simpler—and it will be cheaper too. Is that OK with you?"

"Anything is OK with me. I leave it to you."

For a couple of days after his call I actually toyed with the idea of keeping the baby. Maybe it was just spite, maybe I hoped my parents would accept me, maybe I felt it was what I needed—someone to call my own as the cliché goes. But Anjali was quick to dismiss my fantasy when I brought it up with her.

"Don't be crazy," she said. "A baby is a lifelong responsibility— look at Mimi. Are you prepared to tie yourself down for ever? Get a pet puppy or a kitten if you are feeling all that motherly—forget about a kid. Besides, you won't be able to handle the scene. You aren't cut out for a single parent situation. You can't go around with an Orphan Annie–like kid, with no father on the scene. By the way, does Krish know the developments?"

"I didn't tell him—what's the point? He'd probably ask for compensation—or a present to celebrate the news."

"You'd better get your act together," she said, "and stop being flippant about all this."

"I'm not being flippant."

She ignored the remark and carried on. "I don't trust that husband of yours. Let him come up with the goodies he has promised. Have you seen this flat he's supposed to give you? How can you trust him so blindly? The whole thing sounds too good to be true."

"Look, let's forget all that for a moment shall we? I'm worried about the baby. Suddenly I feel protective and concerned. How can I just kill the poor thing?"

"Believe me, you'll be doing it a favor. Now, let's get on with it."

But even the "simple abortion" turned out to be a very complicated affair. While the gynaec was doing her thing, she discovered fibroids in my womb which meant I could never have children. There were masses of the fibroids and she told me later that I nearly bled to death on the table. I don't remember anything of this. I felt dopey for nearly forty-eight hours after the operation. Anjali said I had to be sedated so that I could get sufficient rest. When I was sufficiently awake and alert the doctor came to see me and suggested I have an immediate hysterectomy to get rid of complication from the fibroids. Anjali agreed. "Get the damn thing out once and for all. What use is it to you?"

I knew that logically that made perfect sense—what did I need a barren womb for—but for some ridiculous reason I wasn't in a hurry to part with it. I asked the doctor whether I could postpone the decision. "It's really up to you—but I wouldn't advise it. It will mean a great deal of discomfort, besides you could start haemorrhaging anytime without a warning. If you are alone when that happens, you could black out and bleed to death. As it is, your blood pressure is pretty low and you are anemic." I phoned my trusted London sister. She was of the same mind as well. I didn't even tell the parents about all this. I'd never felt lonelier in my life. Anjali was being very supportive and playing mother-hen to perfection. But I didn't feel comfortable imposing on her time and hospitality. She had priorities of her own. Her Babaji was still rotting in the clink and she'd had to send Mimi to a drug rehab center in Switzerland to dry out; despite all this she stuck around loyally.

We talked on and off about the hysterectomy and one evening I broke down and sobbed. Anjali put an arm around me and I said to her, "Maybe there is something like divine justice. I've never been a believer—but now I'm beginning to wonder. I'm being made to pay for my sins. This wouldn't have happened if I hadn't got involved with Krish."

"Stop feeling martyred," she said sharply and then softened. "I'm not making fun of your feelings—please don't think that but what you're saying is not true at all. You aren't an evil person. You haven't harmed anybody—not really. Your little infidelity whatever it was and with whosoever is so trivial. Don't blame yourself for it. Even your husband has forgiven you otherwise his attitude would have been different. He would have acted like a real swine and cut you off without a naya paisa. These things can happen to anyone. You aren't suffering for any crime. Hysterectomies are very common these days. It's not a major operation. It sounds cruel to say this, but maybe there was no pregnancy in the first place. Maybe, your irregular period cycle was because of the fibroids."

"What about the urine test?"

"Path labs can and do make mistakes. Also, it was still far too early, and in your state, you must've imagined the other symptoms."

"I don't want to think about all that. I'm worried about now—about next week. Imagine a part of you being sliced away. And, Anjali, I can't stay with you forever. You've been so kind."

"Try and relax. And listen you silly woman, you are not a burden to me. You can stay here permanently. Seriously, I would love it. You are good for me—always have been. You are the conscience I didn't have. Why do you want to move out? How can you slum somewhere as a PG?"

"Anjali, you might find this hard to understand or accept, but I wouldn't stay even in my parents' house for free. I'm not a sponger. I feel very embarrassed living off you like this. Hospitality is one thing, charity quite another. I'd definitely like to move out till that flat is fixed up—if it ever is."

"Why don't you pay me what you'd pay as a PG? Would that make you feel better?"

"No, I couldn't do that. It would make me feel worse. I've already made contact with a Parsee woman who had advertised. I'll go take a look at the place and then decide."

"Can you imagine yourself living in someone else's house? Confined to one little room, having to scrounge around for food? It's too depressing."

"Maybe. But I'll get used to it, I suppose."

"And how do you propose to pay for all this? Is he going to finance you forever?"

"No. I'll just have to pursue my theater contacts. Maybe try for a job in the ad agency we use. Whatever it is, it won't be a grand job with perks. But I've got to start somewhere."

"You aren't a spring chicken any longer. Have you thought of the sort of lifestyle you'll be able to afford on some measly salary? It won't pay for your tampons."

"I don't use tampons."

"Why don't you help me in my business instead? I could use one more person—someone I trust. In fact, I didn't tell you this, but I'm thinking of going it alone. No Kuku and no Murty. I feel confident enough. I have made my contacts and things are going very well. Kuku and I worked fine initially, but I find her far too pushy and wasteful. She isn't very cost-effective and in the long run clients don't like to end up paying for the designer's indulgences. She also inflates expenses and stuff like that. And she hogs all the credit. She is constantly lunching with journalists, inviting them to the sites, boasting about her originality, claiming she's the first one to have done this, that and the other. I don't mind her showing off—but it isn't really fair, considering all the slog is left to me."

"That's true, Anjali. But I don't know a damn thing about this game. I wouldn't know a Ming vase from a Ching one."

"That hardly matters. Do you think I know much more? All it needs is a certain eye, and lots of imported catalogues. You could become a buyer. I don't have the time to travel all over India locating craftsmen and placing orders. You'll enjoy the travel, meet interesting people and earn enough not to have to work a boring nine-to-five job in some crummy ad agency. I have big plans for the business. We can organize major exhibitions in Bombay, Delhi, Calcutta, Madras and Bangalore. Book orders for future projects. Supply specialized fittings and decorative objects hand-picked by you. This is a huge market—lots of money to be made."

"Sounds great—but you know, I'm not sure. I'm not sure about anything at all."

The operation took place on a dull Tuesday morning. The doctor looked ghoulish behind the mask. As I waited to go under I was half hoping there would be a complication and I would die peacefully on the operating table. But there are no shortcuts in life. No easy ways out. When I came around, I was surprised to see Mother's face over me. My mouth felt like it was full of cotton wool. I couldn't articulate any words. I thought I was slurring, and my eyelids refused to stay open. I could hear voices, but I couldn't tell whom they belonged to. I saw the soft green paint on the walls, and a tiny spider in one corner. I tried to raise my hand and reach for some water. My throat was dry and thick. I felt Mother's fingers in mine, her unnaturally warm hands, just as I remembered them from my childhood. I felt eight years old and very tearful. But I couldn't cry. I thought I was at my own funeral or someone else's. At one point I felt as if everybody I'd ever known or loved was lying dead around me. Corpses all over the room. And blood on my hands. I could feel blood oozing out of me and knew this was it, I was dying if I was not already dead. Suddenly I felt the urge to hear the sound of the bangles I always wore, I felt the mangalsutra around my neck. But my hands wouldn't move. I must be dead, I concluded.

It took me a week to feel strong enough to talk or even move from the bed to the bathroom. A week full of dulled thinking leading nowhere. Sometimes, I'd just drop off into deep sleep without a warning. Through dense, black fuzz I'd make a slow journey back to consciousness. I didn't feel like eating anything. Waist down I felt all sewed up and stiff. I must have imagined it, but I felt lighter. How much does a uterus weigh, anyway? It felt like I'd shed fifty pounds in one go. Nothing really mattered very much. I'd nibble at the bland hospital food and sleep. I'd never slept so much in my life. In between, I'd flip through magazines and look at the pictures. But not read. I couldn't read. I'd look at the pile of paperbacks on the bedside table and look away disinterestedly. I could barely make conversation with the few visitors who turned up to see me—some of the theater people, the husband with mother-in-law in tow (did I see a triumphant gleam in those mean eyes?), Anjali, of course, with Kumar and Murty, and Mother who'd come every day and sit there staring at me with her eyes full of sorrow. We seldom spoke. There was very little I could say to her, even if I didn't feel so disconnected. But it was comforting to have her there. One evening, after Mother had gone home after her silent vigil, Anjali showed up latish. She seemed very excited about something. She had more blush-on over her cheekbones than usual, and her nails looked like they used to in the past—tapered and polished to a professional bronze sheen. She was waving her hands in the air, as she did when she was particularly enthused. "It's a special day today, darling, and I bet you've forgotten what it is," she said producing a small gift from her Gucci bag. "What is it?" I asked. "I knew you wouldn't remember, but I was looking through my things today and I found an old diary. In it was the year and day I first met you—remember now—and I'd written a short remark—'met a sweet kid today.' You were just growing out of your teens and I envied you, your youth and innocence.

"Life was just beginning for you—and mine was already over. I wanted to protect you and keep you a virgin forever. Seal you off from the world of men. Warn you about them. Tell you never to get married and make the sort of mistakes I did. In a way, I'm glad I kept my trap shut. You had to do it your way." I was only half listening. I could hear the sea outside my window. I preferred to listen to the sound of the waves as they crashed against the rocks. Again—it was an image straight out of a mediocre film. I'd begun to view my own life in cinematic terms—frame by frame. This evening it was a series of freeze shots. I stared at Anjali almost blankly, without really seeing her. I noticed the new gray in her hair and was glad she wasn't going to hide it under an ink-black dye. There were additional lines around her mouth and eyes. And furrows in her forehead. They made her look beautiful and dignified. Like an attractive school headmistress.

Suddenly it came home to me. What I was thinking was this: Anjali had acquired a personality. Even the knotted choli didn't look provocative anymore. Her white chiffon with pastel poppies sat like a soft cloud around her body. I sniffed, yes, there it was, a whiff of Nina Ricci which filtered through the hospital antiseptics and bathroom disinfectants. Eighteen years. Difficult to believe. I took her hands and looked at her rings—there was a new one on her middle finger, the size of a doorknob ("anniversary gift"). I wanted to luxuriate in her presence, her smell, her touch. She had on a new watch, the gold Panther series from Cartier. It was all so reassuring and comforting. Even the rudraksha mala around her neck, which she wore so easily along with her favorite Bulgari chain. Nothing seemed incompatible about her life.

"Here," she said, pushing the gift toward me. "Open it. Go on, take a look." I felt shy as she thrust the packet into my hands. I took my time unwrapping it. "You like?" she asked. I just stared. It was a beautiful manicure set in silver and gold, neatly fitted into an embossed burgundy leather case. "What on earth am I going to do with this, Anjali? You know that I don't manicure my nails." "I know you don't. But it's about time you started. I can't possibly have a partner with grubby fingers. Before I forget—here's the varnish. You might as well start on a dramatic note—it's a fire-engine-red. Red for danger. Go for it."

I accepted Anjali's polish. But not her offer of a job. I couldn't see myself running around the countryside picking up wooden masala boxes from Saurashtra and dowry chests from Kutch.

For the next couple of months I recovered slowly in Anjali's house (where I'd gone from the hospital), desultorily phoning contacts in the hope of landing a job, every day hoping my parents would call and with the constant thought that I couldn't accept my friend's hospitality much longer. Then one evening I had a surprise visitor: Ritu. She looked wonderful: the lard was nearly all gone and there was a glow about her. After her suicide attempt, she said, she had gone back to live with her husband. He had, to his credit, accepted her without any questions asked and they'd gone off to the hills for two months to get away from everything. She talked about Gul with her old spirit. "Did you hear about Gul-e-Gulzar's latest move?"

"Do we really have to discuss that worm?"

"Don't worry, darling. He doesn't affect me anymore."

"Even so."

"He has gone off to London—taken that light-eyed actress with him. Not the one who was at Anjali's party—no, not Ms. Bubble Dress. The other bitch who also sings."

"You mean Rehana?"

"That's the one. Must say she's smarter than her dumb-dumb appearance, got him by the balls, I believe."

"Does he have any?"

"Come on—that's far too obvious a dig—you can do better than that. Anyway she's doing well for herself. Mink bedspreads and a channel-sized solitaire for her nose."

"Is she a cow?"

"She may look like one, but this fancy nose-stud actually illuminates the room when she walks in."

"What about one for her belly button?"

"She hasn't earned five carats as yet—but she's getting there. Oh yes—he has also set up a recording company for her—and ordered a chartreuse-colored Rolls-Royce to match those glassy eyes."

"Ritu—he still matters, doesn't he?"

"No. But sometimes I feel murderous just thinking about that phase. I got had, and it makes me feel like such a fool."

"Forget it. Tell me what you're planning to do now. How is the husband?"

"As boring as ever—but at least it's a familiar kind of boringness. And he was so sweet about everything. I don't have to stretch myself—living with him isn't a strain and that's what I need right now. A tranqui—by the way—I have quit the real stuff, stopped popping pills, no booze either. The weight will take a while to melt off—but I'm working on that too. Nothing like a month or two in the hills to cleanse the system."

"You make your holiday sound like a laxative. Anyway what did you do there besides listening to the birdie-wirdies doing their thing in the morning?"

"Well—to start with, I rested or tried to. There was this great withdrawal symptoms battle to struggle through. Oh God! That was the worst part. I would get pretty aggressive at times, and poor husband was the only one around. He and the mali. Between them, they'd physically wrestle me to the ground and keep me there. But that wasn't half as bad as the depression which would follow. I'd weep for hours together and sweat worse than all those little piggies outside my window. A couple of times I threw up in bed and messed up the rugs. I couldn't keep any food down either. The mali would bring me fruit from the nearby orchards—I'd take one look at the apples and want to puke. Actually it was the mali who finally succeeded in getting me around. Can you believe it? This Garhwali unpadh did more to heal my wounds than all the pricey psychiatrists and doctors in Bombay."

"Sounds very impressive. How did he do it? Witchcraft? Black magic? Don't tell me you believe in jaadu-tona?"

"Don't be crazy—he didn't do anything of the sort. Yes—he got me hooked all right—but not on tantrik mumbo-jumbo—but on the real thing—nature. We'd spend hours in the garden planting seeds and saplings and watching them grow. The whole experience was so therapeutic. Initially, I hated getting mud under my fingernails, but gradually I couldn't wait to get up at the crack of dawn to see whether anything had sprung up in the night. I really miss all that in this wretched city. It's not the same thing fooling around with stunted plants in pots and giving them fancy Japanese names. Up there in that small village near Mussoorie, where the air is clean and sweet, you feel energetic and alive planting a bed of sweet peas or watching cherry tomatoes growing in the veggie patch. In fact, I'm seriously thinking of turning into a full-time farmer. I have to convert hubby first. I think he got a bit bored once his anxiety about my health was over. He's not one of the back-to-nature types. I would sit contentedly by the fire in the evenings knitting a sweater I'd probably never wear. And he'd be obviously restless, flipping through three-month-old issues of *India Today* and asking about dinner. Anyway, I've convinced him to at least apply for a loan so that we can buy a small place of our own next year. I tried the oldest trick. 'Do it for our sakes, darling,' I said in my sweetest voice. I'm not sure but I think I threw in a hug and a kiss as well. It worked."

"I've heard all about the sweet peas and the hollyhocks, the pigs and goats and the call of the koel—but you haven't mentioned the one thing that would convince me about your serious intentions to move to the hills eventually. Men. Or have they become a dirty word?"

"Well, now that you're asking—and I've always been honest with you—there is this divine gentleman farmer who lives down the road. Don't know much about him. He's a man-mountain, all of six-foot-four, not counting the turban."

"A sardar?"

"Yes—one of those foreign-returned idealists with a string of degrees in agricultural research. He's doing amazing things in the area. But all I'm doing for now is just looking. And I'm not too sure I ever want to go beyond that."

It was a reassuring encounter. Ritu was on the mend, that I could see. And I was pretty certain that it wouldn't be long before Ritu took off for her newfound, sylvan paradise again—with or without the sardar. The original Earth Mother had finally come home to roost.

CHAPTER 17

EVENTUALLY I MOVED OUT OF ANJALI'S HOUSE INTO PG ACCOMMO-
dation. I hadn't heard from my parents. My soon-to-be ex-husband
was dragging his feet on the flat and I knew I had to do something de-
cisive about my life or go mad. Scarcely a week after I'd moved into
my new digs I had my first visitor—and of all people it was Krish.
Funnily I didn't feel a damn thing (perhaps I should have kicked him)
when I saw him standing on my doorstep with a foolish grin on his
face and faded chamelis in his hands. Nothing. Not even nostalgia.
Even his teeth went unnoticed. He looked smaller and shabbier and
altogether uninteresting. And like a *Woman and Home* heroine I asked
myself, "What did you see in this man?"

"Is it OK to come in? I mean does your landlady allow you to
entertain visitors—male visitors?"

"This isn't exactly a convent with a Mother Superior. And I'm a
big girl now, Krish. Yes—you can come in." He walked in with his
typical swagger. I used to find it sexy in the old days. Mrs. Jeroo
Mehta, my landlady, sitting in her favorite chair stared at him through
her bifocals—the first man who had come a-calling for her brand-
new PG. I had been told at the time of finalizing the deal that I could
receive friends. ("But not too many. We like our privacy.") There
were certain house rules I'd have to follow. Girlfriends in my room
(door to be shut), gentleman friends in the living room (no "hard
drinks" to be served). Krish walked up to her and bowed. With great
charm he extended his hand, said a musical "good evening" (using his

theater techniques) and waited for her to ask him to sit down. The house dog came around for a friendly sniff. Mrs. Mehta carefully put her feet into red velvet slippers, got up with an arthritic creak and said, "Please be comfortable." I felt very silly standing there with Krish. I knew I'd have to explain him to her later, even if she didn't ask. And I felt ashamed of my bare feet. On the very first evening at the Mehta home, the old lady had stared pointedly at my toes. "We Parsees think it very rude to show our toes to strangers. We never leave the room without footwear. I suppose it's different for you Hindus—your customs are not the same as ours. It's all right, dear. You needn't wear chappalls if you don't want to. But please wash your feet before going to bed. The dhobi is a lazy bugger, he doesn't take stains off the bedsheets." I'd nodded obediently and rushed off to find my rubber chappalls, but the dog, an indeterminate Pom-mixture, had chewed them to pieces before I got to them.

It was a quaint household. Three lunatic women and a dog ("the only male in our life, dear," Mrs. Mehta had joked, but I'd had a weird feeling that maybe there was something more to that remark). She'd introduced me to her daughter Shireen. ("Do you know a good diet, dear? My Shireen eats all day. Such a lovely figure she used to have, very nice legs and all that. Then she started to eat. Brutus and Shireen finish a kilo of mutton a day—and you know what the price of meat is these days, dear? I'm not complaining. By God's grace, we have enough. Shireen's father—may his soul rest in peace—has left us more than enough—but I worry about her weight.") Shireen was piglike—pink and fat. She lived in flimsy nighties ("only from St. Michael's, dear") and ate her way through the day. The third woman was the servant, Savitri, who had been with them for twenty-five years ("I got her as a wedding present, dear"), and ran the house. Brutus was her companion and obsession. She would talk to him for hours, complaining bitterly about the shabby treatment she received at the hands of her "Jeroobai." I was scared of Savitri. Once, I'd seen her threatening the butcher. He was a sturdy Muslim youth from the nearby mohalla. Savitri stood over him, brandishing his awesome knife, threatening the obviously nervous fellow with instant castration if he put another bone into the meat. Between the three of them, they lived a life of heightened sexuality, seeing phalluses everywhere. "Look at that," the mother would giggle, holding up a cucumber after Savitri came back from the market. They'd exchange meaningful glances and dissolve into hysterical laughter.

Jeroobai woke the house up with the BBC. "Dance music, dear," she'd say, foxtrotting around the place in a faded housecoat. This was at four forty-five a.m. Savitri would produce hot chocolate for Shireen, milk for the dog and tea for the rest of us.

"I'm not like the others, dear," Jeroobai explained to me one morning. "I am not greedy for money. I keep PG's because I like company. They make our life interesting. But, frankly dear, I prefer to keep men. Don't feel bad. But they are less fussy and cleaner also. Oh yes, please do not flush down your you-know-whats, dear; every month. Once we had a girl who choked up all the toilets by flushing her you-know-whats. It was very expensive to get the plumber. With men there are no problems of this type. Only thing is they eat much more. But don't think I'm lenient with men—they are also not allowed to bring ladies into the room. Once, a PG did that and closed the door. I sent Savitri to bang on it and order them to open up. We are decent people, dear. There's a young, growing girl in the house. We have to set the right example."

"So you do, Mrs. Mehta," I said and tried to go to my own room.

"Don't mind my asking, dear, but—no husband? Don't answer if you don't want to. Savitri saw your mangalsutra, so we were just wondering." I took the option not to answer. In any case what on earth was Savitri doing snooping around in my cupboard? But then, the cupboard wasn't really mine at all, I realized. And it made me think—actually I didn't have very much that was "mine." I didn't have "my" room in my parents' home (my sisters did). I didn't have my cupboard there (my sisters did), I didn't have my bed (my sisters did). There was nothing that was mine apart from what I was wearing—and the odd piece of jewelry in the cupboard (not "my" cupboard). Such a depressing thought. And it seemed too late to do anything about it now. I wished suddenly that I'd been more acquisitive in my youth like some of my friends. I thought of a schoolmate who had started working in some women's magazine then moved over to a film rag. Within a year she'd organized a "loan" from an actress she was publicizing in her magazine, borrowed some more from her employer, arranged for another bank loan and bought herself a two-bedroom apartment in a cooperative housing society at Bandra. All this before she was twenty-five. Now she was sitting pretty on an asset worth thirty lakhs. Her actress friend had written off the loan long ago—they were quits after all. And the young woman had a roof over her head and enough money stashed away in the bank not to have to worry about her future. And here I was—no money, no job, no nothing. Not even a cupboard to call my own.

And now here was Krish sitting easily in the stuffed armchair under the lamp, listening attentively to Shireen playing a prelude on the piano. She was still in her nightie and I could see her enormous panties. They'd crawled up the cheeks of her bottom and buried themselves inside. "Why don't we go for a walk?" I suggested. I couldn't bear to sit in the flat with three hungry women hovering over us. "No, no, dear, let the gentleman have his tea first," Jeroobai interrupted, placing a firm hand on his arm, pinning him to the chair. "Oh, I feel more like a beer actually," Krish said. I felt like killing him. Shameless jerk. "Sorry dear, when my husband was alive—God bless his soul—we used to keep hot drinks in the house. But not now." With her eyes she indicated Shireen. "Why leave temptation around?"

"Quite right, Mrs. Mehta," I agreed.

Krish stood up and took my arm. "OK, let's go, babe." Once outside the door I jerked my arm away. "What the hell are you doing here? And how did you find me?"

"Kid stuff, babe. What are ex-husbands for? Ran into the old boy at the club bar—nice place—nice and friendly. He was a bit sticky initially, but there's nothing a couple of stiff ones can't thaw. Got the dope from him—and here I am. Glad to see me?"

"You must be joking! I don't know why I'm bothering to be civil to you."

"Because you're still in love with me."

"Go to hell, Krish. I can't stand your corny humor anymore. What do you want?"

"Nothing, babe. Just relax. I was in the neighborhood, so I thought I'd pop by and see how things are. I still care about you."

"Like hell you do. In any case, it doesn't matter a shit to me. I'm OK and I really don't have anything to tell you."

"Well, your old man gave me all the news—too bad about the operation and all that. How are you keeping now?"

"Listen—you are getting on my nerves. I don't feel like discussing my body or my life with you. I only agreed to go for this walk to get you out of that house."

"I thought we might have a spot of dinner somewhere. Lots of new restaurants in this area I hear. My buddy—your ex-hubby— recommended a few. By the way—did you know he's planning to get married?" Now, that was a new one on me. I hadn't heard anything about his marriage plans. But I didn't want Krish to see my curiosity. I kept my voice carefully neutral.

"Good for him."

"Know the woman? I believe you do. She used to hang around in the same crowd—Vinita—Winnie to friends."

Good Lord! Winnie and him! I could see what was in it for him (she was an attractive, sophisticated party girl)—but why was she getting involved?

Reading my thoughts, Krish went on. "He's a good catch, you know. To some women, these things matter—family, education, success, money. Not all of them are foolish enough to throw it all away on account of some passing fancy."

"Don't flatter yourself, Krish. I didn't leave him because of you—ask him if you don't believe me. Anyway what's the point in raking all that up? Especially with you. And if he's getting married to Winnie that's really their business. It doesn't interest me."

"I believe the old bird is very happy. Winnie has all but moved in—taken over the place, in fact. The servants adore her, and she has changed the whole show all around. It's unrecognizable actually."

"How would you know?"

"Oh, I had a couple of drinks with them last night."

"Really? And did you remember to take chamelis for her—or did she fling them back on your face? I bet you didn't spend on an extra gajra for me—is this last night's reject?"

"Oh-ho. So it does matter. The Ice Maiden has some feelings left after all. For your information, I'm not such a heel. No, I didn't take chamelis for her. But, if you must know, I did pick up a rose on the way."

"And did you flamenco into the living room holding it between your teeth? And did you then fling it at her feet and shout olé?"

"You must be a witch. This is spooky. How did you know?"

"Because I'm a witch."

"It turned out to be an interesting evening actually. The two of them seem very well-adjusted. She drinks quite a bit, smokes too. So there were no disapproving glares to cramp our style. Did I tell you my wife was with me? She's still here. I've left her with some friends."

"Isn't that fascinating? A cozy foursome. How cute! And did you switch partners and dance to Tina Turner?"

"Well, Winnie is the one who is heavily into dancing—but we didn't do it at home. As I told you—she has turned the place around. The old music room has been converted into her office—she's a management consultant—you know that. So, anyway, she suggested we go off to the 1900s which was fine by us—we had to be dropped that side of town as it is."

"And nothing like a fancy evening at someone else's expense— right Krish? I bet your wife was most impressed."

"You are still bitter, my love. Don't be. We had a good thing going. It's over now. Why can't we be friends? Be nice, woman. You are on your own now. A grown-up girl, all alone in the big bad world. You could use some charm. You aren't planning to knit sweaters night after night, are you? Word gets around. Single women are in great demand. If you wanted it—there would be three parties a night to go to. Think about it. Unwind. A smile can take you to places— provided it's beamed at the right person. What are you planning to do with your life now, babe? You've got to get your act together. Ask me. I'm an expert on survival. You are in your prime—a ripe pear ready to be plucked. There aren't too many available women in your age bracket—make the most of the situation. And if I were you, babe, I'd get myself a new look. I notice you are painting your nails these days. But that's not enough. You need a total makeover—new hair, new clothes and, mainly, a new set of expressions. Fix yourself up nice and pretty. Trust me—I'm not such a heel. I'm your buddy. Maybe the only one you have. And I know you—every bit of you, babe. So, just let go, loosen up, and feed me some dinner. I'm famished."

"Krish," I said, slowly and deliberately, "I find you an unfunny, superficial, wreck of a man. I'm surprised you don't see that. Now why don't you be the creep that you are and creep the hell out of my life."

I walked home pensively, having refused Krish's offer to see me home. More than anything else I was surprised by my lack of emotion at the encounter with him. Where was the rage? Where was the loathing? Where was the sorrow? The only thing that disturbed me at all was the thought of Winnie in my home. I still thought of it as "my" home. All my dreams were located in it. I could recall the complicated pattern of the floor tiles, remember the corner of the coffee table that always hurt me, the spot on the carpet where I'd once spilled red wine, the hole in the curtain which the husband had caused with a carelessly held cigarette, my secret drawers under the dressing table full of trinkets from my teenage days, shelves full of old photographs and school report cards, a suitcase filled with trophies won through college. What would Winnie do with all this? Call the raddiwalla and dispose it all of? I wanted to phone and tell her not to throw important portions of my life away. But I didn't dare. Besides, I didn't have any place to keep my things. Jeroobai kept complaining about the few possessions I'd installed in the room as it was. Winnie—imagine! I couldn't picture her in that setting at all—the music room turned into an office! What had she done with the enormous chair which we used to joke was large enough to stage an orgy in? And the books? Records? Framed wedding photographs? Madhubani paintings? The Pichwai on the wall? Oh God! I didn't feel like thinking about it. I didn't resent her, it was just that I didn't approve either. The common theory about second marriages was obviously wrong—the husband hadn't opted for another me—Winnie and I couldn't have been more different. She was assertive, bossy and flagrantly sexual. Her first husband had been a mild German with blond eyelashes and bad breath. She had produced three children with him. Unable to keep up with her, he had fled to Cologne taking the kids with him. She had then attached herself to a five-star hotel as a top bracket PR person and consultant. I would run into her every now and again, as she strode around the lobby, ticking off nervous juniors, a docile secretary at her elbow taking notes. I also remembered the husband being most impressed.

"Quite a woman, this Winnie," he'd commented once while following her with his eyes.

"Yes—if you are an admirer of Attila the Hun," I'd remarked.

"What's wrong with efficiency? That doesn't make her a monster?"

"I wonder whether she performs as ferociously in bed," I'd said and got a dirty look in return. And now, there she was, installed in my room, on my side of the bed. I wanted to go back and reclaim the Jaipuri razai that had been my security blanket. Unless of course, she'd thrown it out by now and replaced it with a silk quilt. I wondered, if I should believe Krish about the servants reacting positively to their new memsaab. Or did they disobey her out of loyalty to me? Did they refuse to turn down the bed, just to spite her? Did they think of me with affection and sympathy and consider her an intruder? Somehow, the matter of Winnie hurt far more than everything that had gone before. It's not because I'd expected the husband to spend the rest of his life pining for me—far from it. But this seemed obscenely soon. Barely had I picked up my hair brush and vacated the place—than there was this new woman installed in our home. And not just any woman—Winnie!

"You're just jealous, darling, it's natural, don't fight it," advised Anjali. She was looking radiant after a quick trip abroad. "Any other woman in your place would feel the same way, even if she didn't care a shit about the ex-husband. The only thing you have to worry about is safeguarding your own interests. I'd told you not to sign all those papers till you'd got everything you'd been promised. But you didn't listen. Now that he's free and with a new woman, you'll be last on his list of priorities. Forget it, kid. If he hasn't come up with anything so far, it's unlikely that he will now—particularly with that woman around. Maybe she is just what he deserves. She'll take over the place and kick him around in his own house. He needed a bully. You were too much of a lamb for him." Anjali was right of course. She was so much shrewder in such matters. She understood the ways of the world and men in particular. But even with her tutoring I still had a lot to learn.

She was still being a considerate and thoughtful friend. Often, her driver would come around with things to eat, dishes she knew I liked and could never hope to get in my present setup. Each time she came over the three crazies would gherao her. She handled them beautifully, with great tact, but I would seethe at the imposition and take her to my miserable room quickly. There was barely any space in there even to move. There were no chairs, and the bed was a high and narrow old-fashioned one—the sort of bed you climbed into with the help of a stool. We'd sit on it and chat and then she'd suggest a ride into town or a shopping spree.

Krish called once after our unfortunate meeting. I was pretty stupid in not hanging up on him, considering the purpose of his call: he wanted me to meet Rini, his wife. As he spoke I thought about the woman whose existence I'd once tried to obliterate from my memory. To my astonishment I now found myself discussing her. I asked him what he'd told her about me. There was no masochism in the question—just curiosity. What does an unfaithful, wanderer of a husband tell his long-suffering wife about the other woman? Everything it seemed. Or so it was in Krish and Rini's marriage. They had discussed me threadbare at the height of the big romance and Rini had read every single one of my letters! Krish admitted all this readily and unashamedly. I asked him whether she sometimes scribbled off replies on his behalf when he was busy otherwise.

"No, she didn't actually do that, but she would remind me if I was behind."

"Then why all the farce about secrecy? Why the no-calls-on-weekends pact?"

"I did all that for you—you would've found out about Rini and me earlier, and you weren't the sort of woman who would have played along with our game." So that's all our romance was—their little game. I asked him wryly if he'd met other women who enjoyed their roles. "A few. In fact, we all ended up friends later. That's why I was wondering whether you'd be willing to meet Rini—after all, there's little she doesn't know about you." It was then that I finally hung up on him. I never saw or heard from the man again. But the phone call took me back to his visit at my PG lodgings. What was it he had said? You've got to get your act together. Yes, I had to. Melodramatic as it sounded I had no one to rely on but me.

I seriously started to hunt for a "proper" job. I'd been freelancing with the theater crowd, doing the odd thing—model coordination for agencies, small scripts for television pilots, organizing props for photography shoots—but that was far from lucrative. And I hated the poverty, this meager income forced on me. I suppose I was a bit too old for the drastic changes I had to adjust to or perhaps I just wasn't cut out to be middle class, lower middle class. For a start, there was the matter of transport. I'd never traveled by bus since my schooldays. Or waited in queues for anything. Getting into a local train and commuting to town was a major trauma. I could not relate to the other women in my compartment. I felt revolted by their small concerns. I'd watch with horror as they squabbled over small change and petty issues. Their conversations depressed me. It was all so stomach-turning, their talk of vegetable prices and milk strikes. Sometimes I'd overhear a husband being discussed, but it was invariably in servile terms. Every problem of theirs seemed trivial and insignificant to me. The quotidian detail of their lives—spats with the mother-in-law, a child with mumps, school admissions and donation money, husbands' stalled promotions, office gossip, a crisis at the neighborhood crèche, an ailing parent, a relative's hernia operation, sari sales at Kala Niketan, haldi versus cold cream, Garden Vareli at a suburban store, discounts at Sahakari Bhandar—I hated to be in that environment. Rubber monsoon sandals and drippy raincoats, the musty smell of old saris, BO camouflaged under cheap perfume, the sickening smell of stale flowers and coconut oil. I didn't belong to this world. I felt nauseated, physically sick. I'd sit there staring at a spot on the partition hoping none of the women would attempt to strike up a conversation with me. I'd watch them devouring cheap novellas as greedily as they dug into their station-bought wada paus. I'd listen to their comments on the latest exploits of popular film stars and all the while feel sick at being there, forced into a lifestyle that I'd rejected twenty years ago.

Yet was I not also one of them? I'd remember my ex-husband sneering, "You are so afraid of your middle-classness aren't you. You were born into the wrong bracket. You think like a memsaab, try and behave like one, but scratch the surface—and your true colors show. Why don't you chuck away old shoes? Why do you spend so much on getting clothes darned? Why do you dig into lipsticks even after they are finished? Why can't you throw away things you don't need any longer? Why should you be so familiar with the servants? They aren't one of us, you know. They must be kept in place." In my tolerant moments I'd laugh with him and agree that it was impossible for me to discard old stingy, thrifty habits. Given the choice, I would have saved the tops of milk bottles, plastic grocery bags, strings, gift-wrapping papers, even the ugly straw baskets that the florist delivered flowers in. ("We can grow money plants in them.")

The other side of me violently rejected all this—I even hated my own self for indulging in these little saving exercises. And sitting in that train I really couldn't stand those women. I needed to make some real money soon.

Anjali understood my predicament perfectly. "Of course you can't stand it, darling. It's easy to get accustomed to the good things in life. Luxury is like a narcotic—you can't get enough of it. Today it's an air-conditioned bathroom, tomorrow it's a Jacuzzi. You have tasted the forbidden fruit and liked it. How can you now go back to eating raw vegetables? We must do something about this, darling. I offered you a chance to make money, but you were far too hoity-toity to take it up. Never mind, let's see what else we can do. I'll ask K to speak to his ad agency contacts. Or his film friends. Everybody is into television these days. You have already done some work in it. Why don't you go all the way? There are plenty of assignments to be had. Interesting people too. Let's work on it."

Work started coming my way gradually. But I wasn't tough enough to push for money. I discovered the insecure world of freelancers; living from one uncertain check to the next, one payment to another. The three witches at home had lost all interest after they discovered that there were going to be no more exciting visitors or phone-calls (of the Krish sort). It was only the sight of Anjali's fire-engine-red Standard 2000 that would perk them up. "That rich friend of yours had come while you were away, dear. Nice lady, very cultured." Which in their vocabulary meant only one thing—moneyed . . .

The only thing I really looked forward to in this phase of my life was theater. I'd rush to Prithvi at the end of each busy day to rehearse for the small role I had in the Hindi version of *Desire Under the Elms*. The director was a hysterical Delhi woman looking to make good in Bombay. She had come up with her own interpretation of the play as a result of which there were usually loud arguments, tantrums and tears at each rehearsal. I kept out of these squabbles, but they added a lot of excitement to the monotony of waiting in the wings for my lines. Our director, Swapna, was certain this play was going to cause a stir. She would tell us confidently, "Give of your best—this is the opportunity to prove your worth. All the big names from the industry are coming to the preview. We all have a lot at stake." What she didn't say was that of all the people in the play she had the biggest stake in its success. Prithvi attracted the nearby film and TV crowd and talent scouts congregated there nightly to check out the shows. If she succeeded here she would be in clover. She'd managed her pre-publicity pretty efficiently and journalists drifted in and out of rehearsals. And there was enough anticipation in theater circles to ensure a full house for at least a week. Because of all this we were all quite tense.

The opening night was a complete disaster. Just about every-thing went wrong—the lights, sets and lines. I fluffed a few my-self. During intermission Swapna addressed the cast backstage, "I want those claps at the end of the show. I've worked hard for them. I'm used to applause. I'm not going to allow a bunch of bumbling Bombay amateurs to ruin my reputation at one stroke. Are you all trying to sabotage my career or something? Did you see who was in the audience? I saw him—I was sure he'd walk out after the first fifteen minutes. But he stayed. He's still there. It means he has liked the play."

"Who are you talking about?" I asked timidly.

"You mean you have to ask? Couldn't you recognize Girish—Girish Sridhar? He was there! I saw him—and he saw me too. He was staring." We heard the third bell and got ready to perform. The second half went off a little more smoothly and more than half the people had stayed on, much to our surprise, including the great art filmmaker, Mr. Sridhar. I was removing my makeup when a shy, young boy came up to me and said, "Excuse me. Miss. I have a mes-sage for you."

I was surprised, but Swapna was even more surprised. She nudged me and said, "Silly—that's Girish's son. What does he want with you? Must be some mistake."

She asked the boy sweetly, "Is the message from your father? Then it must be for me—I am Swapna, the director. I'm dying to meet your dad."

"No ma'am. The message is for this lady. My father pointed her out to me during the play."

"Well, what does he want?" Swapna demanded aggressively.

"He wants to have a word with her if she's free."

Swapna turned to me. "Imagine that! A word with you! There must be some mistake. I'll go with you—come on."

"Hold it, Swapna. I'm still in costume. I can't go out with all this gook on my face."

"Don't be crazy. You think he has all the time in the world to wait for us? He'll go away. I'm sure he is used to seeing women with stage makeup on. Come along, don't make such a ruddy fuss. I'll go."

"Go ahead then. I'll take a while to change."

Swapna rushed out with the young boy. It took me about ten minutes to wash my face and get into my sari. When I came out of the green room, I saw them in the café. Swapna was doing her heavy number on a bored-looking bearded man and his son who had carried the message to us. She signaled to me energetically. "Hi there. Come on over. I've just been telling Girishji all about our play."

I was exhausted and hungry. I was wondering whether I'd make it to the last bus home. Reluctantly I went to join them.

Mr. Beard got up and made a namaste. His son stood up too and made a place for me.

"Irish coffee?" asked Swapna with a friendliness I'd never experienced before.

"No, thanks. I'll have some chai."

"I've just been telling Girishji how hard all of you worked for this production. Of course, we had a few goof-ups in the beginning but the second half was fine—wasn't it, Girishji? It's just that Bombay and all you people are so new to me. I'm used to my own crew, my own setup in Delhi. There one can control everything perfectly. Anyway, as I told Girishji, you people did a good job, even though we didn't have much time to rehearse together."

Girishji just sat there staring glumly into his glass. I was getting restless. There was an awkward pause, my chai was on the table. I said, "If you don't mind, I'll just gulp down my tea and run along or else I'll miss the bus."

"Wait," the bearded one said and put a restraining hand on my wrist. "I want to talk to you."

Then looking at Swapna, he added, "Please excuse us." I thought she'd fling her coffee at me. She recovered fast enough, smiled sweetly and said, "Oh, I beg your pardon. Well, the night is young. I'm sure you have a lot to talk about. Enjoy yourselves."

Bitch! I hated the insinuation behind those remarks. Embarrassed and mad I started to chip away at my nail polish.

"Don't do that. It looks ugly," the Beard said, and I promptly hid my hands like an errant schoolgirl caught stealing someone's pencil.

"You were good, you know. Very good. I don't say that to every-body. Small role, badly directed—yet you came through. How much experience do you have?"

"Hardly any. Actually this isn't my line at all. It started as a time-pass hobby a couple of years ago—and I just do the odd role from time to time. Not seriously—just for fun."

"Have you thought of acting seriously at all—say, in a movie?"

"Movie? No, never! In fact, I don't feel comfortable on the stage or in front of a camera. I prefer to direct, or write."

"Really? That's interesting. Have you any experience in that?"

"Nothing much. Just a couple of small-time assignments—you know, a TV episode here and there, that sort of thing."

"What's your background? Do you work somewhere?"

"I'm a freelance odd-job woman these days. I take on any assign-ment I can handle."

Just then I realized how late it was and jumped up. "Listen, I've got to go. I'll miss the bus . . . besides I don't have my latch-key with me."

"Where do you live?"

"Just down the road."

"Come on, I'll drop you."

"No, really. I mean, you needn't bother. It's OK. I'll find my way home—it's only a few minutes ride."

"Please, I'd like to. My son and I are going home as well—and it's in the same direction."

"How do you know that?"

"I checked with Swapna."

We got into his jeep and I tore my sari as I tried to clamber in. "Shit!" I exclaimed instinctively. Mr. Beard laughed. "My, my! We do use strong language, don't we? Somehow, I can't associate that word with you. You belong to the classical mold. You should be conversing in Sanskrit."

"Are you suggesting I am Kalidasa material?"

"Yes, I am. How did you figure that one out? That's what I wanted to discuss with you. I'm working on a modern-day adaptation of *Shakuntala*—I saw you in the title role the minute you walked on stage. Interested?"

"No, I'm too old to run around in a blouseless sari with garlands around my neck. Neither can I see myself conversing with deer and singing with birds."

"You don't listen, do you? I said a modern-day adaptation. There are no deer and no birdies in this version. It's set in contemporary times and I'd like you to at least audition for it. You have the right expression—and like I told you earlier you fit into its classical framework."

"Thanks, but no, thanks. I'm flattered but frankly I know I'm not cut out for this. I'm sure you will come up with something fascinating but I'm not ready for it. I'd love to work on the script with you though. But I guess you aren't looking for someone in that department."

❖

We arrived on the Mehtases' shabby doorstep. "Is this where you live?" he asked.

"Yes—at least for the time being."

"Meaning?"

"I don't intend to spend the rest of my life in this hole."

"Are you . . . I mean . . . do you . . ."

"Am I single, and do I live alone? The answer is yes to both."

"Well, I don't suppose we can sit and talk for a bit in the jeep. Cigarette?"

"No, thanks. I really must go. I have an early morning call tomorrow."

"What kind of call?"

"Nothing major. I help out with modeling assignments sometimes. I have to go to Chor Bazaar to look for some props."

"Perhaps we can meet up later in the day—lunch?"

"I don't really know. I'm going to be on the other side of town. I doubt that I'll be back before late evening."

"Dinner, then?"

"May I keep it open? My timings are pretty uncertain. Tell you what. I'll call you if I get back at a respectable hour."

"Great. Any hour is OK by me. I won't eat till I hear from you."

"Please don't do that. I'll feel tense all day thinking of you sitting there starving," I said, thinking he was being quite forward.

"That makes it all the more worthwhile then," he said and laughed. The laugh transformed him. I could finally see something beyond the beard. And his voice. I liked that as well. As I changed for bed I realized the best thing about him was the obviously genuine loving relationship he had with his son, Kunal. They were easy with each other and their mutual fondness was touching.

I didn't know too much about Girish. I knew he had lost his wife a few years earlier in a tragic car accident on a family trip to Pune. Apart from that, even though he was pretty high profile in the movie world, he was said to be a loner, someone who kept to himself, had few friends and concentrated on his passion—films. I'd read the odd interview and honestly most of what he said went right over my head. He was counted amongst the "angrier" filmmakers who made powerful statements through his films. I'd seen some of his work and liked the first two award-winners immensely. He seemed particularly adept at dealing with women's subjects. It was said that nobody could extract such sensitive performances from heroines. (The central figures of all his films were strong women fighting the system.) I was definitely interested and flattered by his offer, though not in a superficial sense. As I dropped off to sleep, I didn't know whether it was *Shakuntala* that intrigued me or Girish.

I was woken up in the morning by a phone call from Swapna.

"Well?" she demanded in her usual aggressive way.

"Well, what?" I asked, though I knew perfectly well what she was after.

"Well, you know—what happened last night?"

"Nothing."

"What do you mean nothing? You were talking to him. He must have dropped you back. What did he say? Did he like the play?"

"I don't know. We didn't discuss it."

"Then what did you discuss?"

"Other things."

"Stop being so pricey. Tell me—I'm dying to know. Did he comment on your performance?"

"Sort of."

"Why are you playing so hard to get? What did he say—has he offered you a small role in his next film? I know he's planning something big—really, really, big. All the heroines are dying to get the main role. Did he tell you anything—I believe Anjana is really working on him. They've been the big item in the gossip columns. She said she'd do anything to get the role—anything at all. Isn't that something? He must've mentioned his new film, did he talk about Anjana?"

"No, Swapna. I don't think he waited for half an hour to meet me because he wanted to discuss Anjana."

"What then?"

"I don't really feel up to discussing it right now, if you don't mind. I haven't even brushed my teeth."

"You are just *lagaoing bhav*—it's OK. If you want to be so secretive about it I won't ask. But Girishji was definitely interested in the play, you know. He told me so."

"Then maybe he'll get in touch with you."

"I'm sure he will. I was only wondering whether he'd said something definite to you, because I have a few other commitments. I was planning to go to Delhi after this play but, of course, if Girishji has something in mind for me, I'll stay on. I think I'll phone him directly and ask. Maybe I'll invite him to dinner after the show tonight—let him tell me in person."

"Do that Swapna—and good luck."

Our second performance went off better than the first show. I didn't see Girish in the tiny auditorium. I hadn't expected to either. Swapna had been very cold when I rushed in a little late, about half an hour before we were to go on. I hadn't been near a phone all day, so there was no question of calling Girish. And it was with some regret that I got ready, for maybe I'd let go of something interesting if not important, by not getting back in touch with him. Swapna's hostile vibes didn't help my mind, and I felt too intimidated to ask her whether she'd made contact with him and fixed herself up for dinner.

When I came out of Prithvi and into the narrow lane outside I saw Kunal standing at the corner of the road with a huge smile on his face. "Baba is waiting for you at home—we haven't had our dinner yet." The relief! I got into the jeep and we drove off.

CHAPTER 18

GIRISH'S HOUSE FITTED HIS PERSONALITY PERFECTLY. OR MAYBE IT was the other way around. It was artistic but not oppressively so. It was traditional without resembling Cottage Industries. There were old-fashioned brass lamps ("my wife used to collect these") and em-broidered wall-hangings ("these are mine"), Shekhavati furniture, and antique dhurries. It wasn't chaotic, but it wasn't very organized either. There were books and posters everywhere. And lots of "co-lonial" tables. I liked the warmth of the place, its informality and its vibrant colors. Orissa applique blended with Andhra Kalamkari, but gently. There was nothing contrived about the ambience. There was clutter all right, but a clutter that was the sum total of the lives of the occupants. It was a home, not a showroom. And Girish obvi-ously loved it. Bhimsen Joshi was singing, as Kunal and I walked in. "Welcome," said Girish. "So glad you could make it. Since you didn't phone, I wasn't sure you'd come—but we were both hoping . . ." Kunal looked at me and smiled. I felt right at home, as I settled down on a low divan and hugged a cushion to myself.

Kunal fetched me a nimbu pani. Girish said, "I hope that's OK with you."

"Just fine."

He got himself a tough whisky and sat down next to me. "So—busy day?"

"The usual."

"How did it go?"

"What?"

"*Desire.*"

"Better than last night—thank God! I was so ashamed of our miserable showing yesterday."

"Happens all the time. Have you thought over what I proposed?"

"You proposed something?"

"*Shakuntala.*"

Impulsively, for it was certainly not the lime juice, I said, "I'd like to get involved."

"But you are involved. I thought it was all settled last night."

"Really! That's wonderful. I think I'll drink to that—what do you say?"

"You don't have to ask me, go ahead—fix her a drink, Kunal. Vodka?"

"No, champagne—if you have some going. I think this is a very special occasion. Am I being difficult?"

"Not at all. I'm not a champagne drinker myself. Hate the stuff—and no, there's no Moët et Chandon in this house—but you're right—tonight deserves nothing less. Come on, let's go—we'll find champagne somewhere and I know just where that's going to be. Kunal?"

"Thanks Baba, but I think I'll stay home. Got some stuff to catch up on—if that's OK?"

"Sure, son. See you later."

Girish flung the jeep down the deserted streets at high speed, while I clenched my fists on the leather of the seat, thinking—*Dear God what have I let myself in for.*

"We'll drive forever if need be to find champagne," he laughed, as we finally hit South Bombay. "Rendezvous?"

"Perfect," I said relaxing as we slowed to a more sedate pace.

It was already pretty late and the restaurant was dead, with a few old couples shuffling around on the floor while a bored rock group reluctantly played a waltz. But the view was spectacular with countless ships crowding the busy harbor. Nobody was keen to serve us just champagne, but Girish was obviously a popular regular.

"To us," he said.

"To *Shakuntala*," I replied, and knocked back my drink in three easy swigs.

"I am not dressed for champagne." I giggled stupidly, three glasses later.

"How does one dress for it?" Girish asked.

"Glamorously. Like Anjali. She'd be shocked to find me here like this, dressed so dowdily in a crumpled workday sari."

"I think you look beautiful—and who is this foolish Anjali?"

"Oh, an old friend—very stylish. She taught me to polish my nails. It was a bit late in the day by the time I started—but now they're doing fine."

"Show."

"See." He took both my hands in his and asked for an extra candle at our table. "This I have to examine thoroughly," he said with a solemn frown.

While my nails were being inspected closely, he asked, "How old are you?"

"That's a very rude question to ask a woman you barely know—but I'll tell you." I told him.

"Perfect."

"What do you mean by that?"

"I mean the age difference between us is perfect—eight years."

Nail inspection over, we drank some more in silence. "Do you know that second marriages invariably turn out to be stronger than first? There's an interesting study done on this—maybe you ought to read it."

"Really? Who conducted it?"

"Someone very prestigious—but don't ask me who. I believe in that strongly myself. We also share a lot of cultural affinities—did you know that?"

"No—but it's you who are telling me."

"What's your mother's name?"

"Why?"

"Do you mind telling me—it's important."

"You're never going to believe this—it's Shakuntala."

"It had to be! I call that my first good omen—let's have another drink. I'd like to meet her—your mother. Possible?"

"Sure. But she is very old and reticent. I don't know what you'd talk about."

"That's my problem, really. When can you arrange that—tomorrow?"

"You do seem to be in some mad hurry."

"I am."

In retrospect I blame it all on the champagne.

I didn't go to the Mehtas that night. And Jeroobai brought the roof down. "You should have informed us in advance, dear. Those are the rules in my home. We run a respectable place. Besides, it isn't safe these days to keep the front door unlatched. We could have been robbed or murdered. This is most irresponsible, dear. You should at least have thought of little Shireen sleeping alone in her room. Thank God, we have Brutus to protect us. Anyway, this is my final warning to you, dear. Next time you do this, I will have to ask you to leave."

"I have already decided to do that, Mrs. Mehta," I said firmly. At that moment all I wanted to do was to get the hell out of that place. I didn't care about the deposit I'd have to forgo or anything else. I didn't even know where I'd go. In any case, last night's champagne was still crowding me. I could feel a massive headache coming on.

We'd left the Rendezvous at three a.m. and had gone to Apollo Bunder across the road.

"Let's watch the sunrise—and then eat hot waffles at the Shamiana," Girish had suggested. I hadn't thought twice before accepting. We'd talked, sitting on a hard stone bench. Rather, Girish had talked and I'd listened. He spoke about his life, marriage, the death of his wife, his son, his career, the rest of his family, his childhood, his dreams—just about everything came tumbling out in a champagney rush. His accent had changed and he seemed far less sure of himself. He'd stop every now and then to check my reactions, to see whether I was laughing at him. I wasn't. I had felt weepy at one point, but I sure as hell hadn't felt like laughing at the life and time of the unusual bearded man by my side. And so it went until dawn and waffles.

On the spur of the moment, I decided to go to my parents' home. My sister Alak, I knew, had been shifted permanently to a nursing home at Swati's, my doctor sister's, insistence (she paid most of the costs as well) and I knew there'd be room. Somehow, despite everything that had happened, I was confident they'd be happy to see me. I wasn't wrong. Mother's eyes shone when she saw me on the doorstep with my suitcases. There were no questions, no explanations. Just a mugful of Mother's tea and butter biscuits from the Irani down the road. We sat in the kitchen as we had done in the past in a quiet and companionable silence. She did not urge me to talk. After a while I said to her, "I met a man last night." She looked at me sweetly and said, "I know. I could tell from your smile." I leaned over and hugged her and just at this point Father walked in. "I heard some noise in the kitchen—oh—it's you!" He was leaving when I said, "Oh, Baba, I just felt like coming home—is it all right with both of you?" He stood and looked at me for a long moment before replying. Finally he appeared to come to some decision. "Let me just say that our doors are always open to our children." He left and I wept. Mother said nothing but simply took my hands in her strong callused ones.

It was wonderful to be looked after once again. To have someone make tea for you, wait up meals for you, get the bathwater ready for you. I began to notice the "cultural affinities" I had with my family, the affinities Girish had spoken about at length. My calling my father "Baba"—now that was something I'd never thought about before, a constant that had remained through every phase of my life. But other things came back naturally too. The flying of the hands into a namaskar when the lights were switched on at dusk (the ex-husband had found this gesture ridiculous and primitive and I'd given it up early on in the marriage). But I'd noticed Girish doing the same and not feeling at all self-conscious about it (another plus in his favor).

My living nearly twenty miles away from both Prithvi and Girish was turning out to be a bit of a nuisance. The play closed with fairly good reviews. Swapna, of course, flattered herself into believing it had been a colossal hit. She was headed back to Delhi, but had managed to swing a couple of assignments in sponsored programs on television. I was asked too—a minor acting role in a soap and a chance to work on a lengthy script. I was happy to accept both. Girish wasn't pleased about my decision. "You don't need to waste your time on such faltu projects," he told me as we sat over coffee at the Sea Rock.

"They aren't faltu, besides I need to work."

"That's rubbish. You could join my unit—you know that. It's really a full-time person I'm looking for. *Shakuntala* is going to be a major production. I want to work on the screenplay with you and you haven't even found the time to read the first draft."

"I'll do it over the weekend—promise. But I don't know why you're making me this offer when you aren't familiar with my work—not that there is too much of it."

"Are you fishing for compliments? You know you are bloody

good—or you should, if you don't. I need you, dammit. In fact, I want you to come location-scouting with me next week."

"I can't do that, Girish. I have a few modeling commitments. I'd promised I'd help out with that suitings campaign. In fact, I might have to go to Jaipur with that unit if they want me to coordinate things on the spot."

"Sooner or later you will have to make up your mind what you want to do with your life. You are much too talented to waste your time on these trivial jobs. Aren't you tired of looking for hair-styling mousse and arranging eight identical leotards for a bunch of cretins jumping around singing an asinine jingle?"

"Look, all this may not be intellectual but I enjoy it. Some of the kids are lively, bubbly, crazy. I love listening to their mad comments and zany plans. I feel relaxed in that setup."

"But life is about more than just goofy kids and surfboards. I want you to get involved. Commit yourself. Get into the mainstream."

"The mainstream of what? Cinema? Life? I find all that very complex."

"You are just running away from reality. Don't you see the super-ficiality of your existence? How long can you continue to live with your parents? And scrounge around for work? Don't tell me you enjoy sweating it out—you are too spoiled for that. You don't have the time for anything meaningful. There's a festival of Tarkovsky films next week that I'd like to go to with you—but can I be sure you'll ac-company me? The French Film Festival is after that. Everybody dies to get passes to it. Kunal and I were hoping you'd come with us—I asked for an extra pass for you. But you are so indifferent. Stop run-ning, for Christ's sake. Stay with me—you won't regret it. We enjoy so many similar things. I can't remember when I last looked forward to a lassi on the beach, or reacted to a hibiscus garland, or noticed the fragrance of champak flowers—don't laugh. You think I'm mak-ing an ass of myself, don't you. But listen I'm not feeding you a line. I can understand your being wary of smooth-tongued charmers. But believe me, I'm not doing a number on you. So why don't you just relax and leave things to me?"

"Girish, I appreciate what you're saying. But I feel all closed up and insulated. I need a little time. I'm discovering stuff about myself. I enjoyed this little patch of independence. I'm reconnecting with my parents—they need me. I'm enjoying their presence. We may not talk very much, but it's a lovely feeling to have them at home when I get back. Don't rush me, please."

"Have it your way. *Shakuntala* goes on the floors in four months—we'll see how you feel about it then."

"Thanks Girish. I know I'm probably testing your limits. I'm sorry."

"What about my friend Varun's dinner tomorrow night? Coming?"

"Should be fine—but I've nothing to wear. And besides if it's going to be a filmi affair count me out—I'd feel terribly out of place."

"No, dear girl, it's not one of those dinners. You know who Varun is, don't you?"

"Hotshot magazine editor."

"Right. And he's an old school and college friend. We were at La Martiniere together—in Lucknow. And then at St. Stephen's."

"I've seen him at the club a couple of times. Attractive wife, nice kids."

"Have you read him? He writes quite well, actually, but poor chap doesn't get enough time."

"How come? Isn't that his job?"

"Well, *Outlook* has a team of correspondents but as the editor he gets very bogged down with the administrative side of the magazine. And being a weekly he has to be on the go constantly. Plus, he spends a lot of time in Delhi—he is very close to the high command these days. Did you see him on television the other night? Thought he spoke rather well on the Tamil situation."

"I saw the program toward the tail end. He has an impressive vocabulary, good voice but I thought he was inappropriately dressed."

"Why?"

"Wasn't he wearing a paratrooper's jacket or something?"

"It wasn't a paratrooper's jacket. It's the sort of informal jacket a lot of international journalists wear these days. I'm sure you've seen photographs of the foreign press chaps in Beirut. I think Varun picked it up on one of his jaunts."

"He's always zipping around, isn't he, this friend of yours? No wonder he doesn't have the time to write."

"Now, now—that's also his job. He has to travel to get his stories, and he is one of the best guys for on-the-spot coverage."

"He strikes me as being terribly opinionated and pompous. He smokes a cigar bigger than his face and goes around in a chauffeur-driven Maruti. That's yucky."

"Come on, don't hold such things against the guy. Look at what he has done with the magazine. He has taken the pants off everybody else. Today, whatever he writes carries a lot of weight. Nobody has been able to beat his scoops. He has terrific sources, here and abroad. He was the first one to break the gun-running story, plus the other one on defense deals. His exposés have brought down ministries. You must have read some of his interviews—deadly. There's no doubt about it—Varun is a dynamite. You'll see when you come to the party—he gets the best crowd. Everybody's there—politicians, journalists, film people, dancers, singers, authors, even a couple of underworld types. And mind you, Varun is very selective about his guests. They come there for him. His wife may be attractive, but she's no great hostess. They don't bother about the khana daana. His parties are most informal—you help yourself to drinks at the bar, and dinner generally consists of cold cuts and cheese, with maybe a salad thrown in. That's left on a side table, and people fix their own sandwiches. If he's feeling particularly generous then he throws in a handi full of biryani with a dekchi full of raita—that's it. On very special occasions, a few cans of rasgullas are opened for dessert, otherwise there's a plate full of ready-made paans. Guests prefer to arrive there after finish-ing dinner—he's well-known for his lousy table. But in any case, those who are there haven't come for an eight-course meal. It's important to be on his list—a lot of wheeling and dealing goes on at these affairs. Varun has the knack of getting the right mix to-gether. Things hot up sometimes. I remember a very volatile eve-ning once, when an opposition leader came to blows with a local Congress guy. A lot of glasses were broken that day."

"Sounds almost as riotous as one of Anjali and Kumar's parties."

"Possibly, except these are supposed to be cerebral altercations—issues are battled, policies get born, reputations made or broken. Everybody courts Varun—including his enemies."

"Does he have lots of those?"

"Every powerful person does. He is far more proud of the number of people who detest him than those who think he's a great chap."

"Didn't he write something nasty about Kumar once? Yes, of course he had. I remembered Anjali showing me the item and weeping over it. Pretty awful stuff—this was soon after Kumar was raided."

"Oh, that's all a part of the game. He's carried a few scandalous tidbits on me as well—you know, linking me to this and that actress. But one has to learn to take these things in one's stride. For all you know, you might find yourself in his gossip column after tomorrow night. You'd better look your best. I don't want to be linked up with some frump. Kunal and I have a reputation to live up to."

"That does it—I'm not coming with you. I don't need to be listed among your conquests, Mr. Sridhar—thanks, but no, thanks."

"Come on, I was just kidding. It will be fun. I assure you, you won't get bored. Besides, maybe a bitchy little piece is just what you need to get you out of that ruddy rut of yours. I'm dying to incrimi-nate you. If you don't come I'll tell Varun to fix an item about us, anyway. Kunal can supply the pictures. If you think I'm blackmailing you—I am."

✦

Varun's party was pretty much the way Girish had described it the previous evening. Unlike other parties in the city, where people tended to float around at random, throwing "hi"s and kisses all around, this one was more structured. It had easily recognizable power centers. The biggest was in the study. "That's the real adda," Girish said as he steered Kunal and me toward Varun who could barely be seen behind his cigar smoke. The room was already stuffy and my eyes started to water. By the time we reached the host, I had streams of tears trickling down my face. "Good heavens, Girish! What have you done to this poor woman," roared Varun, drawing everybody's attention to us. "Don't tell me you've been ill-treating her, as you do the rest?"

"Shut up, yaar. Stop showing off."

He introduced us and Varun winked at his old buddy. "*Yeh to achchi cheez hai, yaar.* Not like the other filmi chidiya." I didn't have a hanky on me and was busy blowing my nose into my sari pallav as discreetly as I could.

"*Chhodo, yaar,*" Girish said. "She's not from the industry—at least, not yet."

Kunal reached over and silently offered me his handkerchief.

"But why is the lady weeping?" Varun asked.

I managed to gasp, "I am not weeping—just gagging to death on the smoke in the room."

"Terribly sorry," he said though he didn't sound sorry at all. "So," he said turning to Girish again, "what's your new project—besides her, that is."

I was beginning to feel like a "chaalu cheez" by now—someone picked up from the sets and brought along for the party to add color to it. Except that I was wearing a drab sari. I left the two men and moved off, with Kunal at my elbow. "Don't feel bad. Varun uncle always talks like that—he doesn't really mean it. And you know how

people behave with film persons. They feel they have to make remarks like that. Baba isn't that type of a man. He never brings casual
girls to parties. Please don't feel bad about all this. I'm sure Baba is
angry too, but he can't say anything to Varun uncle."

"Why not? Because they're old friends?"

"That and something happened a few years ago—but don't tell
Baba I told you. It was when Ma died, and Baba was in a terrible
state. He had a major film release at that time, a lot of money was
locked up. Baba had borrowed quite a bit—the film had gone over
budget. He had an argument with Varun uncle over something, it's
a long story, and they stopped talking. We were not invited to any of
his parties and it was difficult for us to face mutual friends. But when
Baba's film was released, Varun uncle really showed what power he
had. *Outlook* did a cover story on the film and hacked it to pieces.
It interviewed the people Baba had borrowed money from and had
them say things like they'd kissed their money goodbye. Bekaar film,
things like that. Baba was finished! Varun uncle also has a lot of influence with other press people. He got bad reviews planted in several
papers and magazines. Baba was written off by the industry—totally
shunned. Nobody wanted to work with him—not even technicians.
We didn't have money to pay our bills. Baba pawned Ma's jewelry.
He tried to pay back his creditors. Fortunately, the film wasn't really such a flop. After the initial adverse publicity, it picked up and,
eventually, we came out of the crisis. But everybody advised Baba to
make up with Varun uncle before thinking of launching his next film.
That's why he's here today—to make peace. He has a lot at stake
with *Shakuntala* and he needs Varun uncle's support right from now,
he also runs a trade paper called *Hits and Flops,* which is required
reading for the industry. A positive mention in its columns makes all
the difference. If *Hits and Flops* backs a film, financiers part with their
money readily. Baba hopes to get Varun uncle to give him a write-up.
That will make all the difference." As Kunal came to the end of his
monologue we looked around for Girish. He was at the far corner

of the room talking to some people but I noticed uneasily that Varun was following him with his eyes. Just then he switched focus and our eyes met. Varun waved his fat cigar and gave me a thumbs up signal. I didn't know how to respond—I smiled weakly in return.

I was introduced briefly to Varun's wife—a pretty, little thing in black—before she drifted on. Vivacious, energetic and fresh-faced, she looked no older than one of the teenage starlets hanging around. Kunal explained, "She looks and behaves like a kid, but she isn't all that young. Her dad's the one with the money. He set up Varun uncle—bought him the press, introduced him to important people. Of course, Varun uncle is now someone in his own right, but when he married he was just a bright, ambitious man looking for a break. My Baba had already established himself by then, he was a known man. In fact, he tried to introduce Varun uncle to all his contacts in the film industry. We had so many parties at our home for him. Things changed once Varun uncle made it. You know how powerful press people are these days. We used to hear stories about how *Hits and Flops* used to extort money from people, or how it would black-mail producers, but initially Baba always defended Varun uncle and said that he was not such a man. He felt that Varun uncle's reporters were probably doing all these things behind his back. So one day he decided to tell him about what the industry was saying. Varun uncle got furious. He told Baba to stay out of his business and that's when they fell out. Actually we were all stunned by his reaction. Ma was alive then. She told Baba not to interfere but by then the damage was done."

"After your Baba made up has there been any trouble?"

"Not really. The odd gossip item linking him with this and that woman. This used to upset Ma when she was still alive. She'd tell Baba to leave this line and take up something else. But Baba really loves films. They are his life. How can he change to something else? He doesn't know any other way of making a living."

"Do you also want to join him in his company?"

"I don't really know. He sent me to California to do some courses in filmmaking—you know, to pick up the latest techniques. When I came back, I checked out the scene. But, I didn't think I really fit into the local film industry. My temperament is different. I can't play all these games. The atmosphere is so unprofessional and uncouth here. People work erratically, depending on whether there's money or not. We are at the mercy of the stars. If they don't show up, there's nothing we can do. We have to dismantle the set, lakhs are wasted just waiting for stars to report. I find all this very frustrating. Baba is used to it by now and he can control his temper. I feel upset and go into a depression."

"Maybe you should have a go at ad films. There's a big boom on at present because of television. Good filmmakers are so much in demand. You, with your fancy US training, could easily make it big. And, you know, you could work with me. I can write the script and handle the creative part and you look after the production. Organize a camera crew, fix schedules, that sort of thing. I think we'd have a lot of fun together. But before that let's get the green signal from your father. I don't want to sabotage his plans for you."

"I'd really appreciate that. By the way—Baba really likes you. Don't pay attention to Varun uncle's cheap comments. In fact, you are the first lady Baba has brought to our home after Ma's death—so, please don't misunderstand him. And don't believe a word of what you read about him in film magazines. It's not true at all. Baba is a fine man—a gentleman."

"Well, all I can say is that he has produced a very loyal son! Thank you Kunal. Your father doesn't require a character certificate, but I really appreciate your staunch defense of him. And yes—I will do my best to swing the ad thing. That's a promise."

On the way back from the party, Girish was very moody and quiet as was Kunal.

"Tomorrow?" he asked as he dropped me in the driveway.

"I'll call," I answered.

"When am I going to meet the original Shakuntala?" he asked.

"Tomorrow?"

"I'll call."

We left it at that.

We couldn't meet for nearly a week for a variety of reasons. I got busy with a new film and he went to Pune for three days. Kunal called a couple of times and I enjoyed talking to him. The new film I was working on was interesting. It was supposedly "new wave," like the music video clips from LA with plenty of computerized graphics and special effects. The script was to be catchy and hip. We spent hours looking at some of the American commercials waiting for inspiration to strike. (The agency's brief was to filch the best elements from the lot and splice them together after adding the obligatory Indian touch.) My eyeballs were rolling in their sockets after two days of nonstop viewing but I'd finally seen everything I wanted to. All I needed to do was write the script.

The first thing I did when I reached home was climb into my favorite nightie, oil my hair, put cucumber juice on my eyes to relax them and sit down to work. The doorbell rang. Mother went to answer it. Ex-husband was standing there looking stupid.

"May I come in?" he asked.

"Seeing that you are here—why not?" I said to help out my embarrassed mother.

There goes my script, I thought. But his visit turned out to be a blessing for even as he talked, the script came to me in a flash. I rather enjoyed the reason he'd come but the moment he left I began writing furiously.

The script has little to do with this story but the ex-husband's visit is worth recording. What it all came down to was this: Winnie was a bitch. Winnie was a slut. Winnie was out to screw him. Winnie was a gold-digger. Winnie had no class. Winnie was after his money. Winnie insulted his mother. Winnie had sacked his favorite servant. Winnie couldn't cook. Winnie smoked too much. Winnie ran up fantastic bills. Winnie had no taste. Winnie was so obvious. Winnie was rude to his relatives. Winnie wore dirty bras. Winnie served bum whisky in Scotch bottles. Winnie was a cheapskate. Winnie didn't do her underarms.

What else? The whine went on and on. I sat there pretending to listen. My parents made out like he wasn't in the room and did not look away from the TV. Girish phoned. Anjali phoned. The ad agency phoned. He just sat there. I didn't know what to do with the guy.

Finally, I said, gently enough, "But why are you telling me all this?"

"I thought you'd understand."

"Sure, I do. But I still don't see the point."

"I was hoping you'd tell me what to do."

"What to do about what?"

"About Winnie."

"Good heavens! How should I know? I mean, don't you think it's rather funny that you should be asking for my advice?"

"What's wrong with that? We were married once. You do know me better than anyone else. Can't I come to you as an old friend?"

"Look, I think that's a bit much. I don't believe in this kind of friendship. What friendship? Why don't you go and ask your mother for her opinion, as you used to in the past?"

"Things have changed."

"In what way?"

"I can't talk as freely to her as I used to."

"How come?"

"Something happened after Winnie came on the scene. We stopped communicating. Mother and I."

"That's too bad, isn't it. But she's still your mother and I'm only an ex-wife."

"But it's easier to talk to you. How do I get rid of Winnie?"

"This is ridiculous. I can't possibly answer that. But I'd think it should be simple enough—you do have experience in that department, after all."

"Don't talk like that and make me feel like a heel. That's behind us now. I want to discuss our future, not the past."

"Did I hear 'our' future?"

"That's right. My eyes have finally opened. I've been such an ass. How could I have been taken in by someone like Winnie? Nobody ever warned me about her, not even that bastard Krish."

"You are not a kid, you know. And she isn't a witch who cast an evil spell on innocent you."

"That's it—she is a witch. My mother thinks she practices black-magic. Even the servants were saying something like that. She is a very strange and powerful woman. I feel ashamed to admit this, but I'm scared of her. I can't do anything because I know she will destroy me. She has that power."

"Then you'd better just sit back and suffer. Or call in your own voodoo men to outspook her—what else can I say?"

"Why can't you talk to her?"

"Me? Talk to her?? What about???"

"Explain the whole situation. Tell her that you want to come back. That might make her leave—we aren't married as yet."

"You are mad—totally mad. You really have some nerve intruding into my life like this and suggesting what you just did. Give me one good reason why I should help you."

"Because I was once your husband. You nearly had our child. And because you are basically a good person."

"I don't believe this—and you are disgusting. How can you even make a reference to the child? Now, it suits you to convert it into 'our' child. I thought the reason we split was because you were convinced it was Krish's." I was so angry I'd totally forgotten my parents' presence. But they might have been blind and deaf for all the notice they took of the nasty revelations tumbling out like a river in spate. Thinking about it now I can only surmise they loved me very much for they never brought it up.

"I have to confess something to you. I really feel very small saying this—but I discovered it couldn't possibly have been his," the husband continued.

"How are you so sure?"

"Because he had himself tied up years ago. Soon after he and Rini got married. It was a part of the deal. He told me so himself."

"And you waited all this while to tell me. Just get the hell out of my house and life. I don't ever want to see you again. I let you in this time—but never again. I'll call the cops if you try and invade my home in future. You are even more of a worm than I thought. You deserve Winnie—I hope she's got a wax doll of yours. I'll send her some extra pins to stick into it. Now take your frigging pipe and OUT!!" My parents didn't take their eyes off the screen.

The ad worked wonderfully. It was a complicated shoot but things fell into place for a change and the coordination was perfect. I was very pleased with myself and so was the agency. They came up with an offer they thought I couldn't possibly refuse. But that's exactly what I did. I didn't want to get stuck with just one agency, no matter how creative. I was enjoying my freelance status despite its pitfalls. The money was beginning to come in regularly and I no longer felt coy about thumping a few tables and demanding it. Surprisingly enough, nobody objected. I bought an air-conditioner for my parents' bedroom. They nearly froze to death for a week, but dared not tell me that it didn't really suit them. It was only when I found my Mother shivering under two blankets that I realized I'd made a boo boo. I shifted it to the extra room—mine, for the moment—and decided to get them something more useful—like a VCR. It changed their lives completely—my parents became video nuts.

When Girish returned I started to help with the rewrites of the *Shakuntala* draft. It was still a problem coordinating our schedules, but we managed particularly on weekends. I suppose we were beginning to be noticed as an item but I didn't pay this much heed until Anjana, a second rung star, lashed out at Girish in a "no-holds-barred" interview in a film magazine. I still have the clipping and it deserves to be quoted from.

"He took me for a ride," screamed the headline. Below it was bombshell Anjana clad *à la* Shakuntala of the classics, in a thin white sari. The interview began with Anjana claiming that Girish had strung her along for two years by dangling this role in front of her.

"I did whatever I could to please him. I even took Sanskrit lessons. He wanted me to change my lifestyle. He asked me to give up smoking and boozing. I promised to change my image. I started wearing saris. I even broke up with my steady boyfriend—and, then, he ditched me without a warning."

This was the cue for the reporter to ask, "Who did he ditch you for? Can you name the other woman?"

Anjana purred. "Yes, of course I can—but I'd rather not. Why should I give her so much bhav? Who is she? Nobody and nothing. If I reveal her name she will become a somebody. A celebrity. I will not do her the favor. But why don't you ask Girishji? Or his son Kunal? Or any of his unit people? They'll tell you. I hear she's there in his bedroom all the time."

"Did she snatch the role away from you?" the reporter asked.

"I don't know whether Girishji will give her the role—how will he get distributors for his film if he casts a middle-aged divorcée? He will be mad to do it. But it is because of her that he broke up with me."

"What does she have that you don't?" the reporter continued.

"If you ask me—nothing. She is a big zero. No looks. No figure. No talent. Just some chhota mota roles in theater—bas. But if he wants to risk his career for her sake, who am I to say anything? If he takes her, *Shakuntala* will be his biggest flop."

"What do your fans say about all this?"

"They are naturally very angry. I have received hajaar letters from them saying they'll boycott his film. Serves him right. Let this be a warning to other girls. Anyway, I'm not sitting back and crying. My brother Babu has told me that he will launch his own *Shakuntala*. We will show Girishji what we are capable of. It will be my way of saying, "I don't need you. *Mein bhi kuch kam nahi hoon*, Mr. Sridhar.""

"Will there be any nude scenes in your film?"

"Look Baba. Don't ask me such questions. But simply I have read *Amar Chitra Katha*. In fact, Shakuntala is shown in the forest with animals. Now you tell me, where can a woman get clothes in a forest? She is natural, no? She can wear leaves and animal skins, but she can't get silks and chiffons. Our nudity will be very dignified and classy. I am ready to strip if the role demands it. In this case I am convinced it's in keeping with the character of Shakuntala. I have already started going to the health club to work out for those important scenes. Like the one in the river, when she loses the ring given to her by that king—what's his name?" The reporter didn't know.

"Never mind—that's a very important scene. It has to be well presented, but it must also look sexy. We will shoot it from the back—no frontal shots—chee chee but it will look ekdum gorgeous, yaar. My brother calls it the paisa vasool scene in the film."

Girish took the piece in his stride. "It has happened before," he sighed, "and will happen again—you'd better get ready to face the onslaught." I was shattered. How could any woman, even a brazen film star, talk about her private life and settle scores through the printed pages of a rag?

"That's the way the industry functions, dear girl, and whether you like it or not, you are now a part of it," Girish said.

"Heavens no! I'd rather opt out right now," I said in a panic.

"Too late for second thoughts now. Brace yourself—chin up. This is only the beginning."

And so it was that I was sucked into a ruthless world without any scruples as I knew them. I saw a side to Girish that was both fascinating and frightening. When he cut deals, he was like a cold-blooded killer. He could be so emotionless and steely. I hated it. "You'll toughen—everybody does. Think of some of the other women in the industry. The ones who are in the spotlight constantly. There's nothing they can do which doesn't get around. Even some of the things they don't do are invented by the film press—it's all a part of showbiz, dear girl. One develops a thick skin sooner or later." I wasn't so sure. I agonized over Anjana's cheap comments for weeks. Each time I stepped out into the street I would wonder whether people "knew." I felt ashamed to meet my acquaintances, imagining they'd be condemning me.

Another item appeared soon after. This time in Varun's paper. While the first few mentions had been blind ones (no names) this one identified me as the new woman in Girish's life. It went on to talk about Kunal's involvement with the ad scene, implying slyly that I was having an affair with both, Father and son, and that I should make up my mind who to go for. My hands were shaking while I read this piece of filth. Just then the phone rang. It was Anjali. "What's going on? What on earth are you up to? Have you seen *Hits*? Are you really having a torrid affair with the Sridhars? I can't believe it, just shows how out of touch we've been. What are you doing today— let's meet up for a quick lunch."

I couldn't speak. My voice refused to emerge.

"Are you there—heh? Hello." I put the receiver down and rushed back to my room, flung myself on my bed and sobbed. If even Anjali could buy that bilge, what about the others? How was I going to face the agency people? I had an appointment to see a new client tomorrow. It was an important brief. The creative director was going to handle the presentation himself. How could I walk into the conference room and face all those people! I didn't even feel like phoning Girish. I couldn't talk about it to Mother—she wouldn't have understood.

As my weeping subsided the incessant drumming of Ganesh worshippers began to filter in. It was the tenth day of the festival, and the immersion of the elephant God had already begun. I could hear the raucous cries of "*Ganpati bapa morya*" and the rhythmic clanging of cymbals as the processionists made their way to the sea.

I felt like drowning myself with the deity. My mind came up with increasingly morbid images. Would I end up at the bottom of the ocean? Or continue to float, belly-up, at low tide like the plaster images of the rotund God? I stood at the window watching a small family negotiating its way through the throngs, carrying their little Ganpati carefully, a small white handkerchief on his head to protect him from the sun. A large group of rowdy mill-workers were accompanying their idol—a mammoth Ganesh straddling the globe— on its final journey with a motley brass band playing the theme from *Come September*. Right behind them was another crowd from a cooperative housing society. Their Ganesh belonged to the 21st century. He was dressed like an astronaut. A tall cardboard rocket was fixed behind him. To go with his space-age image, these people had dispensed with the brass band. They'd hired a rock group with a Moog synthesizer. Their choice of music was also very au courant—George Michael and U2!

The noise, the bustle, the energy eased the sorrow from my mind as I recalled Ganesh Utsavs from the past. From the age of five till my days of trying to be a sophisticate I had participated enthusiastically in them. It was my favorite festival, even more special than Diwali. Though we didn't bring the moorti to our house, it didn't really matter since it came to my father's older brother's home. We were expected to be present for the aartis, which took place twice a day. I loved the rituals that went with the puja. I enjoyed watching my aunt arranging the gleaming silver and brass thalis alongside the altar, heaping one with flowers, one with fruit, one with prasad, and one with diyas. The smell of incense combined with the aroma of sandalwood paste and coconut oil. Wonderful. I'd watch with fascination as the potbellied priest chanted the "*Sukha karata . . . dukha harata . . .*" and the elders joined in the chorus. I'd be given tiny cymbals of my own to beat to the tempo of the prayer. It was almost hypnotic.

I felt in a trance once again as I watched the believers from my parents' home. I wanted to join them downstairs and go to the beach to perform the farewell aarti where dear Ganapati would be given a tearful send-off. Back to his watery home he'd go on the head of an urchin willing to wade into the sea for ten rupees and all the coconuts he could retrieve from the waves. I stood at the window for a long time, gazing at the various images of the Benign One, wondering what the hell to do with my life. Then I saw a familiar figure elbowing his way through the crowd. He stuck out because of his trendy cap and the Nikon around his neck. It was Kunal.

Soon I heard the doorbell go. I didn't feel like meeting Kunal, or anyone else for that matter, right now. But it would have been mean to get Mother to lie that I wasn't in. Kunal looked so sweet and sad as he stood at the door, pleading with his eyes. I held out my hand and took him in. "Baba asked me to come for you. I've parked miles away since the street is blocked, or I would've got here earlier. Are you OK? He asked me to bring you home. He said to tell you to get your things."

"Get my things?"

"Yeah—you know, all your stuff."

"Why?"

"He thinks you should come and live with us."

"Well, now, does he really? How come he didn't think about asking me how I felt about it?"

"You mean you'd rather not?" he asked in consternation. What a sweet boy, I thought, my voice softening. Sometimes it was easy to forget he was still a child.

"It isn't that, Kunal. I just haven't considered the possibility. I can't shack up with you two guys. That's crazy!"

"He doesn't expect you to shack up with us. He wants to get married—he told me so."

"Thanks a lot, pal. But don't you think he should have consulted me before making all these plans?"

"He felt shy or maybe he was scared."

"Of what?"

"I think he was afraid you wouldn't agree. Actually, he'd made up his mind long ago. Remember the night both of you went off to drink champagne? He told me the next morning."

"He didn't tell me anything of the kind. Don't you find that funny?"

"No, I don't. I understand Baba. You will, too. He is like that— very sensitive and afraid of rejection."

"I still think this is no way to propose—or proposition. How can any man do it via his son?"

"Why not? I am the one he trusts the most. He knows I will represent him correctly. And he knows that you and I understand each other. That's very important to him."

"This is a very major decision, Kunal. I can't make it so lightly. Besides, are you sure it doesn't have something to do with that awful gossip in Varun's paper? Is your Baba feeling guilty? He isn't obliged to make an honest woman out of me, you know. Times have changed. I can handle it on my own."

"Don't say things like that. It has nothing to do with that muck. He was worried you'd take it very badly—which I can see you have. But, apart from anything else, he loves you, he really does."

"That's news, Kunal. He hasn't ever told me so himself. That's carrying reserve a bit too far, don't you think—at his age? Do I have to hear even his declarations from you?"

"Don't judge him so harshly. He is a wounded man. I am not playing on your sympathy, believe me. I'm only trying to explain a few things. After Ma died, he went into a total tailspin. He became so uncommunicative and depressed, spending hours locked up in his room, listening to music and drinking. I never thought he'd pull out. I wasn't much help either, being in a state of shock myself. I didn't want to see Baba in that state. I wanted to escape, get away from the scene. Forget about the whole thing. I should have stayed with him but I ran away to California. I want to make it up to him now. We are friends, he and I. We discuss everything freely—one to one. I know how deeply he cares about you. We will both try and make you happy. I promise you. Please give us a chance."

I tried to stop the tears, but they kept rolling down my face. I felt confused and happy at the same time. But was this what I was look-ing for? Did I want to take the line of least resistance? Wasn't all this far too pat and easy? Did one marry on the basis of a gossip item? And how could I convince Kunal that I liked his father too—and him, but that this wasn't reason enough to get married. Not now, at any rate. Living with my parents had opened up a new dimension for me. I felt like a responsible, caring daughter for the first time in my life. They needed me. And I needed them. We had arrived at a happy situation. They didn't have a son to look after them in their old age. They had the enormous burden of an invalid daughter to cope with. Each day in their life was a major struggle to just get on with the liv-ing that remained. How could I abandon them at this point? It would have been a callous, cruel thing to do. Walk in. Walk out. No. There was just no way I was going to stride into my room, fling my few belongings into a suitcase and take off.

CHAPTER 19

Girish didn't react badly. Fortunately. I suppose he understood or at least tried to. The gossip continued and soon I began receiving calls asking for "my version." It didn't take me long to figure out that this was nothing more than a cheap trick designed to prolong a controversy. I consistently refused to talk to any of the reporters, which surprised Girish a bit. "I know you aren't like other women, but most of the girls I've known have not been able to resist the lure of publicity—good or bad."

"That's what separates the girls from the women, Girish. Perhaps I would've fallen for it too ten years earlier. But now I don't need to mess up my life. This kind of exposure is foul and destructive. On a practical level—what am I going to get out of it? I'm not an aspiring actress looking for a break. I don't wish to be a household name. My living does not depend on publicity and I don't get cheap thrills being featured in the glossies. On the contrary, I value my privacy and wish to guard it. All this must sound very schoolmarmish to you—but I'm really not in the market for scandal."

"Neither am I. It's just that I've taught myself to regard it as nothing more than an occupational hazard. I refuse to react to all the garbage these people print. A lot of things hurt deeply—you cannot imagine what I've been through in the past. But now, well, you might say I'm immunized. My life is more important to me than what I read about it."

"How could Varun do this to you? I thought you said he was an old pal."

"I didn't want to prejudice you at that point. Yes—we have known each other over the years—but there's no love lost between us. He can be a vicious son of a bitch."

"But what have you done to him for him to be such a brute?" I was beginning to add that Kunal had told me about the film that Varun had wrecked and why he'd done so when I caught myself. Kunal had sworn me to secrecy. Girish was saying pensively, "I really don't know why he dislikes me so much. I've been told he was in love with my wife in college and that he never forgave her for preferring me. But I couldn't say how true this theory is for neither of them ever spoke to me about it. She used to behave very normally when he was around—as he used to be in the early days."

"But didn't you ever ask her anything directly?"

"The matter didn't arise. I didn't want to give this stupid story any importance. And I think you should learn to ignore gossip too. Remember, if it doesn't hurt you, the gossip writers get deflated. If you react, victory is theirs."

"I am a long way from being that mature. To me, gossip is a very painful reality. It haunts me. I feel marked. I also feel a sense of outrage—why should I be dragged into all this dirt? I am not a movie star. For them it may be an inescapable part of their business—but why should I get caught in the quicksand? I refuse to get sucked in and dragged down."

"Take it easy. Where is your usual cynicism? How come it isn't there when you most need it?"

"I reserve it for bigger things, real things."

"I suppose I should apologize. Had it not been for your association with me, you wouldn't have been in this situation. Now why don't we cut out this discussion and get down to some work."

What made up for the personal anxiety was the fact that things at work were beginning to really perk up. Besides Girish's script, the firm I worked for bagged the Ad Club award for the Best Ad of the year, and I got an individual citation as Copywriter of the Year. My market was up and other colleagues kept urging me to go full time and professionalize—whatever that meant. I decided to find out.

"Set up your own shop," I was advised.

"Start your own boutique agency. Fork out the jobs. Hire other freelancers and get your show on the road. Keep your overheads down by doing most of the stuff yourself, including visualizing. There's money to be made—don't blow it. Capitalize on your award—now is the time."

Even though I could see the common sense in which all these suggestions were rooted, I still resisted them. I suppose my real concerns were different. It wasn't money or success I was looking forward to in my life at that point—it was the freedom to do what I wanted. My part-time job gave me that. Running an agency, however small its size, would involve a major reorganization of my priorities. It would increase my tensions, responsibilities and headaches. I didn't care enough for the big time to tie myself down this way. It would also have cut into my theater activities—and *Shakuntala* of course.

When Girish finally arrived to meet "The Original One," as we had both dubbed Mother, he was on tenterhooks. I'd laughed and assured him that my parents didn't really notice or care anymore about most things. Whether he wore his kurta pajama, jeans or a Savile Row suit, I was sure they'd barely look up or take notes. I was wrong. Mother commented later that she liked his shirt and his neat appearance. "He has nice hands, clean nails."

"Mother! How did you notice all that."

"I'm not blind yet and he was sitting right next to me. He didn't smell of coconut oil either."

"Why? Did you expect him to?"

"Yes, most men from that background and community smell strongly of coconut oil."

"But what about the rest of him."

"He is all right. Doesn't have a big stomach or anything. Isn't too hairy either. Color is all right also. Not too dark. His boy is fairer, must have taken after the mother."

"You noticed him too?"

"He was in the house for nearly fifteen minutes. Isn't that long enough to make out his complexion?"

"You astonish me sometimes. But what did Baba think of Girish?"

"Well, you know your father. He doesn't talk very much: He doesn't understand people who do not work for the Government. Or who are in different professions. He can understand doctors, officers, engineers, chartered accountants—even certain types of business people. But all these fellows acting in films, television—he is not sure how stable they are."

"Girish doesn't act in films or television. He makes films. It is a very creative field."

"Yes, but your father feels suspicious of these sort of men. Can they be trusted? Do they make enough money to support a family? Do they keep their families happy? Are they steady people?"

"But Baba and you watch television all the time—surely, you know how much work goes into each program? And that it requires a director to direct a serial?"

"Yes—but these people do not belong to our world. They are different from us. We are not used to their ways. Does this man drink?"

"Well, no more than other people. I know of several doctors and engineers who drink much more."

"Does he bring home money regularly?"

"I have not asked him such a personal question—but his home seems to run well enough."

"As long as you know what you are doing."

"But I'm not doing anything. Besides, I don't even know why I am defending the man."

"Well, we thought, your father and I, that you were planning on getting married again."

"I don't really know about that. I am happy here and I hope you feel happy having me at home. I haven't yet made up my mind about marrying—him or anyone else."

"A woman cannot live alone. It is not safe. We are here today—but who knows about tomorrow? A woman needs a man's protection. Society can be very cruel. Today you are still young enough to get a good husband. A few years from now it might be too late. You will regret not having your own home and family. You must not feel that you have an obligation to look after us. We can look after ourselves. Look at your poor sister. Look at her miserable condition. I am not saying that will happen to you—God forbid it! But we would like to see you settled in our lifetime. Your father and I both feel a woman's real place is in her husband's home—not in her parents'." But I'm not saying that you should marry this man. You can wait for two more years and then decide. Nowadays you girls are lucky—you can choose. You meet so many men. Take your time, but marry. And marry the right one—that is important. You cannot repeat the earlier mistake. This time it will be far too costly—and you won't be able to afford it. Even if you decide to marry—what is his name—Girish—we will not oppose you—it is your life now. You are old enough and more experienced in these matters. But we also believe in parents' instincts. Nobody else in the world can have your well-being at heart in the same way—remember that. Before we die, we want to see you secure and at peace."

"But Mother, why does security rest with a man? I feel confident now that I can look after myself. I am earning as much as any man. I have a roof over my head. I don't really have any responsibilities. I am at peace with myself. I'm not answerable to anyone. I don't feel like complicating my life by getting into a second marriage. I like and respect Girish. We share a lot of common interests. But I am not sure I'll make a good wife to him. Or he a good husband to me. Perhaps we are both far too selfish for marriage. I can't make any 'sacrifices'—not now."

"Well then, since your mind is made up, I think you should be frank enough with this man—again, I've forgotten his name. Tell him your decision so that he'll be free to find someone else. He has been through a tragedy. He looks lonely. So does his son. They both require the presence of a woman in their lives. I think they are hoping it will be yours. So if you don't want to be married to him please let him know. Poor man, let him not feel let down."

"Mother, I can see you are trying to make me feel awful. I know you mean well—but don't push me into something I'm not ready for. Girish is a good man but I'm not in the frame of mind to consider marriage. But you are right—I must tell him. And Kunal. I love both of them, especially Kunal. But not enough to change the way things are and become a part of their family. I think they'll understand."

But when I did muster up the courage to finally tell them, neither of them seemed to understand. At least, Kunal didn't. I suspect Girish only pretended to. I could tell they were both sore at me. And, as such things normally go, our friendship began to crumble and my involvement with *Shakuntala* began to wane. Girish talked less and less of my playing a role in the film. Oh sure, we met, we discussed changes in the script, we talked about the casting, but it was all very lifeless. There was no soul left in the project. I thought it was time to opt out. One day as I sat wondering about how I would break this to Girish, Anjali phoned. "Babaji is released!" she announced. For a moment I thought she was talking about a film. "We are planning a party to celebrate. You have to come and please ask Girish and that handsome boy of his to come as well. There is so much joy again. I haven't stopped laughing. K is on top of the world."

"Where's the little creepo—Murty?"

"He's away in Europe—business trip."

"Sounds wonderful. But, Anjali, I'm feeling so out of things. I'm not in a party mood. Would you mind terribly if I didn't come this time."

"Yes, I would. This happens to be a very special occasion in our lives. Mimi is back home too. She's going straight. I've got her involved in the business. After a long, long time the family has got its act together. Happy days are here again. And you must share this with us."

"Let's leave it open."

"Let's not. But before that—I'm coming into town for a massage and perm and we should meet."

"You mean after all these years in Juhu you still haven't found a good enough hairdresser there?"

"You know how it is, sweetie, one gets used to one woman. I can't dream of leaving my head to anyone else. Besides, the car makes the trip in that direction daily—so, it's only a matter of my spending extra time—not money. I can afford that. And while I'm at it, I might as well get a facial. Also I have to pick up my ring from the jewelers."

"Another one? At this rate you'll outshine Liz Taylor."

"This one's not for me—it's for Babaji. Just a token to show him how happy we are. He had mentioned that a navgraha ring is useful to ward off evil. K and I thought he'd like it if we gave him one."

"Very thoughtful of you. I could do with one myself."

"What evil do you have to deal with? You're such a goody goody."

"You'd be surprised."

"So, what is it? Are we catching up or aren't we? I can buy you a cold coffee and some salad. You can have your face fixed too."

"Thanks, but no, thanks. My face is beyond fixing. Actually, I'm quite happy with it. Tell you what—let's leave it for another time. And I'll see you at the party."

"Great. You'll really like it. It's Guru Purnima that night, so we'll be celebrating it by the pool. It's important to have the moon's rays shine on you—your body's batteries get recharged for the rest of the year."

"Oh and by the way I'm not sure about Girish and Kunal—but I'll pass on your message to them . . ."

I wasn't really surprised when they both declined—politely of course.

I nearly didn't make it myself to the party and thought of wriggling out of the whole affair at the last moment. But as I always seemed to do, when one of Anjali's dos were concerned, I went.

The first person I spotted was Varun. I nearly turned and walked out. But it was too late—Anjali had seen me.

"Alone?"

"Yes. Do you mind?"

"Not at all, sweetheart. Maybe just as well—who knows whom you might run into tonight? Always best not to have hangers-on."

Varun came up to me. "Why, hello there Ms. Celebrity, going solo?"

"Why don't you look for some other victim tonight? I'm sure there's no shortage. Or is your paper that hard-up?"

"My! My! We are getting prickly, aren't we? Why don't we get ourselves a drink and talk this thing out. I have nothing against you—in fact, I rather fancy you."

"Go take a walk, Varun. Your schoolboy lines don't impress me. I wouldn't like to create a scene—Anjali is an old friend of mine. Just leave me alone."

"Get off your high horse. I told you—I have nothing against you. My reporters tell me it's all off between you and that pseudo fart."

"It's none of your stinking business."

"No? Maybe it is, maybe I have chosen to make it so. In fact, I was hoping we'd meet tonight. I have something for you to do."

"There's nothing I'd care to do for you. I wouldn't spit on you if you asked me to."

"You are reacting like an emotional teenager. Mature people don't behave like this—they keep their opinions to themselves. They play clever games. They try and swing things to their advantage. Don't be a fool. Can't you see how easy it would be for me to destroy you? I wouldn't bother—you are small fry. But I can do it. Now be sensible and listen to what I'm saying." He caught hold of my arm and started to steer me toward a marble bench near the shrubbery.

"Let go. How dare you. I'm not afraid of your threats. You can bloody well go ahead and print what you wish."

"All I was suggesting was an exclusive from you. It's not you I wish to fix—it's that bastard. Now that it's all over between the two of you the time's right. You get your own back—and I help you to do so by printing your story. That way both of us get what we want."

"What makes you think I want to fix Girish? I don't. I'd rather fix you but then, I don't waste my time on worms. I leave them to grovel in their own dirt. Excuse me—I'm getting out of this toxic zone." I walked away swiftly. Almost without thinking I landed in my old room—the one that had seen me through my breakdown. I locked myself in and sat on the bed, my own words ringing in my ears. I'd made an ass of myself. All that bravado—how foolish really. Yes—Varun was going to get me—I'd asked for it. I could imagine him on the phone, right this minute, dictating a mean piece to his minions. But then, I said to myself, what the hell does it matter! A splendid thrill of defiance surged through me and I decided to go back to the party and have fun.

Babaji glowed in the moonlight as did the mother-of-pearl throne he sat on. Two beautiful foreigners stood behind him fanning imaginary flies away. K was clad in a dhoti—he looked beatific too. Anjali had rigged up a small tent for her Babaji made out of mogras and jasmines. Besides looking utterly pretty, it was divinely fragrant. Enormous thalis strewn with rose petals were placed all around the garden. She'd even managed to get lotuses to bloom in the lotus pond. The setting was exquisitely done and Varun started to slip from my mind. I started to float—it was all very heady—I half expected the moon goddess to descend from the sky and scatter stars on the gathering. Was I hallucinating? Had Anjali put something into the thandai? I wasn't worrying. I noticed a man talking earnestly to Babaji. He had a very high-tech tape recorder in his hand. In the dreamlike state I was in, my normal diffidence disappeared. I walked up boldly to investigate. His accent was peculiar. He looked Indian but spoke American. He was asking Babaji about his experiences in jail. So he was a journalist. Not a local one, obviously. One could tell that from the way he phrased his questions. Babaji's nubile fanners pitched in from time to time, helping their guru out with some of the more complicated questions. Babaji handled the whole show with supreme confidence. His answers were delightfully esoteric and charmingly vague. He cleverly dodged those relating to money matters or to his ashrams and investments abroad. The reporter was relentless without being rude. I was enjoying myself and I suppose it showed for the reporter asked pointedly, "Are you a part of Babaji's entourage?"

"No," I laughed.

"Excuse me—but we are in the middle of an interview. This is private. I was given forty-five minutes with him—exclusively. So, if you don't mind, I'd like to carry on with my job."

"Maybe I could help you out with some of the questions—I noticed you were quite off the track on some points."

"Are you a journalist?"

"No."

"Lay off, lady. It really isn't any of your business how I conduct my interviews."

"I was only trying to be helpful."

"Thanks. But I can manage perfectly without your help. Now I'd like to get back to my story, so beat it. You're cutting in on my time."

"What if I refuse to budge?"

"I'll have you thrown out."

"Try."

"Look, what's with you?"

"Nothing. I'm enjoying your interview. And I'd like to sit in on it—why don't you relax and get on with your job?"

"You are behaving like a bloody bitch. I'll have the host himself get rid of you." I sat tight while he went off in search of Kumar. When they returned Kumar looked astonished at the sight of me. "You?"

"Yes, me!"

He turned to the reporter.

"She's OK. I thought it was someone else. She's an old friend of Anjali's—perfectly harmless. Just ignore her and carry on."

"Look buddy, I don't work that way. I don't care a shit who she is or whether or not she's harmless. Get her out of here, or I'm leaving. Our deal's off—no interview—you understand?"

"Easy. You are insulting a guest." Then K turned to me nervously and held out his arm with a flourish.

"Shall we?"

"Are you asking me for a dance?"

"Why not?" We moved off, but not before I made a rude gesture at the reporter whose face resembled a thundercloud. He silently mouthed "B-I-T-C-H" before switching on his machine and returning to his interview.

"Who's he?" I asked Kumar.

"Oh—that's Ranbir Roy from *The Washington Times*. He's well known—a roving correspondent. It took a lot of work to rope him in for this interview."

"Help! Did I blow it for you?"

"Too late to think about that now, dearest."

Just before I left the party, I saw Varun, enshrouded as always in a cloud of smoke, holding forth to an eager crowd of admirers. He looked not a little sinister, only the paunch and goatee spoiling the general effect. I shuddered a little despite myself.

Ritu phoned some days later to say that she had finally decided on a property in the hills. The place was being renovated and she would, she said, henceforth spend the better part of the year there coming down to Bombay only for the winter. She was throwing a farewell party to which she said I must come. I went, happy for Ritu but sad for myself. One more friend gone and how many left to make? Ritu was looking lovely in an ash-gray sari and a vermilion bindi. Anjali had departed on a scouting trip and because Ritu was being mobbed by the crowd, I wandered off as I usually did.

Perhaps because I'd been seeing or colliding with too many journalists lately I began to notice how much of the conversation had to do with journalists. And wherever the Press was mentioned there was one name that stood out: Varun.

"It wasn't worth taking him on," a senior journalist was saying to an agitated industrialist who had been the target of a Varun operation. The polyester king was full of contempt. "This is a town full of gutless people. Here is one of your tribe indulging in gutter journalism and what do you people do? You flock to his parties, drink his Scotch, screw the starlets he provides and feature him in your own publications. I have been counting—in the last four months one weekly has carried three articles on this man. Why? What are his achievements? Does he have any credibility?"

Another media man interrupted, "Fear. That is the explanation. Fear."

"What are you afraid of? Unless all you fellows have dirty secrets to hide."

A small-time politician explained, "Arre baba, it's not that. This man is capable of inventing stories. Ruining reputations. Damaging business. Who wants the jhanjat of annoying him?"

Soon it appeared that Varun had become the theme of the party. Even Ritu seemed content to just listen to the Varun stories that evening. A respected and respectable film-critic from an established nongossip film journal talked about how Varun had hounded a talented filmmaker who had refused to grovel at his feet. Eventually, broken both in spirit and financially, the man had committed suicide. Varun had capitalized even on this tragic death by making it a dramatic cover story for *Outlook*. "He sent those snoopy girls of his to interview everybody from the Gurkha of the building to the jamadar in his house. Even close family members weren't spared. One of those bitches went to the school and tracked down Deven's kids. A photographer clicked away as the children broke down and cried remembering their papa. He wrote about his ex-girlfriends, present wife and future affairs. The headline said 'Who really killed Deven?' It was so sickening."

"Why doesn't someone do something to fix this man?" a bearded art filmmaker from the South asked.

"How do I fix him—I don't own magazines and newspapers? My own editor is too scared or won't stoop as low to muckrake. Who will carry my story?" the critic said.

"*Achcha*—let's leave that aside. Tell us Samtani saab, why didn't you take him to court for defamation?" an industrialist asked.

The polyester king told everybody what everybody there already knew. "Are you joking? Ask any press-wallah—is it worth going to court? My lawyers told me to forget it. Apart from anything else, I would've done Varun a favor—his paper would have sold even more copies—he thrives on these defamation cases—don't you know that? The case would've gone on for ten years, twenty years, then what? It was not the money—I would've spent any amount. But who has the time to waste in courts?"

The Southern filmmaker turned to the senior journalist and

asked, "Why do you people chamchofy this man so much? Why does your group keep writing about him, promoting him?"

"It's simple, yaar. It's better to keep good relations with Varun. Take my example. Who knows when I might need a job? Varun pays the highest salaries. He looks after his staff very well. He offers all sorts of perks—soft loans, driver-ke-saath gaadi, air-conditioned cabins, generous expense accounts. All journalists like to flatter him and he likes to flatter them. Nobody respects Varun, but they like his money-power. Do you know he even sends his editors abroad for holidays? How many proprietors do that?"

The polyester king stared at him sadly and said, "*Afsos hai*, yaar. You people have no integrity. You will sell your soul for a free trip to London."

"It isn't that. Varun has made himself very powerful. If he takes a khunnas against anyone, he can go all out to finish off that person. He doesn't forgive any of his editors if they decide to leave him and join someone else. He carries out an organized slander campaign and makes the person's life miserable till he or she is forced to quit his new job and return to him."

"But can't people do the same thing he does to them. Find out what the skeletons in his closet are?" the filmmaker persisted.

"Plenty, yaar," said the film critic. "We all know that Varun is actually a homo. Forget all that wife-shife front. He prefers young, chikna boys. Just notice how many pretty boys he has successfully launched. All these aspiring heroes have a price to pay—but they don't mind. They know that if they please the boss they are made. He picks them up from nowhere and then starts to build them up. A few who fall out with him talk about his sadistic kinks—but who will listen to them? We all know that he takes these boys to his bungalow on the beach. He is terribly discreet about the whole thing.

"But I must say it's strange that he has managed to keep all this out of the gossip press for so long? I'm sure there must be some enemy of Varun's who has the guts to write about him," the chiffoned wife of a businessman said.

"Who will dare to write? Varun has a dossier on just about everybody in town. You pick on him and he'll get you for something or the other. Could be a tax default or some long-forgotten scandal—after all, every person has something or the other to hide in a city like Bombay. Varun is a vindictive man—like all aging queens, he is very insecure," the critic said.

"And yet all you chamchas flock around him. Didn't I see a big color feature in your weekend supplement?" said the filmmaker who was becoming quite drunk and belligerent. His question was directed to an attractive young editor with a huge bindi on her narrow forehead.

"I was only following orders from the top," she cooed. "It was really a complicated tie-up. Some sort of a swap deal with *Outlook*, with ad spots on his video films. My instructions were to do a soft story, a glamorous lifestyle piece talking about his gorgeous homes, his gorgeous wife, his gorgeous kids, his gorgeous parties, his gorgeous clothes and his gorgeous success. He paid for everything—so we even saved on photography costs. Now that he is losing his hair and has just had an expensive hair transplant job done, he's very careful about his angles. Rather than take a chance with an unfamiliar photographer, he prefers his favorite blue-eyed boy to photograph him. He has an impressive collection of stock pictures which he hands out to any reporter interested in featuring him. God! That guy is so vain. I know the beautician who works on him weekly—his beauty routine is something else. Do you know he spends at least five hours every Saturday getting his face and nails fixed? The works, you know. Apricot face packs, cucumber eye masks, almond oil hair massage, malai body massage, manicure, pedicure, even threading and waxing and a dye job."

I was dying to know what he threaded, waxed and dyed but felt embarrassed to ask her in front of everybody. When I got the chance, I quickly inquired. "Oh—he threads the hairs off his toesies and his fingers. He shapes his eyebrows and dyes just about everything—I mean EVERYTHING down to his eyelashes and you can guess what!"

Varun had so dominated the evening that the only time I managed to have a few words with Ritu was when I was leaving. We promised to write each other regularly.

About a month after this party, I was amazed to receive an invitation to Varun's annual jamboree—the anniversary party of *Outlook*. I vaguely thought about calling Girish and asking whether we should go together just to score a point off Varun and then put the thought out of mind. Anjali then. I'd go with her for she would probably be going. And if she hadn't been invited, I'd go alone. Thinking about it now, I wonder why I was being so obsessive about Varun and the only reason that seems in any way plausible was his dangerous reputation which held me in a sort of thrall. The sort of hypnotic effect some spiders have for flies. Which is as good an analogy as any for that was what I was going to do. Go to Varun's party and be the proverbial fly on the wall. As things turned out, Anjali was going.

"Wouldn't miss it for anything in the world darling," she said with much excitement in her husky voice.

"You are behaving like it's an invitation from Buckingham Palace to Charlie-boy's coronation."

"Oh, baby—this is much better than that, don't you know? Now stop talking rubbish and let's decide important things—what are you wearing? What shall I wear? I can't think of a thing! I don't want to wear a sari—so boring. K is also very excited. This is our first time—what do you know! We rate, darling! Just about the entire city will be there. I'm told lots of politicians fly in from Delhi. This year they're saying the PM's wife might decide to put in an appearance. Can you imagine? In any case, I've been looking for a way to make a breakthrough with Varun. K and I are very keen that Babaji gets featured in *Outlook*. K is willing to pay for the write-up but that's not the point. We feel that more and more people should be made aware of Babaji and his work—especially now, with all the international chapters opening and his plans to start a World Peace Center near Hollywood."

"I don't know about all that but as to what I'm going to be wearing, as usual I've nothing to wear. And there's no time to go out and buy a sari."

But Anjali wasn't listening.

"You know, I saw a gorgeous outfit in London. I wish I'd bought it then. I could always telex K's office there but will there be enough time? Even if I send out the message today, it will take at least five days for the dress to make the flight. And then, with the time difference and everything—it might be a touch-and-go situation. If it doesn't get here by Saturday the whole effort will be a waste. And K will get most upset."

"Why don't you do something really sensational?"

"Like what?"

"Like go ethnic with a vengeance."

"Like how?"

"Like dress up *à la* Amrapali—remember Vyjayanthimala as the court dancer?"

"Are you mad? She was practically nude in the film. You know very well that I don't have boobs. Are you being bitchy?"

"No—I just had this flash in my mind, and you were dressed in that sort of a costume. At least in my imagination you looked sensational."

"Something's happening to you in your old age. It can't be menopause-related, surely? Varun isn't throwing a fancy dress party, remember? There will be all sorts of very posh people present—and you're telling me to go dressed like a cabaret dancer."

"I'm sorry Anjali, I was feeling weird—it was just a thought. Forget it."

"I won't be able to sleep till I can decide on my look for the evening. Do you know *Outlook* carries lots and lots of photographs of the anniversary party? It's considered very prestigious to be invited and then featured as a VIP. People die to get in. I want to make sure K and I make it to that feature. Varun doesn't publish just anybody's picture. If I'm wearing something outstanding his photographers will definitely notice me. And I've heard this year he's planning to bring out a special cassette of the function. Imagine—everybody who owns a video will see this."

"What makes you think anybody is that interested? I wouldn't pay a hundred bucks to watch some stupid publisher's party."

"He isn't going to sell it, stupid, it's for private distribution. A PR gimmick. Varun is apparently going to send the cassette free to all the people who featured in it. Isn't that a great idea?"

"Really, Anjali. I'm already depressed at the thought—maybe I'll just chicken out. I don't want to die of anxiety wondering whether or not I'm good enough for Varun's video show."

Anjali pretended she hadn't heard a word. "I hear he's announcing something big this year. People are speculating. Could be another magazine. Or maybe he's launching his own movie production company."

"Perhaps he's joining politics. Wouldn't that be the next logical move."

"Hey! Maybe you're right! That must be it! I'll ring up Sheila who knows someone who knows his wife. I'll find out. I bet that's what it's going to be."

"Weren't there strong rumors that he was lobbying for a Rajya Sabha seat? I remember reading that somewhere. Then he backed the wrong mentor and lost. Now that he has switched sides and there is a seat coming up—that must be it. Judging from his recent editorials and columns he has certainly been playing his cards well."

"You read his magazine?"

"You mean you don't? Don't you let him hear you say that. He'll cancel your invitation."

"Well, K does bring it to the house and I do glance through it—but that's all. I read all the gossip columns, look at the pictures, a few headlines and captions—bas."

"Can't really say you've missed anything. That guy can't write for peanuts. I suspect he gets someone to ghost-write his pieces—including the editorials. Plus, for me at any rate, he has lost whatever little credibility he once had. It's so obvious he's doing chamchagiri—and nobody does chamchagiri for nothing. He has been supporting even the most absurd policies of the PM. Other editors have hinted that he's going to be rewarded with a plum assignment. A future ambassadorship maybe? In any case he has already extracted quite a few concessions. Someone was saying he's constructing a huge Outlook Towers on prime property. The CM has given him all the go-aheads on a platter. There are charges of land scams—but of course, he'll manage to get out of everything—since he has the government in his pocket. Can you imagine, he got the President to come here especially for the foundation stone laying ceremony?"

"Wow! I must tell K all this. I didn't know Varun was so influential. You are right—he is a future politician. This party must be for that announcement. But do you think he'll actually stand for any elections?"

"He doesn't have to. But even if he does—he has the machinery to win. He can buy any number of votes—particularly if he picks his constituency carefully. Who knows? Of course, once he wins an election, the sky is the limit. But I'm told he is waiting to be inducted directly into the PM's secretariat. He's hoping to become his press advisor. Or to head a special media cell to monitor everything—television included. Or a slot in the Information and Broadcasting ministry in some sort of a special capacity."

"Who will run his business if he goes away to Delhi?"

"Oh, that's not a problem. He can make any of the established editors an offer they couldn't refuse. Or he could plonk his wife at the helm of affairs. There's also an obliging chachaji on the scene—he's the person who handles all his financial matters."

"All this khabar is most exciting. K will be kicked by it. How do you get to know so much? Don't tell me it was all because of your association with Girish?"

"Well, let's just say I'm a good listener. And, darling girl, it also helps if you read the newspapers occasionally. Try it. At least on the day of the party. Make sure to memorize the headlines if nothing else. The place will be crawling with opinionated asses. You'll feel very left out."

"Do you think the PM's wife will really come? Gosh? If she does—who will look at us?"

"Not us, say me."

"Oh, all right. You know you are turning into a crotchety old maid. What you need is a good screw. When was the last time you had one, anyway?"

"You are beginning to sound as trashy as Varun's rags. I think you'll be the biggest hit at his party."

Anjali did become the star of that party. In a manner of speaking. And it took Anjali years to recover from the aftermath. To start with—her dress drew attention and not of a particularly complimentary kind. Well, what can one say about a white georgettey number that made the wearer resemble an extra from a mob scene in *Spartacus*? God knows what it was supposed to be—a gown? A blouseless sari? I couldn't resist asking.

Anjali giggled, "I haven't a clue, darling. I got that sweetie-pie Xen to design it."

"Who's Xen?"

"You don't know? He's the hottest guy in films today—he dresses everybody!" That more or less explained the concoction. Yes, now that she'd told me, I had heard of Xen—he was the absolute rage

ever since he draped a buxom starlet in five kilos of bugle beads.
Period. He was fat and funny and gay as a coot. His drag act more
than anything else was what had attracted all the attention initially.
Xen dressed in either virginal white or devilish black. He loved
makeup, masses of it, and ostrich feathers. He'd insisted in an interview somewhere that he only felt inspired after he had bathed
with his client. "A lovely, long shower, or a good soak in a tub full
of bubbles. Nothing quite like the intimacy of a bathroom to drop
all inhibitions. And that's when I can really look at the tits and ass
and decide on the lines. Most of our women have atrocious figures
which they conveniently hide behind miles of sari. I like the new
breed—they are daring. They love their bodies—and I love them."
His costumes were truly bizarre but in their own crazy way they
worked in the movies. But here was Anjali trying hard to pass off as
a screen queen. She looked so comic I was embarrassed. He'd even
persuaded her to sprinkle glitter dust over her shoulders. Her hair
was up in a spangled mess and her eyes were done up Cleopatra-
style. "Where's the asp?" I hissed, but she missed it.

Outlook's anniversary parties were always held at different venues.
This time Varun had picked a stationary concrete training ship at the
southernmost tip of Bombay. I remembered visiting it with Father
as a child. Getting to the deck involved clambering up a narrow,
near-vertical ladder. There was a strong wind blowing and I kept
wondering how many women would make it to the top in their sti-
lettos and billowing saris. And, more interestingly, how many people
would make it back to ground level at the end of the evening without
breaking a couple of limbs. (Varun's bar was legendary.)

By the time K parked, we were halfway to the ship. After getting
out, as we headed to where the party was, I realized we were march-
ing unconsciously to martial music being played by the enthusiastic
police band. We must have looked pretty funny. But so were most

of the other people who were also making their way to the ladder. There was a long queue waiting to clamber up and many women were attempting an acrobatic maneuver to make it to the top without their panties showing.

The harsh light of sun-guns flooded the place as several video cameras whirred, capturing "golden moments" for posterity. Idly I wondered whether people might not find the footage more memorable if at least one cameraman had been positioned at the bottom of the ladder.

We managed to totter up without a mishap. The deck was already full of glamorous city people. A rock band played in one corner while a few self-conscious couples boogied awkwardly. Varun was at the far end. He had two good-looking, light-eyed bouncer types on either side of him. They were dressed like maître d's in a fancy London hotel. One of them was his latest "star discovery." I scanned the place looking for a dark corner to disappear into but Anjali grabbed my hand and commanded, "Don't run away. Stay with me." In retrospect, I'm glad I did.

Lots of booze, lots of foods, lots of action. Each time the police band broke into a Sousa march, I peered below to look at who'd arrived. Varun had actually rolled out a red carpet right up to the ship which little chokra boys brushed from time to time. Most of the people were familiar-looking though I couldn't put a name to every face. Anjali could. Just about everybody was there that night, including the two reigning cinema superstars—male and female. The male had obviously patched up with Varun after a prolonged and ugly war. The female was in a golden Xen creation straight out of the *Arabian Nights* or *The Ten Commandments*. Anjali gasped at the sight of her.

"Just look—isn't she something! And her eyes—hey—look at that—she's wearing golden contact lenses!"

"Yes—they make her look like an owl or a blinded cat."

"I think she looks gorgeous."

Varun saw us and waved. "Look. Look. He's waving. Did you see that? Wave back or else he'll think we are very rude. And, K, your kurta has climbed up at the back—just pull it down."

Kumar was all dolled up in an elaborately embroidered zard-ozi-style kurta pajama, which looked as if it had come from Anjali's wardrobe. I could've sworn he was wearing mascara and some other discreet makeup. His hair was freshly dyed, blow-dried and gelled into place. His jewelry exceeded his wife's. He wore a gold biscuit encircled by diamonds on a thick chain around his neck. Two heavy-duty bracelets on his wrists. A gold Cartier watch, and diamond buttons completed the look. I peeped to see whether he'd dared to wear gold anklets or something—he hadn't. He didn't know too many people and stuck around with us. And his nervousness showed in the steady stream of paan masala he popped. "Where's Murty?" I asked Anjali. "We've left him to look after Babaji. He wasn't feeling very good and wanted a massage. Murty wasn't invited in any case." I saw Kumar eyeing Varun's bouncers.

Potbellied, dhoti-clad ministers with folded hands and fake smiles floated around the place with their lackeys walking two steps behind them. One or two Delhi VIPs were conspicuous by the presence of machine-gun-toting bodyguards around them. "The best accessories to show off these days," said Kumar looking very impressed. A reclusive industrialist made a grand entrance with two or three of his vice-presidents flanking him. "Wow!" said Kumar. "He never goes to any function. This is quite a feather in Varun's cap."

"Maybe he threatened him with an exposé if he didn't show up," I said, half to myself.

On the other side of the ship was a gigantic screen made out of flowers. It said *Outlook* in red carnations. Disco lights and laser beams made holes in the night. There was a lot of activity going on at the other end of the deck. Obviously someone or something was attracting a great deal of attention. (I felt tempted to stand up on a chair to look.) The video boys rushed there with the long wires of their equipment trailing like snakes behind them.

We eventually made, rather squeezed, our way to where it seemed the action really was and discovered that everyone was focusing on the dance floor. An ugly, diminutive man in a ridiculous brocade jacket was gyrating drunkenly with a nubile starlet. She was giggling uncontrollably at all the attention, while he slopped and flopped and nearly collapsed with the effort.

"Who's that creep?" Anjali asked.

"Not sure. But looks like that obnoxious expat writer. The one who lives in London and writes pornography which passes for literature."

"Never heard of him."

"I forget his name. But I think that's him. He comes to India once a year and makes a complete nuisance of himself. Revolting chap. I remember meeting him years ago at a writer's home. He'd puked all over the carpet."

This evening the writer was sloshed to the gills (as he usually was) and at his exhibitionistic best. With a grand sweep, he tore off his jacket and requested the band to break into the "Spanish Gypsy Dance." He looked like a vicious little dwarf as he swung his shiny jacket around like a matador's cape. The young girl didn't know quite what was expected of her so she continued to shuffle her feet and giggle stupidly. Exasperated by her lack of response, he dismissed her with a rough shove and looked around for a new partner. His eyes fell on Anjali as she stood on the edge of the dance floor watching. Without warning he rushed toward her with a wild expression in his eyes. "Helen of Troy herself," he announced with a deep bow. "Here's one ship you won't be able to launch, my dear—do you know why? Because a concrete ship can't sail." Then, holding out his arm, he suggested, "Shall we?"

Uncertain about what she was supposed to do, Anjali accepted and went on to the empty floor. I wanted to pull her off but didn't dare interfere. Kumar stood around looking miserable and clapping feebly to the rhythm of the pseudo-flamenco music. Almost all the guests had converged on the spot by now. The floor was lit up like a movie set. Under the bright lights Anjali's dress had turned transparent and one could see all the way up to her crotch—not a particularly pretty sight. Someone threw a long-stemmed rose at her. The Brat swooped down on it and savagely stuck the stalk between her teeth.

"There—that completes the picture," he snarled. "Come on, shake that ass of yours—what's the matter with you? Relax, unwind, let's go." She was almost immobilized by all the attention. He started to circle her, still flourishing his jacket. "*Toro! Toro! Toro!* Come on," he urged. She looked around desperately—I suppose for Kumar, and attempted a halfhearted charge in the direction of safety.

Just as she nearly cleared the extended jacket, the Brat stuck out a foot and tripped her. We all saw him do it. She went sprawling across the floor, her legs spread-eagled at a ridiculous angle. Before anyone could stop him, he pounced on her after chucking his jacket away. To the tempo of the music he started a lewd, simulated love dance—the sort one sees in two-bit peep shows. "Move! Move! Move!" he said. "*Ole! Torero.* Now I am the bull, baby!" Even though he was much shorter, she seemed paralyzed by his weight. Her eyes were tightly shut, and her lipstick had smeared all over her face. The Greek Goddess dress was torn and mucked up. One could see her underwire-cupped bra clearly. It was a horrible sight. "I've never fucked an Indian woman before—never. This is fun. Move it, bitch. Never had it done to you before? I knew Indian women were cold—just my luck that I had to land on the coldest one."

I searched the crowd for Kumar. He had disappeared. There was just one thing to do—get the bastard off Anjali. I ran up to them and attempted to haul him off. He leered up at me. "Aha! Another cold fish! Come on in—join the party. Maybe you can thaw together." It must have been the sight of his reptilian pink tongue and the drops of saliva trickling down his goatee that did it. Something snapped inside my head. I wanted to lift my foot and land it hard on his bony backside. I could almost hear him yelp like a kicked mongrel. I was lifting my foot when my courage failed me and the nervousness poured in like a flood. Anjali was still groveling on the floor. Awkwardly I found my voice, but the rest of me refused to move. I heard myself saying weakly, "Anjali, it's time for us to leave—let's go." She tried to struggle up but couldn't. "Clumsy bitch," the dwarf taunted. "Bastard," I mouthed silently. He wagged his bottom in Anjali's face and made out like he was about to pull his pants down as well. The band continued playing. It was "You Better Come Home, Speedy Gonsalves" now. Finally, tiring of the sport, the Brat walked off with an exaggerated swagger. Anjali wobbled up to me.

"Where's K?"

"No idea."

"He must be furious."

"Don't worry about him. Let's get out of here first."

The crowd parted silently. Not one person came to our help. Anjali was bruised and had tears streaming down her face. I must've looked quite a sight myself. You must have the same sort of feeling in hit-and-run cases or in street fights, I remember thinking, as we traversed the agonizingly long way back to the edge of the ugly ship. A new worry presented itself. Would Anjali be able to make it down the steep ladder on her own or even with my help? People seemed to jump out of our way like we were deadly killers or sickening lepers. Bombay society lived up to its reputation that night—nobody "interfered." Nobody helped. And nobody cared. People had got to watch a tamasha for free. They'd got their money's worth. We had provided them with something to talk about, laugh about, for at least a fortnight to come. I could almost see the blurbs and the captions in Varun's own rags—oh yes, he wasn't going to miss out on this one. How could he—it had happened on his own turf, at his own party.

And it was recorded evidence. I still don't know how we made it to ground level. Anjali was clutching the wispy shreds of her dress around her, and I was trying hard to keep my sari on.

The car park was full. We didn't know where to begin looking for her Merc for the narrow road leading to the training ship was choked with cars parked at crazy angles. Besides, it was ill-lit and full of idling chauffeurs and I certainly didn't want to linger long enough to be the object of the stares and comments of the assembled drivers. We just stood there, holding each other, wondering what to do next. Finally someone came up to us. He was an elderly man dressed in an old-fashioned suit. I recognized him vaguely—but was far too disoriented to get his name.

"May I help you ladies?" he asked in a soft, refined accent.

"About time," I growled and instantly regretted my rudeness.

"Terribly sorry about what happened," he added. "Are you looking for your car or shall I drop you home in mine?" He pointed. "There's Tukaram—that's my driver. He can at least drop you to your car, if that is all right with both of you." I nodded quickly. He held out one arm for me and placed the other around Anjali. She must have shivered at the touch for he quickly removed his jacket and gently placed it over her shoulders. Tukaram drove up in a magnificent old Bentley. The gentleman stepped aside and held the door open for both of us. We drove along the narrow side-lane looking for Anjali's car and then turned onto the main road which was also lined with cars. There was no trace of Anjali's metallic green Mercedes. I kept wondering about what had happened to Kumar. When we reached the big traffic island, Tukaram turned to his master with a questioning, "Saab?" He, in turn, looked at us and said, "Please allow me to drop both of you home. It's no trouble at all." I told him that "home" in Anjali's case was a long, long way off—Juhu to be precise. With a warm smile, he placed a hand on my wrist and told me, "Well, now, isn't that a coincidence! I have a long way to go myself. I was on my way to the airport. This won't be a detour at all. Please do not think anything of it. I'll be very happy to see you both to your residences—and I have plenty of time to spare. My flight leaves at some god-forsaken hour. I would have read a paperback or dozed off in the lounge anyway. So, please." I sank back into the deep seat thankfully and looked gratefully at our host. As I relaxed I recognized him: he had once been a popular governor of the then Bombay state!

We found Kumar cowering at home, Murty applying Tiger Balm to his forehead. He refused to meet my eyes. I was far too drained to get involved anyway, so I led Anjali to her bedroom and helped her remove her sandals and lie down. "I made a complete fool of myself, didn't I?" she asked pathetically.

"Drink a warm glass of milk and go to bed," I said. My mind wandered over Kumar's cowardly reaction. He had fled, leaving his wife to fend for herself and make her own way back. What a caddish thing to do!

Anjali's hair, under my hand, was a tangled web, teased and sprayed and stiff like wire. Gradually she felt calm enough to open her eyes and lie still, staring fixedly at the ceiling.

"Don't leave me," she said flatly. "Stay. Stay the night. Call your parents. The driver will reach you back in the morning."

I didn't have the energy to go back all the way anyway. I called Mother, who responded impassively, "Are you safe?"

"Yes."

"Will we see you tomorrow? Shall I boil your egg in the morning?"

"Yes."

"It's the dhobi day tomorrow—what about your clothes?"

"Mother—can we discuss that tomorrow?"

"All right, I was only asking whether I should give your towels and bedsheets. Also, your sari petticoats should go to the bhatti."

"In the morning. Mother, in the morning."

"Don't blame K," Anjali said when we awoke. "He's a weak man. He can't handle scenes. He has to escape. He didn't mean it. He ran away because he was so embarrassed. I understand him."

"Well, then, that's what counts. What does it matter what I think? He's not my husband."

"Don't say anything to him when you see him at the breakfast table."

"I'll be gone before that. I'm not dying to meet him."

"Don't say it like that. He really didn't want to dump us—but he's like that. He finds such things terribly painful. He gets completely disoriented. Scenes give him bad vibes."

"Don't make stupid excuses for him, Anjali. It's OK. You don't have to explain anything to me. I'm concerned about you—not him."

"I'll be all right. I was stunned at that moment, but really, I can handle it. I'm stronger than you think."

CHAPTER 20

MONTHS LATER I RAN INTO THE REPORTER FROM WASHINGTON again. The one I'd insulted at Anjali's party. This was at a recording. I'd graduated from writing to making ad films and to my great relief I was doing very well. As a result of this and my work on the *Shakuntala* script I'd even been asked to script a major TV serial sponsored by a soft drink company. This morning we were scheduled to complete a jingle for a new brand of jeans. When I got to the studio, the gay music director was preening all over the place.

"Guess what, darlings? I'm being interviewed today. This is big, I mean BIG. He's from *The Washington Times*—now ask me dumb questions like, 'Why is an American paper interested in you?' If you chaps want to run along and dab some lipstick, rouge or whatever—feel free. He might even do you."

Someone joked, "Well, baby, you've got on sufficient makeup for all of us—by the way, isn't purple mascara a bit much even for a foreign paper?"

"Piss off—you're just jealous. What mascara! This is natural color, poppet."

The reporter walked in scratching his thick mop of hair. He spotted me and said wearily, "It's you again! Are you following me around or what?"

"Yes—I'm a KGB agent pretending to write for *Pravda*. De bosses have told me to tail you during your visit to India."

"Smart kid, huh?" He turned to the gay music man and demanded,

"Who is this broad? Why doesn't she get off my butt?" There was an embarrassed silence. Nobody in the unit had ever seen this side of me. In fact, I used to wonder what they imagined I was all about since I preferred to keep to myself. Probably, the speculation was that I must be a lonely spinster with a dark secret.

"You can't talk to her like that," said the director flapping his hands nervously.

"Oh, yes, I can. She almost screwed up a previous interview too."

"Who let you in here?" I asked.

"Why?"

"Because I call the shots. This is my unit and we are recording a jingle for my film. I can throw you out, you know."

"I don't believe this."

The music director was almost weeping. "I'm sure we can sort all this out, darlings," he said stroking my hair.

"That depends on the spoiled brat here," I said.

"OK lady—let's call a truce," he replied holding out his hand.

"What story is this anyway?" I asked.

"Oh, I just got a telex to do a longish piece on the television boom in India. You know—the ads, the soaps and serials, their impact, the people behind them, what the villagers make of the stuff they watch nightly, how much money is involved, the small-screen stars and their lifestyles—that kind of stuff. I've been given a few leads—not much to go on actually. I hear there is a series in the offing that everyone predicts is going to be big, real big, something *à la Dynasty* with a bit of *Miami Vice* thrown in. Do you know the woman behind it? Very successful ad film career and now poised to break into the soaps."

"What's in it for me?"

"You drive a hard bargain—don't you? Forget it, baby. I can locate her on my own. Problem is, I have a pretty tight deadline. This has got to be wrapped up in four days, pictures and all." The rest of the unit watched this exchange in silence. I said, "Best of luck, buddy, and now, if you don't mind, I have to get on with the recording. We have to wrap it up too—and we don't have four days for it—more like four hours."

"Mind if I hang around and talk to the musicians, ma'am?"

"Fine. So long as you don't disrupt the session—it costs, you know."

"Right."

The next evening I got a call while I was washing my hair. The parents were engrossed in a TV show, so with dripping hair and cursing I answered. It was the reporter again asking very formally to speak to me, making sure he got the pronunciation of my name right.

"It's you again," I said.

"I beg your pardon?"

"I said, it's you—the relentless reporter strikes again. What can I do for you?"

"Have we met?"

"Have we met? Are you kidding! You nearly botched up my recording yesterday."

"Hell! I should've recognized your voice. You mean it's you? You are the Soap Queen in the making."

"Yes, and if you want your quotes, you'd better be nice to me. No rough stuff."

"Hey! This is fantastic—how about a drink tonight? How does that sound?"

"Sounds complicated. First, I'll have to kill my husband. Then, dope my lover. Maybe I'll drug my six kids and tie up my mother-in-law while I'm at it. After that, I'll give my blind parents their evening meal—and then I shall be ready for the big date. How does that sound, smart ass?"

"Terrific. Can't wait. Eight-ish?"

"Yes. Got to go. Lots of suds in my eyes."

"Soapy days are here again . . . ?"

"Something like that."

The relationship started off all right. The light banter, the pj's and smart comments. He talked. I talked. Plenty of cute talk and "in" references. I found him attractive in a boyish kind of way. His stream of corny jokes and labored puns made me laugh. There was a serious side to him but for some reason he preferred to hide behind his buffoon mask. I envied him his nomadic life. He talked about cities and places I'd only read about. He was regarded as a whiz-kid—or so he claimed. He'd got his breaks early and fast. He hardly knew India and saw it through American eyes. I found this disconcerting in the beginning since I couldn't think of him as an "American"—which is what he really was. Second-generation American. But, like a good Brahmin boy, he'd married a good Brahmin girl selected by his parents. And, like any other Indian man, his wife had been converted into a fixture in his apartment. She could've been a microwave oven or a compact disc for all the difference it made. Yet, he repeated rather lamely that he loved her and that she was a good wife. Which to me meant just one thing—he played around while she stayed put at home. They'd produced two kids who loathed India. He mentioned how his wife would start loading suitcases for their annual "native" holiday, months before their departure. "She's crazy. She brings enough food supplies to feed the marines."

"Does she bring American toilet paper?"

"Sure she does—but how did you know?"

"Your kids must be used to the texture."

"Cut it out. You can be such a bitch."

"Don't you know any other terms of endearment?"

"Say, why don't you come back to Washington with me?"

"Oh God! That's all I need. No way. I've done that number once, years ago—and it's not for me."

"Why don't you help me with some of my stories? I have a huge list—I could do with a research assistant. Can you type? Can you load a camera? Take notes? Reference material? Come on—think. I'm sure you could make yourself useful if you really wanted to."

"That's it. I really don't want to. Why should I hang around with you? What's in it for me? Besides, I have stuff to do here."

"I'm offering you an out. Think of the options. You'll be able to travel, write, have fun—at someone else's expense at that. In fact, I'm thinking of quitting my job and doing a book. I also have plans to get into documentaries with a talented filmmaker I know—she's terrific. You'll get to meet her. Both of you could do great things together. I can fix all this for you. What the hell are you doing, busting your ass and wasting time? Here's your big chance. Get out of this environment. Put yourself on the line. Find out what you're all about. I think you've got the stuff in you. If you let it go now—you'll never do it later. Remember, a Ranbir Roy doesn't walk into your life every day with offers you'd be crazy to refuse."

"You are cocky, aren't you. I hate people who refer to themselves in the third person. It stinks."

"I could play humble—but why should I? I'm special, baby, and you know it. You're special too. I think we should team up together. And look—no funny business. I'm not chasing a piece of ass—you know that. I ain't one of dem hard-up natives always looking for the nearest available tail. If you want—I want. If you no want—that's OK too."

Truth was, I did want. But not in that crude way. What I really wanted was a Grand Romance with violins and roses. Ranbir had no time for such stuff. Nor was he cut out for it. His wooing was done via one-liners—which, incidentally, had never been particularly good.

And he was usually never there. He was invariably onto half a dozen stories, many of them outside Bombay. He'd phone from wherever he was, often booking lightning calls, only to say, "Heard the one about . . ." These calls would follow me to the studios and sets, and I'd find it very difficult to keep a straight face and pretend they were business-related. He made a quick trip to London and back during this period. Again, I got a call from Dubai airport, another one from London and they carried on at the rate of three or four a day, with funny notes ("Why do you reduce me to marmalade?") and doodles posted at regular intervals. He was a Beatles freak and so was I. One call from London was devoted to "Yesterday." He hummed the lyrics. "Yesterday . . . Love was such an easy game to play." It became "our song" and I would feel all mushy and sentimental, when I heard it. "I'm just not the man I used to be . . . there's a shadow hanging over me . . . Oh yesterday . . . came suddenly."

If the parents were puzzled or curious they didn't show it. They hadn't asked me about Girish's abrupt exit either. Perhaps they just didn't find me at home enough to talk to me about it. For if Ranbir was busy so was I. I'd discovered soon enough that making serials was no cakewalk: trips to Delhi (to deal with unyielding bureaucrats and idiot ministers), budgets, crews, schedules—and while all this went on Ranbir flitted in and out of my life. Our usual meetings would be in coffee shops between engagements and seldom went beyond jibes, wisecracks and a retailing of woes. The sole evening we went to the Sea Lounge was typical. "You guys live in such a primitive state—how do you function? No working telexes, telephones, typewriters and no public conveniences. Hell—ever tried moving your bowels in an open field with three curious cows staring at your exposed butt?"

"What are you cribbing about—there—you've got your story. Or, at least, one paragraph for your future book. File it all away— you never know when you might be stuck for five hundred words on 'shitting alfresco.'"

"You have a filthy sense of humor—it stinks!"

"Thank you. I take that as a compliment."

"You would, you pervert. How do you get your kicks anyway? Pulling wings off butterflies—or is that far too innocent?"

"I graduated from that a long time ago if you must know. These days I specialize in castrations."

"Balls to you."

"You may not have any left by the time I'm through with you— you stand warned."

"You talk tough. You must be butch. Admit it—you prefer girls, don't you? You are far too macho for the natives. Ever thought of making it with a big black American? Don't knock it till you've tried it."

"This is so juvenile—grow up, Peter Pan. Brush up your locker room jokes. Next you'll be singing soccer songs and expecting me to laugh."

"No, I wouldn't. Those might be far too subtle for a lowdown broad like you."

This was the usual pattern and very rarely did we get down to serious talk. I suppose this was more Ranbir's fault than mine—perhaps because he was afraid that being serious or taking anything seriously would boomerang. But as a professional he was good. He managed to file respectable copy. His byline rated. Very, very infrequently he expressed his misgivings. He was walking me home one evening when he said with some bitterness, "I'll never make it to top dog—I can't. Unless the color of my skin changes miraculously."

"That can't be true—what are you saying?"

"Simply this—I can't lick the system. It's been fun while it lasted, but this is the end of the road for me—careerwise. I'll never make it to the editor's slot—not a chance. I don't want to die a reporter. Can you imagine me at fifty still flying round the countryside doing stories on population explosions and gas leaks forever and ever? I must be realistic. If I don't break out of this rut now—I'll be stuck till doomsday."

"What are your options? Do you feel the call of the Motherland? Are you in search of your roots? Has India cast its magic spell on you? Are you ready to chuck it all up and get into low-cost housing in mud or some such thing? Tell me—maybe we could do a documentary or something."

"No. Much as I love being here—loos or no loos—there's nothing here for me. I can't see myself fitting into any of the existing newspaper chains. I don't have the resources to start something of my own. I couldn't afford to live in Bombay—and my wife would divorce me."

"Is that good or bad?"

"Good and bad."

"That doesn't answer me."

"Does it make any difference?"

"Maybe."

"I'd better run. Didn't know you were such a predatory female."

"Some bitch said that to me years ago—I hate that word. Don't call me that."

"What else should I call you? Here you are, to all appearances a well brought up, conservative Hindu woman, wrapped up in yards and yards of sari, propositioning a married man and trying to break up his marriage. Disgusting! Aren't you ashamed of yourself? This only happens to the likes of Michael Douglas. You really are something else."

"Don't flatter yourself too much, bozo. I say this to every man whose name begins with an R. My astrologer has told me that's the one to go for."

"Is that right?"

"Right."

"That begins with an R too."

"What does?"

"The word right."

"Is that relevant?"

There you go—R again."

"Say, what is this, a new twist to Scrabble or something?"

"Don't be dull."

"How about a dirty weekend to hot things up?"

"How about getting lost? Why don't you go chase some wild asses in the deserts of Kutch?"

"I prefer mine civilized."

The conversation had degenerated again and as I went to bed that night I remember thinking there was no future to the relationship—had never been, would never be. Ranbir was relaxing and fun but that was it. It was good to have him around because, unlike the locals, he knew where he stood. He didn't misread signals, and most important, he didn't behave like a horny teenager in heat.

We kidded around a great deal, but we also knew the score. The undercurrents of a possible affair were always present, but they did not preoccupy us nor did they cut into the friendship. This was a huge relief because I'd always found it a strain relating to my other male colleagues. I suppose I made them as uncomfortable as they made me. After a point, some silly tension would intrude, spoiling the delicate balance of a fastidiously created facade. Particularly while traveling on assignments out of town, this intangible unease would become very pronounced. After an exhausting shoot, while the rest of the unit met up in the hotel bar, or in someone's room, I'd stay put in my own, watching cable TV or just catching up on lost sleep. I'd tried fraternizing with the "boys" once or twice. It hadn't worked. I didn't enjoy their brand of boisterousness or the familiarity that crept in after a few down the hatch. I hated the leering expressions of men who had maintained a formal distance through the day but thought it was OK to drop the mask in the evening and take a chance. I resented the presumptuousness of it all. The snide, insinuating dig behind a seemingly innocent question like "Madam, don't you feel lonely after the work is finished?"

The crews weren't the only problem. At parties or other functions, if I didn't have an escort, men would zoom in hungrily—not because they found me irresistible—oh no—but because they imagined I was "available." One of them even said: "But what have you to lose? You are a free bird." Perhaps it didn't occur to these mutts that even free birds could be selective! I didn't find any of these men attractive—it was as simple as that. And though I felt guilty and sorry for Mother as she worried herself silly over my single status, I wasn't about to relinquish the status for some cretin or weirdo. After all, even if it may sound snide, I wasn't Anjali. Single was good for me. It was this attitude, stated one evening over a heady bottle of champagne at the Rendezvous (Ranbir had sold a big story), that initiated something that has ruled my life this past year. He said: "Is it usual or unusual for an Indian woman to feel this way?"

"Don't know, I mean I haven't conducted a survey or anything. But, offhand, I'd say it isn't the standard attitude. For instance, I can't think of a single school friend in a similar situation—however good or bad it may be."

"Hmm. Just a thought—why don't we do an update on the status of the urban Indian woman, using you, babykins, as the central figure. Tell you what, I'll send an outline to my editors. Fill me in on all the goriest details of your life. If they buy the piece—we are in gravy. I see it as a longish, generous spread—maybe we can hawk it to someone else. I'll also telex my agent. We can go the whole hog, make a documentary perhaps—take you back to school, or sooner—didn't you tell me you were born in some remote dusty district of Maharashtra, where your father started his career as a lowly civil engineer or something? Think of the photo opportunities. We will locate the guy who delivered you—was it in the bush? Or in your mother's old-fashioned four-poster bed? Maybe at a dingy, far-from-sterile village clinic? Great. Then we'll cut to your early school years—what was it—a municipal patshala? Your switchover to a Scottish Protestant Mission—the horrific experiences of growing up with glassy-eyed spinsters teaching you the gospel according to St. Mark. Your mousy adolescence. Your father's rise up the bureaucratic ladder. College. A Jesuit hangout yet. The Beatles and the Vietnam war. Elvis Presley and Blue Suede Shoes? Your first love and jam sessions at Bistro's. Learning the Peppermint Twist and jiving to Chubby Checker. Conforming to parental expectations, toeing the line of authority. Forays into modeling—the Anjali character will be a sure-fire winner, the 'safe' marriage—do you think hubby dearest will agree to an interview? Or the Old Bird—is she still alive? Breaking out of the holy bonds of matrimony, finding your feet in a career you happened to drift into. The success story that followed—hey, how did she do it? Did she have to sleep around, compromise herself? Work her way to the top on her back? I just love this part.

"Anyway—cut to you as you are now—disgustingly self-assured and revoltingly self-sufficient. Baby—you'll give one of those padded shouldered Wall Street American broads a run for their money! This is going to be a terrific project. I can see it—maybe we can throw in an Indira Gandhi angle, link it up with the desi-lib movement. Get your half-baked views on dowry deaths—perhaps coerce you into saying stuff the American media will lap up—like your refusal to remarry since you don't want to end up as a heap of kerosened ashes—will you say that? I'll give you a few bucks more for it! We can sit in on your shoots, have you sip martinis in exclusive clubs, get you to smoke a cigar and talk about your lovers—you do have some, don't you? Or else, we can always hire a few. That gives me an idea—what about a gigolo—just a suggestion—nothing crass, maybe a sly reference to how you pick up guys as and when the libido works itself up. I can see this turning out into an eyeball-popping shocker. Here we have this Bombay socialite all parried out with nowhere to go. And to imagine where she actually sprang from, wow, the potential. And you must stick to your drab saris and horrible tikas throughout. Let the externals remain. Zap them with your inner landscapes. So what do you think, love of my life?"

"I think it's a great idea. In fact, I think I'll steal it. There may be a documentary in it but I'm going to give a book a shot. I've always wanted to write one—so you can go take a walk, Yankee agent. I know when I'm on to a good thing and the good thing is me. If anyone is going to cash in on this, baby, it isn't going to be you. Thanks for the lead, though. I'll try and write you in somewhere. Nothing major, maybe a paragraph or two. Now get lost, I have work to do. The opening line will read, 'I was born in a dusty clinic in Satara, a remote village in Maharashtra . . .'"

EPILOGUE

The woman rose from her typewriter and walked to the window of her study. It had been very hard work, this packaging of her life, and quite often it had almost seemed impossible to finish the book. But now that it was over she felt a certain sadness, autumnal in its intensity . . . Outside the day was almost gone and the streetlights of the Queens Necklace had begun to glow—a string of old sunflowers against a field of gray. She loved this time of day and she willed herself to relax. Tomorrow's anxieties could be dealt with later, today she would rest.

Socialite Evenings

Shobhaa Dé

A CONVERSATION
WITH SHOBHAA DÉ

Q. Socialite Evenings *was your first book. How did your life change when it was published?*

A. The writing of *Socialite Evenings* came about under rather dramatic circumstances when a tall, dark and handsome stranger walked into my home and made me an offer I couldn't refuse! That person was Penguin India's first editor/publisher, David Davidar, who now heads Penguin's operations in Canada. I was flattered but puzzled. He wanted me to write a nonfiction book on Bombay (which is now Mumbai). I was pregnant with my third child and big as a house, but keen to take a crack at writing a book. We decided to make it a novel instead. I wrote furiously and at a demonic speed—and totally loved the experience. The novel created shock waves across the subcontinent when it was launched. Looking back, I'd say the book spoke about the sort of urban Indian realities that were taboo subjects at the time— divorce and adultery.

Q. How has Mumbai changed in the twenty years since your writing Socialite Evenings?

A. Mumbai has not changed as radically as some of the other, smaller cities in India. Mumbai was always ahead of the curve. But India in its present-day avatar is virtually unrecognizable from the India I grew up in. It is affluent, glamorous, aggressive and ambitious. It is now a world player in every sense of the word.

Q. What inspired you to write this particular story?

A. A first novel remains the most self-revelatory one for most authors. You write about the world you know and understand best—your own. That is your territory, your unique turf—you cannibalize your own life, and the lives of people you know. *Socialite Evenings* reflects my immediate world—it remains a fascinating one. These are urban realities that make Mumbai such a magnetic city. The story of Karuna could so easily be my own story or the story of countless upper-middle-class girls who get sucked into a crazy world filled with crazy characters. I was keen to track Karuna's trajectory—it's really an old-fashioned morality tale at the end of the day. *Socialite Evenings* remains a personal favorite with all its raw edges—there is so much truth in it.

Q. Are the characters in this story based on people you know? Do you feel that you need to be a part of the world you write about in order to be an authentic voice in this genre?

A. Some of the characters are people I know, some are loosely based on people I'd met, and others are created. But I also believe most fictional characters are based on the writer's experiences and observations. They don't jump out of hats. For me, it is important to know the world I am writing about. I need that level of intimacy with the subject. No false notes or missed cues.

For me to connect with my reader, I want to provide the real thing—draw him/her into my world. Make the person believe in that world and get involved with the lives of the characters. A good storyteller must know how best to exploit these rich, personal resources.

Q. *When did you first realize you wanted to be a writer? If you could speak to yourself back then, what advice would you give?*

A. I joke that I crawled out of my mother's womb with a pen in my hand! I have been in love with words from the time I uttered my first one. It is the one love affair that I trust implicitly! The only advice worth giving is to say, "Write from the heart and you can't go wrong." I did it then. I continue to do it now—there is no other way. Remain true to yourself. Take ridiculous risks—you must! Above all love what you do.

Q. *What is the writing process like for you? How much do you write a day? How long does it take you to write a novel?*

A. I am an obsessive-compulsive writer. I need to write every single day. I go into withdrawal if I don't. I love the process of writing and watching words as they fill a page. It gives me an incredible high each time I start a fresh project—be it a column or a book. I write for approximately eight hours a day, with small breaks in between. On a good writing day, I can easily produce twenty-five hundred words—they pour forth in a torrential, un-stoppable way. I take a year or so to complete a book.

Q. *What kind of experience do you hope your readers have when reading one of your books?*

A. I hope they will be able to crawl into my mind and heart and get totally involved in the narrative. I want them to feel for the characters, weep, laugh and cry with them. I want my readers to beg for more! I want to convert them into Shobhaa Dé junkies.

Q. *What's your favorite thing about Bollywood? Least favorite thing?*

A. Bollywood is adorably bizarre. It is an insane world. Surrealistic almost. We produce the maximum number of films in the world. Bollywood has its own magic—I hope it never changes its unique formula. What I detest about Bollywood is its lack of professionalism and its chaotic method of making movies. But the OTT nature of our movies dictates a certain system that makes no sense to the outside world.

QUESTIONS
FOR DISCUSSION

1. *Socialite Evenings* was considered controversial and shocking in India upon its initial release in 1989. What, if anything, shocked you about this story?

2. Is Karuna's rise to the top an admirable achievement?

3. Whom do you most relate to in the story?

4. What do you think the moral of the story is here? Is there one?

5. What are the most prevalent themes of the story?

6. Do the characters ever suffer any consequences for their actions?

7. Who is the happiest, most content person in the story?

8. Who is the American equivalent of Karuna?

9. What do you think of Shobhaa Dé's depiction of women? Of men? Of Bollywood?

10. Shobhaa Dé considers the city to be a character in the story. What experience did you have reading about Mumbai?

11. What are your feelings about the ending? Were you expecting something different?